CREEKWOOD SERIES

Blind Spot

A. MARIE

Editing: Sarah Plocher, All Encompassing Books
Proofreading: Judy Zweifel, Judy's Proofreading
Cover Design: Okay Creations
Illustrator: Apryl Bielejeski
Formatting: Champagne Book Design

Playlist

You can find the full playlist on Spotify

Suit And Jacket—Judah & the Lion

Play With Fire—Sam Tinnesz

Ember—Katherine McNamara

ok on your own—mxmtoon, Carly Rae Jepsen

All My Friends—AJ Mitchell

I Don't Exist—Olivia O'Brien

Hurts Like Hell—Madison Beer, Offset

Heaven—Julia Michaels

Bad Boy—CARYS

Fuck Away the Pain—Divide The Day

Lost My Mind—Alice Kristiansen

burning bridges—Bea Miller

Honestly—Gabbie Hanna

Anywhere—Sigma, Louis III

Dance Monkey—Tones And I

Real Friends—Camila Cabello

Flames—MOD SUN, Avril Lavigne

Damaged—Britton

idfc—blackbear

2 Souls on Fire—Bebe Rexha, Quavo

Higher—The Score

Small Doses—Bebe Rexha

Thief—Ansel Elgort

My Heart's Grave—Faouzia

Love in the Dark—Leroy Sanchez

Brother—Sam Tinnesz

Paralyzed—NF

Almost Touch Me—Maisy Kay

Collide—Rachel Platten

Fantasy—Bazzi

talk is overrated—Jeremy Zucker, blackbear

Seeing Blind—Niall Horan, Maren Morris

warmer—Bea Miller

Go Crazy—Leslie Odom Jr.

Bitter Love—Pia Mia

Cry for Me—Camila Cabello

I Fall Apart—Cimorelli

Burn Me Down—Sophie Simmons

Do You Miss Me At All—Bridgit Mendler

Where Your Secrets Hide—Klergy, Katie Garfield

I R L—DYSN, Prelow

Dark Side—Phoebe Ryan

I Still Wait For You—XYLØ

Twenty-Somethings—Judah & the Lion

Ocean Eyes—American Avenue

Author Note

No artificial intelligence was used in the making of this book.

This is a 119k-word secret relationship romance. Although this is the third book of the Creekwood Series, it can be read as a stand-alone. It contains content that may be triggering and/or disturbing to some readers, such as, but not limited to: foul language, alcohol use, graphic violence, explicit sexual situations, domestic abuse, raw sex/sex without a condom. Any on-page sex between the main characters is consensual. The full, updated list of triggers can be found on amarieauthor.com

For the ones holding two swords.
May you never forget you have them.

Blind Spot: an area where a person's view is obstructed, keeping something or someone out of sight.

Chapter 7

Marc

EASE UP, DAMMIT.

She comes tearing around the final turn of the track, ahead of all the boys, of course—just like I taught her—and it's the same one I've had my eye on since we pulled in at six o'clock this morning. The hay bales holding it up look unstable as shit, and as soon as the tires on her 50cc blaze across the top of the turn—unlike how I taught her—the loose bundles wobble enough to make her sway unsteadily and I grip the flimsy two-by-four railing I'm standing behind even tighter. Luckily, Rebel's straightened left leg helps stabilize her fast enough so she can shoot out of the curve smoothly, her long, blonde hair flying out from beneath her maroon helmet like a superheroine's cape.

Even though she's competing in the correct age bracket, she's smaller than every other rider on the track—easily—but racing dirt bikes isn't about size, it's about heart, and Rebel's determination is unmatched—also easily.

I wait until she's safely across the finish line before stalking over to the track master and getting in his face.

"This track is shit! Someone could get killed."

It's bad enough this run-down ORV park is the only one around, forcing anybody serious about racing to make the fifty-minute drive outside of town, but it's poorly run and in need of major repair. It's by far the worst one I've been on and it's only getting worse as time goes on.

"Isn't that your daughter accepting the first-place trophy up there?"

Over on the joke of a stage that's comprised of wooden crates that have also seen better days, Rebel stands proudly, holding up her trophy and most likely cheesin' beneath the helmet she's still wearing.

Fuck. I gotta get over there. Her mom will want a picture. Or twenty.

I narrow my eyes and turn back to the man in charge. Yeah, she got a trophy, that she earned fair and square, but that doesn't change the fact that this track is run by somebody who doesn't even respect the sport, let alone know what riders actually need. Safety during an extreme sport may seem contradictory but it's vital—literally.

"Fix this place up or I'll have it shut down." Which honestly, should probably happen anyway before anybody dies out here but it really is the only—somewhat—legit place around. It's the same track my boys, Coty and Beckett, and I used to ride when we were growing up, except now it holds an air of decay, of despair, that wasn't here before that makes me want to stop coming here just so it can't taint the memories, too.

"Then where will everyone go, huh?" He lets out an irritating little chuckle that has me grinding my molars together.

That's one of my main problems with this fucking town. There's enough open land around for people to ride wherever the hell they want but nowhere with actual practice jumps, let alone a full race course. Fuck if I'll admit that to him though.

Instead I pin the guy with a glare, then turn on my heel, needing to snap a pic of a little girl worth more than the hunk of metal—or whatever the fuck it's made of—in her grasp.

Trophy. Shit, she'll laugh at this pathetic excuse of a trophy when she makes it pro one day. We both will.

If that's what she wants.

Heading over to the winners' stand, I pull out my phone and start clicking away.

Satisfied with enough pictures to fill one of those sappy scrapbooks my mom used to make for me and my sister, I put my hands under Rebel's arms to lift her off the rickety crate and her chest protector clunks against my wrists as she squirms in my hold. Kid's ticklish as shit.

Once she's back on the ground, I pull her helmet off to reveal a huge-ass grin on her flushed face showcasing her missing front teeth. Ruffling her already staticky strands, I grin down at her, so fucking proud my chest hurts.

Then some guy rushes over with a camera saying something about a picture for the newspaper and I drop the smile to slip Rebel behind me before throwing a twenty and a quiet "fuck off" at him.

Isn't there a rule about taking photos of kids without permission? There fucking should be.

Turned back around, I tell her, "Good job out there. You 'bout gave me a heart attack on that last berm," I drop down on my knee to help with her gear, "but you pulled it off."

"Thankth. Can we get ithe cream on the way home?"

Ice cream? Only a six-year-old would be thinking about ice cream right now.

I hood my eyes at her which only makes her gap-filled smile grow wider. She knows she's not supposed to have ice cream first thing in the morning.

Screw it. She just burned off a ton of energy competing against boys that've probably been doing this since they were toddlers…and she won. Ice cream for breakfast it is.

We gather her dark maroon Yamaha TTR50 and load it into my trailer.

After switching both the trailer and truck out for my BMW tucked away at my dad's, we head home while Rebel fills the silence with excited conversation. We're talking over-the-top excited. If it weren't for her being strapped into her booster seat, I have no doubt the girl would be levitating right now.

The ice cream might've been a bad idea.

Her scoop of double chocolate cherry chunk drips down her hand wrapped around the cone, landing onto my custom leather seat with an audible *smack*, making my jaw clench hard enough to hurt my temple.

Ice cream was definitely a bad idea.

Back at Creekwood Apartments, I swing a hard right to park in front, far away from my place, and as soon as I pull the e-brake up, I spy Rebel through the rearview mirror, mouth wide open, breaths heavy and slow. Little mama passed out—with the half-eaten ice cream cone still in her fist. *Naturally.*

With a shake of my head, I set the cone on the pile of napkins she ignored, then scoop her up in my arms, taking the stairs without her so much as stirring.

Kary opens the door the second I hit the top step, her light blonde hair matching her light eyes.

"How'd it go?"

"Fine," I mutter, rearranging the limp body in my hold so we can fit through the doorway easier and fighting not to roll my eyes in front of her.

Like I'd ever let anything happen.

I lay Rebel down on the couch, then stand back a minute to just watch her sleep. Kids are crazy, man. She's got chocolate coating her top lip, both eyebrows, and at least one of her ears.

My own lips twitching, I turn around, going back outside to grab her riding gear along with her snacks, water bottle, tablet, diary with matching fuzz-covered pen, picture book, two bracelets, and a partridge in a pear tree.

Fuck.

Why did she need all this shit again? It's a far cry from the two, maybe three, things I always carry with me and she didn't even use any of it. Did she?

The diary falls open to a dog-eared page showing the number one sketched across the top with a shit ton of hand-drawn smiley faces and hearts underneath. A full smirk pulls at my mouth. I guess she did.

A breeze blows through the open car door, rustling the paper to an earlier entry, a drawing there jumping out at me before I can slam the frilly diary shut and add it to the growing stack piled on the booster seat.

Kary's suppressing a smile when I deposit it all upstairs but I just hand her the trophy, careful not to let our fingers touch as I attempt to stare directly at the floor.

She makes a noise in her throat and our eyes finally do collide in time for me to watch her lose the rest of the battle as she lets out a laugh to say, "You know this is your fault, right?"

My eyebrows plummet. *What part?*

"Chocolate…ice cream, I'm guessing?" She gestures to Rebel's face. "Really? I bet that left a mess."

"I needed a car wash anyway." I shrug, AirDropping her the rest of the pictures now that I have a better signal before sliding my phone back into my jeans and realizing she's the one refusing to meet my eyes now.

Time to go.

"I'm sorry," Kary whispers even though we both know it's pointless.

On my way out, I peer over at Rebel one last time, feeling some of the tightness leave my shoulders, and nod.

I'm not.

Outside, I do a quick scan before pulling around to park beside Paige and Beck's street bikes alongside our building.

Creekwood is broken up into three sections, forming a broken U shape with a pool in the middle of the complex. Our unit—soon to be my unit—is in the central hub while Kary's is in one of the outer buildings, the front one to be exact.

With Paige about five months along in her pregnancy, she doesn't ride for the time being, so she drives Beck's Tahoe which is also parked in the lot, even though I thought they'd be gone already.

By the time I do a half-ass wipe-up of the backseat, they're both descending the stairs hand-in-hand.

I honestly don't know how my roommates haven't noticed Rebel yet. That's all I can see.

She's all I see.

The thread holding me to Creekwood is clutched by a tiny hand with glitter-painted nails caked in dirt and probably even a little double chocolate cherry chunk ice cream now.

With Beck and Paige set to move into their own home soon, she's the only thing keeping me here anymore. I don't see that changing anytime soon, even with my own group of properties sitting idle, waiting for me to do *something* with them.

"Where were you?" Beck asks with a shit-eating grin on his face but I don't bother with a reply. I don't answer to him. I don't answer to anyone.

Fortunately, he knows the deal and laughs lightly, changing the subject like only he can. "Come with us. Paige wants to hit up the farmer's market."

I'm about to decline when Paige speaks up, asking if we can swing by Pop Two, the second location of our joint venture auto repair shop, Pop The Hood. "I need to give my brother the ultrasound results so he knows which color powder to buy." Her gaze drops immediately, probably checking to see if she can still see her feet or some shit. She's been talking about that particular change a lot lately but I'm pretty sure it'll be a few more months before she has to worry about that happening.

Despite all that though, my ears perk up. Not for the gender reveal part. A kid's a kid, and as long as they're born healthy, they'll see that's all that really matters. No, it's because I need my car washed—bad—and Angela's the only one I trust with cleaning the interior as well as the exterior.

As soon as the words leave my mouth suggesting my plan of dropping my car off too, Paige offers to drive it there for me, so I jog upstairs and grab my helmet. After watching Rebel tear up the track, I'm ready to do some riding of my own.

With both my rides custom painted to be the exact same color, my Ducati Corse 899 parked next to my BMW looks like its hotter, nastier, younger sister and the shot of almost visible energy shooting up my arm when I turn the key settles over me like a low current of electricity. I keep all my toys the same color, the same garnet red, for a reason—as a warning of upcoming danger.

An hour later, I'm narrowing my gaze on a boy that reminds me of Rebel as he studies the snow-cone stand with a deep wrinkle in his brow before I tune back into Beck. Or I try to anyway. He won't shut the hell up about how much better my family's farm is than every other tent at this farmer's market. *No shit.* My dad may be a world-class dickhead but he knows his shit when it comes to his life's work. After moving here from Mexico with his family as a kid, he dreamed of being his own boss and doing what he loved, which was grow things with his hands, so he made a risky investment on a large piece of land when he was barely nineteen. Over the years, he's added to it, working his ass off to grow his produce farm into the successful business it is today. I'm surprised he's not out here himself actually. *I'm glad he's not out here himself.*

The little boy in front of the stand is now holding a pencil up to his mouth, deep in thought, and I glance around for his parents, coming up empty. What the hell's he doing? He's got messy, sand-colored hair with several cowlicks all over the place and his clothes are filthy with tears every-fucking-where. Not the kind I shell out a ton of money to already be on my jeans either. These are real tears that make me think of the kids I grew up with on my family's farm. Before my dad opened an onsite daycare for his employees, they'd sometimes bring their kids with them and we'd run absolutely wild.

He squints and I eye the snow-cone stand again.

Just as I'm getting to my feet, cash already in hand, he marks something down on a piece of paper and runs off in the opposite direction.

I trade the money out for my cigarettes instead, scowling over at my roommate as I sit back down next to him. We're sitting at a table in the parking lot cleared out for shoppers and I'd rather be anywhere else. Literally anywhere. Stuck in the middle of a human tornado is not how I wanted to spend my day.

"Are you just gonna talk shit the whole time?" I snap at Beck for no real reason but he just shrugs unapologetically, pushing his blond hair out of his eyes to say, "Yeah, probably."

I roll my eyes, sticking a cigarette between my lips.

"You know it's my favorite hobby."

Guy could carry on a fully animated conversation with spackle, I swear.

A passerby screws up his face in disgust at me, making me wonder why the fuck I agreed to come here again. Ever since Washington banned basically all cigarette smoke—not marijuana though—I get even more heat than ever about my…habit. Like I care. At least I'm open about it. I'm not pretending I'm good like those shit-for-brains taking hits off a stupid flash drive lookalike.

Staring the crusty-lipped jerkoff right in the eye, I bring up my lighter, holding it to the tip with my thumb just waiting to fucking roll, but then his starry-eyed kid being pulled in the wagon behind him blinks up at me and I rip the cigarette clean off my mouth.

"What are we doing here anyway?" I ask. "I could've grabbed all this shit yesterday." Or this morning technically, but I keep that to myself.

Vega Farms is also where I spend most of my days, not for the crops, but for the vehicles transporting the people tending to the crops. Cars, trucks, ATVs, golf carts, hell, even an occasional scooter—I can handle. Things with engines I can actually fix. Crops though—hard pass. People—fuck that. Things that don't require a lot of hovering, that's my bread and butter. And jam, because jam's fucking fire, especially grape jam.

"Paige was craving pickling cucumbers."

I quirk an eyebrow up at him. Beck's a half foot taller than me but his loud-as-fuck personality makes him seem even bigger.

He drops a hand on my shoulder. "Don't worry. I'll give her the full-size thing later." His eyes widen seriously as he tilts his head down to add, "King size."

I bite back a smile, shaking him off me. Like I don't already know my roommates go at it night and day. *I live on the same planet, brother.*

It's no wonder Paige ended up pregnant by the guy less than a year into their relationship. That's one thing I won't be missing when they move into their own place next month.

First our boy Coty gets taken off the market by our old neighbor, Angela, now Beck's locked down by his baby mama.

At that moment, Paige, wearing shorts and one of Beck's idiotic motorcycle tees saying *If you think I'm cute now, wait until you see my motorcycle* that does nothing to hide her growing baby bump, walks up to us in her thick-ass combat boots, laces bouncing with every step, and Beck rushes to take the tote from her shoulder, saying proudly, "What my wife wants, my wife gets."

She shoots me a flat look. "Some daddy you are." My eyebrows nosedive as my heart picks up speed. "I thought you're the one that's supposed to be in charge here."

Oh. That.

"Daddy? Ha!" Beck elbows me when I make it to my feet, saying, "Bet you've heard that one before," while I try like hell to keep my expression neutral.

"Seriously, I leave you two alone for five minutes and he's already got himself a wife?"

Her eyes are aimed my way but her snarled words are all for Beck, so I just sidestep them, hoping to see myself the fuck outta this entire situation as quickly as possible.

"You," he tells her, dropping all traces of humor. "You're my wife, dream."

With a flick of her wrist, she passes us both, saying simply, "No."

Beck and I share a look and while he seems thoroughly confused, I can only shrug my shoulders, my heart still not moving at normal speed. Last I checked, you had to actually do shit to be married. Certificates, signatures, witnesses, the whole nine. Some people even—get this—have a wedding. Beck knocked his girl up and assumes it's a one-label-fits-all kind of thing. Yeah, he's a dumbass.

But not for long. He'll make it right with Paige. He'll make it official. And sooner than she thinks.

The three of us make our way through the packed crowd but it all starts to be too much, so when they stop to buy some cupcakes—cucumber craving, my ass—I find myself alone, leaning against a wall down a side alley, watching as faces blur beautifully together until I can't even make out one from another.

This cigarette I do get to light, turning the end a deep cherry red with a labored inhale.

"Give me that!"

Cheeks hollowed out, I glance over my shoulder to see a group of kids, maybe ten years old, maybe a little older—most of them anyway—with the kid from earlier standing in the middle.

Thick smoke billows from my lips as I turn back around, keeping an eye out for my roommates. I don't want Paige to get too close. I won't even smoke in my car and I quit smoking at the apartment as soon as I found out Paige was pregnant. I don't want whatever the fuck thirdhand smoke is affecting Rebel, Paige, or her unborn child, so I basically only smoke at work, when I travel, or if I'm outdoors far from Creekwood.

"No. I need it."

Something—the kid's voice maybe—has me facing the group again. Twisting until my back is pressed flat against the brick wall, I kick one foot over the other and take in the scene as it unfolds. The older ones surround the youngest as he continues inspecting the paper in his grasp with determination.

"What is it? A love letter to your mommy?"

Amateurs.

"A drawing of your imaginary best friend?"

Shitty, but still pretty tame.

"The back-to-school list you can't afford?"

Maybe I was right about the snow-cone thing.

The tallest of the group leans down, trying to snatch the sheet but little dude holds firm.

"A wanted poster for a new dad?"

Little shits.

"Hey!" I bark out, then smirk as they scatter like deer in a field.

Pushing off the wall, I dab out my cigarette on the sole of my unlaced high-top, tucking the still hot butt into my palm.

"You a'ight, little man?" I ask the boy from earlier when he's by himself.

Some sort of mumble comes out of him as he peers down at his paper, squinting again. I chance a peek at it, not really wanting to stick my nose into the dude's business, then frown. It's a handwritten list. Nothing like what those kids were saying either, but a scavenger hunt for items around the farmer's market. He's got almost everything marked off, even the tasks that seem more like errands than actual items. Who made this?

And who the fuck does he belong to? I haven't seen a parent for him yet.

Maybe he ran off. Or maybe he just got carried away while searching for whatever it is he's supposed to be looking for.

I try again with, "Hey, you okay?" while glancing around.

"I can't find this one."

I follow his finger to see the last item on the list. *Something that runs but isn't moving.*

Runs?

Runs…

It's not technically part of the market but it should work.

"What's your name?"

He finally looks up at me with a heavy dose of suspicion, which he fucking should. I am a stranger after all.

Where are his goddamn parents?

"Gunther," he says slowly like I'm the fucking problem. *That'd be whoever's supposed to be watching you, kid.*

"Gunther." I nod, telling him, "I'm Marc. I got an idea for that last one but you gotta get permission first."

Without another word, he turns, so I follow, keeping my eyes peeled for anyone that might be in a panic from losing him. If Rebel got away from me here, this whole fucking place would be shut down 'til I found her.

We merge back into the heaving flow of foot traffic and I can't help but regret every decision I've made—starting with agreeing to that damn ice cream cone—that led me here with this kid, and these stinky fucking people. Mainly the people. Did Washington ban showers, too?

Switching to breathing through my mouth, my heels drag a little harder as I weave through the crowded market, trying to keep up with him, then Gunther pulls away suddenly, running up to a pop-up tent stock full of dairy products sitting in buckets of ice.

"Mom. This guy needs you. Mom. Mom!"

My feet freeze on the spot.

What the fuck?

A woman, that could easily pass as my age, is helping a customer as she waves off her…son? That can't be right.

I take Gunther in again, realizing he's gotta be close to Rebel's age, if not a little older.

Could be.

She's really pretty. The part of her I can see anyway. In a home-grown, girl-next-door type of way—if your neighbor had a half sleeve of tats of…are those weeds? Actual weeds, not the drug. With a strange-looking butterfly flying to a moon set behind those weeds even though I thought butterflies slept at night.

Her light jeans hug every bit of a peach of an ass, accentuated nicely without a shirt trying to cover it. The hem of her basic tee is tied at the waist to show just a slice of naturally suntanned skin while both sleeves are rolled up to her shoulders, exposing muscular arms and the tattoo covering one. She's also wearing boots. Rain boots? It's sunny as fuck out even though it's only ten thirty in the morning.

How is it still morning?

To top it all off, captured in a bun that looks like an octopus with way more than eight arms is dirty blonde hair. For real, there's a clump of dirt in her legit dirty blonde hair. How do you not know there's a clump of dirt in your hair? What do you even do to get dirt stuck in your hair?

In rapid-fire succession, images flash in my mind with several scenarios that could definitely explain away the dirt-in-the-hair look and my dick stirs in my jeans.

I haven't seen her face full-on yet and I'm already imagining her rolling in the hay, literally. I'm also gonna go out on a limb here and assume she's married since I can't see her left hand from where I'm standing.

Suuuper inappropriate.

Shoving the hand still holding the cigarette butt into my pocket, I drop it, then dig my bike key into my thigh through the thin cotton and take a huge inhale, this time using my nose.

Down, boy.

Finished with the customer, Gunther's mom, or whatever she is, side-eyes him, asking, "Did you find everything already?" Taking the list, she shakes her hips back and forth in a celebratory dance that I wish was for my eyes only. *Damn.* "I finally came up with one you couldn't find? I stumped you? Whoo!"

Despite him trying to hide it, a small smirk slips out as Gunther tries to ignore his mom's over-the-top show.

Oh, uh, right. That's where I come in. I'd been so busy watching them, watching her joke around with her son, I almost forgot why I was even here. That I don't actually belong here.

I clear my throat, inching forward. "I thought maybe I could help him with that last one but I wanted to check with his parents first. Is that you?"

My voice stops her dead in her tracks as her body comes to an abrupt halt, locking up like she was just caught doing something wrong and the word "sorry" is out of her mouth before she's even facing me.

Um. What? Sorry for what?

Then she finally does turn around, her gaze reaching mine and I forget everything else because holy fucking shit. I never knew that combination existed. I mean I did, but not in an eye color. Blue-violet and nuclear green. Only at Blue Lake in New Zealand did I see those colors so vibrant. And together? Get the fuck out of here. They gotta be contacts. Right?

I had to hike two days just to get to that lake, and because of the locals' belief that it was sacred, I couldn't even touch it. Not that I wanted to once I got there though. You could *feel* how special the water was just by looking at it.

Kinda like now.

"Mom, this is Marcus," Gunther says but his mom doesn't react. She doesn't do anything actually. She just stares at me, that contagious energy from before bleeding out at an alarming rate and being replaced with something I can't pinpoint.

What's happening right now?

"Er, what?" she says, blinking the moment away to look down at Gunther, her nose ring glinting from a streak of sunshine touching the half of her face not covered by the tent. I miss the colors beneath her lids instantly.

"It's Marc, actually," I say, just to see if I can get her focus back on me. "Short for Marcos, but close." Except not. At all.

I knew a kid named Marcus once. He ate the dried-up glue balls off all the classroom glue sticks. And I've gone by Marc ever fucking since.

People swear kids forget stuff like that but I'll never not remember glue-ball-eating Marcus—unfortunately.

"Where's Sydnee?" Gunther's mom asks suddenly, her voice rising as she searches around. Around me, like I'm not even here.

Gunther's eyes widen for the first time since I spotted him and he drops his gaze to the ground.

"Hunter, where's your aunt? She's supposed to be watching you."

Hunter? This whole time I thought he said his name was Gunther. Maybe he's got a speech impairment like Rebel with her missing teeth.

His downturned face turns the same color as his mom's as she becomes almost frantic next to him.

Or maybe he outright lied. *Smart.*

A younger woman similarly dressed to Hunter's mom walks up and narrowly avoids being chewed out when I step forward again, explaining how I had my eye on the boy. Initially I was wanting blood as well for Hunter walking around this place alone, now I wouldn't mind a reward. I did return him safely, unlike Sydnee here.

"I'm sorry. How do you know each other?" his mom asks...I guess me, but I stay quiet, waiting until she looks back at me. I like those eyes too much to continue talking when they're not on me and she's now avoiding my general direction. She wants my words, she's gonna have to show me. Instead though, she speaks to her son, asking, "Why did you bring me a," her gaze falls down my body, her face turning an interesting shade of pink now that she's over her initial panic, "man? That wasn't on the list."

"I didn't. I brought you Marcus."

"Marcos. Marc," I say again to clarify. "And I am a man," I add to also clarify. Was that actually in question though?

I scowl at the kid, not sure what to make of him. Or his mom.

I should probably leave but for some reason I can't. My feet literally won't let me. My feet...or something else.

Beck's voice booms next to me, saying, "It's you," and everybody turns to my skyscraper of a friend, unsure who exactly he's talking to as he gapes like he's seeing a hallucination. "You were there, weren't you?"

What the hell? Do we know her?

"What are you talking about, Beckett?" Paige asks, appearing beside him.

Without taking his eyes off Hunter's mom, he tells her, "She was at the hospital."

Pain seeps out of the couple at the shared memory. Something happened between them before our roommate went AWOL on his dirt bike last year out at my dad's property, landing himself in the emergency room. It wasn't his first time pulling a stunt like that but something tells me it was his last.

We all face the person in question, wondering the same thing.

Those mesmerizing eyes of hers crinkle at the edges as she smiles warmly at Beckett while reverting back to openly ignoring my presence.

"Of course, yeah, sorry. We didn't get to meet, I guess. Not officially. You were pretty out of it." She steps around a giant cooler, stretching out a toned arm and says, "I'm Bentlee. Bentlee Graham."

Now why does that sound familiar? And why wasn't I offered a handshake?

"How'd you make out?" she asks, looking him up and down, taking stock. "Seems like you're all good."

Beck shakes her hand silently, frowning like he's trying to piece together a lopsided puzzle.

"You're lucky I found you when I did."

"How did you?" I ask.

She finally drags her eyes back to meet mine and, after a moment, waves a hand around to gesture at the tent she's under, her blush spreading to her tanned chest. "Isn't it obvious? My family's farm is next door to yours."

Graham as in Graham Dairy, one of the biggest dairy farms in the region. But what does that have to do with her being at the hospital with Beck? And how did I not know she was our next-door neighbor? Although, next door in farming terms is like miles and miles down a never-ending road of crops so high you can't see past, a couple of unmarked turns, a silo, and a pile of hay bales holding up a handmade street sign. I never made it my business to investigate who else lived and worked out there. Not when I was just trying to get the fuck out.

Had I known we had neighbors like her though, maybe I should've. I know better than anyone, those tall crops hide *lots* of things.

But she still didn't answer my question.

"How did you find him?"

"Luck." She drags a thumb across her bottom lip, biting the tip briefly. "I saw his headlight." She nods at Beck. "Then I didn't, so I went to investigate and found him laid out. Got him on my RANGER and hauled ass back to my parents'. From there it was more of a group effort to get him to the hospital since we didn't know if his neck was injured or not."

Beck and I shoot each other identical looks. *Excuse me, what?*

"You *got* him on a UTV? Alone? How?"

Beckett Meyers is 6'6" and built. This girl's like 5'7" and that's with her ugly-ass boots on.

She lets out a light laugh, glancing down at her son. He just shakes his head, smirking.

"I've handled heifers bigger than him. Meaner, too."

"Heifers are cows, right?" Beck asks.

"Females, yeah."

"You work at your parents' farm then?"

She visibly flinches, saying, "I do now."

This is news to me. Every single bit of it. I've never seen her. I would've remembered. Wouldn't I? Sometimes when I'm in the zone though, I don't notice anything. That's the whole point.

Her eyes lift to lock on to mine, and unlike the lake in New Zealand full of the world's clearest water, I can't see the bottom of these. They go on forever—endless pools of the untouchable.

"I'm glad it all worked out, even if you did flip me," her gaze touches on Hunter, "the bird." She laughs like she's ending the conversation but for some reason I'm not ready. Not ready to say goodbye.

Luckily Beckett rushes to apologize, saying sheepishly, "I thought you were someone else."

Who? Who the hell did he think was at the hospital?

Then it clicks. Blonde hair, blue eyes—kinda like Beck. Did he think it was his mom—the mom that abandoned him when he was only ten—somehow?

Fuck, that sucks. But he flipped her off? That's…interesting.

"Don't worry about it. It's not the worst way I've been thanked for my efforts."

The other woman, Sydnee, laughs knowingly but Bentlee doesn't let her off the hook so easily as she glares at her sister.

Paige steps up, latching on to Bentlee's arm. She's been friendlier these past few months. At first I thought it was just the pregnancy softening her up a bit but now I know it has more to do with finding her place in life. With her blood family coming together, along with making a place in ours, she's right where she's supposed to be. It helps—finding where you belong.

"Thank you so much for what you did. I don't even want to think about what would've happened if you hadn't found him." After making introductions, she says, "We're having a gender reveal party next weekend," gesturing to her stomach. "We'd love it if you would come since without you, we might not even be expecting."

Beck throws his hands in the air, saying, "I said I was sorry. Thrice!" He holds up three fingers, looking over at me again for help but I hold my free palm up. *Switzerland, man.*

Keep me out of it.

"I wasn't gonna die," Beck maintains before dropping his voice to grumble, "I don't think," and earning a glare from Paige.

"You can bring the whole family," Paige adds, waving at Hunter, then looking around.

Automatically, I follow suit. She didn't say if she was married or not but she's not saying much of anything. She's purposely ignoring me and dancing around my questions.

Now that both hands are on display, I can see she's not wearing any rings. There's not even a tan line on her ring finger and I'm willing to bet she's got a nice tan everywhere. Everywhere a t-shirt and jeans don't cover anyway. Fucking farmer's tans.

Wait, weren't those kids saying something weird about Hunter's dad?

"That's sweet but I don't know. It was nothing, really."

Again with the dancing. I didn't mind the first dance she gave, that was nice, but this shit, her dodging around information I'd like to know…it hits a little too close to home and I'm wondering what the hell she's hiding.

"You carried a 220-pound giant. That's not nothing," Paige tells her with a snort.

"Yeah, I think I broke my RANGER doing that. It hasn't run right ever since."

"Oh, well, Beckett can fix that."

"I'll do it." The words are out of my mouth before I even realize what I'm saying. It *is* my specialty but Beck could easily pitch in. We're pretty evenly matched in the skills department; I just prefer to work at different locations. Locations away from the masses.

He's a people person. I'm not.

But this person, I'm definitely interested in.

Paige glances over at me, her green eyes sparkling like sea glass before she speaks to Bentlee. "Say you'll be there. I need all the help I can get. There's set to be more men than women by a disgusting ratio."

Bentlee releases a strained laugh. "Maybe I should then."

So…no man?

"Perfect." *Perfect.* "Marc will give you the address."

"Mom, what about this one?" Hunter points at his paper, reminding her of the unfinished scavenger hunt.

"I can help with that," I tell her, trying to catch her eye.

"Something that runs but isn't moving." Paige eyes the paper, then looks up to me with a smirk. "Clever."

They say their goodbyes, then the couple leaves us alone and a moment passes as we watch them go except, when I turn to Bentlee, she's not looking at my friends. She's staring right at me.

Fucking finally.

Chapter 2

ARCOS VEGA.

Marcos freaking Vega is right in front of me. *What? How?*

The boy I watched for years, tearing up the outer parameters of his family's farm, is all grown up and standing in front of me like I exist and he sees me too for once. Like I'm not just the creep that used to spy on the hot motocross boy down the road.

And he's still got that way about him. Like he's bigger, better, like he's worth keeping an eye on. Except now he's looking back at me, no, *staring* at me, waiting for me to…what again?

"What exactly did you have in mind?"

His lips—lord, his lips—pull into a secretive little smirk, practically crushing any dream I ever had about them to bits. My high school fantasies featuring the neighbor's son were softer, too soft for the man before me today. All hard edges, sharp angles, and severe dips—there's nothing soft about Marcos Vega.

In a deep voice that raises the hairs on my arms for the second time, he says, "Follow me," and it's like I'm seventeen all over again. I would've given anything to have him say that to me back then. To have him say anything to me at all.

Is this really happening?

Hunter and I look at each other, and after waffling for an entire minute about if we should or not, Hunter grabs my hand with his and we do. We follow him all the way out to the parking lot. All the way out to a fiery red crotch rocket—a huge upgrade from the dirt bikes I used to secretly watch him ride but still the same fierce color.

Hunter and I stand next to the bike while Marc starts it up without climbing on. After getting things just the way he wants, he smiles down at Hunter, making my chest warm. Making all of me warm.

Something that runs but isn't moving.

I was talking about a generator—a lot of tents inside the market have them—but this works, too. This works better because… Marcos Vega.

I fan myself as inconspicuously as I can.

"Want to give it a try?" he asks Hunter but looks to me for permission.

I nod, telling Hunter it's okay, and he goes right for it, cranking the handle without any hesitation whatsoever. The engine instantly whines at an earsplitting level and I jolt forward, saying, "Sorry," but Marc puts his hand up, only to eye me confidently, telling me, "Don't be." So simple.

Why can't I stop already?

My blush from feeling the need to apologize blends into a deeper, heated blush at having him tell me not to. It's a habit I wish I could quit. I'm trying to quit. I'm trying. I will. I will quit.

I'm quitting.

Hunter experiments with trying to achieve different frequencies while Marc watches on, his lips pursing to the side anytime there's a momentary sputter but doesn't say anything otherwise, just lets Hunter continue uninterrupted.

He's patient. Didn't know that either.

Technically, I didn't know anything about Marc before this. Not that he has a scar above his right eyebrow. Or that when he smiles, really smiles—like he's doing right now—he has blindingly white, straight teeth like a model. Not one chip, one stain, nothing. Just a sexy mouth full of perfect teeth any orthodontist would be proud of.

I've only ever seen him from afar and having him this close is like a whole new experience. His skin is like the first glimpse of sunbreak when the warm, golden haze bathes the earth in new sunlight, letting you know it's going to be a good day. *A really good day.*

I take in the motorcycle, wondering if he rides it the same way he did his dirt bikes—like he's trying to outrun something. Or someone. Then I focus on Hunter, his face lit up with more excitement than I've seen in a while. Eight months, to be exact—eight and counting.

Tears fill my eyes before I can stop them and I have to blink them away.

"Alright, I think that's enough," I say after another few minutes, gently tugging on his arm. "Tell Marc thank you."

He mumbles out a half-coherent thanks while I stifle a sigh. He's adjusting. He'll get better. We'll get better.

We're getting better.

Trying to give Marc privacy to mount his bike, I stare down at my son, wondering what he's thinking right now. I'm always wondering what he's thinking and he never tells me. He used to talk more. He used to laugh. He's much more serious now. And it kills me. Every minute of every day.

Will it always be like this? Will we ever have a chance at happiness again?

Was that really happiness though?

"Do you want to try?"

Marc's still standing beside his motorcycle, his dark eyes watching our every move.

"Excuse me?" I ask and he jerks his chin at the handle Hunter was just twisting. "Oh, no thanks. I'm good."

He studies me for a beat too long, then asks, "You sure?" *No.*

The silence stretches and I fumble to say, "So, more red, huh? Is that your color or something?"

His eyebrows sink.

Shit. Why did I say that?

His face morphs from suspicion to…something else, as he asks carefully, "You've seen me?"

"Um, yeah, your dirt bike. I think I've seen it before." Lots and lots of times actually. From a spot I don't typically tell people about because I like having one place where I can go and not be around anybody—except the one that used to tear across the land on his searing red dirt bike. Sometimes I'd envision him doing the same thing as me. Him escaping, me escaping. Us escaping—together, but separately.

He doesn't say anything, so I say, "Red bike, red pads, red helmet?" Like a flame licking across the horizon, lighting everything up in its path. Yeah, I'd know him riding anywhere. "That's you, right?" I tack on in my last-ditch attempt to not sound like a complete troll but he doesn't even move or breathe. *Is he breathing?* "I only saw you briefly. You know, the property lines out there…it's hard to tell whose land is whose sometimes." I know exactly whose property it was but I just shrug, sticking to my story. With no real markings or fencing it is hard to tell where one farm ends and the other begins. Sometimes my dad will point to a bush and say that's the only marker he needs but I swear it's a different bush every time, especially after burning season.

Someone somewhere knows exactly where the property lines are but I don't particularly care to find out. Not if it means losing my favorite view while I'm back at my family's farm.

My hand comes up to touch my tattoo and Marc tracks the movement, asking thickly, "Land?"

I drop my hand and shift so my arm is out of his view.

"We're neighbors, remember?"

It can't be news to him that Graham Dairy is Vega Farms' neighbor, can it?

"Right." The grip on his helmet relaxes a fraction. "I practice out there from time to time."

Now I'm the one not breathing. He rides out there *still*? I haven't seen him recently. The only person I've seen since I've been back to Graham Dairy after being gone the last eight years was his friend Beckett when he crashed, but that was last fall. Now that I am living with my parents again, I've been out there several times, never seeing anyone else. Or so I thought. Did he ever see me?

I hold my breath, waiting for him to say as much but he doesn't.

Then I remember he's supposed to actually go out to Graham Dairy and my breath comes out in a rush just like my next words.

"I was going to take a look at the RANGER myself, so I don't think you need to stop by." Ever.

"Do you usually fix UTVs?"

His question is hand dipped in humor, deep-fried in doubt, and presented to me like a prize-winning creation on the same flimsy little stick of misogyny that I've been fed too many times to count.

But I've fixed a lot of machines on the farm. Graham Dairy has two workshops full of tools, so I can make almost anything work if I have to. If I try. Which I haven't. Yet.

"Sometimes," I say. I did fix one of its tires before.

"Okay," he draws out. "Well, maybe I'll swing by next time I'm out that way anyway. Just in case."

Finding out he doesn't live at Vega Farms full-time, being groomed to take the reins over for his dad one day, doesn't make me as happy as I once thought it would. That's what's expected of all firstborns after all. We inherit the responsibilities, the expenses, the obligation, the weight around our throats that lets us know we're never truly free because we were born first and therefore must pick up where the generation before us left off.

Maybe it's because while he may have gotten out from that crushing weight, I just settled back under mine.

My heart starts the race it's been performing for the last year anytime I think about my current situation. That thread of thought leads directly to my ex which is even worse—makes me *feel* even worse. Unfortunately, my heart is so tired, tired of reacting to thoughts of someone that doesn't deserve half the attention I give him, and it rebels to the point that I worry it'll quit entirely. Just go on strike until I can find someone new, someone better for it to pump for. It's not that unfathomable.

Everyone talks about the broken hearts but no one ever mentions the tired hearts. They're just as tricky, if not trickier, because while broken pieces can always be stitched back together again, tired hearts struggle to find the will to try at all.

Hunter complains about being thirsty at the same time Marc finally mounts his motorcycle, probably ready to make his escape.

"I don't want to trouble you," I tell him honestly. "Thanks for all your help today though and, uh," I meet his eyes one last time if not just to make sure he is in fact real, "take care."

Take care? What am I? A widow handing out stale caramel chews to the handsome fella next door?

I hear him rumble out a laugh, saying something about liking trouble but I don't bother looking back on our way out of the busy parking lot. He's real. He's real and now he's free to go back to his life while I go back to mine. I can't have him out at my family's farm, walking around in the same space I walk around in, smiling with those teeth. Oh God, the teeth! I never could've guessed hidden under that dust-covered helmet of his was a commercial-worthy smile tucked between lips that look like the devil himself designed. Very, very naughty things happen with mouths like that. Looks so clean, but I bet sounds so dirty.

I can't help but wonder what it *feels* like though.

No. That's not even close to possible. Just like back then, I'm older than him. And unlike back then, I'm a mom. Two strikes in a long list of other strikes against us, starting with I'm just not ready.

My fed-up heart is not ready.

Why am I still thinking about him? I haven't thought about him in years.

I rub my left arm again, knowing that's not exactly true.

But I've been trying. Trying to forget about the Vegas' son, starting when that little blue line appeared in the window that felt more like a door and all the way up until last September.

As soon as my younger sister spots us, she starts waving maniacally, bouncing on the balls of her feet.

"So? How did it go?"

"Fine."

Her eyebrows nosedive and I busy myself with shuffling some stuff around on the table, making the pens look more scattered. I'm still pissed at her for leaving Hunter unattended. I'm not about to spill about the hot guy down the street that I may or may not have stalked in my very limited free time when I was a teen.

"I got to rev his motorcycle," Hunter says around his water bottle.

"What about you, Bentlee? Did you *rev his engine?*"

I frown at her. "Why are you saying it like that? No." At least I don't think I did. How could I? I barely even spoke to him. He's nerve-wracking up close. More than I anticipated. "And I tend my own engine," I mumble as if she and everyone else isn't already aware that I'm running on absolute fumes all by myself.

"Everybody needs a mechanic for a professional tune-up every now and then. Maybe you should've added one to that list."

To everyone else it's *already* been eight months, but to me it's *only* been eight months. Eight months piggybacking on eight years. Eight years of buildup I have to chip away at before letting anyone even get a peek at what's under my hood.

"What do you know? You're only twenty-one." The words sound harsh to my own ears and I apologize immediately, wincing through that, too. I was only seventeen when I got pregnant with Hunter, not because of how much "tuning" I was getting, but because the safety precaution we put in place broke.

And now here I am, left to figure all this shit out alone. Adding someone, anyone, to the mix is not an option, even for something like a basic "tune up."

I can't even pretend to care about another person's feelings right now. Hunter is my first priority with my own wants and needs falling far, far below his. I can only do so much with the time I have to protect his innocent, malleable heart.

Blows are coming. Hard blows that could knock him down and make him question everyone around him, maybe even himself, and when that happens, I don't want to be the one he looks at with cynicism and distrust. I want to be the one honest thing that never failed him. Everything—*everything*—can fall apart around us and I'll still be the one person in his life standing, if only to hold him up.

He is my world and I am his gravity. My love for him will never falter.

The rest of the day continues on one endless loop of overstretched smiles, counting and recounting cash, and repeated sales pitches about why milk straight from the source *should* cost more than the stuff sold in stores. By the time we close up shop and start to head home, my cheeks hurt, the back of my shirt is more sweat than cotton, and Hunter's whining about literally everything. The hunger eating him alive, the pebble in his shoe, the sweat dripping in his eyes, the mannequin looking at him through a store window—it's all extremely upsetting and I need to hear about it over and over and over again.

My love for him will never falter.

Chapter 3

Bentlee

With my shoulder pressing my phone to my ear, I stick my hands inside the front of my bibs, leaning against the wall of the maternity barn and listening to my ex come up with yet another excuse why he can't take Hunter for the weekend. There's always something. Something and nothing.

He didn't want us to go to court for a custody agreement because "we're grown adults," but the last eight months it's been one thing after another with him and I'm starting to rethink that decision.

"Bent, it's not like I can control the weekend traffic. You act like I want this." I roll my eyes. "Unless you want to make him stay up past midnight?"

And there it is. The opportunity to somehow make me look like the bad guy. *Go ahead, Bentlee, deprive your child of sleep for your own selfish reasons.*

"We can just switch weekends. That's fine."

Every time Shawn does this, it's a whole song and dance. Every time Shawn does anything, it's a whole song and dance. He wears me down until I'm too exhausted to fight just so he can get his way. It used to work for a lot of things. It doesn't anymore. Well, it does sometimes, but I'm at least aware of his underhanded techniques now. I'm just trying to figure out how to navigate around them better and not let them—*him*—control me.

Breaking up with someone usually means breaking up with all their bullshit, too. Not with a child involved though. Everything's more complicated when children enter the picture and you can't just walk away when someone's being an unreasonable asshole, even if you really want to.

I thought everything would get easier after I left him but this shit's hard.

Living with him was even harder though.

"Bentlee! Are you around?" Sydnee calls out from inside the barn.

An apology sits on the tip of my tongue but I swallow it down, mumbling out a quick goodbye instead, then hang up, freeing a hand to catch my phone before pocketing it.

"I'm here," I tell her as I make my way down the hay-covered walkway between dozens of pregnant cows. I worked out here from the day I turned eleven years old until I told my family I was expecting as well, so it's like second nature really. I became calf manager at fifteen and kept that title right up until I quit. My family wanted me to stay. They wanted me to work but Shawn didn't want me to work at all, and if you live here, you work here—those are Graham Dairy's rules. Have been for all three generations the farm's been through.

Work. Work. Work. That's what matters. That's all that matters to them. If you're not working, you're not useful and everything on a farm has a use.

They couldn't comprehend that something else mattered to me more. That something else matters more. He did then and he does now. He always will.

Hunter.

I know my ex thought it was him I chose. That *he* was more important to me.

He was wrong.

But so was I for ever letting him believe that he might've been, even for a second, because it was a second too long.

Hunter's trying to coax a new litter of kittens out from under a tub in the corner when I pass and I tell him, "Hey, be careful, okay?"

He just nods, lowering his head into the messy straw to get a better look and I shake mine, thinking about the bath I'll have to give him tonight. With his dry skin, I used to be able to draw it out to every other day but I'm lucky if I don't have to bathe him twice a day nowadays. He's seriously covered in eczema but he goes to bed every night with a sense of belonging which is more than I can say for myself.

My son's name may be Hunter but he is anything but. He's always taking care of some four-legged critter or another and I know it'll be hard for him when school starts back up in two days to leave behind all the furry friends he's accumulated since we moved here.

Although moving back into my childhood home felt like diving into a wave pool and then trying to swim against the current, I can't deny how good it is for him to be around all the animals. For both of us. I missed them. Caring for the many animals running around, loving them, nurturing them. That's one thing Graham Dairy is never short on—living things in need of round-the-clock care.

Technically I was hired back for office work, or so the story goes. I'm *supposed* to be Graham's full-time bookkeeper but the other positions around the farm that my parents need me to fill continue to increase—daily. Now I just wear my bibs and go where they tell me. If I can find the time to run some numbers, I do, otherwise I'm mostly out here, lending a hand where needed. I don't mind tending to the cows. What I do have a problem with is my paychecks not showing how much I'm actually working or how hard. And I always find time to run those numbers, so I know I'm being underpaid. It's just enough for me to support myself and Hunter...here. If we moved out, I could never get by with what my parents are paying me.

The hands of manipulators are only open in the beginning, to shuffle you from one to another, then they close so tight it's hard to escape. Shawn, my parents…their hands are all starting to feel the same and I'm not sure why I can't seem to break the cycle. Or how. Especially if the money I'm finally making won't allow for it.

I didn't know it at the time because Shawn was always careful to lay the guilt on thick enough for me not to see clearly about staying home full-time to be with our son. As amazing as it was to spend those first years with Hunter, it wasn't until he started kindergarten and I tried to find a job that the shame-coated glasses were ripped right off my face to reveal Shawn's tricks. Well, most of them. Shawn didn't want me to work because I'd have my own money, and if I had my own money, it'd be easier to walk away. I had already refused to marry Shawn. No matter how much he pushed, it was the one thing to which I never backed down. It never felt right.

It didn't feel right that I had to sneak online classes just to get my bookkeeping certification either but I did it anyway. I only wish it were being put to use the way I'd imagined. The way I'd hoped.

"What's up?" I ask Sydnee. She's leaning down, helping the minutes-old newborn calf struggling to stand next to the heifer that just gave birth to it. Dairy cows are notoriously disinterested in their young but good dairy farmers swoop in and take care of the calves from their first minute, so it's not a big deal.

"Can you take this one while I help the momma?"

"Sure," I say, helping get it into a box. It's not exactly a box—we just call it that—more a huge crate on wheels so we can keep the newest ones warm in another area while we get them situated with everything they need to start off as healthy as possible.

Within their first thirty minutes we try to get them fed their first feeding of colostrum along with a batch of probiotics and vitamins. We'll mark their head with a special crayon afterward, letting everyone else know they had their most important meal.

Wheeling the newborn—*looks like we've got a…boy*—bull to the back room where the temperature is carefully regulated just for the babies, I get the bottle all set up. Even though the bottle is gigantic compared to a human bottle, it brings back memories of feeding my own baby. I fed hundreds of calves during the six years I worked here, but when I fed my son for the first time, it was like nothing I'd ever experienced. Even with my background, for whatever reason, we just couldn't come together to get him latched on well enough to actually breastfeed. So I pumped for the first six months and gave Hunter bottles of breastmilk instead. Attaching milking equipment to heifers isn't all that hard once you get the hang of it but trying to breastfeed your own child is difficult as hell. I think the lactation nurses chalked it up to me being young at only eighteen but I'm as unconvinced now as I was then. I tried and tried and tried. I tried until tears soaked both me and Hunter, then I tried some more. I just hope I get another shot at it one day.

One day.

I want more kids. Of course I do, but it's not going to be the way I'd originally thought. One husband, one father for all my kids, one dependable man to uphold both titles simultaneously.

Maybe that's why I dragged my feet whenever Shawn brought up marriage. Some part of me knew he wasn't capable. I just wish that part announced itself sooner. So much sooner.

"Alright, come here, cutie."

Standing above the baby bull, I lean over his head and stick my middle finger in his mouth to relax the jaw muscles enough to get the nipple in. As soon as it is, he begins sucking heartily, the sounds making me chuckle.

"Hunter!" I yell, looking over my shoulder and smiling. "Wanna feed the calf?"

His body is practically a streak of motion as he darts around the corner and I laugh.

"I thought you might."

I've been careful to always pose this kind of thing as a question. An option. A choice. Not a chore. Not an obligation. Not a job he won't get paid for but is expected to complete nonetheless.

Basically the exact opposite of my time here.

Farm kids are helping hands, expected to lift everyone and everything up without ever considering where it's putting them and from a young enough age that they don't even fully understand the repercussions.

My son walks, talks, and acts like a farm kid but isn't. Not really. This is only temporary—hopefully.

But if he ever does choose a life in farming, it'll be his choice and it'll be when he's old enough and educated enough to make it for himself, not because I swaddled him in those expectations from birth.

Climbing into the box as well, Hunter drops to his knees and takes the bottle from my hold, keeping it angled correctly as I watch his little lips pull into a grin while he feeds the bull. They're a tad smaller than mine but have the same cupid's bow on the top lip. Shawn used to complain about Hunter looking so much like me. He was mad Hunter didn't have more of his features but I guess my genes are stronger. *And better.*

He didn't get my eyes though. Not all of them anyway. I have central heterochromia which means I have two different colors in my irises, one color near the border of the pupil and another for the rest of the iris. Blue and green while Hunter just has blue. A steel blue that's seen way more than I wish it had to. Hopefully not as much as he could've seen though…at least for now. Everything will be revealed one day, then the blue might even harden to real steel. Betrayal leaves a chaotic path of destruction in its wake, and it's anybody's guess how any one person will fix the damage when their time comes to face what happened.

I stand up straight, blowing a hair out of my eyes and crack my neck side to side, asking, "What should we name him?"

"Marcus."

"What?" I drop my head to look down at him but he's staring behind me.

Someone else speaks, saying, "Better him than me."

Swinging my gaze around, I find Marc with his hands in his pockets, leaning against the doorjamb.

How long has he been standing there while I've had my overalls-covered ass on display? That kind of wedgie is as far from sexy as you can get. Not that I'm trying to look sexy for Marc Vega. That'd be impossible.

Him, on the other hand, he looks like he couldn't *not* look sexy if he tried. With a muscle tee showing off his toned-to-perfection abs, dark jeans hanging off his slim hips, and high-tops, he doesn't look like he was born and raised on a farm at all.

He looks lost.

I thought if we ever met, we'd have a lot in common, that we'd be able to empathize with each other. But looking at him now, I don't think we could be any more different except for the tattoos decorating our arms—his on his forearms, mine on my upper arm.

Then I wonder if he has any piercings and my face starts to feel flushed for the first time all day.

Don't go there.

"Er, what are you doing here?"

This feels like one of those out-of-body experiences right now. Like I'm hovering above my own body, watching as I move in slow motion to piece together what's real and what's not. Is he really here? Am I still wearing the ugliest outfit on the face of the planet?

Did we really just name a Graham calf Marcus?

Yep, yep, and yep.

"I was out at my dad's and thought I'd stop over. There's," he grimaces, pointing his thumb behind him, "a lot of blood…or something." His eyes fall from mine down the rest of me and he starts forward suddenly, his shoulders bunched like he's ready to fight. Ready to kill.

He asks, "Are you okay?" and I realize I'm not the one he's prepping to take on, to take *out*.

My heart performs this little staccato that I've never felt before. He thinks I'm hurt and that upsets him. It upsets him *for* me, not *because* of me.

Snapping out of it, I follow his gaze, already knowing what I'll find—blood…or something. More like afterbirth. Lots of it. Everywhere.

I swing my legs over the side of the box, planting both feet on the ground and try to wipe some of the mess off my pant legs. This is nothing new—to me. Obviously it's a shock to Marc.

Is getting dirty really that foreign of a concept to a guy who rides dirt bikes?

Getting dirty…

Do. Not. Go. There.

"Sorry," I say before I can stop. "I'm fine. Thanks."

Pushing the goop around my thighs is doing nothing, so I give up—it'll dry eventually—and grab a towel off an overhead rack to dry my hands instead.

"You didn't need to come all the way over here."

"Is the UTV fixed yet?"

I tense and peek at him out of the corner of my eye but don't find any actual mockery in his stance. Not like Shawn. *Nothing* like Shawn.

Eyeing him a moment longer, I stuff some more hay in the box, under the bull. He won't be staying here long term—we only keep females since you can't milk a bull—but we still treat them all the same starting out, aside from the kind of vaccines they get at first. He'll eventually be sold to another farm, and in order to get top dollar for him, he needs to be in good health. Everything at a farm has a purpose. Everything and everyone.

"Do you think you can finish feeding him for me and I'll be right back to wash the bottle?" I ask Hunter. He can help with the fun part but I'll complete the chore portion since I'm the one getting paid. *Barely.*

I wait until he nods, not even sparing me a glance as he focuses on the bull guzzling milk.

My sweet boy. Steel eyes, elastic heart.

After planting a kiss on the top of his head, I pass Marc, expecting him to follow. At first I don't hear any footsteps behind me, so I turn around, noticing him glued to the same spot, eyes fixed on Hunter and the calf. He takes a tentative step toward the two before getting permission from me.

With a wave of my hand, he leans against the top of the box

and watches. Just watches. After a few more minutes, he says, "Bye, *Hunter*," with a light chuckle and pushes away from the box.

Embarrassment colors my son's face and every hair on the back of my neck rises like a cat ready to pounce.

"What's going on?" I ask as Marc finally approaches me.

Marc's smirk widens. "You got a good boy, that's all." Only half of the hairs lie back down, somewhat placated. "How old is he?"

"Seven."

"Which makes you?"

"A mother of a seven-year-old."

His smile wanes to a solid frown but he drops it. As soon as I tell him my age, he'll judge. They all do. Sometimes I like the look of surprise on people's faces when they realize I'm a young mom. Sometimes I hate it. Mostly I hate it.

"When we met, he told me his name was Gunther. I don't know if a lot of kids his age would think to give a fake name to a stranger."

I could kill Sydnee for putting my son in a position that he felt he had to lie about his identity. Actually, after Marc leaves, I think I will. I've always told Hunter that if we did somehow get separated, to find someone he could trust. Looking over Marc now, I'm wondering if he succeeded.

"Come on," I say, changing the subject and spinning on my heel. "It's this way."

It's only when we're walking again that I realize Marc's been looking at me the same way.

"You should be good."

I jerk my head over to him, eyebrows raised behind my round sunglasses. "That's it? That was like…ten minutes."

He shrugs, wiping his hands off on his own rag and sticking it in his back pocket. "I'm quick."

I push my bottom lip out, impressed. I would've spent at least an hour messing around with it before slapping some duct tape in a few places and calling it a day.

After a slight hesitation, he adds, "On engines."

I'm quick on engines.

My bottom lip is sucked back in and bitten between my teeth.

With his hands tucked into his back pockets, his biceps bulge out to his sides, drawing my eyes to the veins shimmering with sweat like rivers of volcanic lava—*hot.*

"We should test it out, make sure it runs all right."

"I trust you." As soon as I say it, I regret freeing my bottom lip at all. Trust is not something I have in spades anymore, especially not for a man I barely know. I *don't* know. Not really.

"You trust easily."

"It's a character flaw." That's the truth if I've ever heard it. "So, you don't live at Vega Farms but you…work there?" He said he practices on his dad's property but I'm not sure what that means exactly.

He nods once.

"What do you do?"

"I work on cars. Engines…" He gestures to the RANGER. "Of all kinds. Farming equipment is my department and my dad's our biggest client."

"Are you a…"

"Mechanic."

Oh. *Oh.* That's what this is. Probably just a house call in hopes of landing another big deal. Got it. As if there was any other reason for today's visit—a Cher Horowitz-sized *as if.*

"And you? You work out here?" His gaze takes in the cluster of buildings with a frown etched on his already hardened face.

"I quit," comes out on a whisper. "Almost eight years ago." I don't know why I feel the need to confess to him. I guess I just want him to know it's not as simple as what he's imagining.

I watch the loose dirt kicking up around my Mucks as I bat at a rock with one, noting the irony. No matter how you look at it, I'm nothing but a dirty girl to everyone. Farmer—dirty. Teen mom—dirty.

Farmer that quit—dirty. Teen mom that couldn't hack it on her own—dirty.

"Hunter gets it from you then."

"What?" I bite the word out, preparing to spit a follow-up insult back in his face.

Waiting until I meet his eyes, he answers, "All of it," but it doesn't feel like an insult. Instead it feels like a compliment. One I don't fully understand but let in anyway.

He slides into the RANGER's driver's seat smoothly, nodding me over to join him but Hunter and Sydnee come out of the maternity barn, both of them holding the kittens from earlier.

"We're going to go get them some milk," Sydnee calls out, grinning from ear to ear. "I'll keep an eye on Hunter."

"Be careful." Then because it's fresh on my mind, I say, "Remember last time." A look of genuine guilt washes over my sister's face and I decide not to kill her after all.

I slip into the spot next to Marc on the small bench seat, propping one foot on the dashboard and wrapping an arm loosely around my bent knee.

"Thank you. For fixing this," I say as he starts the engine and cranks the wheel, pulling out of the dirt-packed driveway.

"It's the least I could do for Beck's hero."

"I'm nobody's hero." Not even my own.

"Heroine then."

"No," is all I say.

"My brother being alive and well with a baby on the way says otherwise."

"Brother?" I know for a fact Marc only has a sister for a sibling. A fact I'm beyond grateful for. One Marcos Vega is enough. Enough to rob all coherent thoughts. Enough to keep you up late, late into the night using those same fickle thoughts for fantasies. Lots and lots of fantasies.

Two would be too much for any sane woman that'd like to stay that way.

"Not all families are predetermined, some are forged," he states like it's a fact.

Okay...

"I thought you had a sister though. A younger sister?"

His grip on the skinny wheel tightens but his eyes remain focused ahead.

"Do you keep tabs on all your neighbors?"

"It's kind of hard not to when we went to the same school."

"I think I'd know if we were in the same class."

I abandon my knee to grip the bar above me as we fly over a bump, rocking us from side to side, our shoulders brushing. Instinctively, I unroll my shirt sleeves, covering both shoulders again. I was too caught off guard at the market to do anything then.

"We weren't the same grade."

His head whips sideways and his eyes drop for a split second like he's looking for something, then he meets my gaze, confident enough not to look where he's going.

"Older or younger?"

Like he really has to ask.

I sigh. "Older."

"By what? One grade?"

Enough to keep every part of me away from every part of him growing up. Physically, he didn't look like a teen ripping across the horizon but that didn't change the fact that he was just that. I was on the cusp of becoming an adult, and, unbeknownst to me at the time, a mom, while he was…not. Not even close. And so, I let him be. I never made myself known even if I really wanted to.

"Try two."

His Adam's apple bobs.

"Who did you hang out with?"

I spread a hand out at the vast space surrounding us for my answer. Not who, what. Cows, cows, and more cows. And sagebrush, of course.

I was one of the youngest seniors in my graduating class because of my summer birthday and it mattered. It mattered to a lot of people. Not only that I was younger and more inexperienced with actual people but that I didn't care to *try* to fit in with anyone else. A lot of farmers went to our school and I think they could tell that I wanted out. That I wanted *different*. I wanted to want and be able to chase that want, but in farming, that's not readily encouraged. That's probably why I was swept up in a different crowd altogether, from a different school.

Obviously, Shawn didn't have the same reservations about being with someone that was underage, or inexperienced.

This close to Marc, I smell something other than sweat from working all day and it helps quiet everything else circling in my head. It's almost like a nature scent with a hint of smokiness and…sweetness? Like a campfire in the woods with a basket of s'mores off to the side. It's enticing and relaxing all at once. When he said he works on engines, I assumed he'd smell like oil and rust but that's not even close to how he actually smells.

I probably smell like cow shit and desperation. An effective combo for scaring off our new friendly neighborhood salesman no doubt. Although, the night I conceived Hunter I remember smelling both as well, so what do I know.

"So, what? You're twenty-six?"

"I just turned twenty-five last month," I say, then wait. Wait for the judgment. The look. The one not easily hidden. The one that always tells what everyone else is thinking but they don't typically say because spoken words can turn into living, breathing omens with the ability to bite them in the ass and they'd rather not risk it.

Except it never comes. Nothing about Marc changes, like this news is not a shock to him whatsoever. Like a teen parent is not as abnormal as everyone would prefer to think.

The wind cuts a harsh angle, blowing the loose bits of hair sticking out from my messy bun around my face and a couple get stuck to my lip gloss as I point out where to turn. I do it without giving any real thought but Marc listens before I can fix my mistake.

As soon as we're near the spot I found his friend all those months ago, I tell him to park. *That's close enough.*

He turns the key, silencing the RANGER and we sit here motionless, breathing in the flat land before us. On this side of the knoll, all the eye can see is Graham land. On the other side…Vega land. I don't know for sure if the knoll is ours or theirs but I've always treated it like it's mine. Mine to escape to. Mine to hide on. Mine to get lost… in him. It didn't matter if he was riding during the day or at night, I only ever saw that red streak of rebellion.

That's what I thought he was at the time anyway, what I needed him to be back then. Anything to hold on to that little sliver of hope that it was possible. That there was more. More than what I'd only ever been shown. More than what I am today.

Whether that's what he actually was or not is irrelevant. *Just like my plans to make it out of here.*

He does still look every bit the rebel though. That part hasn't changed at all—thankfully.

"It works," I say about the RANGER, hating how fake my tone sounds. How fake I feel.

Staring out at the tumbleweeds rolling over the land, he says, "It does."

"But you knew that."

He doesn't answer because it's not a question.

After a while, he asks, "Where's Hunter's dad?"

I rein in my surprise fast enough to answer honestly. "Home."

Shawn won't let me go anywhere near there anymore even though I'm fairly certain what I'll find. He tries to blame me, of course. I left him so I shouldn't be able to visit the home I abandoned in the process. We either meet at an agreed-upon location for visitation handoffs or they don't happen at all.

Always on his terms.

"But not yours?"

"That's…incredibly fucking presumptuous of you."

He looks at me seriously. "Am I wrong?"

I scoff for answer. *Presume that.*

"Why does it matter? You brought me out here to ask about my son's father?"

He doesn't answer either and I sigh, laying my cheek against my still bent knee.

"We're not together anymore, if that's what you're wondering." Is he? Wondering?

He's quiet for a long time, back to studying the landscape again.

"You left for your boy and you moved back for your boy?" *How did he…* He turns to me and I can only nod. "And you're not happy about it?"

It. Two inconspicuous letters sitting atop a whole lot of layers hidden underneath.

I take longer to nod this time. The answer is just as layered and I don't feel like peeling any back right now.

"What did he do?"

That, I really don't want to explain. Not to him. Not to anyone. Not unless I have to.

Instead, I whisper, "What if I'm the bad guy?" It's a possibility I don't like considering, especially knowing how Shawn liked to pull the villain card on me more often than not, but I had to have been at least a little bit, right? Isn't that the belief? That it takes two to tango—always. Once one stops dancing, it's no wonder another dance partner starts to look more appealing.

Or maybe the appeal was always there and it didn't matter what anyone did, least of all me.

People are who they are regardless what society tries to label them. Right and wrong is not a group mentality issue. It's a person-by-person case but humanity swallows pills of disappointment better when there's someone else to blame.

Marc's eyes alternate between mine, searching, and I close them. I don't know what he sees but I know what he *might* see and that alone is enough to shut him off.

"Stop doing that."

"What?"

"Keeping your eyes from me."

I open them slowly, grinning when his frown only increases.

"You like my eyes?" Marc doesn't say anything. "What do you like about them?"

"Everything."

Those very eyes widen when he follows that up with a headshake before abruptly climbing out of the UTV.

"How don't I know you? Why?" he asks suddenly.

Eyeing him carefully, I sit back, the pad of my thumb pressing into the top of my palm.

"Because we never met. I was busy as I'm sure you were, too."

"I know I've been out this far before." *Umm.* "Probably. Shit. I don't know."

The only person that I'm aware of ever attempting to climb the knoll we're parked at the bottom of is Beckett. It's deceptively high and the loose dirt that's more like silt at the top isn't ideal for tires. It's practically untouched. Except by one—me.

But eight years ago I did move away and he very well might've pushed the invisible boundaries I alone set.

I simply nod like it's anybody's guess. Maybe he did. Maybe he has a whole life I know nothing about.

No, not maybe, he does. We don't know each other. And I should start acting like it.

I slide over to the driver's seat and start it up, then pull up directly in front of him. Sticking my hand out, I wait while he looks from it to my face then back again.

"I'm Bentlee. Due to unforeseen circumstances, my son, Hunter, and I live here at Graham Dairy with my family and about six hundred cows, and I think we might be neighbors. Or were once upon a time."

His lips twitch like he wants to smile but doesn't want me to know. But I do know. Oh, I know.

When he still doesn't take my hand, I shove it into his, touching the side of a very strong thigh in the process. I give him a firm shake, then go to remove it but his hand grips mine even tighter, yanking me out of the vehicle entirely. I stumble into him at the exact moment the RANGER rolls forward without a foot on the brake but Marc shoots his left arm out to the side without so much as blinking, grabbing the front bar of the frame and stopping its progress.

Our fronts still touching with our clasped hands caught between us, he says huskily, "I'm Marc. Short for Marcos. Not Marcus, *never* Marcus."

"Noted."

"My family owns Vega Farms, somewhere nearby, but I *don't* live there and I *don't* work for them. I work for myself and sometimes it lands me out this way."

I nod my head once, swallowing loudly but not making any move to detach myself from him.

"Do you like it?" His gaze drops for the briefest of seconds to my left shoulder. "Your job?" I say quickly. "Do you like your job?"

Our eyes connect again and hold, then he measures his words by saying, "It gives me plenty of freedom. And it pays well enough."

I almost snort. "Must be nice."

A shadow crosses his face similar to the one when he thought I was hurt.

"Yours doesn't?"

I pull back finally, putting some space between us. Marc doesn't let go at first but then he does and I wish he hadn't.

"It pays enough."

People think having the last name Graham is illustrious but it's always felt more like a condemnation to me. Why won't they let me go?

Without further explanation, I sit back down, depressing the brake again and say, "Let me show you around," all the while keeping my eyes straight ahead. If he wants Graham as a client, he'll need to know where everything is.

I give him the full tour, then park the RANGER back in the front lot, thanking him again for fixing it. I think he made it faster somehow, too. All in ten minutes…dang.

"So, I'll see you on Sunday?" he asks, walking to the BMW that's the same deep red as both of his bikes.

Even after all these years, he's still just as easy to spot.

"For?"

"The gender reveal."

Oh. "I, uh, no."

He chuckles, almost to himself. "Good luck with that." I frown and he says, "My roommates don't really take no for an answer."

"I can't. Really." I motion behind me, lowering my voice. "His dad just backed out of visitation this weekend, so I'll have Hunter."

Marc studies me, then glances past my shoulder, saying easily, "Bring him."

My heart trips, landing face-first and eating a healthy serving of dirt only to pick itself back up, coughing up dust.

My heart isn't just tired, it's out of shape, too.

"I think there'll be a bounce house or some shit."

"Wow. You guys go all out," I joke, trying to calm my nerves. I can't go to a party with Marc. Will I be *with* Marc? No. I'll be with Hunter. And we'll stay for the reveal portion and then leave Marc and his friends to their celebrating. And lives.

Is this official? Am I really going?

"You need me to pick you up?"

Looks like I am.

When I shake my head, telling him I'd rather drive myself, he lists off his number for me to save in my phone, and with unsure fingers, I finally get it in after misspelling his name three times. Hunter isn't the only one that thinks he's Marcus. Stupid autocorrect.

Distractedly, I roll my short sleeves on my tee back up. It's too damn hot out for sleeves now that there's no wind.

Marc stands with an arm draped over the top of his car and rakes his gaze up my body, lingering on my left upper arm.

"See you then. Nice ink, by the way," he says, the half-sleeve of flames tattooed on his exposed forearm that much more noticeable before he climbs inside his car.

The air in my throat expands, turning to fat cotton balls I swear, and I choke out "you too" after he's already gone from sight.

Like a flame licking across the horizon…

Chapter 4

TOSSING A FEW LARGE—REALLY FUCKING LARGE—BILLS on the counter, I scoop up all five outfits for Prince What-The-Fuck-Ever, then grab Rebel, giggling and squirming, and toss her over my shoulder. No way was I waiting in line to stuff a fucking unstuffed teddy bear—what in the actual fuck?—with a thirty-five-cent crown on its head, so we came to the mall first thing this morning but now I'm late. Sort of.

They won't start without me.

Little did I know the nine-thousand-dollar bear that we had to fucking stuff ourselves—again, what the fuck?—needed an entire wardrobe, too. Guy started out flaccid and sad but now he has a week's worth of outfits to cover his new lumpy-ass body. Yeah, I overstuffed the fuck outta him. Who cares?

Swear his clothes cost more than mine.

I was supposed to be at the gender reveal party thirty minutes ago to help set up. Thankfully I stole the discreet package of colored smoke from Paige's brother, Tysen, to guarantee they couldn't start without me in case this shit ran over. Ty's a great shop manager for Pop Two but he's still as preoccupied as he was when we first hired him last summer. He's been locked in a nasty custody disagreement with his ex for their son and even though I don't know all the details, it's not hard to tell it's eating him up. Can't say I really blame him. Lawyers, courtrooms, judges, everyone packed in there listening to and then walking away knowing all your business…I'd rather stuff a hundred more bear princes. Some couples can get by without taking their cases to court, some can't—Tysen and his ex, Clarise, are one of them.

I start to feel a little bad he's probably shitting his pants right now on top of everything else, so after I drop Rebel back off to her mom, still giggling but upgraded to full-on bouncing now, I press my foot on the gas until it's practically touching the floorboard.

The party's out at our original roommate, Coty's house. He had it built for him and his girlfriend, Angela. Their property is perched directly below Beck and Paige's, which is still in the process of being built. It is built, it just needs all the finishing touches for them to be able to live there comfortably—like faucets and backsplash. And since it doesn't have any actual landscaping yet, Coty suggested we use their stained concrete back patio. I don't know if I'd be offering up my stained concrete for burnouts but it is our brother and luckily Angela's pretty understanding of what all that requires. Our makeshift family doesn't hold out on each other.

Except…

But that's different. Some things *are* bigger than self-constructed bonds and it's only a matter of time before they realize that for themselves. And when they do, maybe they'll be more likely to forgive my sins, should I decide to confess them. Should *we* decide, since it's not just me.

Until then though, we're not on the same playing field. Not fully. Which hurts more often than I care to admit, but ultimately, it's for the best. I'll do anything for Rebel. Out of everything, my friends should at least be able to respect that.

I make it out to the canyon where all our properties are located in record time, parking behind the white Jeep Angela refuses to upgrade despite her now being able to afford to. She doesn't like any type of materialistic item whatsoever but is overly sentimental about the 1986 CJ-7 for some reason. We keep up with all the aftermarket upgrades we can find for it, so it runs like it's brand new but…it's not. And it doesn't have doors. Angela does have the doors somewhere but she just chooses not to put them on; and since Coty lets her do whatever the hell she wants, she drives it around in the dead of winter like that, too.

Her resolve runs deeper than the Mariana Trench, but luckily, Coty's love for her runs even deeper.

She's on me as soon as I arrive, directing me where she needs me most. The dumbass that set up the inflatable water slide left a blown-out motor for it, so I head there first, stopping to hand off the color packet to Tysen as he talks anxiously into his phone, probably to one of our technicians he's got searching Pop Two for it right now. I don't explain how or why I have it and he doesn't ask, just pockets it along with his phone. In his other arm, he's trying to hang on to a baby that could pass for a slobbery roly-poly that's chewing on a set of toy keys. His son's around nine months now but ready to move out and take on the world one sharp, non-baby-proofed edge at a time. It's actually a good thing he's got all that baby fat to cushion his many falls. Little man's never content sitting still, and the day he takes his first step, we're all in trouble. I despise those kid leashes passed off as backpacks but Tysen's son, Diesel, is a prime example for why they exist in the first place.

"What are you feeding him?" I joke on my way past.

"Man, it'd be quicker to tell you what he doesn't eat."

I chuckle under my breath almost saying, "I hear ya," but that'd open a door and I keep all my doors shut and locked.

The next forty minutes are spent taking apart and rebuilding the entire fucking motor with red corn syrup melted down to the wires that aren't supposed to be exposed. The only tip I'll be giving at the end of today's reservation is to the proper authorities who are in charge of these assholes' safety certifications. It's supposed to be constantly running next to water—water kids are playing in—for fuck's sake.

By the time I'm finished, my shirt's drenched, so I take it off and throw it on the back of a chair in the sun to dry.

I'm hooking the hose up to the top of the eighteen-foot double slide when a pickup worse off than Tysen's vintage Ford rumbles up the gravel driveway. Tysen loves himself a run-down, diesel anything, hence his kid's name, and the truck parking next to his looks like its twin. Behind it, someone dressed like my boy Coty pulls in on Paige's Honda CBR. The rider dismounts and takes their helmet off to reveal it is Coty. I already spotted Beck's Ninja—you can't fucking miss the neon green street bike—when I arrived so I'm not sure why the hell he brought Paige's bike here, too. Beck wanted to use his own bike for the big reveal, so he rode it today while Paige drove the Tahoe. I know because I was supposed to drive Paige myself but had to back out when Rebel called me last night, telling me all about the latest princess movie she'd just watched. She was so excited, I thought she should have a coordinating toy first thing today.

Did Coty see me dropping her back off at Creekwood though?

My hand slips and the sharp threading on the metal adapter slices my pointer finger. Another violation, another reason for me to gut this goddamn slide like a fish when we're done using it. They can charge me and get a new one to rent out. One that won't put their customers in danger just by setting it up.

Beck appears, coming out of the sliding glass door, so I call down for him to turn the water on and after rinsing the blood down, I descend the built-in stairs between the slides and push the tainted water pooling at the bottom out.

"Oh my God, bro, did you finally get your period? This is such an exciting day." Beck holds his face to the sun, grinning.

"Yeah. Think Paige'll teach me how a tampon works?"

His face drops to pin me with a murderous glare and I laugh, lifting my finger to show him the cut and he pretends to dry heave, saying, "I'd rather you be on your period," around a gag.

"What are you going to do when your daughter has her period?"

"My daughter," he says loudly for no real reason, "whenever she decides to bless us with her presence, will sweat glitter and fart rainbows."

Every word of that is as far from reality as you can get—even him acting like he knows the gender already—but I think it's better to let Beck find that out the hard way.

"Whatever. Put that shit away before you scare off our guests," he says suddenly.

"No one's even here."

He eyes me, another grin sneaking out. "She's not here yet?" He rubs his hands together in front of him. "Ooh, this is gonna be fun. Okay. Hurry, lie down and smear the blood all over you so she can rush over to give you mouth-to-mouth when she shows up."

He shoves me but I shove him back, frowning. He can't really think that's how mouth-to-mouth works, right? His girlfriend's a nurse.

"And keep the shirt off. That's believable." He tries to push me again but I don't budge this time. "Just make sure you cover back up before Paige comes outside though."

Beck keeps spouting some rule about me not being allowed to leave my room back at our apartment unless I'm wearing a shirt. Something about bringing down the patriarchy but I'm pretty fucking sure it's because he knows my abs are better than his. Naturally, I prove that fact every chance I get. Paige grew up with four brothers, one more shirtless torso isn't going to bother her—even if mine is cut like a fucking diamond.

"Who the fuck are you talking about and why would I want mouth-to-mouth from her?"

His hands drop from me as he says seriously, "Bentlee. And why *wouldn't* you?"

"That's not even..."

"Dude, you gonna tell me she's not a total M.U.L.F.?"

"It's M.I.L.F."

"No, it's M.U.L.F. Mom *you'd* like to fuck. Not me. I'm not allowed to look at other women in that way. Gross." He fakes a shudder before sobering to stress, "But you are, so you should."

"You starts with a Y, not a U."

His eyes thin as he tilts his head back, peering down at me. "Grammar Police, huh? That's how you're gonna play this? Okay,

Deputy Spellcheck, what took you so long out at her place the other day? You get a good look at some udders while you were there?" His eyebrows do an idiotic wiggle, bouncing the backward hat on his head.

"That's something I wanted to talk to you about. In all the times we rode out there, did we ever see Graham Dairy?"

His face falls, probably because it's not some sick detail he thought I was about to share but he should know better by now.

And udders? What the fuck?

"Nah, not really. Except for the last time I was out there when I sailed over that sand trap death hill. I could've sworn I saw a barn or something in the distance. Think that was her place?"

"Could've been," I say distracted. Bentlee took me to a hill too but I didn't see the top of it to know for sure. If it was the same spot, how would she have seen Beck though? It was far enough away from the main drag of her family's farm that she would've had to be out there for some reason.

Glancing behind me, he asks, "You wanna explain that?"

I give him a flat look and sidestep him, going straight for the slider. I need a Band-Aid, and maybe if I'm lucky, I'll find one big enough to cover my best friend's mouth, too.

"Aye, at least get dressed before you go in there."

Smiling, I close the door behind my back—my bare back.

After taking care of my cut and finding some disinfectant cleaner, I wander downstairs to find a variety of food covering the counters along with the backyard now full of guests.

Angela's floating around the kitchen trying to hide lids that'd give away everything here is store-bought. Her cooking is bad. The worst. Before us, she didn't know the difference between an apple and a to-mato. Honestly, she *should* leave the lids out so nobody has to worry if she cooked anything.

Drinks are a different topic entirely from working at a coffee stand for a while. She's a fast learner when something interests her, it's just that food never really did. Her mom thought kids were self-suffi-cient from birth, or didn't care enough to learn otherwise, and made her youngest go without for most of her childhood until Angela fig-ured out how to take care of herself. If she hadn't, we would've never got her though, so it worked out the way it was supposed to I guess.

It's crazy the turns life takes in order to get you where you were always gonna end up anyway. Sucks that hers was so shitty.

Sucks that anybody's is.

She looks up when I enter the kitchen, pointing at the bottle in my hand. "What do you need that for?"

"The slide." I doubt the rental company even does that much.

"Ah, let me do it. I was just heading out there."

I don't bother arguing. Angela likes things clean, if not for the simple fact that it keeps her busy. She never stops moving. Ever.

"Why's Paige's bike here, by the way?" I ask when Coty comes through the garage door, joining Angela at the counter and giving her temple a kiss.

They smile at each other, then at me.

I look between the two of them, not liking what I'm seeing. What don't I know? And why don't I know it?

Coty says, "It's twins. B's having twins. Can you believe it? That lucky fuck."

Angela's face visibly flinches while my breath comes out in one long exhale. What? How?

I know *how*, but again, how the fuck didn't I know?

"And…they don't know either?" I ask slowly.

Angela shakes her head. "Paige does but she wanted to surprise Beckett. Well, try to. He hasn't said anything to you, has he?"

"No, he didn't say anything." *And neither did you*, I think. Or Coty, who's more brother than friend. Even Paige. Why didn't my own roommate tell me? We live under the same roof. I could've helped her more or kept the apartment's kitchen stocked better—since she's eating for fucking three. "That's great," I say, feeling a tight knot in my stomach like I'm gonna be sick.

What a shitty way to find out you're at the bottom of the totem pole in your own family. I keep things from my group of friends but only when necessary. Not out of some popularity contest, or whatever the fuck this is.

Coty's eyes narrow. "You alright, man?"

"Fine. I got shit to do." I raise the cleaner in my hold, beelining to the back door.

Angela tries to get my attention but I ignore her and the way my stomach hurts.

I don't have a lot of ground to stand on, I realize that, but they don't know that. They don't know…a lot about me these days.

The older Rebel gets, the harder this whole thing is. She *wants* more now than ever. More time with me, more from me in general, and I don't know how to give that to her without taking away from the other members of my family anymore. It was easier to balance when she was younger. Time apart isn't as noticeable to toddlers. She just started kindergarten and she has actual hobbies now besides staring at the TV or shoveling puffed rice in her mouth. She rides. She wants to learn how to swim, fly a kite, blow a bubble with the gum I always keep in my center console just for her. How the fuck am I supposed to teach her those things without ghosting everyone else in my life in the process? Kary's social paralysis sure as fuck won't help Rebel learn any of those things. It won't help Rebel at all. Not at this stage. She barely even agreed to let her go to a public school, but things are different now. This isn't seven years ago when Kary assumed she'd be doing all this alone. Rebel's got me. No matter fucking what, that little girl's got me and the rest is manageable. The rest is fucking cake. Cake that tastes a little off now that I know I didn't make the original cut today in my family hierarchy but it's still cake.

Twins. My boy's having twins. As soon as their house is completed, Beck and Paige will be moving into it, starting their own branch of our family, and leaving me on my own for the first time in…ever. Will I be on my own?

Finally dragging my gaze from the ground, I stop dead in my tracks, the sliding glass door at my back…open? Closed? No fucking clue. All I see is Bentlee, smiling, and holding a baby—a sight I didn't even know I needed but soak in just the same, letting the image settle my nerves.

Diesel's wet fists latch on to Bentlee's hair, pulling, but her smile only grows like she's completely unfazed by her hair being yanked out of her head. Her blonde hair's down and curly this time, hanging loosely around her smiling face and down the top of her dress—a navy blue dress with two thick straps that get just wide enough on each side to cover her tits. Another set of straps wrap around the torso of the dress just below those same tits, making them stand out like a dessert being presented on Thanksgiving while the bottom flows freely, brushing the tops of her sandals. And her arms, those are on full display today. No shirt sleeves in sight. Just ink and suntanned skin.

Christ. How is this the same girl from the farmer's market? Or in those grimy overalls?

Her lips are still shiny though. Like a small bow decorating a present, just that little something extra that isn't needed whatsoever but makes it all the more appealing.

Tysen rushes to help disentangle his son, apologizing, but also smiling to himself while Hunter looks at the baby's feet, squinting at the chubby little toes scrunching and unscrunching.

Someone taps my hand with the cleaner in it and I look down, noticing Angela trying to pry it from my hold. *How long's she been here?*

She holds up a couple of rags, taking the cleaner off me. "Why don't you go welcome our guests?"

"They're not here for me," I call to her back a little too late, then frown thinking that over.

I glance over at a grinning Beck and he mouths the word udder at me so I flip him off, scowling even more. Beside him Paige looks green, probably nervous about the reveal. The double reveal.

Triple, if everything pans out the way it's supposed to.

So many secrets floating around nowadays.

Slowly, I drop down a step. Tysen's having a hell of a time getting his son off Bentlee and Hunter's still squinting, this time at nothing in particular. Diesel's restless toes get tangled in the front of Bentlee's dress, bunching up a good portion and pulling—down—effectively threatening to give everyone in attendance an entirely different reveal.

Shit.

Keeping my steps quick but measured, I slip my hat from my head down onto Hunter's with the bill facing forward, then step directly in front of Bentlee, blocking her from view of everyone else—everyone but Tysen, whose hands fall away from my close proximity.

Bentlee looks up, oblivious to the show she's about to put on.

"Uh, hey," she says, still smiling but not as easily as a moment ago and focusing on my…chin?

"Hey," I reply back. "Need a hand?"

"We're fine. Aren't we?" she asks the baby in a soothing tone.

"His teeth are coming in and he's looking to chew on anything," Tysen says as Diesel puts a fistful of Bentlee's hair in his mouth, smacking loudly on the strands. "Sorry about that." Tysen grimaces, trying to squeeze his hands between us again but quickly realizing he can't with me standing so close.

"It's a'ight. I got her," I tell Tysen without taking my gaze off Bentlee's. She still isn't exactly looking at me but those colors draw me in just the same. *Do I got her?*

With everyone occupied, I reach out to blindly work the fabric at her hip from Diesel's toes, brushing her hip bone with the back of my knuckles. Her eyes widen but she doesn't say anything as she tries to surreptitiously back away. I get it. I'm standing less than inches away from her with a baby squirming in her hold. Her hair's being munched on by a tiny terror and her hip's being fondled. I would've already laid somebody out by now, starting with Tysen.

Why's he touching her again?

"Come on, Diesel. Let go already," he says, nervously laughing and trying to retrieve some of Bentlee's hair with his hand on her tatted shoulder for leverage. *It better be for fucking leverage.*

I free the fabric from all of Diesel's toes, sliding my right arm between Bentlee and Diesel to pull gently.

"I got you," I repeat, and the moment Bentlee eases her hold, I take all of Diesel's weight while Tysen works to get the chunk of hair still in the baby's fist. At the last second the kid folds in half like a fucking chip clip over my forearm though and latches on to one of Bentlee's dress straps instead. Before anyone can react, the material stretches taut before going completely slack at her collarbone in the next instant, and without thinking, I mash my front to hers, tucking Diesel against the side of my rib cage like a football.

Bentlee's entire body stiffens and she tries to retreat again, but I match her step with one of my own, keeping us glued to each other.

"Don't move," I whisper against the side of her neck, wrapping my left arm around her back to keep her in place.

I feel for the strap behind her neck, holding it tight against the other one. It's a halter-type dress and both straps are now hanging limply down her back. I'm not sure if Tysen saw anything but he will if Bentlee takes one more step.

"I'm so sorry," he says off to the side of us, snapping out of it enough to take Diesel from my hold. "Do you need any help?" he asks once his son's back in his arms but I shake my head, wrapping my other arm around Bentlee, wondering how it can feel so normal— hugging her without really even knowing her.

"We're fine. Aren't we?" I parrot back against the side of Bentlee's hair, biting back a grin when she jerks out a nod.

Her hair smells like peppermint and something else. Something fresh. Nothing like what I smelled at her family's farm. Goddamn, cows smell bad. I thought people stunk until I went out there.

Ever so slowly, one of her hands goes to my bare hip, resting above the top of my shorts and my fingers freeze, the skin-on-skin contact bringing our position to the forefront. I acted on instinct, forgetting I wasn't wearing a shirt but now it's hard to ignore—my body touching hers. My naked chest pressed to her almost naked chest.

With hot fingers, I retie her straps beneath her curls, keeping my elbows tucked tightly against her so she's still covered, even from Tysen who's lingering. *Lingering.*

What does he want?

Aside from the obvious.

The straps now tied in a knot so tight she'll probably have to cut them apart to get undressed later, I pull back, my eyes immediately searching for hers. Bentlee looks like she's in a trance though, not even realizing what she's doing.

"All good?" she asks, eyes refusing to come anywhere near mine. A hell of a lot surer than her voice, her middle finger dips into the top of my Adonis belt, rubbing back and forth like she's memorizing the crease.

My eyelids threaten to close but I shake it off with a head nod, telling her, "All good."

Her hand jolts as her eyebrows crease and she mumbles out, "Sorry."

She does that a lot. Apologizes for shit she shouldn't.

"Don't be," comes out more natural than anything else I've ever said in my life. Of all the things she doesn't need to be sorry for, touching me should be bumped to the top. She'll get zero complaints from me on that front.

Bentlee puts some space between us, taking her hand with and glancing at Tysen, a small blush streaking her cheeks. "I guess I picked the wrong thing to wear."

Why is she looking at him? Tysen did jack shit besides stand here and gape.

Gaping? That earns a look and a blush now?

I open my mouth but Tysen beats me to it, saying, "You look great," and I almost snort. Great? The grass seed finally growing in front of Coty's house looks great. Bentlee looks…better. Way better than anything I could ever come up with, so I remain quiet, watching as she takes another step away. Away from me.

Another scowl makes its way onto my face while Bentlee full-on smiles at Tysen, showing off straight white teeth made even whiter against her tanned face before she looks down at Hunter, seeing the hat on his head for the first time.

Instead of asking him about it though, she finally—*finally*—brings her gaze back up to mine to say, "You didn't have to do that."

What am I supposed to say? Sorry? I'm not. It's okay? It is.

But also, how the fuck did she know it was my hat when this is the first time she's bothered to even glance at me full on?

A moment passes, neither of us so much as blinking, then Paige and Beck step into our little circle, breaking the connection.

"You made it. I told you it was quite the drive out here," Paige says to Bentlee.

She did? When?

Paige takes her nephew from her brother before Beck steals him right out of her arms, as Bentlee waves her off, praising good GPS.

The kid doesn't so much as blink being shuffled from person to person, just grabbing for anything he can get his mouth on in the meantime. With Beck's head cocked from Paige glaring at him, Diesel takes the opportunity to latch on to Beck's jaw with both hands and bite my friend's chin.

Paige laughs at her boyfriend trying to act like he's not in pain when we all know those few teeth Diesel's got are sharp as fuck while Tysen tries to hide a chuckle.

Bentlee gazes down at Hunter with a tender smile, saying, "You used to do that, too."

This ruses Tysen and he jumps on the topic like a kid at a party that just broke the piñata wide open. "Your husband couldn't make it?"

Bentlee clears her throat, still staring at the top of Hunter's head. "I'm not married."

"Oh, sorry." He doesn't even bother to sound sincere though. "Your boyfriend?"

Her eyes meet mine for a split second before they land on Tysen, a tight smile making the edges crinkle. "There's this new thing, maybe you've heard of it, I don't know, but women can actually go out in public without a man attached to them now."

Paige punches Tysen in the arm, talking to Bentlee. "Oh, he knows all about independent women. He's just digging for answers from the new pretty girl."

Bentlee's cheeks grow pinker as do Tysen's. Fucking gaping *and* blushing?

This shit's for the birds.

"Could've fooled me with Marc here stuck to you like a cardigan," Beck mutters loud enough for all of us to hear but I don't bother denying it.

Paige eyes him suspiciously, asking, "You know what a cardigan is?"

He shakes Diesel off his chin to say, "It's one of those bodysuits that goes up your butt crack, right?"

"You're so full of," I glance at Hunter, "it." I wasn't anywhere near her ass and he knows it. Guy is always talking shit. Al-fucking-ways.

"Mom, I'm hungry," Hunter says beside his mom, ending this dead-end conversation. Bentlee's single. I wasn't up her ass. What else is there to say? Fuck off, Tysen?

I wish.

I like him well enough. He's just…irritating me today. Right now specifically.

Beck shuffles Diesel to hold him in one arm while tickling him with the other and says over the laughing baby, "Follow me. Baby D and I will show you where the food is. The food Angie didn't cook anyway. If it looks homemade, don't eat it. Okay?"

"Hey, I brought a salad," Paige says.

Beck beams at her, then drops it to pin a serious expression on Hunter, telling him, "Don't eat that either." Paige swats his back as he passes but he ignores her to murmur, "Stick with me, kid. I'll show you how it's done."

"I can show you around, if you want," Tysen suggests to Bentlee after an awkward pause.

She nods politely, following him without a backward glance as they go after Beck and Hunter.

Paige turns to me as soon as they're out of earshot with a similar grin to Beck's when he's up to something. "They'd make a cute couple, don't you think?"

"No," I say honestly.

"Really? But, they're both so hot."

I tear my gaze away from the back of Bentlee's dress, noting there's not a single panty line, or bra line—which I already knew—to be found and frown at Paige, asking, "You think your brother's hot?"

She only laughs, saying, "He's attractive, to other attractive people...like Bentlee."

Bentlee's hot, yeah. So? What's that got to do with Tysen? Two attractive people can still be attractive separately.

"She could use a good man in her life."

What does that mean? That her ex wasn't? Her lips were sealed when I tried asking about him, but that was away from everyone else.

I cock an eyebrow, asking, "How would you know?"

"I made a run out to Graham Dairy a couple days ago. I wanted to thank her privately and make sure she was coming today."

"And you didn't think I needed to know that?"

"Did you need to know?" Her green eyes sparkle.

I scoff, pinning her with a hard stare. "There's a lot I don't need to know. Right?"

"Shit. Angela told you, huh?"

I nod my head, crossing my arms over my chest.

"Look, I didn't even tell my brothers, except for Ty, so don't take it personal. I just," those same eyes fill with unshed tears, "this is really hard. And scary. And big. So big. Two fucking little Becketts will be running around in my new house, with my *boyfriend*," she says the word like it's a curse for some reason, "and it's just...I'll be doing it alone."

The fuck she will. How can she even think that?

But then she continues and it all makes sense. "I thought I'd always have her around to help me out with this sort of thing, ya know? Even if just to call her in the middle of the night to cry. So, when I found out we were having twins, I chose to focus on that instead of..." She gestures vaguely.

Her. Paige's mom has Alzheimer's and lives full-time in the same facility Paige works at that specializes in Alzheimer's and dementia patients. Paige and her four older brothers have come a long way in the last year dealing with their mother's diagnosis along with her rapidly declining health, but they all still miss her—bad.

"They're both boys?"

Her shoulders lift and fall, defeated. "I don't know. You have to admit, it'd be just my luck."

I pull her into a side hug, saying, "You will never be alone, in anything, ever. You're going to be an amazing mother and Beck will be the best father. And if he's not, I'll kick his ass. Twice. For both kids."

She coughs out a watery laugh, resting her head on my shoulder and covering my entire chest with her burgundy waves. "I'm sorry. I should've told you. I just didn't want to freak you out."

Freak out? Why the fuck would that freak me out?

"Well, my phone's always on, day or night, if you need…anything."

Green eyes clash with mine as she peers at me, and after a moment just past uncomfortable, she asks, "Is it?"

Not looking away, I nod slowly. While my phone is technically never off, that doesn't mean I'm always readily available, but I do try to be for my family…*all* of my family.

"How did you find out it was twins without Beck knowing? Guy never misses an appointment."

"At the first one, when it was time to hear the heartbeat, he had to take a call just before, something at Pop One, I don't know, but he ended up missing it. So, after hearing two heartbeats, I brought my OB and Angela in on it and we had it set up that Angela would call him with some emergency or another after that. I wanted to surprise him at the ultrasound, but when I had to go in early for," she eyes me, "some concerns, my doctor just did one right then."

"Put a shirt on or get off my woman!" we hear Beck call from behind us as he walks over sans Hunter. "Actually, you know what? Just get off my woman."

We pull apart on a laugh at the same time the rest of Paige's brothers come around the corner, the oldest one, Jesse, saying, "God, Vega. Put that shit away, would you?"

The youngest of the Christensen brothers, Nick, raises his eyebrows, whistling appreciatively as his eyes fall down my bare chest. "I don't know, Marky-Marc. I'm into it." Paige shoves him before I can though and he stumbles off the stained concrete into the grass. He recovers quickly, letting out another whistle that I know is directed at Bentlee without needing to turn around to check.

Every muscle in my body locks up and I feel like pushing him all over again.

Beck hands off Diesel to Jesse, then hangs his head to say, "Nick, don't be uncool, dude. We don't catcall chicks anymore."

Nick looks around the group, truly confused, asking, "Who's we?"

Caleb pulls his attention away from his phone long enough to say, "Our future ex-brother-in-law's all about women empowerment now," and Beck mutters, "Rude."

"What would real feminists say about your infamous shirts though?" Nick goads.

"That they're funny?" Beck shoots right back. "Jesus, they lost their patience with us, not their sense of humor."

"Stop speaking for women, okay? None of you have any room to talk, so drop the superiority complexes and just try to be better. All of you. That's all *we* are asking for." Paige gives each of us a pointed look.

I'm not sure you have to be a feminist to treat women with respect. I think that's more so being a decent human being but I'm not an expert on either to know for sure, so I stay out of the argument, keeping my opinions to myself.

"Jeez," Nick practically gripes like Rebel does when she needs a nap.

The oldest brother says, "You can't be serious. Are you really gonna make your kid call you Poppa?"

We all look at Beck's shirt with *Poppa* scrawled across the chest.

He showcases one of his biggest smiles and spins around, saying, "Poppa Wheelie, motherfuckers," as he reveals the wording *Poppa Wheelie* on the back.

The Christensen men collectively groan, knowing they walked right into that one while I just smirk.

"Watch your mouth," Paige chastises him, gesturing to Diesel when he turns back around.

"The kid thinks my chin is a tit but he's gonna understand the word motherfucker?"

"He will if you keep using it, motherfucker," Nick retorts, earning himself another shove, this one from Beck.

"This is fun. My shithead brothers dragging my shithead *boyfriend*." Her voice rakes the word boyfriend over hot coals again and I eye Beck, wondering if he has it in him to actually practice patience just this once.

"Two quarters in the swear jar for Paigey-poo," Nick singsongs, righting himself.

"Put me down for five bucks and we'll call it even," she tells us all like we don't already know she cusses like a drunken sailor. "Oh, and Nicky, leave Bentlee alone. Ty called dibs."

I feel my shoulders bunch together. When the fuck did that happen?

"Dibs?" Nick sounds out the word, shaking his head and the chocolate hair threatening to get in his eyes. "Nope. We tried that once. It didn't work out. We'll have to fight for her, plain and simple, and I intend on winning no matter what it takes. Bentlee…I like the sound of that."

I follow his eyes, watching as they size up her body from where she and Hunter sit with Tysen on the other side of the patio.

"She's got a kid," I say since no one else will and he's clearly not getting it.

"Yeah, I'm out. She's all Ty's," Nick says, then pulls out a cigarette, forgetting all about Bentlee like a fucking tool.

"You can't smoke that right now, assface. Your sister's pregnant, Diesel's right here, and there's another kid running around now, too," Beck scolds him. It's one of his favorite things, maybe his only favorite thing, about having Nick around—to scold the absolute fuck out of him.

"This party officially blows."

Nick is an immature little shit but the vibe definitely has changed recently from the parties we used to host. Much tamer, more family friendly. It makes me wish Rebel was here but Kary would never go for it, so I don't put the pressure on her by asking. One day. Maybe one day.

"I'll be in the front," Nick says, putting the cigarette between his lips.

Coty passes him, saying, "Don't smoke out front either. Go out to your car, dirtball." When he reaches me, he asks, "What about you? You wanna go out there with him?"

I shrug, taking the clean shirt he's offering since I don't know where mine went. I haven't actually thought about smoking once since I got here and the last cigarette I had was…yesterday? Fucking shit. Maybe I should.

But then I catch sight of Bentlee again and smoking's the last thing on my mind.

Chapter 5

Every sixth word out of Tysen's mouth is in reference to his ex-girlfriend in some way or another. He's pretty funny but is hung up on the mother of his child like nobody's business. And I mean nobody's, including mine. Honestly, if this were a drinking game and Clarise, his ex, was the trigger word, I'd be absolutely hammered right now, and I've only been talking to him for what feels like several hours but I doubt has even been one. Everything circles back to her somehow. The dimple on his son's cheek, the sound of my sandals slapping against the concrete when I walk, the color of the lid on the jar of mayo—everything.

If he's this miserable without her, why aren't they together? They have a beautiful baby boy together and were a couple for several years starting from a young age.

Doesn't that sound familiar.

But I don't know what else to do. The only other people to talk to are couples I don't know or Paige's other brothers who are all intimidating with their matching dark brown hair and stern expressions that only soften around their sister or their nephew. There are several other single guests as well including a man who looks like the older, somewhat shorter version of Beckett but nobody else has so much as even looked my way. Then, of course, there's Marc.

Marc.

After his visit earlier in the week, I put a lot of thought into what's happened so far and what could happen. Outwardly, I haven't given much away—I don't think. Inwardly, I'm a ball of yarn starting to unravel. So I decided to forget the party and attempt to forget all about Marc. Paige also surprising me with a visit made that plan vanish into thin air but I thought I'd still give the portion pertaining to Marc a solid try.

Which is…not working out either. I'm aware of everywhere he goes, everyone he talks to, everything he does. I thought if I didn't look directly into those charcoal eyes of his, I'd stand a better chance. I should've known. I've been drawn to Marc for years and I never even saw his eyes up close until a week ago. Now it seems like the more I try not to look at him, the more I look at him. He's different than I expected him to be. So different. He's kind. Really kind. Not openly kind either where it draws attention to his good deeds, but in hidden gestures that people don't even realize. Like giving Hunter his hat to block out the sun. I told Hunter at least a half dozen times to bring either a hat or a pair of sunglasses but, of course, he forgot both. We just had an appointment at the eye doctor a couple weeks ago after Hunter told me some things were blurry and we're waiting on the prescribed glasses to arrive so he can start wearing them full-time. Since his eyes are more susceptible to damage from the sun, we opted for transition lenses—despite Shawn's objections—but until they come in, we're on our own trying to protect his eyesight. Today, Marc helped with that and he doesn't even know it. Probably doesn't even need to. He doesn't talk a lot. He watches though. He's been watching just as much as I have, if not more, because he's not trying to hide it like I am. Like now. He's perched against a garden wall, one ear tilted to a guy next to him while he scans the entire crowd in the backyard, coming to rest on the table I'm seated at every other glance around. His gaze touches on me, Hunter, then Tysen, before flicking back to me again. I know because I've been staring at a patch of long grass just close enough that I can see him out of my periphery without making direct eye contact.

At least he has a shirt on now. When he didn't, well, I made the biggest mistake yet—I reached out to him. Him being pressed to me was one thing, he was trying to stop me from flashing my breasts to everyone in attendance. Me deliberately reaching out to stroke his mouthwatering muscle dip, or whatever it's called, that was all on me. I cannot, absolutely cannot, touch him again because I don't think I'll be able to stop. I didn't want to stop today. I wanted to follow where it leads and see what other muscles Marc's been hiding under all that riding gear. I want to right now.

I fist my hands in my lap, bringing my attention back to Tysen bouncing Diesel on his thighs.

He finally stops talking to look over at Paige, asking, "Ready?" when Beckett rolls his motorcycle onto the back patio.

Her eyes go round but she nods her head, saying something to Coty. He disappears inside and his girlfriend, Angela, discreetly grabs an unmarked packet from Tysen, tucking it behind her back and standing off to the side of Beckett.

Excusing himself, Tysen stands, pulling out his phone set to video mode. Paige's other brothers follow suit as well as Marc and the rest of the attendees as they gather closer.

Hunter and I just sit here, unsure what to do. As exciting as this is for the expectant couple, I don't know anyone here well enough to record this on my phone. What would I do with the video? Watch it when I'm lonely to remind myself just how lonely I am? Zoom in on Marc should he accidentally take up the entire frame?

No. No video for me.

Pulling Hunter onto my lap so he can see better, we watch as Paige approaches her tall boyfriend, tears already forming in her eyes and I can't help but consider how different this all feels compared to when I was pregnant. The only tears shed were when I was forced to make the decision I didn't know I'd be making so soon. I thought I'd be much older and wiser when I finally walked away from Graham Dairy. I thought it'd be on my terms, not what felt like someone else's. My parents negotiated with Shawn like they were selling off livestock, not letting their daughter go her own way to start her own life, her own family. Pregnant at seventeen, a mom at eighteen, it wasn't the way I'd planned, but then again, nothing ever is.

If I do get another chance though, I hope it's something like this. Something meaningful…to everyone. You can see the excitement on all the faces gathered around, especially Marc's closest friends.

My own eyes get a little blurry, so I blink repeatedly, trying to focus on the soon-to-be parents as Beckett places a packet under the back tire of his bright green motorcycle that's nearly identical to the one Angela just hid for whatever reason. Maybe it's a backup in case the first one's a dud. Maybe we're all in for some kind of prank. Beckett has mischievous written all over him.

"Boy or girl, dream?" Beckett asks Paige.

Dream?

Nobody else reacts to the nickname, so I don't either even though I'm dying to know the story behind it.

She shakes her head, grinning at him as he straddles the bike and starts the engine. "Maybe both," she says, surprising me and, from the looks of it, everyone else.

Beckett's eyebrows touching, he asks, "What?" but she only nods over his shoulder, her grin growing even bigger. Coty appears then, walking alongside a white and gray motorcycle and parking it beside Beckett's before mounting it and turning the key, too. Angela removes the packet from behind her back and puts it under the back tire just like Beckett did for his.

Paige stands between both motorcycles to announce, "We're having twins!"

There's a lot of pushing and shoving and jumping and shouting between all of Paige's brothers as three of them bombard her, Tysen hanging back to get it all on camera. But his ear-to-ear smile says it all—he's happy for them. They're all happy for them. And even though my chest pangs with jealousy, I find myself being happy for them, too.

Paige pushes them back enough for a slack-jawed Beckett to ask, "Are you serious? Twins?"

She nods and with a hand on the back of her head, he crushes her to him, pressing his mouth against hers. Whoops and whistles sound across the backyard while Marc silently approaches them, clapping his friend on the back and telling him, "Congratulations," when the couple pulls apart. "Let's see what we got."

We. Another pang.

"Alright. On the count of three," the soon-to-be-daddy says, then taps knuckles with both of his friends.

With Angela on Coty's other side and Paige in the middle of both bikes, Marc is the bookend as they all look between each other, counting together, "One, two, three," then the revving begins and two clouds of smoke simultaneously erupt—one blue, one pink—causing everybody to go crazy.

A boy and a girl.

Angela has Paige in a hug in the next instant, squeezing her as they both openly cry. Marc catches Beckett's bike as he hops off to immediately drop down by the hugging girls.

The bikes go silent as does the rest of the party and I try to sniffle as quietly as possible.

Paige turns around to find Beckett, bent on one knee and holding up an open ring case. Her hands fly to her mouth, the tears flowing freely.

"You were the first woman to sneak into not only my bed but my heart. Somehow you managed to sneak both a son *and* a daughter into our life and I couldn't imagine being any happier than I am right now…unless you say you'll be my wife. Dream, will you marry me?" he asks, his voice catching at the end as she beams down at him.

"Yes," comes out on a whisper every person in attendance can hear. Then Beckett stands to lift Paige off her feet, kissing her mouth and cheeks before burying his face into her neck, his back to us shaking as they cling to each other.

Coty stares at Angela, longing emanating from him before she sets about busying herself.

"What happened?" Hunter asks. "Why is everybody crying?"

After wiping under both eyes, I rest my forehead on the back of his head, taking a deep breath and saying, "We just witnessed somebody get their happily ever after." And it was more magical than any fairy tale could've ever predicted.

And smokier.

I'm standing off to the side of the massive water slide, watching Hunter continuously play on it…by himself. I thought there'd be more kids, but aside from Diesel, Hunter's the only person under twenty here.

Angela comes up beside me fanning herself and says, "It's hot, right?"

Tysen introduced us earlier but she's been busy ever since. She's got straight caramel hair that's now in a high ponytail and hazel eyes that look like they're always watching. Watching for what, though? From what I've seen so far, this group is a tightknit crew that has each other's backs, fronts, and sides.

"So hot. And this heat isn't letting up anytime soon according to The Farmer's Almanac," I say fanning my own face and chest.

She groans, then shrugs. "At least it'll be good for business." During our impromptu tour of Graham Dairy, Marc told me about their setup, about the guys owning and running a couple of garages where Angela takes care of the attached car washes. "This turned out to be a good idea though." She gestures to the slide just as water splashes over the edge, spraying our arms with fat drops.

"I'm sure you're not the first ones to rent it for adults." This group definitely fits the bill of grown kids. Some more than others.

Her laugh has me looking over at her.

"You're a genius. I should've thought of that sooner. We could totally go down this."

"Was it just for Diesel then?"

She faces me, those observant eyes staring into mine. "I don't think so. But I didn't rent it. Marc did."

He did?

"So, should I get us some swimsuits?" Angela lets the question hang in the air.

Well, if Marc was the one to rent it, he must've gotten it for everyone, in which case, it'd be rude not to use it.

When we were together, Shawn would never let me do something like this, and even if I chose to anyway, he'd make snide comments carefully disguised as harmless fun until I stopped. Until I gave in. Until I gave up.

But Shawn's not here and he doesn't have a say, any say, over what I do anymore.

"We don't need them," I tell her, going over to the stairs.

She laughs, calling out to her boyfriend, "Coty, will you get us some towels?"

Standing on the patio with some friends, his face splits into a grin but Paige pushes from her chair, saying, "I'll get 'em. It's not like I can do anything else anyway."

Before she's even past the threshold, Beckett stops what he's doing to jog after her, saying something about having another idea on how to get her wet.

"It might be a while before we get those towels."

Now I'm the one laughing. "Fair enough. We'll just have to keep moving so we don't get cold." Like I could with Marc nearby. He's like looking directly at the sun—dangerous. And hot. So damn hot. Every time our eyes connect, I have to look away just as quickly.

Meeting Hunter at the top, I hold his hand as we slide down together with Angela going down the other one at the same time, our laughs all mixing together like a perfectly tuned chorus.

Hunter beats us to the stairs and hustles up them, not wanting to be left out now that there's someone else to play with.

Stopping at the first stair though, Angela waits for me as I quickly tie the bottom of my dress just above my knees. Without underwear on I have to be careful not to reveal anything but still be able to climb the stairs a little easier.

"I'm starting to rethink keeping spare rooms for the guys here,"

Angela says when there's still no sign of our towels, or the people supposed to be getting them.

"Do they use them often?"

"Beckett and Paige have a couple times but Marc never has. He prefers to stay close to Creekwood when he's in town."

"What's Creekwood?" And what does that mean, "when he's in town"? Where does he go?

"That's a good question," she muses, then says, "I'm kidding. Kind of. It's an apartment complex. The boys all lived there together before I moved next door. Coty and I only moved out together last year, then Paige took over his room and, obviously, you know how that turned out." We both glance over at the pink, blue, and slightly purple explosion on their patio. "And if all goes well with their house, they'll be our new neighbors shortly. But all three of them have land out here, so they'll always be together. It's really their love story and we're all just distractions."

"A damn good distraction, too," Coty says suddenly, propping his elbows at the slide's pool wall and scaring the hell out of both of us. Or maybe just me. Am I digging for info or are we just chatting? I honestly can't tell the difference anymore.

His girlfriend rolls her eyes but he just winks at her, causing her cheeks to turn pink.

"Why hasn't Marc moved out here yet?" I ask quietly.

She tilts her head down, pinning me with serious eyes. "Another very good question."

Her gaze jumps a second before Marc appears out of nowhere, standing way too close behind me, so close I can feel his chest touching my back. This time he's at least fully covered but my back…isn't. The maxi halter dress doesn't have a back, hence why I'm not wearing a bra either.

With nowhere to go, my eyes fly to Angela for help but she simply smirks down at me conspiratorially as she makes her way up the first couple stairs, leaving me on my own.

"Going up?" Marc asks, his breath moving the curl by my cheek.

"I was going to but, um, I-" I prepare myself for the camouflaged criticism, the whispered reprimand, with an apology already propped on my tongue and ready for launch.

"I'll come with."

I shake my head, swearing I misheard him but he only gives me a gentle nudge, urging me on. *Encouraging me.*

While Angela's black clothes absorbed most of the blue smoke from earlier, Marc's short hair and white V-neck is covered in pink. There's even some on his eyebrows. The pink does nothing to lighten his dark features, only enhances them somehow, and I find myself unable to respond as I climb the stairs, Marc's pink-dusted arms caging in mine as he matches my every step up. Goose bumps sprout along the skin touching his and I fight a shiver.

Once we're halfway to the top, Hunter yells at me mid-slide to watch, so I halt where I am to give him my full attention. Not realizing I stopped, Marc runs directly into my ass. With his crotch. And warmth spreads—*everywhere.*

He curses quietly, pulling back but only an inch or two. I can still *feel* him without really feeling him and he's still very much right there. At least with him this close nobody can see up my dress.

I peek back at him, making the mistake of looking directly at his face. Those gray eyes of his, so deep and warm, find mine instantly and hold steady. Seeing them again, I lose my train of thought until Angela goes down the slide to the left of us, splashing us on her way past.

Turning around, I climb the last couple steps and position myself at the top of the right-side slide.

"You're not sliding down?" I ask when he remains stationed at the top stair. I thought he was joining me.

Wait.

With him this close nobody can see up my dress.

My initial instinct was right. Mostly. He wasn't encouraging me; he was maneuvering me. So fucking sly.

"Beep, beep. You're holding up the line, Marc," Angela says from below, Hunter just above her on the stairs and waiting to get by.

"Move to the side," he tells her, and I tear my eyes away, irritated I abandoned my original plan to ignore him.

Angela laughs incredulously. "There's not enough room. Just go up the rest of the way so we can get by."

After a beat, I hear him take the last stair to perch behind me, letting Hunter slip past to go to the other slide. Hunter drops down to sitting and looks over at me, smiling brightly, and just like always, the irritation starts to melt away.

"Wanna race?" I challenge him with my own smile.

Before he can answer though, Angela appears, suggesting we all race.

Marc says, "I'll just see you at the bottom," and heads for the stairs but Angela pushes him toward me at the last second saying, "Not if we see you first," then he and I are tumbling down the slide—together. We're a rolling ball of limbs with water going up my nose and I don't even know what I'm grabbing, just that I'm grabbing and pulling, trying to right myself with no luck whatsoever. By the time I recognize what I'm gripping, we're slamming into the wall at the bottom of the slide and landing in the shallow pool with a final splash—still together, with him on top of me. And, it's his forearms I'm holding. The forearms that are tensed from being wrapped around my back, putting our faces inches apart. With our fronts mashed together, I can feel every firm part of Marc and for a split second it's hard to care that we're in such a compromising position. Or that my legs are falling further apart the longer we stay like this.

My eyes rove his face, taking in the sharp angles and smooth skin and committing it all to memory while I can. His throat contracts with a hard swallow at the same time as his arms tighten around me like he's doing some memorizing of his own.

But, no, he's probably just mad. Shawn would be.

"You're dead, neighbor girl," he grits in a menacing tone without opening his eyes, pink-tinged water dripping from his head and shoulders onto me. My breathing hitches thinking he's talking to me. I knew he was mad.

Angela lets out a small laugh as she grabs Hunter's hand, saying, "Uh-oh. I think I'm in trouble." Pulling Hunter after her as they tiptoe to the stairs, she calls out, "We'd offer you a rematch but it wouldn't be fair to pick on such slow pokes."

Marc's eyes pop open like Pandora's box, full of secrets and wonder, and the next instant we're moving—still together—as he pulls me out of the pool then guides me toward the stairs as he follows immediately after, telling me, "We can't let them win."

What? I thought…

Angela used to live next door to him, too.

But that doesn't explain him covering me on the stairs. Why else would he do it if not for some sort of personal gain?

Trying to climb with him stuck to my backside again, I point out, "They're already at the top," my teeth close to chattering from something that has nothing to do with the cold water.

"Hey," he yells behind him, not missing a beat on our ascent. "Make sure they don't cheat."

Coty releases a husky laugh, saying, "I don't know, man. She's ruthless."

Already seated next to Hunter on the left slide, Angela says, "You won't say that to my face."

A chuckle rumbles behind me, the movement setting off aftershocks in my own chest. If only my body could get on board with my mind.

"Bet?" Coty throws out there, the challenge as clear as the sky above us.

Her lips spread, and staring him in the eye, she says, "Bet," then her boyfriend hops into the bottom pool, gripping the semi-dry sides and tearing up the slide, his flip-flops kicking against the current of cascading water as he takes big strides, heading straight for her.

She squeals, helping Hunter to standing. I intercept him just as I reach the top step and Marc and I get him over to the slide on the right just as Coty catches Angela, yanking on her ankles and causing them both to slide down in a heap similar to the one Marc and I were just in.

"Should we still see who wins?" I ask, looking over, but am met with the backs of both Marc and Hunter as they slide down without even waiting for me.

After storing that mental picture somewhere safe, then going down myself, I take my time at the bottom, trying to let Marc go up ahead of me but he just waits patiently, like he's got nothing better to do.

"I can do it by myself," I say with a nice little bite at the end, and silently, his lips purse to the side before he leans back for me to bypass him.

I make it exactly three steps up before the air hits my ass through the thin cotton, chilling the wet skin almost in spite of the material stuck to it, and it's then I realize my dress is most likely see-through as well.

Marc wasn't trying to control me; he was trying to protect me—again.

If I want to make a fool of myself, that's my choice, and choices haven't always been granted to me, so I had to sneak them, hiding them away whenever I could just so I'd have *something* to make me feel like my own person once in a while. Slowly, I've started taking those choices back, claiming them as my own again, claiming *me* as my own again. While it's obvious that Marc didn't want me to make a fool of myself, I appreciate that he ultimately still respected and honored that it was in fact a choice and that it was mine.

Hesitating, I grimace as I look over my shoulder, totally prepared to eat crow.

"Don't say you're sorry," Marc tells me before I can, catching up to me easily by taking two stairs in one stride, and just as the apology turns to hot liquid in my mouth, I almost choke on it at his next words. "Just…wait for me."

Done and done.

The five of us continue taking turns racing down the waterslide and eventually others join in, making the waits in line a little longer. No matter how many people end up on the slide at the same time though, I never go up the stairs without Marc behind me again.

A little while later, when Paige and Beckett reemerge, Beckett pushes through several bodies on his way to the top, then dives directly onto the slide I'm sitting on as I wait for Marc to join me, making us both go down from the bounce his tall body creates.

Once we're back on the ground, Beckett peels off his shirt and takes the stairs three at a time, leaving me alone for the first time.

Shirtless as well now, Marc pauses at the top, asking, "You comin'?" His hands are gripping the sides, completely prepared to jump down just to help me back up.

The entire party goes silent at that exact moment. Everyone except Paige beside me, who murmurs, "Holy shit. If you're not, I might."

I shake my head at him right before Beckett tackles him from the side, both friends falling down one slide while Coty and Hunter go down backward on the other.

Angela joins us on my other side and asks, "Is this what life will be like for us from now on?"

I turn my head to see her gaze glued to her dark-haired boyfriend all while wondering who exactly "us" is.

"God, I hope so," Paige answers, not taking her eyes off the scene either.

And maybe, just maybe I do, too. But even I know that's impossible, so I stop that thought in its tracks, putting one of those tire boots on it before it can gain any traction. This is *not* my life. Far, far from it, and it probably never will be. According to Shawn, I'm spoiled goods, meaning because I have a kid by someone else, no man will want to take that on.

Finally breaking the moment, Paige says, "Anyway, let's hide their shirts so they can't get dressed after this."

Angela and I look at each other and shrug. Sounds reasonable to me.

Chapter 6

"SO, BENTLEE, WHAT DO YOU DO?" ONE OF PAIGE'S brothers asks as all of us sit around a large table, drying off. I didn't catch his name yet but he somehow knows mine. I know he smokes though. I can smell it from where I am four seats away.

Beckett answers, or tries to, by saying, "She milks cows."

After taking a sip of my iced tea, I tell them both, "We have machines that do that mostly." He's probably imagining the whole milking by hand into a pail scenario but that's not even close to re-alistic. For an operation the size of Graham Dairy, it's downright laughable. "I'm actually a part-time bookkeeper."

Coty joins in, asking, "Why part time? Don't you live where you work?"

My gaze touches on Hunter still going down the slide much to Diesel's delight as Tysen holds him near the bottom to watch. Every time he lands in the pool, he splashes Diesel, making him squeal in that adorable drooling-baby way.

Paige props her feet on Beckett's lap, ignoring the way his face mock-blanches at them, and says, "Bentlee showed me some of what she does on the farm actually. Let's just say she does a little bit of everything."

How I wish she was wrong. How I wish my paychecks actually validated that more.

"That's a good way to put it—a little bit of everything. For the time being anyway."

"You don't plan on staying at Graham long term?" she asks with a furrow to her brow.

I shake my head gently, not wanting to share too much. The spotlight's already been on me for too long, so I ask her about their house in the distance, hoping the subject change sticks. Luckily, it does and soon it's as if I'm not even here as the large group talks about final walk-throughs and moving companies.

"Are all your lots the same size?" Paige's oldest brother, I think his name's Jesse, asks Beckett, Marc, and Coty.

Beckett says, "Yeah," at the same time the other two answer, "No."

"What?" he bursts, asking Coty, "What do you mean? How big is yours?"

Angela shouts suddenly, "That's what she said! Yes! Got ya finally."

Coty sobers from a chuckle to tell his friend, "Not much bigger than yours. Sixty acres."

"Sixty? I got twenty."

I run my thumb along my bottom lip, biting the tip to keep from laughing. He's acting like that isn't still a ton of land. The house Shawn and I lived in was on a quarter acre in a cookie-cutter neighborhood. Twenty acres will still provide lots and lots of privacy.

"What about you, Marc?" he asks, sounding downright insulted. "How big were your lots?"

With his eyes on my mouth, Marc tips a shoulder, saying, "Four hundred acres in total."

A couple whistles fill the otherwise silent table as everyone stares at Marc. The noise breaks his reverie and he looks up, meeting my eyes before glancing around at everybody else.

Coty's eyebrows lift as his head jerks back. "I didn't think they sold them that big."

"They don't. But you knew I bought a bundle."

A large bundle, like industrial size. What's he going to do with all that land? Coty and Angela already have some areas on theirs that look like they're preparing to plant some sort of crops on.

Beckett double blinks, saying, "The fuck? You dipped into your father's money to buy four-hundred acres? For what? What are you gonna do with all that land?"

Marc's face transforms into a deep scowl. "I didn't touch any money from him. I never have and never will."

I recognize the dissent right away. It's embedded in my every fiber.

"How can you afford that much land then? You make as much as me."

If we were inside right now, I'd swear all the air was just sucked out of the room. It's silent. Like you can hear the streams of water spilling from the slide's pool into the already drenched grass below it.

Immediately, I push from the table, not wanting to impose any longer. It's none of my business. I'm not a member of this group. Their lives are interconnected, intricately woven together, while I'm just here, enjoying the coleslaw.

Just as I reach the waterslide though, I hear Beckett's voice as he calls out, "Exactly how part time are you, Bentlee?"

"Very."

"How about you come work for us the days you're free? We need our books checked."

Angela speaks up, saying, "Lucinda looks them over for us."

"Angie! Your friend's freebie Friday ain't gonna cut it anymore. We're getting too big for that. Plus, I need to know if someone's taking from the community pot."

"You know that's not true, Beckett," she says seriously, and Coty shifts beside her while Paige just frowns, narrowing her eyes at her fiancé.

Acting oblivious to it all, Beckett just meets Marc's silent stare head-on, saying, "We'll see about that."

The rest of the table's eyes fall on me, so I nod. "Yeah. Sure. Just let me know when you need me." The sooner I start making real money, the better.

Tysen cranks his head over his shoulder, asking, "Can I have her?"

Marc's voice cuts across the yard like a sling blade as he says one word, simple yet final, "No."

"But Pop Two's in the weeds."

Finally tearing his gaze from his friend's, Marc looks directly at Tysen, telling him, "You and Angela should be on top of that."

Paige's brother, the one who smokes, mumbles, "He's gonna be on top of something." But even from where I'm standing, I hear it and glare at him. Another choice that is very much mine, another man acting like it's not.

Paige slaps the back of her brother's head at the same time Angela speaks up, saying, "Actually, Tysen's right. It makes sense for Bentlee to start with us so I can catch her up on what Lucinda's already done." Then she tells me, "We could even have you start tomorrow, if that works?"

"Um, I mean, I can…if that's okay?" Because it doesn't seem like it is. Marc only takes his eyes off Tysen to stare at Beckett who's now smiling like a thief after a successful heist.

"It is. I'm so ready to have another girl in the shop with me."

"You didn't even interview her," Marc practically spits and I feel my spine stiffen.

"Pop Two is mine, right? Or were you guys just talking crap?" Her hard gaze falls on Marc, Beckett, then Coty. "I run it the way I want and you don't have a say. That was the deal. If you want to break it over this, I don't think you'll like where that leaves things between us all."

Coty warns, "Babe," but she stands too, cutting him off.

"No, you boys decide. Either you trust me fully or you don't. But know that sentiment goes both ways."

Beckett doesn't skip a beat, saying, "I trust you with my life, Angie," and someone else says, "Dead man walking."

"Christ, Angela. It's not you. It's him." Marc points at Beckett whose smile grows even bigger, completely relaxed amongst the chaos erupting around him. "He's the one that brought this all on."

"Whatever's going on here, you two better figure it out. Now," Coty cautions as he stands to pull Angela against his side. "You got my girl over here threatening me over what? Who cares if Bentlee starts at Pop Two? We could use her at both, so what's the issue?"

"Yeah. What's wrong, bro? Worried about something?" Beckett taunts but Marc doesn't bite as he remains locked in a staring stand-off, his hands balled into fists.

For the first time I actually consider it. That he might be trying to cover something up. Is he really stealing from their company? And if so, how has no one noticed? You need money, a lot of money to buy that much property around here. While the rest of the country is having real estate problems, southeast Washington is not. We're flourishing in our own little bubble as people continue to leave the bigger cities like Seattle and Portland for simpler, quieter lives. With the world turning to more remote jobs and everyone wanting space to spread out, property values in the area have skyrocketed. I know firsthand because I've been house hunting for the better part of the last year. Even apartments that don't cost an arm, leg, and a piece of your soul are hard to come by these days.

But that doesn't exactly make sense. If that's really how Marc paid for his large investment, then they wouldn't have been able to open their second location so soon after opening the first. You don't even need a bookkeeper to tell you that; it's common sense. Something feels off about that excuse. Flimsy.

And I'm supposed to work alongside all of this? Their friendship is practically a visible life force that keeps them afloat but it could also bulldoze if not navigated properly and I don't want to be in its path. I can't afford to.

I can't really afford to turn down a paying job either though.

Catching Hunter before he can climb the stairs again, I tell him we're leaving and, together, we quietly find our shoes, the voices behind us dissolving into white noise.

"Are you leaving already?" Tysen asks unfortunately, making me have to lie.

"We have a thing."

"What thing?" Hunter questions, his face morphed in confusion.

"Dinner?" It is coming up and we'll need to figure out what we're eating—eventually.

Still not convinced, he asks me, "Didn't we just eat lunch?" to which I just shrug noncommittally while nodding at the same time. The pure innocence and honesty that comes out of kids' mouths can be so cute. Just not right now. Right now I need a cooperative accomplice so we can exit stage left as soon as possible.

"Yeah, well, it's a continuous loop. It never ends." Especially not for kids who need snacks around the clock on top of regular meals.

Hunter reaches for Marc's hat on the ground and I freeze, unsure what to do. Do I let him keep it? Did Marc even give it to him? More importantly, does it smell like him?

Oh. No.

We have to give it back—now.

I shoot my hand out, swiping it before Hunter can and shove it toward Tysen, mumbling in one long breath, "Canyoureturnthisthanks," but he doesn't take it. Paige does.

"Bentlee and Hunter are off to find some dinner," Tysen tells his sister with a knowing smile on his chiseled face.

She just laughs. "You can't beat that early bird special, can ya? If I didn't drive Beckett's Tahoe here, I'd go with you. These babies are *always* hungry." Her hand cradles her bump in a move that used to be so familiar I almost reach out to do the same but then I remember how much I hated when other people would do that to my stomach when I was carrying. "Listen, don't let that stuff bother you," she tells me. "This always happens. Angela makes them fight for every ounce of her trust. She makes all of us actually. And we give it to her because she deserves it but those three like to give a little pushback before they fold completely. It's their thing, I don't know."

Tysen nods. "It's true. You get used to it."

"I don't know." About any of this.

"Yes, you will because starting tomorrow, you'll be working side by side with her and my big bro here."

Paige leans her head onto Tysen's shoulder revealing the space behind her. Marc, still in his chair, sits casually with his arms crossed and nothing on him moves except for his eyelashes as they slowly blink once, only once, as he stares loudly in my direction.

I blink too, trying to get my bearings, then tell Paige congratulations again. She promises to text me and Tysen later so he can have my number before we wave out the rest of our goodbyes.

Finally at my truck, I'm struggling to get Hunter's booster seat buckled when a thick voice behind me says, "Can I help?"

My fingers freeze as I mutter out, "No, thanks," hearing a hint of a buried chuckle coming even closer and I turn around to face Marc. He's wearing the hat I just shoved at Tysen, the brim covering some of that devilish tilt of his lips that isn't quite a smirk but a trace of one to come.

Removing the hat as he slides by me, he places it on Hunter's head once again before buckling the seat belt with ease. Too much ease.

"Happens all the time," he says vaguely, then looking over my truck asks, "So, this is yours?"

"It's mine." My Cummins that I've had since my sixteenth birthday but have been driving since my fourteenth. It's probably got more miles on it than all the cars here put together and leaks more oil, too. I parked it next to the other beat-up truck in case it took the liberty of embarrassing me by proving that fact.

"Thanks for earlier." I motion toward the house, hoping I don't actually have to spell it out. "I definitely did not dress appropriately."

I wanted to look nice today. These people are around my age but it doesn't feel that way, not when I have one eye on Hunter the entire time.

And the other on Marc.

"You look perfect."

My eyes jump to his and he releases the chuckle I previously heard building. "I'll see you tomorrow."

Turning back to his friends' house, his hands in his pockets make the muscles in his back more pronounced.

"I thought you worked offsite," I say to that back, wishing I could rub my hands over it, dig my nails in it. Wondering if he'd let me.

We aren't going to be working together, are we?

The tense lines between his shoulder blades soften minutely as he tips his head back, calling to the sky, "I do what I want."

If only the rest of us could say the same.

Chapter 7

Bentlee

WHAT AM I DOING HERE? AND WHAT WAS I SUPPOSED to wear?

My black and red kimono paired with cutoff shorts seemed like a good idea this morning before I left but now that I'm here, not so much. I guess I got a little excited at the prospect of being around other adults that I'm not actually related to. At least I'm not wearing my usual Mucks. I've still got boots on but they're a bit more stylish. They even have a thick heel.

Again, a choice I'm rethinking as I scour the other people milling about in front of the garage, and by people, I mean men. Angela wasn't exaggerating. We're the only girls.

If I ever go in.

I haven't quite worked up the courage to go inside yet, so I'm sitting in my truck, trying to ignore how bad my stomach hurts while practicing smiles in the cloudy rearview mirror. I don't want to come off too eager but I don't want to seem ungrateful either. It's a thin line that I'm afraid I don't have the skill to walk. Not with these anxiety cramps. And heels.

After Tysen was able to relay all the important information I'd be needing, thanks to Paige connecting us, I let him and Angela know I'd be running late. I just didn't think I'd be *this* late.

The cramping grows almost unbearable as I hop down from my tattered bench seat, landing on the asphalt with an echo courtesy of my boots, and I swallow the rest of my nerves down, hoping the acidic whirlpool awaiting them will disintegrate every last one of them on contact. There's nerves and then there's *nerves* and I've got the latter in spades right now. Have ever since I left last night's party if I'm being honest.

Tysen says, "Good morning," effectively scaring me on his way past. He spins to face me but continues walking backward without breaking pace. "Nervous for your first day?"

"Morning," I practically squeak, then laugh when he does. "Terrified," I admit, following him.

"That's understandable. Marc has that effect on people."

"Oh, I don't know about that." I do actually. The only scary thing about Marc is the way I react to him, especially when I'm trying *not* to.

It'd be a hell of a lot easier if he wasn't a watcher himself, picking up on stuff others typically don't—a trait only another watcher can spot. I can identify one when I see one, and Marc, he's definitely a watcher.

Will he really be here though? And is he my boss now?

"How was Hunter this morning?"

I shake my head, breezing through the door when he opens it for me. "Good. Excited really. He even packed me a sandwich for lunch. It's more peanut butter than jelly but if I chase it with a quart of milk, I should be okay." Which he also packed me. Graham Dairy or die—there is no in between.

He gives me a pity laugh. "Well, if it's not, I'd be happy to take you out for lunch to celebrate your first day."

We both watch a door scraping open beside us with Marc coming through it, dressed in all black. Black hat, black muscle tee with the armpits cut halfway down his torso, black pants, black sneakers. A far cry from yesterday's pink-tinged ensemble.

This is where I eat my words about Marc not being scary. The air around him practically screams it—danger, danger, danger. And those muscles peeking out from beneath his shirt that were pressed against me less than just twenty-four hours ago, they're definitely a threat…to my overall well-being if I have to stare at him all day. Even his sides have muscles.

How am I supposed to concentrate on numbers when the only thing I feel like counting are the abs Marc doesn't even have the decency to cover up? In addition to him and his friends owning the two garages, they also work at them full-time as well. Or at least I thought the other two did, I'm not sure what exactly Marc does.

"What's up, boss?" The guys bump knuckles, nodding at each other, then I feel Tysen's hand at my lower back as he guides me closer, angling me at his—our?—boss. "You remember Bentlee?"

Marc's gaze starts at my boots, making his way up to my hair and face, before stopping at my eyes. I consider closing them to break up the intensity but then I remember his reaction the last time I did that.

Instead, I pull my kimono tighter at my front and his eyes drop for the briefest of seconds to watch the movement.

"You're late," is all he says as he tilts his head to the side like he's trying to figure something out. Figure me out.

Boss. *Check.*

He doesn't look like one but he's got the whole bossy thing down pat.

"Angela didn't tell you?" I think I might need a little clarification on who I'm expected to actually report to or this will get confusing very quickly. "I drop Hunter off at school."

"You don't make him take the bus?" Tysen asks.

I turn to him, feeling the weight of Marc's scrutinizing stare drop to Tysen's hand still at my back. I like that Tysen asks about Hunter. He's interested. He has a son too, so he gets it, how much space they take in both our minds and hearts.

"We're a little out of district." That's putting it mildly. My parents' house is nowhere near it.

"There aren't any schools close to where you live?"

"There are, but after," *after my world fell apart and I tried like hell to keep Hunter's together,* "everything, I didn't want to pull him out of the only school he's ever attended, so I make the drive every day." The hour-roundtrip drive twice a day was just cut in half though, at least on the days I'll be working at Pop The Hood.

"Hey, I'm sorry about yesterday if I made you uncomfortable. I just went through a bad breakup myself and thought I recognized-"

"Yeah, totally," I say quickly, glancing at Marc then back to Tysen. "It's a difficult situation especially with kids involved but I think for me and any other woman you come across, you might not want to put us in boxes. We don't do well in them and we really don't fit neatly into them with men's names for labels attached to the outside."

Like me, I don't think Tysen knows how to be separate from his ex yet. High school sweethearts can be cruel like that. Mine was just cruel to my heart. And my head. But I'm still standing on my own two feet, despite Shawn's many attempts to knock them out from under me, and now I'm working on not letting him define me at all.

"Lesson learned. So, are you and your ex on good terms at least?" He puts his hands up, removing the one from my back. "If you don't mind me asking."

"Great terms."

But unlike Tysen, I don't want to talk about my ex—ever—so I leave it at that. His name alone gives me stomach cramps worse than this morning's, but Shawn and I are not on any terms other than co-parenting our son, or trying to, which still doesn't qualify as great by any stretch of the imagination.

"Why don't you try to get a place closer to Hunter's school?"

"I'm working on it."

"Marc, you should get her in at Creekwood. Aren't you seeing the landlady? Maybe you could get her a discount."

My eyes drop to the ground like a meteor striking the earth and I focus on an oil stain that looks like it's in the shape of a pomegranate. Pomegranates are said to resemble the human heart and right now I think it's pretty damn accurate. Flattened with no hope of resuscitation.

I should've known. Of course he'd be taken. He has an entire life, as should I.

"I'll be right back," I say out of nowhere, covering whatever might be coming out of Marc's mouth next. "I forgot my coffee."

I don't want to move to the same apartments as Marc and the woman he's seeing. And I definitely don't want him to know I don't want to move to the same apartments as him and the woman he's seeing.

Leaning against the side of my rusty Cummins, I drop my chin to my chest, taking a huge breath and filling my cheeks almost painfully, then letting it all out loudly. I could leave right now. I should leave. Work somewhere else. Anywhere else. I need money but I don't need to do this to myself. I tried and failed yesterday. I'm trying and failing today.

Marc is…overwhelming and I'm not sure I'm strong enough to fight the attraction I still feel for him.

Regardless of how much I've grown and gone through and endured, nothing's changed. He's just as off-limits to me now as he was then. Marcos Vega. Forever elusive. Forever out of reach—my reach.

If I'm going to work here, I'll just have to work twice as hard at ignoring him and those charcoal eyes I lose myself in. Yesterday didn't go as planned. Not at all. But starting today, I'll succeed in pretending like Marc doesn't affect me the way he does. That the feel of him between my thighs for the briefest of moments doesn't run through my mind on a constant loop of longing. Longing so strong I wish I could pull him to me just to feel it again. To know if it was as perfect as my memory would like me to believe.

A man that perfect has to belong to someone else.

"Did I hear someone say coffee?"

I jerk my head up, seeing Angela standing in front of me with a hesitant smile as her fingers run over themselves like she cannot wait to get to work.

"Oh, er, I forgot mine."

"Do you wanna grab it and we can get started?"

She eyes the driver's side window and I cringe. "I forgot…to make some."

After a sympathetic sort of look, she turns, waving me to follow her and telling me about her time as a barista. Apparently, she even keeps an espresso machine at both locations for this exact reason and offers to make me a drink.

"Do you like lattes?"

I raise a shoulder, catching the silky material when it slips. "I prefer mocha."

She beams over at me, saying, "Me too."

Upon discovering the sandwich Hunter made me was basically inedible—it was like he sawed the bread to crumbs before using gobs of peanut butter to glue the microscopic pieces back together—I accepted Tysen's offer to take me out for lunch. Luckily, Angela was able to join us so it doesn't feel date-ish. They're both incredibly funny and don't take much encouragement from me to keep the other one going as I sit in the back of Angela's Jeep. Tysen's better at telling entertaining stories while Angela has a quick wit that's unmatched.

Marc took off shortly after I went back inside with Angela and I haven't seen him since. I've also been cooped up inside a private office all morning preventing me from seeing what's going on in the garage, or *who's* in the garage, so that's helped.

Although Angela said her friend's been helping them out, I can tell it wasn't her day job. I have a lot of work to do and I'm kind of shocked that Pop The Hood was getting by without a bookkeeper for so long. There's no question they're a successful business. Without even seeing it firsthand, I was still able to hear enough to know that they don't really have slow times. Every hour is their rush hour. We were only able to get away long enough for drive-thru and now we're eating on the car ride back.

"So, your parents live by Marc's?"

"Pretty much."

"But you and Marc never met or anything?"

Or anything...

I shake my head, swallowing my bite of fried chicken sandwich. "I'm older than him."

"So? Isn't Kary older than Marc?" Tysen asks Angela as she makes a one-handed right turn, a burger in her left.

"Maybe?" she guesses. "I only saw her a few times when I lived there. She rarely left her apartment. And why would she when Marc was more than willing to go to her all the time?"

"I feel bad nothing came from his visit to Graham," I say, changing the subject.

"I thought he fixed something for you."

"Yes, but my parents weren't around, so he didn't get to do his full sales pitch."

Tysen and Angela exchange identical looks, not saying anything.

"To land Graham Dairy as a client…"

Angela breaks out in laughter as she parks in Pop Two's lot, then she turns around in her seat, facing me. "Marc? The one that could melt icebergs with a single look? Yeah, he doesn't do sales calls."

Tysen chuckles darkly. "We should send him to sever contracts. That'd be funny."

"Is that Beckett's job then?"

"Hell no. He'd give everybody some discount or other that he pulled out of his ass."

Okay…

After a moment, she warns, "You have to be careful of those Creekwood boys. They're sneaky as hell and before you even realize it, they're already under your skin like a bad case of flesh-eating bacteria."

"Isn't that stuff fatal?"

She nods, gazing off dreamily. "Sweetest demise you could ever hope for."

"It sounds painful," I note even though I get what she means. She didn't find a cure, she found a way. People that have to fight their whole lives usually do and the more I get to know Angela, the more I wonder what kind of fighting she's done.

"Is it even real love if it doesn't hurt?" Tysen questions and we all fall quiet until I say finally, "It all hurts."

A heavy sort of understanding settles over the car like the first snow of the season blanketing everything into deafening silence. It's beautiful but eerie at the same time. Instead of gauze and medical tape for the world to see, the three of us are staunching our internal wounds privately in our own ways.

I think I might like Pop Two.

Chapter 8

Marc

EVERY DAY I LEAVE CREEKWOOD VOWING TO HEAD STRAIGHT to work and every day I find myself at Pop Two, waiting. Watching. Since Angela always gives me some vague-ass answer every time I ask about what days Bentlee's supposed to work, I've been here for the last week and a half straight, bright and fucking early, kicking around like I don't have a fuckload to do elsewhere. Besides the occasional drop-in, I never spend time at Pop Two. Any tools I don't use for the day are kept at Pop One. In my toolbox. With guys we've had for longer than a few months here and there. Guys we know their wives' or girlfriends' names in case they try fucking around with, say, the gorgeous new bookkeeper. Here though, I don't know these technicians for shit. They could say anything, *do* anything.

Angela isn't even a concern in that regard because of Coty.

That's it. That's the threat—Coty. One name and nobody's messing with his girl.

And pregnant or not, Paige could probably take on any person working at either location. She'd never have to with all those goddamn brothers she's got though, not to mention Beckett who doesn't like her being out of his sight for longer than absolutely necessary.

Bentlee, however, who's gonna look out for her? That's the only reason why I keep coming back. She needs someone to make the rules about her presence clear as glass. We have a strict sexual harassment policy…I think. I don't actually know for sure but it seems like something Angela would put in place. She knows exactly what qualifies as inappropriate, enough to outline a leather-bound handbook and pass it out every quarter as a refresher course on how not to be a vile piece of shit. I don't *think* we have any of those working for us but I don't *know*, and that's the problem.

That and what Bentlee wears to work every day. I've seen her in every type of outfit now from frumpy-ass overalls to that curve-hugging dress to what she's got on today—camo. What in the fuck? I didn't even think people outside of duck hunters wore camo. Shit's so dumb. And yet she's wearing it in hoodie form with a beanie, tight jeans that show off that fantastic ass of hers, and rain boots that are covered in mud. At least I hope it's mud. Fuck. She's all over the place with her clothing choices, and as much as I hate that I notice that about her, I can't stop. It's one of the first things I do whenever I arrive at Pop Two is seek her out just to see what she's wearing. See how good she looks in whatever the hell she's rocking. I always wonder the same thing—why? Why'd she choose that? She's not dressing sexy or flashy even, she doesn't seem to have one particular style, she just wears whatever the hell she feels like. I don't ever ask her though. I can't. Every time she catches sight of me, she disappears into that office she's using as a shield. I just can't figure out why.

Then there's the days I get it wrong and she's not working here. Those are some of the longest. With nothing to break up the monotony, my fingers start to itch. Always fucking itching. I need out. I need air. Any way I can get it.

It's on the horizon though. This weekend. It's not my usual but it'll do.

Rebel's first couple weeks of kindergarten came and went and now she's full of tales of friends and birthday party invites and shit that Kary will never let her have or do. No matter what I say, what I promise, it doesn't matter, she just won't budge, even if it means Rebel misses out on having a normal life. She could, goddamn it. She could and I could make sure of it if I was careful enough. Or not. Rebel's only getting older and bigger—finally.

But times like this, when I'm reminded just how fucking powerless I really am, is when I need to do something to feel some sort of control again. I can go anywhere, do anything, and nobody can take that from me.

I reach into my pocket, fingering my pack of cigarettes.

"There she is," Beck says and I still my fingers as we watch Bentlee enter through the open bay door, her eyes finding mine, then flying to Beck's like I'm as inconsequential as the corny motivational posters with cats on them on the wall behind us.

I run my tongue across my bottom teeth, wanting to call her on her shit. Instead, I tuck my other hand into my front pocket, watching this play out.

Beck splits his time between Pop One and Pop Two but as far as I know he hasn't been here on the same day as Bentlee yet, which should be surprising considering he's the one that hired her—to make sure I'm not ripping off the company. Except, it's not, because that's not the real reason why Beck hired her. He knows damn well I'm not stealing from Pop The Hood and he's probably the only one that knows why I wouldn't need to. His little show at the gender reveal party was just that—a show. In typical Beckett fashion, he ran his mouth through a cocky-ass smile without even meaning a word he was saying. Such a dickhead.

"I heard something about you," he tells Bentlee when she cautiously approaches and I slide my gaze over to my boy. What did he hear? And who the fuck did he hear it from? This is exactly why she shouldn't be at Pop Two.

"Oh, yeah? What's that?" she asks, her lips quirked as she grips an insulated tumbler in front of her. Sticking out from her beanie, her hair's in a thick braid off to one side, draped over a shoulder. That lip gloss she's got on every time I see her shines like a lone star in an otherwise black sky.

One of the hourlies slithers—he fucking slithers—up next to her, whispering something in her ear and she smiles, reaching into her back pocket to hand him a five-dollar bill all without taking her eyes off Beck. She still refuses to acknowledge I'm even here which is starting to piss me off the longer I stand right in front of her, staring at her lips like their sole purpose in this life is to torture the fuck out of me.

Why the gloss? Why the beanie when it's not even cold out?

Why the fuck do I care?

She drops her arm and Beck's head whips side to side as he asks, "Bentlee? Where'd you go?"

The guy that took her money—I'm sorry, what the fuck?—stops to stare at Beck as he spins in circles, pretending to search before coming to a stop and gesturing to Bentlee.

"Oh, there you are. Man, that camo is effective. I thought we lost you for a second."

My lips twitch and I drop my head, shaking it. You can't make this shit up. And that's why I love him.

Bentlee goes to speak but Beck holds up a finger, dramatically shushing her and says to the guy, "Whatchu got there?"

He, I think his name's Peter but I honestly don't care enough to check, looks down at the bill, saying, "Just a little bet."

Beck and I exchange glances. A bet? About what?

And why won't she look at me still? The worst part is her hat is pulled so low that her eyes are practically hidden in shadow and I can't make out any distinguishable color in them.

"What did you hear about me?" Bentlee asks, sounding impatient.

I'm technically her boss and I can invent tasks for her if I want to, starting with greeting me like a normal person.

Greeting… I didn't greet her. I don't think I greeted her on her first day either when I actually had the chance to. I just jumped into asking what I really wanted to know. One small part of it anyway. *Why was she late?* Not because I cared about her being on time, I only wanted to know where she'd been. Did something happen to Hunter? Did she have car trouble?

But it was nothing like I'd imagined—thankfully.

Doesn't her ex help out at all? If they're on such "great" terms, why is she the one making the drive into town every day to take Hunter to school?

I want to know a lot about her. Like why she chose a silk robe for her first day working here? Or any day really. What would it feel like if I ran my hands over the material? What it would feel like to *her* if I ran my hands over the material. Something tells me she'd acknowledge me then. Pretty sure she'd acknowledge the shit out of me.

I do this thing with my throat like a cough but lamer, then say, "Good morning, Bentlee," and while her lips tighten like she hates the very sound of my voice, Beck screws up his face, covering his mouth like this level of pathetic is somehow contagious. I frown at him, glancing over at Bentlee but she's still just as oblivious to me. Absolutely no idea I exist. Just a figment of my own imagination.

Did I also imagine her copping a feel at the gender reveal party? Or the way she waited for me at the bottom of the slide after she realized why I kept insisting on covering her up? Her dress was sticking to *all* her parts, and as much as I might've appreciated that fact, so did everybody else. Paige is lucky she walked away that day with all four brothers still breathing after I saw the way Nick was drinking in everything Bentlee was unknowingly showing.

With one last side-eye in my direction, Beck drawls, "I heard you don't have any plans this weekend."

"Who told you that?"

"Chester," he says, motioning to another employee walking past.

Bentlee follows him with her eyes until he's out of earshot, then says, "That's Colson."

"Isn't that what I said?" he asks me and I nod my head silently. Sure. Whatever. What the fuck do I care what someone's name is? I don't exist.

"Right. Well, I do have plans actually. Shawn's taking Hunter this weekend..." She pauses like she wants to say more, then continues, "So I thought I'd-"

"Perfect. You can come with us. We're going up to The Bar for some camping. In cabins, not tents," he stresses, probably remembering those glamping tents we all tried out last time we did a group campout. They weren't all that bad honestly. I've definitely stayed in worse.

"I can't-"

"Great. I'll have Paige text you the details."

Blowing out a breath, Bentlee leans forward, dodging her head left and right as if she's doing some sort of search of her own.

Beck's shoulders bunch and he looks around as well, asking, "What?"

She straightens, saying, "I was looking for a collar. I'm surprised Paige let you off your leash."

Damn…

Beck's eyes find mine and we share a smile before he says, "Oh, okay, the mom's got jokes, I see. You'll make a great addition." To what exactly, I'm not sure. Looking around, I'd say we've already got plenty of clowns at Pop Two.

"I thought you were against labels," I say, louder than before.

Her body visibly tenses but I don't get why. What did I do? I never said I didn't want her working for us. I just don't want her working *here*, without people I trust that can keep an eye on her at all times.

Staring at my shoes, she answers like it's being pulled from her one letter at a time. "Boxes with labels, no. Leashes for those that require more…supervision, those are okay. Necessary sometimes."

The fact that she's even acknowledging me at all's enough to get me hard but it's the way she keeps talking about leashes like she'd be comfortable holding someone's that's got my cock on the verge of swelling.

"Don't, and I cannot stress this enough, ever say that in front of Paige. We can't give her any ideas like that or she'll have me fitted for a real leash the first chance she gets. Girl already put a GPS app on my phone when she thought I wasn't looking."

"You know about it and you're not mad?" she asks, suddenly serious as she looks at my friend.

"Nah. She could track my every move and all she'd find is that they're all to bring me closer to her. I got nothing to hide."

Except for last month when he left me his phone so he could go ring shopping without Paige knowing, he really doesn't do anything that'd put their relationship in jeopardy. Not that I'd let him. Those two are perfect for each other, and if he even thought about fucking it up, I'd step in. No way would I let either of my boys cheat. Not when they're with the people they're meant to be with.

Bentlee gets a faraway look in her eye that borders on painful, like whatever she's thinking of hurts but she's trying not to let it. Then, with her gaze fixed firmly back on my shoes, she says, "Look, I got a lot of work to do and not a lot of time to do it, so if you don't mind…"

Tysen calls her name and her expression brightens as she changes the direction she was just going.

"Yo, Ty? Are you kid-free this weekend, too?"

When he nods his head, Beck invites him along as well, then we watch as the pair with *so* much in common skip off together, all merry and shit.

I look over to find Beck grinning at me with drool practically dangling out the corners of his mouth like one of those bulldogs.

"What?"

"Dude, Imma get so many brownie points for this."

"For what?"

"Finding my new sister-in-law. Duh."

What the fuck?

"So, you think them working together will make them fall in love?"

"Not love. Well, maybe not right away but eventually?" He shrugs. "Why not? She's definitely ours. Can't you feel it?" He waits a beat while we glance over at Bentlee, then says almost to himself, "We're keeping her."

I don't know what exactly he means, and yet, I do. It's weird but true. I do feel it. But I didn't know anyone else felt that same tug. That pull like she's being drawn into our orbit and there's nothing anyone or anything can do about it. She is ours…or will be soon enough.

But is she really Ty's?

She is happy to see him. Happier than she's ever been seeing me.

"Anyway, we only have one extra cabin left," Beck says nonchalantly, "and those two are getting it, so we'll get to put my theory to the test this weekend."

"Guy can sleep in that truck he loves so much," I all but spit, getting more pissed by the second. Hell, I once slept *under* a rental Jeep in Maui when I miscalculated how long the road to Hana actually was. He'll survive. *Aloha, Tysen.*

Aloha as in *goodbye*. She's ours. Not his. I just decided.

"What's your beef with Ty? I thought you liked him."

I shrug tightly, trying to keep my shit under control. "I did."

"What changed then? Was it the moment he locked those baby-making eyes on Bentlee?"

Could be. Or could be when Bentlee gave him all the smiles I fucking earned. Or even when everyone thought it'd be a good idea for Bentlee and Tysen to get together. It's hard to narrow it down precisely. I do know he can fuck off though and that's as narrowed down as it gets.

"If you're that concerned, maybe one of them should bunk with you then," he suggests, some of the spark in his eyes igniting a little too quickly.

What the hell? Why the change?

"Unless Kary wants to finally come out of that apartment of hers and make things official with you?"

I run my hand over the back of my head, gripping my neck. What is this shit? I never talk about Kary with my friends, not if I can help it. They think I'm just having a fling with her and I let them because it's easier. Or it was easier. But he's never given me shit about her even when I've hooked up with other chicks, so why is he bringing her up all of a sudden?

The skin beneath my hand prickles and I glance over my shoulder to find Bentlee staring right at me. Our eyes hold for just a second before she tears them away, diving back into whatever the fuck Tysen's showing her.

Did she hear what Beck just said?

Judging by the grin he's flaunting, she just might've. I really want to hate him sometimes.

"What's wrong with you?"

"What do you mean? I thought you and Kary were–"

"I'm out of here," I say before he can put something into the universe that can never be taken back.

"Hang in there," he calls, pointing at the wall behind him where a poster of a cat hangs precariously from a clothesline.

I shake my head as I pass to keep from exploding on him but he keeps going, his stereotypical words of encouragement following me all the way out to my car. I'm already running late and the drive out to my dad's isn't getting any shorter the longer I sit here pretending like I don't give a fuck, or wondering why the hell I actually do.

Another shit day in suck city.

"Motherfuck," I grit after unscrewing the blown head gasket.

I remember when my dad bought this four-wheeler eight years ago. The milky oil currently coating the head gasket is a dead giveaway that the oil's never been changed in at least that long, too.

Using voice command, I text Coty so he can order the correct part for me, then I pull the towel out of my back pocket, wiping my hands as I scan the surrounding apple trees, watching a lazy draft rustle the almost florescent green leaves to expose the bits of red hidden underneath. After this weekend there will be more people than trees out here. My dad opens this area up to the public for do-it-yourself picking since the apples in this part don't grow as consistently as the other orchard further out. They're just moody enough not to be reliable for stores to bank on but the families coming out in hordes looking for viral-potential photo ops don't really care about how perfect the apples are. Not like my dad. If something can make him money, it will. And if it doesn't, then he'll still find a way for it to serve him somehow. His way reigns supreme. A supreme pain in my ass.

"How's Coty?" my younger sister, Maggie, asks, skipping up to me. As manager of the DIY section, she's over here setting up the stands with supplies. There were so many customers last year, Dad had to hire parking attendants to direct traffic so no crops got ruined. *The precious crops.* Can't risk those.

"Married."

"Did I miss the wedding?"

Her nearly black hair is up in a long ponytail with a few strands sticking to her forehead from sweat. She's chewing gum like she just learned how, smacking it against her cheeks with each bite, and if she blows a bubble, I'm sticking my finger right in the center, I don't give a fuck if there's oil on it or not.

"They're not married yet but they will be." Eventually…only because the thought of marriage this early in her life scares the shit out of Angela. It shouldn't though. Not with my boy, Coty. He'd never do anything to hurt her or make her something she's not. And she's not her mom, despite her fear of the contrary.

"There's still time." Maggie gazes off like she's picturing a scenario where Coty and Angela don't belong together. She'll be there a while though. There is no life where those two aren't together with the perfect life that they both fought like hell to make. They're two parts of a whole. Period. Even if they weren't, Coty would make it so they were.

Maggie has no chance with him and she knows it, he knows it, I know it because I told them that years ago when she first started batting her eyelashes at him. My baby sister is off-limits.

"Better stop or you're gonna hurt yourself," I tell her.

"Stop what?"

"Thinking."

She throws one of my wrenches at my head and I dodge it just in time.

"What the fuck? You could've killed me!"

"Too bad." She shrugs, unapologetic.

"You're evil. I don't know why Dad likes you so much."

"Probably because you're such a disappointment."

I spit on the ground, returning the rag to my back pocket a little harder than necessary.

"I'm joking. God, you're so uptight. When's the last time you got laid?"

I pin her with an unamused look. We're not going there. I'm not even going there. It's been longer than I'd like but that has nothing to do with this.

"You can't take a joke or what?"

That wasn't a joke and we both know it. I can admit it—if I wanted to—but she, and everyone else, acts like that isn't the truth which is a part of why I only spend as much time out here as I absolutely have to.

"Don't you have some bags to stack?"

"I finished already."

"Change to count?"

"Done."

"Christ, you should come work for us." It's been like an hour, at best, since I saw her last.

"No thanks," she says, fixing the neckline on her t-shirt. "Too much toxic masculinity."

"That's this place." My dad employs a dozen men for every one we have at Pop The Hood—easy. Then there's my dad. He's just toxic.

"That's every place," she challenges and I concede instantly, nodding. She's right. Maybe not out at Graham Dairy where the women seem to run the show though. That was all I saw when I was out there anyway. Not that I'm complaining or doubting their capabilities. I saw Bentlee's sister toss a bale of hay like it weighed nothing and she's smaller than Bentlee in basically every way. Not as muscular. Or as fascinating.

Aside from the stench, it was nothing like I'd assumed. The cows were actually content and treated well. Everyone we passed on the tour was happy to clean, feed, and otherwise tend to the cows like they were a part of the family, too. It makes me wonder why Bentlee doesn't seem too happy to be working there again.

What's she doing right now? And why can't I picture her without Tysen all of a sudden?

Stupid. I'm so fucking stupid. I can't keep thinking of Bentlee, and imagining Tysen up her ass while I'm doing it is even worse. It's hard enough trying to focus when I know they could be getting up close and friendly in that tiny office she's got. I scoped it out yesterday when she didn't show up and it's like a coffin with a vent, mini fridge, and door. A door that locks. I checked that, too. Why would that door need a lock? Who made that decision?

Coty. Fucking genius.

I know exactly what that office with a lock is for.

Maybe I'll dismantle it next time I'm there. Tomorrow. I'll be there tomorrow, dammit. Looking for someone who thinks I'm not even worth looking back at.

She did for a second though. Only when she thought I wasn't looking but she was definitely checking me out. Another *why* I'd like to ask her…to her face, if she'll stop hiding it from me long enough.

"What are you doing? You look like you're about to puke."

"No I don't." I could use a cold shower but that's about it.

"Well, you were smiling and that's basically the same thing."

"What do I have to do to get rid of you?"

"I need lunch money."

"You graduated like three years ago and Mom makes your lunch." Every-fucking-day to be exact. She tries to pawn that shit off on me too but I always leave to eat. I'm not sitting at the same table as my father. Not anymore. My mom knows that but keeps insisting any-way. It's not like she doesn't see why but she somehow makes it seem like it's normal. Like it's okay the way he treats me.

Love for your spouse should only carry you so far until your own moral obligations need to kick the fuck in and tell you that a child doesn't deserve that kind of treatment.

I love my mom and I'd never want to break up our family but she could've done more. She could've done something.

I retrieve my wallet, handing Maggie the first bill I see. I need to finish up here and get to what I really want to do and I can't do that with my sister hanging around.

She looks at it in disgust, saying, "This is only twenty."

"Where the fuck you eatin'?"

She rolls her eyes dramatically, her rose-scented perfume filling the air around us. "You are so oblivious."

I scoff. Yeah. Right. Sometimes I think I'm the only one that actually sees what's going on but I'll let her live in fantasyland. The one where her and Coty fall in love—*fuck that*—and I'm the village idiot. What a fantasy indeed. Maybe my dad being a decent father, or person in general, will join in for a little added spice.

"Whatever. Get out of here." I give her two more bills, then tell her I love her in Spanish. "Te quiero."

"Te quiero *mucho*."

I can't help but laugh at her. Yeah, now that lunch for her and her friends is on me she loves me more.

She finally leaves me alone, so I pull on my pants falling down my boxers before kneeling to replace the head gasket just until I get the new one in. The hot metal burns my forearm with an audible sizzle but I don't even flinch. I almost never wear a shirt when I'm working outside, so I'm used to it by now. I don't wear any actual mechanic clothes. The pants are ugly as fuck and uncomfortable. I try to wear work attire at the shop because we're supposed to appear somewhat professional but even that's a stretch. Jeans and a cut-up tee are about all I can handle before I start to itch too much.

"You should put some ice on that," I hear behind me.

My grip increases with each rotation but I keep my head down, eyes on the four-wheeler.

"I can smell the burnt hair from here. Huele." *It stinks.*

So does having a prick of a father, but ya know, we all deal with inconveniences in our own way. He can leave if it bothers him that much. On second thought, he can just leave. I didn't ask my dad to come over here.

Why *is* he here? We usually keep to ourselves on the days I'm at Vega Farms, meaning I dodge him like Bentlee's been dodging me.

That comparison sits like lead in my gut. Why's she dodging me?

"Dammit," I mutter between clenched teeth.

I accidentally tightened the head gasket past the point I was sup- posed to and now it's gonna be a bitch to get off next time.

Pushing up to my full height, I cross my arms over my chest be- fore facing my father, knowing and not giving a shit that I'm getting dirty oil all over myself in the process. I'm used to that, too.

Neither of us speaks for a full minute as we stare the other one down.

Like always his ego gets the better of him and he breaks first to guilt me. Of course. Like there was ever any question what he was here for. Guilt and disappointment—my lunch of the typical bullshit, hand delivered without anything to wash it down with but my own disappointment…in him. He could've been so much better. He could still. I see it in the way he treats Maggie like a princess. But she plays the part. She is the princess of Vega Farms while I'm just the part-time mechanic that talks back and resents the fuck out of this place.

Some people lean into their conditions, some people lay on the gas. I'm the latter. Always.

"Your mother misses you."

"She's welcome to visit me anytime. I love to see *her*." I don't have to emphasize who's really welcome but I do anyway. I have to get my fun somehow if I'm really gonna sit here and entertain this shit again.

"To feed your friends? That's all she's good for?"

My fists clench under my arms. They're more than friends.

"That's all she does here, isn't it? Keep you all fed. Maybe she'd like to do something else for a change. *Go somewhere else.*" *Be* something else.

But no, not here. Once a farmer, always a farmer. It doesn't matter what position either, once you're in, you're *in* and you surrender to the crops and what they require to thrive enough to earn a profit. My mom took on the role of cook to keep everyone fed which is understandable, admirable even. The life of a farmhand is tough. The work is brutal—long, hard, harsh as all fuck. The physical demand alone is un-fucking-matched from having to withstand the elements—all of them. Just because it rains doesn't mean you go inside to warm up. Working on a farm is grueling and my mom likes to help in her own way by making big meals to keep the energy up and the employees' expenses down. Part of it she orders from local restaurants to pump money into the economy but most of it she wakes up before sunrise to start making herself.

And yeah, when she visits Creekwood she likes to cook for us, too. I don't ask her to or expect her to, that's just what she does to show her love, so I let her. *I'm greedy enough to let her.* But that doesn't change the fact that she should still have something else for herself, too. We all should. Joaquin Vega doesn't believe in that though. It's all or nothing with him.

And me, I'm straight nothing. Always have been, always will be because I'm not changing a damn thing.

I've created the life I want on my own, without ever using a dollar of his money or an ounce of his help. Anything and everything I have, material or otherwise, is from my doing. My hands form my own life and I don't feel the need to explain myself, least of all to him.

As someone who formed his own dream into a reality, he should understand that.

His trek to the top has been at the expense of others' backs he used in the climb but mine won't be there to catch him should he ever fall. I've been out of his reach for a long time and he doesn't respect that. He doesn't respect anything about me which is why I keep so much from him and everyone else. People can't ruin what they can't touch and I need certain things in my life to remain untouched.

"Watch yourself, Marcos," he warns, and I drop my arms by my sides, readying myself in case he wants to take it there. This is how fast things escalate between us. One wrong word, one drop in tone, then we're fighting, not giving a shit what we were arguing about to begin with because it feels too good to finally get some of the anger out. It's been a while though. We haven't had to go toe-to-toe because I've made it so. I avoid him to avoid hurting my mom but my dad doesn't seem to have the same reservations.

"No problem. Been doing it for years," I bite out.

At the end of the day, I don't care what people think of me, all that matters is what I think of me. So I let people, including my dad, assume what they want. I'm detached, fine. I'm cold, sure. I'm a rich boy with a silver spoon from my father's successful farm in my mouth, great. I travel for my own selfish reasons, you fucking got it.

But none of that's true.

While some of my trips are solely to get away from everyday

life, it's not to sit my ass on some all-inclusive tourist-infested private beach to sip piña coladas while getting a nasty sunburn. Everything I do has purpose. Meaning. On the trips I'm not actually grinding, I learn. The cultures, the customs, the cuisine, the overall environments—I soak in everything that I couldn't experience when I was growing up. All I ever knew was on the six thousand acres I'm standing on now and that wasn't enough once I realized there was more to the world than rows upon rows of strategically placed crops. I wanted to go where people didn't look like me, or talk like me, or eat like me. I wanted to see differences and embrace them. It's the one thing that humanity has in common, how different we all are, and I wanted to see that firsthand.

At first, I traveled to compete, to win. Racing dirt bikes came naturally to me once I taught myself how to ride in the first place, so I used that skill to my advantage as soon as I was old enough. I got a taste of the amount of freedom that was provided by doing something I already loved and became addicted, so with those earnings I started traveling even more but to explore.

I don't openly share that part of my life because I don't feel the need to. I don't race motocross for the recognition. I do it for the money. And money I've made. Enough to afford the properties out by my boys, enough to pay for anything I've ever needed or wanted, enough to set Rebel up with everything she could ever need or want, too.

Beck's the only one that knows I race, only because he's too nosey for his own good, but he doesn't know how often I race or the size of most of them or what all I use the winnings for. I've raced professionally since I was seventeen but I've never been signed by a big sponsor because of their…requirements. Sponsors don't just want riders anymore, they want stars, and I'm no star. I don't keep up with social media or speak publicly. I don't even take my helmet off for pictures.

Just like I taught Rebel.

I still applaud the shit out of all of Rebel's wins, no matter how big or small, but I don't want her thinking she should depend on it. You don't need to be applauded for your successes by others. You shouldn't need to. It doesn't make the victory any sweeter and it doesn't make you any different. It doesn't change who or what you are at your core. You're still you whether other people see it or not, whether they appreciate it or not. You stand on your own with the intention of doing it alone or you don't stand at all.

"When you're finished with this, come up to the house," my dad says, interrupting my thoughts.

"I'm busy."

"I'm not asking."

"Of course not." He never has before, so why the fuck would he start now?

He takes a step in my direction and I flex on impulse, my elbows bowing out to the side. I loosen my jaw though, parting my lips slightly. He's gone for a sucker punch enough times for me to know better than to lock my jaw up. I can handle a dislocated jaw but I'll be goddamned if I let him knock me out.

Then he says, "Marcos, *I* miss you," and I'd rather he knocked me out. At least I wouldn't have to sit here and stare a liar in the face. I already do that every time I look in the mirror.

"The DIY is getting too big for Magdalena to take on alone."

"So hire someone," I barely manage to get out as red blurs the edges of my vision. At least now the "missing me" statement makes sense.

"You're the only person that can do both." Someone to take care of the vehicles and the patrons.

Fuck. No. I'm interested in learning about other people, not catering to them.

Besides, I already have two careers. If anything, I'd be open to spending more time at Pop The Hood…Pop Two preferably.

The red recedes as an idea starts to form.

The other day when I was waiting for Bentlee at Pop Two, one of the new hires was chatting me up about his time volunteering at a food co-op, which he actually does for free, or in exchange for a discount on hemp lotion or some shit, I don't know. I couldn't really focus when Bentlee didn't show up.

I relax my arms by my side, feeling the first shred of calm since catching sight of Bentlee this morning. *Maybe I could see her every morning.*

"I got someone that can do both for you," I tell him, and he immediately counters with, "I'll pay you on top of what the garage does. You can get out of that apartment finally."

All the calm leaves my body at once. There's nothing wrong with my place at Creekwood. It just doesn't meet his standards because it's an apartment. What he fails to realize is my apartment holds more than his house ever will. More of what really matters—respect, understanding, acceptance. Things he's never been able to earn from me without resorting to coercion.

But just like with everybody else, I don't care enough to correct him. It doesn't matter what I say anyway. Seeing is only believing as long as people like what they're seeing and my dad sees me exactly how he chooses to.

With spotty vision and itching fingers, I turn for my car but he keeps after me, asking, "Why are you so determined to leave all the time? What's waiting for you, mijo?"

I flinch involuntarily, my BMW in front of me a distorted smear of red as I approach it.

Sometimes when I think about what I want out of life, I can't envision anything past what I'm doing right now but I know that's not realistic. Nothing is forever, and with the apartment on the verge of basically being empty, that's never felt more true. The impatient breath of change has been panting down my neck more and more recently, and even though I've tried fighting it off, it isn't going anywhere.

But where am I going really? *Is* there anything waiting for me? It doesn't feel like it. For the first time in a long time, it feels like I'm the one being left, not the other way around.

What does he have to gain by pointing that out though? What is it about me that's so goddamn threatening to him and his self-sustained status? I'm in my own lane. A lane I wholly dominate with no chance of me veering into his. He should be motherfucking happy. He can remain right where he likes to think he is—at the top. Except he'd prefer to berate me into being his successor so he can hand all that his name's achieved down to me. Down, because I'm always below him.

But what about my name? It's my name lining the trophies I have stashed away, not his. Why can't I be at the top, too?

The confession sits heavy on my mind but I don't actually tell him. He wouldn't believe it. Even if he did, he wouldn't understand it. Riding, racing, he doesn't understand. He doesn't understand me, and I stopped trying to make him a long time ago.

"What day do you want Troy to start? The part probably won't be in for a couple days," I tell him, pointing to the four-wheeler. "If you want him ready for this weekend, I can have him come tomorrow."

My dad studies me for a long time, then nods, saying, "Mañana." *Tomorrow.*

I've been wanting off this fucking farm since I stepped foot back on it but it affords me easy access to do what I love most, so I've stuck it out—for Pop The Hood and for me. If we do switch things up, then I'll need to make some changes that will raise questions. Questions I can answer; I just don't necessarily want to. Not right now. Not because he made it happen.

Because I made it happen though? Maybe.

Giving a nod as well, I get into my car and fishtail away before driving out of the veil of dust my tires create. When he's long gone from my rearview, I slow down, searching for my hidden path between the seventh and eighth rows of peach trees. They've all been harvested already, so it's the perfect place for me to store my shit without drawing notice. I have spots all over the farm where I keep my racing equipment and I move everything as needed. Because my hiding places change so often, I'm able to come and go as I please and nobody so much as bats an eye.

Beck and Coty already moved their dirt bikes out to their own properties. I might even be able to do the same without anyone catching on, too.

What's waiting for you?

Maybe Bentlee's got it right after all. Maybe I don't exist.

Chapter 9

Bentlee

"READY, SET, GO!"

Everyone jumps into the water from the top of the boat while I watch from the bow.

The gang rented the double-decker pontoon boat for the weekend and they tied it up to a couple other, smaller boats full of just as many people, if not more. At any given time there are three different songs fighting for the spotlight and every few minutes Beckett barks out orders for everyone else to shut theirs off but nobody listens. If anything, the other boats turn their sound systems up even louder, making conversations onboard that much more difficult.

Angela surfaces first, splashing at me and Paige as she climbs one of the ladders back onto the boat, saying over the music, "The water's so much warmer here. You both should come in."

I decline but Paige stands, heading to the rear to meet Beckett. Even though the water's not as deep in this part of the river than where we live, it's still deep enough. There could be any number of things down there, waiting to brush against me, to touch me. To touch my toes. No, thank you.

"Yeah, aren't you hot?" Tysen asks, following after Angela. His eyes fall down my body and I shift my legs I've been sitting on.

"I'll survive," I lie, feeling like I'm melting onto the vinyl seat.

"At least dip your feet in with me," Paige yells from the stern of the boat as she sits down with Beckett's help. I spy Marc and Coty treading water next to her fiancé, and as soon as another employee from Pop One opens the cooler, I jump on the opportunity to grab myself a beer.

And avoid Marc.

My approach at ignoring Marc and everything in his general vicinity is going well. So well. Extremely well…right up until I'm in the same room as him, which has been every morning I show up for work at Pop Two. I don't understand why he's there. It's not like he sticks around to actually work, with the exception of yesterday when he put in a full shift, he usually leaves right after I arrive. It's like he really doesn't trust me or something. I haven't seen anything that suggests any missing money so far, so I don't know what his problem is.

And although he did come alone today, I still can't help but wonder why he didn't bring Kary, his…whatever. There's a certain amount of confusion where she and Marc are concerned and nobody seems to know what the real situation is. Not that I've been asking around.

Tysen's got his arms spread wide on the back of the wraparound seat when I go to sit back down and his fingertips brush my shoulder.

We both say "sorry" at the same time, then he rubs the back of his fingers against my skin as if more touching will erase the original touching and I nod it off, tossing back a long pull of beer while turning the opposite way.

We're sleeping in the same cabin tonight which I didn't know about until I arrived. Luckily, it has two beds and they're both twin size, so there's zero chance of anything happening between us, as if I didn't already know that from working alongside him and hearing about Clarise every thirty-six seconds.

After Tysen's fingers bump me for the fifth time, I get up, swaying a bit from the boat rocking side to side over a wave, and join Angela on the top deck.

"I dare you to slide down," she says, pointing at the slide going off the back of it.

"I'm not drunk enough for that."

"Why? You went down the slide at my house. It's the same thing."

We peer over the edge.

"That's a five-foot drop into dark water." The water at her house was from a hose and it was contained and the size of a puddle. This water has things that haven't even been identified yet in it.

"Can you swim?" she asks with a frown.

"Yes." I can, I just prefer not to.

"I'll go in first and wait for you," she says as she climbs the ladder, but before I can tell her that won't help, she slides down, landing in the water with a tall splash. Coty swims toward her and stays by her side when she resurfaces, immediately yelling up at me, "Your turn."

"I'm fine up here," I try to say but my voice falters as my feet begin sizzling on the hot floorboards.

Drops of sweat roll down my temples, and just when I decide to go back down the stairs, Tysen and the guy from the cooler appear.

"I can give you the Christensen treatment if you want," he offers up politely and I ask, "What's that?"

"I toss you over." With a wink, he shrugs like that isn't the worst thing I've ever heard in my life. You can't just throw people overboard. "It's not as bad as it sounds. It'll be over before you know it."

"I'll go," I say through a gulp. I take one final swig of my beer and put it in the garbage bag attached to the railing.

Marc makes his way over to Angela and Coty, making a semicircle below the slide and I squeeze my eyes shut, wishing he were on one of the other boats. It'd make ignoring him so much easier.

Lie.

Tysen brushes me again and my eyes snap open to warn him, "Don't touch me. I'll do it myself."

"Do it for me, Bentlee!" Paige hollers through what are probably cupped hands but sound like a bullhorn straight to my brain.

Tysen raises his hands innocently, saying, "Can you at least hurry? It's hot as balls up here."

Situated on the slide, I stare down, trying desperately to avoid Marc's persistent gaze but it's hard because he's all I see—him and the dark water.

Why am I doing this? Any of this? Why did I agree to even come here at all?

With no wind to be found, and the three different songs blurring together into wordless noise, I take a deep breath, letting this moment wash over me. The sun beats down on my upturned face and there's a brief pause of pure peacefulness that I haven't felt…in possibly ever? Maybe this is why I came. To feel something. To just feel, period.

A hand at my back pushes me to slide before I'm ready and my wide eyes catch on Marc's just before I'm falling through the air, reminding me of the real reason I came. *Like a moth to a flame…*

The water swallows my body whole, my legs overcome by a cold needling sensation as I plunge toward the river's bottom, praying the entire time I don't get tangled in seaweed. I start kicking vigorously as soon as time stands still and break the surface to hear Marc shouting something about beating somebody's ass. Then, next thing I know, I'm yanked through the water and tucked behind a strong back that I've only admired from afar.

A huge splash followed by another hits my face as I quickly recline to float on my back, lifting my feet out of the water while using my arms to keep from sinking. With my ears slightly muffled, I can only make out voices but they're pissed. Or at least one of them is.

I watch the back of Marc's head as he chews Tysen and the other guy out, angling my head so one ear is out of the water.

"What the fuck is your problem? You shoved her off then almost landed on top of her. She could've got hurt."

"She seems perfectly fine to me." Tysen waves a hand at me, sending droplets of water across my face and I have to blink my eyes several times.

Marc turns his face to me and his expression immediately softens before he looks at my feet and asks, "What are you doing?"

"Did you know sturgeons can grow to fifteen feet long?"

He nods. "Longer in Russia."

"Did you also know they're technically dinosaurs and that this river is full of them? They say getting hit by one is like getting hit by a truck."

"And," he glances at my feet again, fighting a smile, "holding your feet like that will keep one of them from hitting you?"

"I'm not worried about getting hit by one, I just don't want them to touch my toes."

"Your toes?"

"Yeah." It sounds so ridiculous. It is so ridiculous. I'm around animals almost every single day but I also wear steel-toe boots or heavily insulated boots that nothing can scratch or nibble through. I have a small degree of control on land when it comes to my toes. Here, I have nothing.

He turns to give me his back again, then says, "Get on."

"What?" I lift my head fully out of the water.

"Get on my back."

I drop my head back down, almost submerging my entire face as it catches fire. "That's okay. I'll backstroke over to the boat." Or sink to save myself further embarrassment, whichever's quicker.

I'm suddenly dragged through the water again as Marc unfolds my body to position me around his. My feet dangle by his legs and I tighten my arms around his neck, squealing when one of his calves brushes my toes.

"Here." He chuckles. "Wrap your legs around my waist." His hands grab my thighs, rubbing along the sensitive skin to help wrap them around to his front and I forget how to breathe. *So much for avoiding him.* With my legs finally in place, he uses his arms to tread water again and I use one of mine to help as well while the other rests across his collarbone. "Are your feet okay like this?"

They're not out of the water but they don't feel as exposed, as vulnerable. Actually, tucked against his hard torso as his abs flex with each kick, they feel safe. I feel safe.

I nod against his shoulder blade, my chin never leaving his skin.

"Alright, good. This way if *anything* hits you, it'll have to hit me, too."

My arm stops paddling and I sit here speechless. He didn't laugh at me. He didn't make fun of me for some unreasonable fear. He offered his own body up as protection after already protecting me from getting jumped on by two grown men.

"I gotta swim or we'll sink," he says, pushing through the water. *We.*

"Oh, you can just let me off at the ladder."

"Are you cold?"

One of his arms reaches back, the inside of his elbow grazing my side and I suppress a shiver.

"No." Not anymore.

"You like being in here otherwise? Aside from the toe-touching dinosaurs?"

There's laughter in his voice but no sarcasm whatsoever and I smile, nodding again.

"Then we'll stay in. Just hold on."

"Hey, Bentlee, I'm sorry for pushing you," Tysen says as we paddle along the side of the boat.

Marc mutters, "Idiot," under his breath and I chuckle, telling Tysen, "It's okay." I can't say I hate where it landed me.

"I don't think he meant any harm," I tell Marc when I know we're far enough away from the others.

"I don't care," is all he grits out and I sit back to alleviate some of my weight on him.

He chances a look over his shoulder, asking, "What's wrong?"

"I'm drowning you."

He laughs, slowing his strokes once we reach the front of the boat. "You're not."

"There's another ladder around here somewhere," I say, looking around for the one Angela and Tysen just used.

"You're going the opposite way," I accuse, tightening my hold on Marc again once he's a good fifteen feet *away* from the boat.

"I finally got you talking to me. I'm not about to give that up."

My hold on him goes lax. He noticed. He knows I've been avoiding him and I don't know if he knows why. How pathetic does this look? How pathetic do *I* look?

"I talk to you."

He scoffs, not saying anything more.

"You're not much of a talker yourself. Has anyone ever told you that?" It's not *all* my fault.

"Maybe a time or two," he says matter-of-factly, his back muscles straining with every stroke.

How far out are we going? He can't keep this up for that long. It must be all kinds of awkward to swim carrying a whole other person on your back. I don't even think lifeguards do that.

"Your friends might worry," I point out when I can't even hear the music from the boats behind us anymore.

"Probably."

"Do you care?"

"Do you?" he asks, turning his head to the side and spitting out some water.

"Will we be able to make it back to the boat okay?"

"Do you want to go back?" he almost stops swimming entirely, leaving the option completely up to me.

I shake my head against the back of his shoulder, my lips splitting on a secret smile. "Not yet." It feels good to make the decision. Really good.

"Fuck."

Without thought I drop my legs and push off of him. "I told you I was drowning you."

I get a couple backstrokes away before he reaches me with the ease of an Olympic swimmer. For every stroke forward though, I match his with one of my own backward, our eyes never straying from each other's.

"I thought you said you didn't want to go back."

"I don't want to drag you down either."

His long arms make even longer strides, bringing him within reach, but instead of grabbing me, we continue swimming like that, keeping the same pace all while watching the other one. The pontoon boat floats in the distance and I'm tempted to just make a beeline for it but I can't seem to turn away from Marc's teasing eyes holding mine as he chases after me. I know he could overtake me at any moment, yet he doesn't. He's playing with me.

Grinning, I splash him but just as quickly he ducks under the water, his entire body disappearing from sight. Every nerve in my body tenses, anticipating him grabbing my feet, or brushing my toes, or...

Suddenly he resurfaces right behind me and my back ends up slamming into him as I let out a scream. I spin around to face him, gasping out, "You scared the shit out of me."

He catches my hand though and pulls me tight against him, his low voice drawing me even closer. "Don't. Move." A dark expression crosses his face, making my heart sputter.

"What? Why?" Instinctively my legs wrap around his middle, my ankles locking behind his back. Small waves hit us from both sides and it feels like we're our own island. Him, me, and the turbulent tide keeping everyone else at bay.

Our breaths mix as my gaze falls to his lips, tiny drops of water clinging to them.

"Why?" I repeat barely above a whisper, unable to look away.

"There's a," his eyes drop too, our breaths mingling as we bob against each other and I tighten my hold on him, "jet ski."

Bringing my chest just under his chin, I'm able to see over his shoulder as the tail of water being sprayed into the air behind the jet ski sputters by.

We're too far from the boat for the orange flag signaling swimmers in the water to notify other boaters of our presence. We could've been run over. I could've been run over.

"Something hits you, it hits me. Remember?"

I close my eyes against the swelling beneath my ribs, trying to make its way up my throat. He willingly put himself between me and the danger—again.

How many times is that now?

Too many.

"You could've just said something." I don't dare open my eyes.

"Could've," he agrees quietly, adjusting us so his lips move against the skin above my collarbone while simultaneously encouraging the throbbing at my center to intensify significantly. "But I like my way better."

With my legs still wrapped around him, I lie back, keeping my head afloat and my arms outstretched to my sides as they help to keep us from going under. Opening my eyes to look him dead in his, I ask, "What next?"

He raises a single brow and I rush to clarify, "You got me here, so you must want to talk about something."

His eyes fall down my body but I don't rush to cover myself to try and hide my imperfections like I did on the boat. Instead I let him look, wondering why it feels so different. Why I feel so different. Every time I'm around Marc I feel different.

"How old were you when you got your nose pierced?"

"Sixteen." Much to my parents' complete and utter disappointment. I did it myself with a safety pin, and up until that point, that was the worst act of rebellion I'd ever done.

"Tattoo?" His gaze drops, wandering along the inked design like a stroll through the park on a lazy Sunday afternoon and setting off a deep chill of jealousy beneath the rest of my skin.

"Last year," I get out somehow, hoping he drops it.

"Does it mean something?"

Shit.

"Yes."

When I don't explain further, a cloud crosses his face that even the sun above us can't chase away.

"What's the deal with your ex? How long were two together?"

"Long enough."

"Long enough for what?" His scowl deepens in thought.

"To learn a few things."

His eyes sharpen on me and I fight a smirk. Probably not the way he's thinking but I'm not spilling all my business like that.

"And Tysen?"

Tysen?

"He's a great manager," I say simply. "Fair and personable. He does well with both the customers and the other employees at Pop Two."

Tysen has this uncanny talent for adapting to any situation. He flows like water but isn't afraid to rise up either. Angela's more of a stickler for order, so she balances him out well enough that the two of them make a great team together.

Coty, Marc, and Beckett are my bosses too but I haven't had many dealings with them. Beckett picks up shifts at Pop Two occasionally but is so busy working under hoods, he gladly lets Angela and Tysen take care of everything else. He's a highly sought-after mechanic as is Marc from what I've gathered. Coty has his hands tied at Pop One, so I've only seen him a couple times when he's stopped by to drop off lunch for his girlfriend.

Marc shakes his head like he's disappointed and I worry I gave something away about Tysen. Sitting up a little, I lower myself directly onto something hard, but before I can fix my mistake, Marc's hand grips my thigh, keeping me in place.

Everything gets fuzzy and I blink a few times, trying to get my thoughts in order and my heart rate under control. Now my heart wants to jump straight to sprinting? How about a little warmup first? Some light stretching maybe.

This is crazy. I'm not fourteen years old freaking out because my crush is giving me the time of day.

"Why was he touching you?"

"When?"

"On the boat."

"I don't…know. Was he touching me?" I can't think past Marc's body. And penetrating eyes. And the solid erection poking my ass despite the cold temperature.

How is that even possible? Isn't there shrinkage or something? Because it sure doesn't feel like it from where I'm sitting—literally.

"Yeah. He was," he spews like an accusation, hot and pointed. It's a tone I know all too well. A tone that still haunts me.

But Shawn and I were together. Marc and I are not. So why does it matter? The few finger brushes back on the boat were nothing. I don't have an attraction to Tysen beyond a detached physical appreciation of how attractive he is. No part of me throbs when his skin comes into contact with mine. Not like this. I swear I can feel my pulse in every part of my body. Between my toes, behind my knees, deep within my core, my stomach, the part of my throat just under my ears—everywhere.

And yet, Marc's trying to talk about other men right now? Really? They, every last one of them that isn't named Marcos Vega, are the last thing on my mind.

Is it jealousy swathing his beautiful face? Not always, but some-times—*enough times*—jealousy masks a person's own indiscretions and wasn't Kary supposed to be here…with Marc?

Wow. Lessons from mistakes really don't stick the first time they're made.

An anchor falls from my chest, its line unfurling indefinitely, and without meeting his eyes, I tell him, "I want to head back now."

When he doesn't release me right away, I assume he's going to take the choice from me but then he jerks a stiff nod, letting me go and we swim back to the boat side by side, neither of us saying anything. Once I'm back on board, I make sure I'm surrounded by enough peo-ple that I can't be alone with Marc again. When we're alone is when his demons try to tempt mine out of hiding but I've already tangled with one devil. I don't want another.

I don't.

Chapter 10

Bentlee

FTER BOTH OF US ARE SHOWERED AND DRESSED—thank God there's a private bathroom in the cabin—Tysen and I make our way to the bonfire set up in the middle of the cabins. It was awkward once we were by ourselves in the cabin, much more awkward than I thought it'd be. When there's nothing else to do but stare at your cabin-mate, you learn every little tic about them. We work together but not every day and not all day either. He does this thing with his knuckles, it's like cracking them but louder, so much louder. And he does it every few minutes, like how much lube do your joints really need? Tysen works with his hands and he works with his hands well but I just wish I didn't have to hear the bones in his body moving in blaring synchronicity as background noise for my first ever solo getaway.

Tall grass brushes my ankles as we cross one of the small dunes separating our cabin from the bonfire and the smell of burning wood hits me at the same time I see the floating embers dancing their way up to the darkening sky, reaching for the same stars they're desperately trying to resemble.

Coty and someone I've never met before set everyone up with roasting sticks and the choice of either hot dogs or brats to cook over the fire. There's ingredients for s'mores, too, and I swipe a marshmallow to eat as an appetizer. That and another beer that I tuck in the front pocket of my hoodie.

Luckily, Paige calls me over before I have to do that overly obvious seat search while trying not to look like I'm doing a seat search.

"Thanks," I tell her and Angela once I'm settled in front of the log they're sitting on.

There's more people than there were on the boats and a part of me wonders if Kary's one of them.

Why was I wrapped around Marc today?

Because he made me.

Because he let me.

Because I wanted to.

Because I chose to.

It was my choice.

Across the fire my eyes find his and hold before glancing to his left and right as surreptitiously as I can. His lips tighten ever so slightly letting me know I failed. Just because there isn't anybody sitting next to him now doesn't mean there won't be later. The night is young and he looks incredible in his gray Henley with the sleeves pushed up to his elbows and black jeans tucked into some expensive-looking black and white sneakers. With a hat sitting crooked on his head, he looks perfectly at ease even if he doesn't seem to notice anything else around him, like he's in his own world and we're all just visiting.

"Babe, you want some?" Coty asks Angela as he lowers a tray, then to me and Paige, "Ladies?"

I grab a handful of grapes, wishing they were actually cold—the colder the better—but Paige blanches like she's about to be sick and Beckett's quick to ask, "What's wrong?"

"God, what is that?"

"What?" He and Coty look down at the tray, both searching it suspiciously.

"I don't know but it smells like pussy."

A laugh bubbles past my lips as several people turn our way, amusement lighting their faces more than the bonfire. Angela grabs her stomach, trying to keep her laughter in and Coty mashes his lips together to hide a smile.

Beckett sniffs, then lifts a piece of what looks like prosciutto, pinching it between two fingers to ask, "This?"

Paige nods, gagging. "Get it away from me."

"It's definitely got a fishy smell to it, but, dream, you think this is what pussy smells like?" There's humor in Beckett's entire stance now like he's gearing up to chase his fiancée with the thinly sliced meat.

Peering up at him, she narrows her eyes. "Well, I'm not the one that buries my face in it almost every night, so why don't you tell me."

Without so much as blinking, he shoves the entire piece of prosciutto in his mouth, pursing his full lips around it while pretending to consider its flavor.

Everyone watching the scene laughs, including me, even though I know I shouldn't encourage him. He's like a naughty house pet that gets away with way too much.

"You're sleeping outside tonight," Paige tells him seriously and he spits it all out into the fire, wiping his mouth with the back of his hand as the flames flare instantly in a brief standing ovation for Beckett's performance.

Maybe he doesn't get away with as much as I originally thought.

"Okay, you win. And for the record, your pussy smells nothing like that," he murmurs for just her as he leans down for a kiss and I direct my attention to the grapes in my hands, popping a couple in my mouth. I hear her gag again, asking him to rinse his mouth with alcohol, then he kisses the top of her head instead and gives her a takeout container someone from a food delivery service ran down a minute ago to hand deliver to him. I guess his height made it possible for him to be picked out of the crowd. He's *so* tall. "Here. Your OB said you're not supposed to eat hot dogs, so I got you something else. I called to check while you were napping earlier."

She thanks him, then he nudges Coty with his elbow all while wearing a dirty grin that further proves my point.

"Thank fuck not all wieners are on that list, huh?"

Coty only hangs his head and shakes it, also trying like hell not to provoke his best friend as they move to leave us girls alone.

"He's so over the top."

"Yeah," Paige agrees with Angela as she watches his back while he wanders away. Beckett turns around as if he can sense her ogling him and she smiles unashamedly, giving him a flirty wink. "About everything." She returns her focus to us with raised eyebrows, saying, "Thankfully."

Angela nods in agreement, her cheeks pinking up a bit beneath the inky sky.

"What about you, Bentlee? Was your ex generous?" Paige asks and I have the urge to laugh maniacally. The word generous and Shawn do not belong in the same sentence.

"In what way?" I feign ignorance as I spear my hot dog with the roasting stick, then hold it over the closest part of the fire.

"The only way that matters?" Paige says, lifting the lid off her dinner and moaning when she sees the hamburger and fries.

"Is sex the only thing that matters though?" Angela asks, rotating her own hot dog with intense concentration as the grease on the skin begins to bubble up.

Paige pauses, pretending to consider the question even though she's not fooling anyone. There's not a doubt in my mind the ever-present heat on full display between the newly engaged couple doesn't hold a candle to the love they share for each other—it's practically blinding. Not unlike Angela and Coty's actually.

"It sure helps," she finally settles on.

Angela smiles warmly. "That it does."

I prolong the moment even longer by opening my beer and taking a long drink. They both look at me expectantly and I roll my eyes, saying, "No. He wasn't."

"Ugh, I hate selfish lovers."

"He's definitely selfish, but with sex he was more so…" I hesitate, not exactly comfortable with what I'm thinking. It is the truth but I've never said it out loud. Not to anyone other than Shawn in the heat of the moment during one of our constant fights about our sex life, or lack thereof. "Uninterested," I finish on a shaky exhale. At least that's how he always acted when I tried to initiate. When he initiated, it was different—kind of. It was almost calculated, premeditated even.

"Do you think he's asexual maybe? Because that's not that uncommon actually. Asexual people often don't experience sexual attraction even if they're in a committed relationship with someone they love," Paige says, reminding me she's a nurse with her nonjudgmental tone as she delivers the facts I already know from doing lots and lots of research on the topic. "It has nothing to do with the other person. That's just who they are."

After everything happened the way it did, and I finally picked up on all the little hints I was blatantly ignoring at first, I know that wasn't the case.

"He's not asexual. He's just manipulative."

Both girls are quiet for a long time, then Paige asks, "So, he used sex as a way to control you?"

More than familiar with its sickening taste, I swallow the pill of shame with a reluctant head nod.

"My mom would do the same thing with her husbands," Angela admits with her own amount of humiliation, almost like she's guilty by association somehow.

"Did he take care of any of your needs? Like at all?"

"Maybe in the beginning. Back when we were young and dumb—"

"You're kidding, right? You're still young."

My hand motions in front of me like a wheel getting away from me. "Even still, he never, like, went…" I drop my gaze, feeling the skin on my face, chest, and arms heat uncontrollably.

"Down on you?" Paige supplies helpfully and I nod again.

Angela drops her hot dog along with the stick, sending ashes into the air. Staring at the ruined hot dog half lying in the dirt, she says, "I'm pretty sure Coty spends more time on his knees than not, and I'll tell you right now, that man is not religious."

Paige blows out a breath. "Fuck, girl. That makes me really sad for you. Honestly? I thought that was part of the dating audition process. If a guy won't go down on you, you should *not* have sex with him. I mean, what's the point? If he's not there to get you off, then you shouldn't even bother with getting him off. Sex should be a mutual agreement between bodies, not a fucking solo mission."

I shrug noncommittally. What is there to say? My ex stooped to any level just to get me where he wanted me…and I didn't stop him. For a long time I didn't stop him and that blame falls solely on my shoulders. I should've known.

But I really was young and dumb. I didn't know what a healthy relationship was supposed to feel like. I didn't know you weren't supposed to feel like a piece of roadkill all the time.

"As much as that sucks, the good news is, it's fixable," Paige says suddenly, and both Angela and I look over at her. "Pick a man, any man." She gestures a hand out in front of her like she's on a game show presenting a high-value prize to the wide-eyed contestant.

Angela smiles and clasps her hands together. "Okay. Tell me which one you like and I'll tell you their current dating situation. I know them all. In graphic detail," she says with a faux shudder. She and I both know the guys at the shop are worse than women, all they do is talk. Some more descriptive than others.

"I can't. It's not that easy."

Paige waves me off. "Listen. It is. It will be. I promise. You're gorgeous, your style is super sexy," I frown, "and your ass puts all of ours to shame." I didn't know any of that but Angela nods solemnly like these are all well-known facts, not just an exaggerated attempt to boost my confidence. "If I wasn't pregnant and madly in love and straight as an arrow, I'd fuck you myself. Now, any guy would be lucky to spend a night with you and it just so happens there's some pretty great eye candy here tonight, so close your eyes and point if you have to, but tonight, we're getting you laid. Hopefully with an earsplitting orgasm, or two, before that even happens. Actually no," she holds up a finger, "that's the prerequisite from now on. Got it? You are no longer sleeping with men until they make you come first."

Angela's smile grows as she looks around, then says, "Just not Coty or Beckett obviously."

"Obviously," I agree easily, feeling a bit of crazy excitement take hold even though this is insane. I can't just shop for an orgasm donor. I haven't been to that kind of supermarket in a long, long time, if ever.

They may have a point.

"Or my brother," Paige adds. "He's-"

"Hung up," I finish for her.

"He's hung up still," she nods, "and needs to take care of that before he even thinks about sleeping with anyone else. Although, if Clarise's glowing endorsement of Ty's oral skills can be trusted, he'd make a great candidate."

Both Angela and I groan and I tell her, "We did not need to know that."

"Yeah, we work with him, Paige. Not to mention that's your brother."

"Hey, for all the shit my overprotective brothers have put me through over the years, they better take good care of their women. I'm kinda proud they're not the selfish shits I always assumed they were. Now quit stalling and choose already," she says to me like it's really that simple.

The second my eyes move from Paige, they find Marc's and both girls notice instantly, chuckling to themselves.

"You're brave, I'll give you that."

I tear my gaze from his.

"I didn't even choose."

The two exchange conspiratorial glances, then Paige says softly, "That's usually how it goes."

How what goes?

"Besides, Marc's taken…isn't he?"

"That thing with Kary?"

Angela raises her shoulders while Paige leans forward, her red-streaked hair even brighter from the fire, and drops her voice to continue, "I don't think he is actually. Marc was always, careful let's say, about going over to her place. Always at weird times and never at the same time twice. We're talking Tuesday late afternoon, not all-day Saturday watching Netflix marathons, or dinner with an extra helping of dessert on Friday nights."

"People have sex on Tuesday afternoons," Angela deadpans and I shrug, completely useless. None of those examples are familiar to me unfortunately.

"Of course they do, but a quickie on a Tuesday afternoon should take, what? Fifteen, twenty, thirty minutes tops?" Thirty minutes? For a quickie? Shawn's take on a quickie was thirty seconds. And that's compared to the minute it usually took him. "He'd be over there for *hours*, and when he'd finally stroll back into our apartment, he wouldn't have a single hair out of place and he was just as stoic as he was before he left."

I'm torn between covering my ears and wanting to hang off every word. Hours?

"He does have short hair though," I argue weakly.

"You know what I mean. A man like Marc?" Despite my best efforts, my eyes search him out again but he's no longer looking at me—thankfully—as he talks with Coty and Beckett who are now flanking him. "You're telling me if you spent hours in bed with him, you wouldn't leave *some* kind of mark to show for it? And hours? If he's wearing anything less than a dopey-ass smile after that, something's off. Something doesn't add up about that situation at all. Not to mention she's a goddamn recluse who never sets foot outside. She's almost as bad as Gary."

"Who's Gary?"

Angela answers, telling me about the notorious neighbor at Creekwood who does bear some similarities with the complex's manager the more they describe both of them.

With my hot dog heated through, I busy myself putting it in the bun while still listening.

"What happened between you two earlier today when you disappeared?" Paige asks after Angela finishes.

"Yeah, I've never seen Marc so…attentive before."

"He was sweet as sugar," Paige agrees.

I immediately shove a gigantic bite in my mouth, mumbling "nothing" around the scalding food and making a show of chewing slowly.

Her eyes narrow as she says, "Uh-huh."

Angela laughs. "Welp, tonight should be fun."

Several beers later and everything around me starts to feel heavy. Like it's all happening in slow motion.

I glance at Tysen gazing into the fire and try to get his attention, not really sure if my face is moving or not because that definitely doesn't feel heavy. My body feels like it's in a quarrel with gravity, scoffing at its trivial existence.

"Tysen," I say, my weightless eyebrows matching my rising tone. "Are we going?" Now?

Before we left the cabin, we agreed on a time to sneak away from the group to make our phone calls. Mine to Hunter and his to…I don't actually know. He didn't specify and I didn't ask. Diesel, I'm assuming—if he's still awake. We made the pact and I intend on keeping it with or without him. I hate going an entire day without talking to Hunter. Even hanging out on the boat today, it felt weird not having him there. To look out for. To worry about constantly. Everybody else is carefree, not on someone else's schedule of meals and homework and device time and "Mom, is there anything in your purse I can have? I'm starving." As exhausting as it actually is, I love it. I miss it. I wouldn't trade it for anything else in the world. When Hunter's not with me, it feels like I'm missing an arm. A leg. A part of me I can't live without anymore, at least not blissfully.

I just want to talk to him, then I'll be okay. This whole thing will pass—all of it. Marc's staring from across the fire. This idea that I'm supposed to get laid tonight. The microscopic bugs I swear are treating themselves to my exposed calves as their own dinner. Marc's staring from across the fire. Not knowing if Hunter is fed and safe and happy right now. Marc's staring from across the fire.

"Wait," Paige speaks up from her spot on Beckett's lap. "Marc, can you walk Bentlee back to her cabin?"

I give her a wide-eyed headshake while watching out of my periphery as Marc pushes to standing with zero hesitation whatsoever.

"How are your knees feeling? Do you need to do a couple lunges first?" She snickers and Angela covers her mouth with a hand, trying to smother a laugh the fifteen-foot sturgeon can probably hear.

"Lunges?" Marc's deep voice surrounds me even from several feet away.

"I got her, dude." Tysen stands finally, sending his hand out toward Marc which Marc openly sneers at. Taking a swig off a vodka bottle, Tysen offers it to me with a slice of a smile on his face that doesn't reach anywhere near his eyes. "Liquid courage?"

I study him for a second. Did he drink more than me?

Rubbing my thumb along my lip, I push the bottle away with my other hand. I'm not the one planning on talking to my ex, but even if I was, the last thing I'd want to be is drunk. I'm more flexible when I'm drunk. Shawn knows that and has no qualms about using it to his advantage.

Wait, am I drunk?

"Where are you two sneaking off to?" Beckett asks with the subtlety of a grenade when Tysen one-handedly pulls me to standing, his front brushing mine.

A low rumble of thunder echoes around us even though the sky's as calm as a still lake.

"Bed," I say at the same time Tysen says, "The beach," and the fire crackling next to us becomes blaring as everybody falls silent.

Angela's eyebrows lift as she relaxes back between her boyfriend's bent legs, her arms framing his knees while Paige's head jerks toward Marc meaningfully. I know they wanted me to have some kind of hall pass night where I escape the only norm I've ever known with someone I barely know all in the spirit of female empowerment, but it's not happening. Not for me. Not tonight. And definitely not with Marc.

I can feel those charcoal eyes on me as strong and sure as the firelight dancing between us and pray he didn't just see Paige's attempt at being a wing woman. Just like with the sun at noon, I avoid looking directly at him just in case he did.

"We're already at the beach, bro. Didn't you notice the sand in your ass?"

"Is that what that is?" Tysen makes a show of shaking his ass near his sister's fiancé and Beckett howls loudly, shoving him away with an incredibly large foot without so much as jostling Paige still on his thighs.

"Why do both of you need to go?" Beckett asks, his voice thick with insinuation.

My eyes meet Tysen's and I shrug. He doesn't have to. I still want to talk to my son though. I'd rather talk to Hunter for one minute than listen to small talk for the next sixty.

But Tysen says, "Moral support," which makes me break into laughter that sounds suspicious even to my own ears. First liquid courage, now moral support? If we really were sneaking off, everyone would know it from those two ludicrous excuses alone. Smooth criminal he is not.

"Come on, Bentlee. Lesss get you to *bed*." He drapes his arm over my shoulders, pulling me along and my reactions are delayed just long enough that I let him get me a couple feet before I'm able to slip out from under his hold.

"Enjoy," Angela singsongs just before Paige blurts, "Remember, female ejaculation before penetration."

Another crash of thunder that no one else seems to notice reverberates through my bones down to my toes as I cringe, too embarrassed to look at Tysen. There's no way he didn't just hear his sister. Everybody did and the laughter at our backs proves it.

A few steps ahead of him, I finally work up the courage to turn around but what I see stops me dead in my tracks. A tear. A single tear in the corner of Tysen's eye as shiny as the moon itself still reflecting the sun's rays, even in its absence.

"She should be here. They should be here. With me."

And just like that, what Paige said slips from my mind. Mostly.

"I know." Trust me, I know. "But that's not what she wants, Tysen. You're just going to have to accept that and move on." *Please.*

I do empathize with the man. I'm walking around without the

beats of my most vital organ all because of a breakup. It's hard to reconcile who the person you thought they were with the person they became but it doesn't mean that it's impossible. We all wear many faces, we just don't show them all at once. We can't. It's too much even for ourselves to deal with, let alone put that on somebody else.

Shawn revealed faces I never wanted to see. Faces I had no idea existed. But they did. They do. And now that I've seen them, I have to internalize that they're real, not lie to myself that they don't just to help me sleep better at night.

Rejection stings but it doesn't destroy, not unless you let it.

Tysen's letting it. He's letting Clarise destroy him one missed memory at a time. He needs to make his own memories and be okay with the fact that his ex removed herself from the mental snapshots.

"We're going to the beach," I tell him, determined. I'm doing all kinds of things I wouldn't normally do but the great thing about my breakup is there's no longer anyone around to tell me what I can and can't do. Right now, I want to help Tysen get out of his head.

"Didn't you hear? We're at the beach." He says it with sadness, the humor long gone.

Reaching the water's edge, the moon's pale face watches from both the sky and the river's surface as I pull my hoodie over my head, placing it on the hard-packed sand.

"Strip," is all I say, then pull my capris off, too. Down to my underwear and bra, I look over at him but he's not looking at me as he removes his jeans and tee, just silent contemplation about a life he doesn't have anymore and maybe won't ever have again.

"The Christensen treatment, was it?"

"What?"

For answer, I shove him with all my might and, catching him off guard, he goes sprawling into the cold water, the vodka bottle flying out of his hold. Cursing and spitting, he pulls himself up onto his knees before grabbing the bottle now full of murky water and chucks it by our clothes but I'm already sprinting past him and diving into the water. Popping back up almost instantly, I float on my back with my toes just barely showing.

My moment of peace lasts for exactly that as Tysen launches himself at me like a professional wrestler shoving off the ropes and I dunk myself to avoid collision. I feel his hands grip my sides under the water just before he hefts me into his arms and tosses me through the air and back into the water several feet away. He follows immediately after me and we take turns trying to dunk the other, screaming out our frustrations each time we land—not at each other, just at the world. At life. At the unfairness of it all.

As soon as I'm above the water long enough to catch my breath, I paddle for the shore, mindful not to let my feet go too deep as I kick vigorously.

Tysen drops down next to me on the sandbar, both of us letting our bottom halves float weightlessly as we lie in silence.

"Does it get any easier?" His head turns to me, little streams of water running down his stubble-covered cheeks. "Being without them?"

"Not easier. It's like trying to kick a ball with your legs tied together. You can do it if you try hard enough but it's not what you're used to. What your mind has been programmed to accept. And so you just…adapt." But I don't miss Shawn, not like Tysen misses Clarise.

"Adapt," he repeats. "What if I don't want to? What if my body refuses? This one fucking time, it's like I know that this isn't how it's supposed to be."

I consider his question.

"Then you fight with everything you got."

He blows out a breath, running a hand through his dark brown hair. "All we do is fight."

"Don't fight *with* her. Fight *for* her."

A few minutes pass, each of us lost in our own worlds of ruined possibilities and missed chances, then I pull myself up, giving him a hand this time.

"Thanks," he says, taking it and leading us back to our clothes.

"Anytime."

This is as close to skinny-dipping as I've ever been, and while it was fun, it's extremely cold now that the endorphins have worn off.

My teeth are still rattling when we stop in front of our cabin.

"I think I'm gonna stay out here a while longer. Try giving her a call."

Our eyes hold, and where I saw wavering resignation before, I now see steady determination.

I close the door telling him I'll keep it unlocked, then go in search of a towel and something dry to wear.

Chapter 77

Marc

WHAT THE FUCK IS GOING ON? I DON'T KNOW WHAT the hell all that shit was with Paige and lunges and female ejaculation, which had nothing to do with anything—right?—then Tysen stole, fucking stole Bentlee out from under me when I had every intention of being the one to see her safely to her cabin.

Their cabin.

And now there's fucking screaming—*screaming*—coming from *their* cabin.

One thing I do know is whatever the fuck they're doing, it doesn't require screaming. There are people sleeping and shit. Everywhere. *Their* cabin isn't the only one here. It's so fucking inconsiderate to act like it is. Not to mention irresponsible. We could lose our deposits.

Not that I give a flying fuck about deposits but they should have a little respect in case I did.

That's why I'm here. Standing at *their* fucking door, ready to tear the goddamn piece of sun-bleached wood down with my bare hands.

Who the fuck do they think they are?

Screaming. Fuck.

Screaming?

Why were they screaming?

Whatever. Fuck Tysen for making Bentlee scream.

He did make her scream, didn't he? I specifically heard her voice… even though it was from far away and over the annoying-as-shit bonfire party I swear kicked up a notch once Bentlee and Tysen disappeared from my sight.

But if he really did make her scream, was it out of pleasure or pain?

That's also why I'm here. To make sure Bentlee's not being strangled to death. It did go completely quiet in this direction a few minutes ago and Tysen could be an undercover psychopath killer. It's always someone you know. The person you least expect.

And on the off chance it's from pleasure, well, fuck. I don't know. That sounds just as bad for whatever reason. Bentlee being choked out or getting dicked down? By Tysen? That's Russian roulette with a fully loaded chamber.

I hear a voice, a single voice, and lean in, my ear brushing the yellow wood.

"Don't just tell me. Show me." *Bentlee.*

And no, I don't think so. Tysen will be showing Bentlee absolutely nothing tonight other than some polite, *friendly* hospitality. This is a work retreat for fuck's sake. With less clothing but a shit ton more alcohol and enough inappropriate conversations to get us all written up. Don't even get me started on the eye fucking taking place when I left.

But here, right now, consider *their* cabin ground fucking zero for enforcing the shit out of some new guidelines I just came up with, starting with no showing—whatever the fuck that means.

At the same time I knock, Bentlee's laughter from inside shakes the door on the hinges. Or maybe that's me. My hand is shaking.

I'm not shaking. I don't shake.

Dropping my hand to the knob when the knock goes unanswered, I'm surprised when it turns easily. I mean, I turned the motherfucker with enough force to break the handle clear off, but I didn't *have* to. Because it's unlocked.

Christ.

I push the door open with a dry "hello," made even drier by the fact that Bentlee's underwear-covered ass greets me as she lies on her stomach across a small bed with her phone strategically aimed at her face. Talking with her son. And some kind of craft project he's showing her that might've been paper but is now mostly glitter.

Cue that infamous screaming.

Falling halfway off the bed as she scrambles to sit up, Bentlee shrieks, "What are you doing here?" and I grimace, hesitating in the doorway.

Still holding up the phone for their FaceTime call, Hunter's voice comes over the speaker. "What's wrong?"

A gust of wind teases my back, ruffling my shirt and I realize the door is still open. With Bentlee in her goddamn panties. She's wearing an oversized tee that goes to her thighs now that she's not flat on her stomach, but still, the panties are still very much visible. I know I'll never be able to unsee them.

With a click loud enough to wake the dead, I shut the door.

With me on the inside.

Tracking her every move.

There's no sign of Tysen and both beds are still made. I search the part of her neck I can see from across the room for bruising but find none.

All of my theories were wrong.

Does that mean I should leave now? One hint and I will. One hint that I shouldn't be here and I'll walk out right now, I swear.

Bentlee glances from Hunter to me and back again before shaking her head. "Nothing. Did you brush your teeth?" She frowns at the screen. "Make sure you brush your teeth and have Dad check it for you."

The whole time her hands pull at the hem of her shirt, trying to cover the skin I've already checked out, I glance around the cabin—*their* cabin. I might've been wrong about the reason for the screaming—what other reason is there?—but they are still set to share this cabin tonight. At least there's two beds, both tiny as fuck, which makes the knot in my stomach unfurl slightly. Slightly because...I wouldn't need a bed.

"I know, I know. I can't help it. I just love you." Her eyes meet mine over the top of the screen for a split second and I shove my hand in my front pocket, squeezing the fuck out of my pack of cigarettes.

A guy's voice I assume is Hunter's dad interrupts, saying, "Okay, that's enough," then the phone goes completely silent. What a fucking dick.

Bentlee's eyes close like she's in pain and I debate going to her. What would I do though? What could I do?

Practically slamming the phone on the salmon-colored comforter, she opens her eyes to pin me with a stern expression that only makes me want to grin. That motherly shit won't work on me but I appreciate the effort.

Soft waves that look half wet at the ends fall over her tits…that once again don't have a bra covering them.

I'm surprised she's even wearing underwear.

I'm disappointed she's wearing underwear.

My scowl returns even though I didn't realize it'd left. "Why was the door unlocked?"

Her scowl matches mine. Tries to. It tries to match mine but I've perfected this shit by now.

"So Tysen could get in," she says sarcastically, and I might be starting to finally understand the screaming, 'cause no. Hell fucking no.

"You were gonna let him in here with you wearing that?" I take a step into the room, bringing me closer.

Her gaze falls down to her lap, and when she looks back up at me, there's straight fire—to my cock. Holy fuck.

"My pajamas?"

"You sleep in that?" I all but yell myself and she rolls her eyes like I'm a moron for not understanding the universal code of sleepwear or some shit. Lowering my voice, I ask, "Every night or just tonight?"

I gotta know. I *need* to know.

"Why are *you* here?" she asks instead, pissing me right the fuck off.

"Where's Tysen?" I counter her question with my own, ready to go for twenty, if needed. I'm Joaquin Vega's son and I'm just getting started. Stubborn runs through my blood more than antibodies. *Let's fucking go, mama.*

"How should I know?"

I glare at her, advancing another step. "Because you're the one fucking around with him."

"Fucking around with him? What do you mean by that?"

"Screaming," I say nonchalantly, like I couldn't care less while also studying her carefully for any clue possible.

Understanding finally dawns and she fights a smile, saying, "Doesn't ring a bell."

So now she's fucking around with me.

Another step and I'm almost within reach. I've got a long reach.

"What about female ejaculation?"

Her eyes go wide and she sputters, "What?"

Exactly. That's exactly what I was thinking when I heard it.

"Before you left." *With Tysen.* "Does that ring a bell?"

Her amused expression falls away faster than a landslide and she brings her hand up to her forehead like that'll stop the destruction in its tracks. With a sigh, she rolls to her back, saying, "Nope. That definitely doesn't ring a bell."

What'd I say? She didn't have this reaction when Paige said the exact same words, so why is she acting like she's remembering something she'd rather forget?

"Kary does though."

I stop short. *What?*

She eyes me right back, saying, "Kary rings a pretty big bell, doesn't she?"

There's a bite to her bark that I find myself enjoying the absolute shit out of. Jealous. Why's she jealous?

Keeping my eyes on hers, I shake my head slowly.

"That's not what everybody else seems to think."

Motherfuck. My friends need to keep their mouths shut, especially about that. That just shows how much they don't understand. They don't have a fucking clue.

"They don't know what they're talking about."

She makes a sound in the back of her throat.

"It's true. I'm not with her." *Not like that.*

Several inches separate her knees thanks to the transition from sitting, revealing more thigh along with the smallest hint of her panties and I can't stop staring at the lace peeking out. Red—my favorite color.

My hand hovering over her bent knees tingles. I didn't even know I was this close. I could touch her.

I could do a hell of a lot more than touch her.

If she wanted me to…

"Bentlee?" My voice feels loud even though it's no more than a whisper. A prayer. For restraint or permission? The choice is hers. All hers.

The same legs I had wrapped around my waist earlier today, not once but twice, are here, open and…waiting? Does she feel this? Is it just me?

It didn't feel like it was just me in the river. There was something there. Something tangible between us, something that made me feel downright primal about Bentlee. I didn't want anything to hurt her, not even a dumbass prehistoric fish. It came on like the motherfucking flu and left me feeling just as disoriented. How? I've felt some kind of pull toward her since I laid eyes on her but that's simple. That's easy. Physical attraction is nothing new to me. At. All. I've been pullin' chicks since I was in pre-k. But today was not that. Today was a glimpse into something I've never had and couldn't wait to get more of. Holding her, looking out for her, damn, I've never felt so high. I've never felt so right.

The glazed-over look I saw when I first walked in disappears almost entirely the second hunger surfaces in her gaze.

It's not just me.

Those same blue-green pools begging, just begging me to come closer, to test the waters, lower to my throat, then to my arms and it's like every nerve-ending goes ape-shit from the contact.

Say the word. Say something.

"Marc?"

A prayer as answer to mine—I'll take it.

Without wasting another second, I grab a handful of the bottom of her shirt and twist the thin material in my fist, exposing even more of her toned body to me. The moan she releases feels like it comes from my own throat, and the way she's looking at me, maybe it did.

I drop my knees to the floor, pushing her thighs out to the side with my elbows and look. Just look. Firm, tan thighs leading to red lace that might as well be my own personal invitation. I can smell her want for me and it smells fucking delicious.

"Bentlee," I say much calmer than I feel. "I'm going to eat you. I'm going to eat you so good, you'll scream. And these screams, they won't even compare to the ones Tysen got from you."

Her thighs tighten and the heartbeat through her skin pulses recklessly.

"Swimming."

My eyes lift, meeting hers again. "What?"

"We were swimming. Tysen was a wreck thinking about his ex, so I pushed him in the water to make him focus on something else."

I wrap an arm around each leg, pulling her ass off the mattress and just far enough away from my mouth that I can't taste her yet but have a pretty good idea what I'll find when I do.

"That's it?"

"That's it."

"Tysen didn't hurt you?" I kiss the inside of her right thigh and she shakes her head quickly. "He didn't try anything with you?" I give a matching one to her left thigh, letting my tongue linger a little longer and she shakes her head again, this time with her breath held. "If you don't want this, you can tell me."

"I want you." She nods, keeping eye contact. "Do," she swallows thickly, her fingers at her sides contracting, "you want me?"

The jitters are sweet but unnecessary. She doesn't need to worry about anything with me. Not right now.

I lick up her panties, wetting the outside to match what I know the inside will feel like. It's excruciating to stop but I have to or I won't be able to at all. "I want you, Bentlee." So fucking much. "Now pull your underwear to the side and hold it there for me."

Those jumpy fingers of hers slide over her stomach, slowly approaching their destination.

"Faster, Bentlee. I'm hungry."

"Oh, God."

Her eyes close on an exhale, so I nip one of her knuckles, getting her to laugh and relax a little.

"I can't believe this is happening."

I can't believe she's talking. I prefer to be encouraged with moans, curse words, and any other type of generally incoherent noises. Not full sentences. How *is* she talking? She should be half out of her mind with need by now. My fucking cock *hurts* I'm so ready to go.

"I'm sorry. This is just my first time."

I sit back on my heels to regard her and ask slowly, "First time for what exactly?"

"Oral, I guess."

"Receiving?"

She props herself on her elbows and looks at me as she closes her thighs together. My hands ache to open them again but this is important. I need to hear her.

"Nobody's ever eaten you out before?"

"No."

Touching her ankles, I run my palms up her calves and knees, gently nudging them apart before climbing to my feet to stand between her thighs.

"A'ight then."

Only breaking eye contact to pull my shirt over my head, I come down on her and a whoosh of air escapes her lips as she drops to her back, making me chuckle.

I was so consumed with wanting to taste her pussy I didn't even think about kissing her actual lips. I've wanted to kiss them since she danced around at the farmer's market.

She's light. The light to my dark and I regret rushing this. Not only for her sake, but for mine.

I bring her arms around my shoulders, draping them over my neck, then prop myself on my elbows to gaze down at her. "Sorry," I say quietly.

"For what?"

"For not giving you the best possible first." I may be an asshole but I'm not *that* asshole. I'd never knowingly take someone's first anything without taking care of them properly.

"You're not my *first*." Might as well be because after this, she won't remember anyone who came before me. Guaranteed. "It's just that my ex was-"

"An idiot that should get his ass kicked. Relax, Bentlee. I won't do anything you don't want me to."

Her thighs on either side of me ease up a bit and her eyes flit between mine. "I want you to."

"Want me to what?"

Licking my lips draws her attention to my mouth and she rocks her pelvis into mine the slightest bit, making me swallow down a hiss.

"I thought you said you do what you want anyway," she repeats the words I once told her and meant with every cell of my existence. "So," against my lips she finishes, "do that."

That's where words stop and moans kick up as I press my lips to hers finally, sliding my tongue inside without waiting to be let in. *Knock, knock.*

This is one of the few times she's not wearing any lip gloss, a fact I'm not sure I like. All I fucking do anymore is stare at those glossy lips, wondering what they taste like. Wondering if they're sticky or sweet or would look just as good wrapped around my cock.

With her lips smooth and pliable beneath mine, I accept every sound she makes like I'm collecting souvenirs and give her my payment of deep kisses that don't feel quite deep enough no matter which way I angle my head for better access. I just want more. So much more.

Still kissing her with my tongue and lips and even my teeth, I grip one of her thighs and hike it up my waist, loving the way she follows my lead so easily.

Drawing my bottom lip out between her teeth, she smirks up at me before sucking the entire thing in her mouth and swirling her tongue around the sensitive skin. If there's not a half-moon of bite marks beneath my bottom lip in the morning, I'll be shocked. The copper taste in my mouth tells me as much and I swear my cock gets even harder as I groan loudly, pressing into her roughly before ripping my mouth away.

Lifted onto my arms, I stare down at her, my necklace dangling below my chin like a pendulum, hypnotizing us both.

"Better?"

She shakes her head shyly and I frown, asking, "It's not?" She sure the fuck feels more relaxed to me. Her hands haven't stopped moving but at least now they've got something to play with—me. Up my biceps, around my shoulders and over my back, the girl leaves no muscle in reach untouched. She's touching *everything*.

"It only feels good…"

"Yeah?"

Don't say something weird. Don't say something weird. Please don't say something weird.

"When you're touching me."

A smile teases my lips. "Am I not touching you?"

"Not enough."

"You don't like all this space?" I nod at our position, laying almost all of my weight below my waist on her and letting her feel what she's done, what she continues to do.

Her heel digs into my ass, giving me the okay to grind into her even more and I do, both of us breathing heavy as tension between our bodies builds quickly—too quickly.

"Fuck," I say, slowing my movements, my elbows shaky as all fuck. It's just like in the river earlier—one graze and I feel like I'm gonna explode. She has no idea how fucking sexy everything she does is. Shit, just watching her eat those grapes at the bonfire had me hard as a fucking rock.

With a hand slid under her back, I drag her further up the bed, nipping the bottom of her shirt bunched at the middle of her stomach when it's just under my face, then ask, "What was it Paige said again?" I fight a smile when Bentlee's face turns red, keeping my voice low in my throat. "Female ejaculation before penetration?" I'm down to uplift the fuck outta this woman…right to my impatient mouth.

Bentlee groans and I feel her thighs start to tense around me again but I'm not having any of that as I pull her shirt up and kiss her quaking stomach all the way down to her panty line.

As soon as those red panties come into view, I lose sight of everything else, even the last shred of patience I was hanging on to and with one bite to the top of the fabric, I pull until I can use my hand to quickly rip the rest of the material off one thigh as they lie useless on the other.

Hope she packed another pair.

Finding her shaved and beyond ready for me, I don't hesitate to lick up her slit, causing her to jump. And she's just like I thought— fucking delicious.

I tilt my head from side to side, placing a kiss on each of her thighs, then sneak a glance up at her. She's got both hands next to her head, clenching the pillow in a death grip.

Quickly, I lean up to swipe my lips across hers just as I yank the pillow out from under her head, saying "sorry" when I take it with me. It does the trick and she laughs, relaxing again as her hands fall motionless to her sides.

I guide her hips up, then stick the pillow under her ass, propping her up higher and putting her pink pussy on full display. I dive down and make out with her pussy, kissing and licking and sucking, just like I did with her mouth, but not with my teeth. I save those for nibbling her thighs when I feel her start to freeze up as a reminder that I'm here. I'm doing exactly what I want, what we both want, and she's got nothing to fear. Not when I'm around.

She's ours but right now she's just fucking mine.

I drop to my side, half off the tiny bed, and push her right thigh over my head as I eat her out from the new angle. She arches automatically, giving me even better access and I swear I don't come up for air until I hear 'em—the screams I promised her. Using my thumb, I press down on her clit as she tries to float off the goddamn bed and a scream gets stuck in her throat as her entire body goes stiff before rolling to the side, both legs encasing my head. I don't care, I keep going, wanting to draw her orgasm out even longer and feeling one of my own coming on even though I've done nothing to get myself off. My cock jumps in my pants and I feel precum smear all over my boxers, but still, I keep fucking sucking as her pussy lips spasm, needing this to be perfect for her. The scream softens to a strangled moan, then to a sated sigh and I finally ease up, wiping my mouth and chin and even nose as I duck under her leg to sit up, taking the pillow with me.

I open my mouth to say something, anything, but her eyes are closed and her breath starts to soften. What the fuck? Is she asleep?

She speaks though, in a small, tired voice, saying, "Thank you."

Thank you? Am I being…dismissed?

"Uh, yeah, you're welcome." My voice scratches every surface in this room, cementing my confusion like a motherfucking crime scene. *Here lies my dignity.*

Silently, I sit and watch her for a minute, mesmerized by the way her back to me rises and falls so calmly, so confidently.

I drag her ruined underwear down over her foot before replacing her leg on the bed and gently pulling her shirt to cover her ass. Pocketing the ripped panties as I stand beside her, I tuck a blanket around her.

"I'm gonna take off," I say even though I don't want to. Not because I think I deserve sex after everything but because I didn't expect for it to end this way. So final. I'm not ready. Not yet.

But she's fucking exhausted and obviously isn't up for anything else. It's not like I wanna cuddle her for fuck's sake but…no, she's right. We're done here. I'm done. I did what I wanted—as usual—and now I can move the fuck on already.

After finding my shirt and tucking it into my back pocket, my hand's on the door handle when I hear her say, "Can you leave the door unlocked for Tysen?" and instead of turning the knob, I turn the lock.

I don't think so.

Sliding my phone out, I send Tysen a text informing him of his new sleeping arrangement, then drop down onto his original bed. And maybe a part of me is happy for the change of plan because at least now I get to spend more time with Bentlee, even if it is just to watch her sleep peacefully—across the room from me.

Or maybe I really am coming down with something.

Chapter 72

Bentlee

I MOAN, STRETCHING MY ARMS ABOVE MY HEAD ONLY TO realize there's no pillow.

Where did it…

Oh, yeah. Marc used it to…

Oh, shit.

Did Tysen see anything when he came back?

There's a blanket covering me at least but I don't remember putting it on before I passed out. I don't remember much of anything before I passed out except for Marc. Everything Marc. His mouth, his hands, his groans. I swear I can still feel his greedy groans against my core, like aftershocks from an earthquake. 8.0, no question. He *rocked* me last night. Me, my world, the definition of what good feels like. It wasn't even just the act of his mouth on me either. It was his eyes. His undivided attention, like there was nowhere else he'd rather be. I didn't have to talk him into it. There was no guilt trip where I felt like shit afterward.

I might've been feeling the beers from last night when Marc came in here but that didn't stop me from searching for what I'm always looking for now—an angle, an ulterior motive. When I couldn't find one, I just kinda let things unfold naturally. I didn't have to try. I didn't even want to. The way he treated me, it was like he truly wanted me for me. I felt good enough exactly how I was for the first time in a long time. Maybe in forever.

Not now though. He's gone and probably already forgot about everything that happened yesterday.

"Morning."

My eyes fly over to the other side of the room and land on the bed almost identical to mine except holding Marc—a shirtless, sleepy-eyed Marc. He's on his back with one straight leg crossed over the other and a hand on his stomach while the other's under his head as he stares over at me.

He stayed? And how does he look even sexier now than when he was buried between my legs?

"Morning," I croak back, wiggling further down under the out-dated comforter. He saw a lot last night. He saw it all, but things are different now.

"Do you have more clothes anywhere?"

"Why?"

"Because I couldn't find any other underwear for you in your bag."

I sit up. "You went through my stuff?"

"Yeah. Tysen'll be coming back for his shit at some point..."

He lets that sail through the air like a tetherball going too fast for anyone to stop. Around and around it goes, neither of us reaching up to secure a win. Or avoid defeat.

What does Tysen have to do with my underwear? *Or lack thereof.*

Marc's reaction to Tysen touching me on the boat rushes back to me at the same time the end of the rope comes into view.

I take a last-minute swing, saying, "I don't have any others." The only two pairs I brought I wore yesterday. "I don't normally wear...them."

A sharp inhale across the room reveals I succeeded in hitting a weak spot. Marc likes me not wearing underwear...as long as others don't see. How familiar.

How disappointing.

"Where did Tysen sleep anyway?"

Marc stares up at the ceiling, saying, "I'd assume my cabin but I haven't been outside. I didn't want to leave."

I wait, thinking he's going to say more, but he never does and I'm left to read between the lines. He didn't want to leave what?

If he left, it'd expose his location to everyone else. I am his subordinate and this doesn't look good. No matter how you slice it, we stayed in the same cabin together—a manager, no, an *owner*, and an hourly associate. We didn't necessarily sleep together but we didn't exactly *not* sleep together either.

I don't even know what we did. Technically I do, but theoretically? I don't know where this leaves us going forward. It was just a one-time thing…right?

"Hmm. Yeah. I don't know how we're going to explain this," I tell him like I'm some kind of expert on one-night stands all while my cheeks heat to an unbearable temperature.

Marc remains deathly still for a moment then says slowly, "We won't," reminding me I'm not the only one that doesn't share everything with everyone.

It doesn't mean there won't be looks though, especially cast in my direction. Marc will look…like the man, while I'll look…bad. It's a tale as old as time—a boss and his employee. Just because we don't want to face the music doesn't mean the track won't be playing on repeat the second we leave the safety of this cabin. He has to know that.

Out of nowhere, he asks, "Do you cook?"

The cabin has a kitchenette but no food. I didn't bring anything more than the snacks for the drive up and Tysen only brought a twelve-pack he took on the boat yesterday.

"I can," I say carefully. "Do you?"

He nods and I perk up.

"Like what?"

One of his shoulders shrugs lazily. "Anything you want."

"Anything?" I ask with a heaping pile of skepticism. "How about waffles? Buttermilk? With chocolate chips?"

The corner of his lips pulls up in a cocky grin.

"Really?"

"Sure."

"Omelet?" I can cook but I can never get omelets to cooperate.

They always end up scrambling themselves and I never bother correcting them.

"Maybe."

"Maybe?"

He turns his head to meet my eyes again, saying, "If you're lucky."

"I'm gonna hold you to that."

The words are out before I can consider them, and when the silence grows an awkward tail that wags like an impatient puppy, the little bit of self-confidence I woke up with quivers just as spastically. *Why did I say that?* There will never be a time where Marc can even make me breakfast.

But then, he says, "I'm counting on it," and I don't feel quite so stupid. Either he's placating me or I'm placating him with this entire conversation. We have to face reality sometime. We can't hide out here, ignoring the outside world forever, as tempting as that sounds.

"What's for breakfast today?"

"I'm not sure. I woke up when you did."

"What happened last night? I mean aside from…" I widen my eyes but he doesn't so much as move, just watches me stagger around my own words like a drunk failing a sobriety test. "Did you pass out, too?"

"Eventually."

"Oh."

"Your snoring kept me up."

My jaw drops.

"Did your family make you sleep out in the barn with the cows when you were younger?" he jokes with a tilt to his devilish lips.

"I do not snore." Now talking in my sleep I could believe. Before I hit my preteen years, my sister and I slept in the same room and my parents recorded us talking to each other in our sleep more than a few times. But I never slept by the cows. Not intentionally anyway.

He laughs to himself and I throw a pillow over at him, watching as it lands directly on top of his face. Realizing a second too late that it's the pillow we used last night, I hold my breath, hoping he doesn't recognize it. When Marc's laughter only increases beneath the pillow, I know he does.

"You're going to regret that," he warns, and I think, *I already do.* I shouldn't have thrown *the* pillow.

Marc doesn't miss a beat as he climbs from his bed, heading straight for mine and I swallow down a scream, scrambling to my feet while trying to make a run for it. With one arm, he catches me easily as we both fall onto my bed, sending dust motes up around us like snowflakes on a lazy, winter morning. They swirl and twirl above our heads just like the butterflies in my stomach as Marc's arm clutches me to him, almost possessively. I know he's only playing around but it doesn't feel like it. It feels like he's trying to keep me safe like he would a cherished heirloom.

Rolling his top half over me, he angles his head to gaze down a second before I feel his other hand on my side, the palm wide and familiar even though it's not. Even though it shouldn't be.

I squirm the opposite direction, trying to avoid his light touch but it's no use, his body cages mine in.

"Say uncle."

Shaking my head, I bite my lips together only to open them again on a laugh when his fingers dig into my ribs.

"Say uncle."

"Reynold!"

He rears back, frowning. "Reynold?"

"That's my uncle."

"That doesn't count." His fingers inch just below my armpit and I clamp my arm down on his hand, arching off the bed and laughing at an embarrassing frequency.

"Yes, it does. *Uncle* Reynold totally counts."

His charcoal eyes darken. "When you're at my mercy, there shouldn't be any other man's name on your lips but mine." The hand at my side goes slack as he drops his stare to my mouth, suddenly serious.

Bringing my knee up, I slide my foot over his lap, brushing his growing erection on my way to switch our positions. He lets me— actually, he *helps* me—mount him, then I'm the one looking down my nose at him. The power I feel in this moment is indescribable. The power both over myself and over him, it's liberating.

"Why'd you want me to say 'uncle' then? Why not Marc?"

His eyes glide over my body sitting atop his, both of us extremely aware of my lack of underwear when he locks on our connection.

"Because then I wouldn't stop at all."

"Stop what?" Are we still talking about the same thing? Tickling?

Marc simply gazes up at me and I'm right back to last night when he looked at me the same way, like he wants me. It's hard to ignore. It's hard to not let the flattery soak through to my bones, strengthening my confidence like straddling him does.

It's also hard to turn down. He is hard to turn down. Maybe even impossible. But this is just a fantasy, one from long ago that's finally come true. Marc Vega in the flesh wanting to see more of my flesh, *demanding* to see more.

What if I don't have more to give though? What if I'm not more? Most days I don't even feel like I'm enough, let alone more.

Gripping onto my shirt, he starts to lift it but I hop off his lap like it's on fire, and he follows me, standing in the next breath to ask, "What's wrong?"

I pull back out of his reach, but that doesn't discourage him, at all, and he keeps advancing until my back hits a wall.

"I'm sorry. I'm not ready to actually like, *be* with someone. This was just a rebound kind of thing." I think. Rebounds, surface level, no real feelings or expectations…sounds about right. I've never had one before, so I don't technically know how they work or what they look like but I'm thinking last night could easily be classified as a rebound—a half-drunken one at that—and that's just not fair to anyone, even a man who gives amazing head.

Positioned in front of me, his legs spread wide so he's eye level with me and he says, "I'm…okay with that."

My voice flees, leaving behind a whisper, a scared, little whisper that holds more truth than a scream ever could. "I don't want to hurt you."

"You can't."

One statement, a confession of sorts, slips past my lips like a breeze coming off a tumultuous sea. "I could."

"You won't." His half-smile doesn't reach his eyes before he drops his head, fingering the hem of my shirt, just barely touching the tops of my thighs. Softer than my whisper, he murmurs, "You don't have to worry about me," and I realize he's just as delusional as I am.

But if we're both lying, who's really at risk?

Watching him steadily, I pull my shirt over my head, letting it drop next to our feet. It takes a while for his eyes to make their way up to mine as he takes the long path, traveling over every dip and valley my naked body holds first, but when he does, it's like they never strayed to begin with. As gray as a cloud about to unleash its pent-up storm, his gaze promises an absolute reckoning.

One hand on my neck, he pulls me to him and my mouth meets his in the middle just as hungrily.

Standing to his full height, he breaks away to say, "Spread your legs," then presses his mouth back to mine at the same time his bare chest brushes my erect nipples, making me gasp and letting his tongue sweep inside.

I separate my feet a few more inches and he growls, nudging one of my knees with his to make my stance even wider. The empty feeling deep inside me starts to pulse like a second heartbeat and the open air does nothing to ease the ache until…until Marc's hand cups my pussy, giving just enough pressure to raise me onto my toes, trying to chase the feeling any way I can.

"Goddamn, you're so wet."

I nod, pulling his bottom lip between my teeth again. Last night he seemed to like it. Today there's no mistaking the way his palm basically lifts me off the ground, spurring me on.

One finger slips inside, another following close behind as he keeps up the pressure of grinding on my clit simultaneously.

Using his other hand, he traps both my wrists, lifting them above my head, and causing my shoulder blades to grate against the wall as my back arches clear off.

A moan swallowed whole, I narrow my eyes at him. Why can't I have my hands? Don't I get to be an active participant here?

"Last night was for you. This is for me," he says against my mouth and I release his lip immediately.

There's always a catch. Always.

While Marc's hand works my body over, my mind checks out completely. I add in a moan here, a shudder there, careful to give a good enough performance to keep him from suspecting but not too good or he'll stop entirely. I should've been a funambulist because I've been walking this tightrope for years.

At some point Marc's hand stops but it takes me a moment to realize and act accordingly with a faked look of concern.

Don't call the circus just yet. Looks like my balancing act could still use some work.

"What's wrong?" he asks again, and before I can even think of a lie, he takes a step back, both his hands leaving my body instantly. "Did I hurt you?"

I shake my head, shrugging loosely. He didn't hurt me—physically.

"You gotta tell me what's wrong. What'd I do?"

"I don't…" I start, then stop.

"You don't want me?"

I bring my eyes up to his, seeing nothing but sincerity along with a hint of uncertainty. How could Marc ever be self-conscious?

"I do," I tell him honestly. "I want to…" How do I say it without saying it? Saying what you want isn't sexy, right? Asking for it only makes you look desperate. That's how Shawn always treated me when I voiced my desires.

"Was your ex the only person you've ever been with?"

I know he can tell the truth without me having to spell it out. It's not that I'm sexually inept, I'm just deprived. The want—the need— is there. I just wasn't given a lot of opportunities to explore it. At least not with a partner.

"Forget about him, okay? It's just you and me right now."

I study his gray eyes, then nod.

"And I only want to make *you* feel good. *That* makes *me* feel good, got it?"

It does? When he said "this is for me," I assumed the worst. I assumed he was like Shawn.

When will I change? *Can* I even change?

I guess that's up to me.

His hands come up again but I grab his wrists this time, holding them suspended between us.

"Can I just…"

Those eyes search mine, then he tells me, "You can do anything you want," making me want to believe him.

And so, I decide to.

Taking a deep breath, I trail my fingers along his arms, slowly tracing the vein up his bicep while Marc remains still, letting me take my time.

His swallow is the only sound in the room and I admit quietly, "I want you."

With featherlight touches, my fingertips make their way over his collarbone and chest, then I dip my head forward, pressing a soft kiss to his left pec, the noise echoing throughout the cabin.

"I want this," I whisper against his skin, glancing up at him through my lashes. That feeling washes over me again, the same one from when I was looking down at him. *Power.* I feel powerful right now and I have no idea why. It's such a foreign concept, I don't exactly know what to do with it but I covet it nonetheless. Whether I have any real power or not is beside the point, the illusion itself encourages me, urging me on even further. We're all imposters anyway and I'm going to enjoy my run while it lasts.

I kiss up to his neck, biting the skin there into my mouth just like I did to his lip and earning more of those groans that drove me wild last night. I think I actually came twice, once from Marc's mouth and once from his groans. They are everything and they increase when I suck as hard as I can, losing myself in the swirling of my own tongue.

I feel Marc's hands grab my naked waist, dragging me until my nipples are mashed against his, so I relax my jaw to say, "Don't," around his neck and his hands disappear just as quickly.

Doing this to him does make me feel good. Really fucking good.

"Just wondering when it's my turn," he rasps.

My tongue savoring the vibration in his throat, I chuckle. "I haven't done anything to you yet."

His dark chuckle matches mine, raising it and I almost fold. Almost, but don't.

I am powerful.

Dragging my nails down his abdomen, I track the crimson scratches streaking across his golden skin with small bites followed by open-mouthed kisses. By the time my chin hits the top of his jeans, he's as wet as I am and I bite the jeans' button, earning a tight smile from him when I chance a look up.

"Relax, Marcos," I tell him, giving a kiss to each of those dips above his hip bones, wishing I had a week to dedicate just to them.

"At least you didn't say Marcus," he murmurs, the hands at his sides restlessly grasping at air.

I shake my head, settling onto my knees. "No other name but yours." Requests I can stomach, it's commands I don't ingest very well.

Something hits the wall above me, and with a peek up, I see Marc's fist pressed into one of the cedar planks lining the cabin from floor to ceiling.

"Say the word, Bentlee, and you're fucking mine."

The threat, the promise, sends chills down my bare spine and the plea to have him follow through on his threat, his promise, sits on the tip of my tongue. What would being Marc's feel like? What would him being mine feel like?

"All mine."

"Stop talking," I say while I can. We just agreed to keep this shallow.

Shallow…right. I like the shallows. Nothing dangerous ever comes from the shallows.

He blows out a breath that rattles with his own longing and a nervous laugh builds in my throat. He's losing his mind and I'm the thief clutching it in my hands…right next to my own.

The laugh curls into a ball and dies the second I unzip Marc's pants and his cock still trapped in his boxers tries to spring free like a jailbreak at midnight. Feeling like a criminal myself, I give the guy a hand—or two—and help with the escape, pushing his underwear and pants down. The material hits the floor with an audible swish causing us both to freeze, the only movement being Marc's hands still trying to figure out whose lead they should follow.

I let the moisture in my mouth build, not swallowing any of it, then wrap one hand around the base of his cock and split my lips enough to suck his throbbing shaft into my warm pool.

"Shittt."

One of those indecisive hands finds the crown of my head, not rushing me, just cradling, but I'm already moving up and down his length to even care.

My hand mirrors my every movement, stroking him in time with my mouth, and the second I hear his signature groan, I pick up speed, going even faster.

And harder.

And louder.

And...*oh shit*.

I moan so loud myself there's no way the cabin next to us isn't awake and listening in by now.

"Fuck," Marc bursts, pulling my hair and head away until I'm forced to release him from my mouth entirely. "I'm done."

What?! There's no way he finished already.

Unless...

"Done with what?" I ask cautiously, both wanting to know and not. *Did I suck...at sucking?*

But Marc says, "Waiting," then I'm lifted clear off the ground the next instant, his mouth covering mine with a blinding urgency.

I hook my leg around his hips and jerk him to me, crying out from the sudden feel of him on my body again, not giving a shit who's in control anymore.

Back on my tiptoes, I fumble through lining his cock up to my entrance, dragging the head through my wetness with a back-and-forth motion as we break apart to watch, our gazes transfixed between us with identical concentration. All at once I drop back flat on my feet, causing his tip to disappear between my folds and time halts altogether, hanging in the rafters above our heads.

"Don't move," he grits and I grin, remembering the other times he said the same thing—the times I was in some sort of danger. This time I'm not.

I'm not.

Right?

With a hot kiss, he mouths against my quivering lips, "I need a condom," and I suck in a sharp inhale, breathing in his air as if it's mine.

After grabbing one from his jeans' pocket, Marc pumps his glistening cock twice, then rolls the condom down over the swollen tip and rigid shaft, with his tongue sliding across his top lip making me grow ten times hotter.

Stepping between my legs again, he grabs my ass with one hand as he positions himself with the other and then…it. All. Goes. Blank. Everything else around us comes to a standstill as Marc pushes deep inside, our bodies joining like one of those blackjack dealers shuffling two halves of a deck of cards together—fucking flawless. Artistic. Significant.

Then, in perfect unison, we start moving. Just like that, where he moves, I follow. Where I go, he chases—vehemently. Marc wastes no time returning the favor of touching and licking and biting everything he can reach all while keeping up a steady pace between our hips, not too slow, not too fast, like a dance between two trained professionals. Except I'm not. I'm not even close to a professional. But he makes me feel like I am. He makes me *feel*. Something I'd almost forgotten how to do.

I'm last on my own list of priorities. Why wouldn't I be on everyone else's? But Marc, he makes me feel important. Like I do matter.

With that in mind, I claw Marc's shoulders, looking for leverage when my legs threaten to buckle. Marc throws one across his hip as he pistons into me from the new angle and an orgasm rips through me and my throat at exactly the same time.

Marc's hips slow and he pulls back to gaze into my eyes. Just when I think he's going to say something, a knock on the door interrupts the moment.

Tysen calls out from the other side, saying, "Hey, Bentlee? You up?"

Hearing him, I lock up, grappling to keep Marc in front of me like his naked body blocking my naked body makes this somehow better even though he can't see us and the door is locked. I think it's locked.

I didn't lock it.

"Shit! The door…" I whisper-shout making Marc chuckle before his arms wrap around my back like an intimate hug, then he rocks into me with small hip thrusts while keeping our bodies mashed to each other's…with Tysen only a few feet away.

My breath catches in my throat as my hips move to meet Marc's despite the severity of the situation. We could get caught.

Knowing that only makes my pussy flood more as it chokes Marc's cock with each firm thrust.

"Holy fuck," Marc groans out, dropping his sweaty forehead to mine. "Ease up or I'm gonna fucking blow."

"Shhh," I shush on a strangled laugh, then continue tightening my muscles as tight as I can each time he buries himself to the hilt. I want him to lose control. I want to see him come undone.

"Bentlee? Is that you?"

"Go the fuck away," Marc growls low and I stifle a giggle, telling Tysen, "Yeah, just gimme a minute."

"Christ. A minute?" Marc whispers as he pulls his head away from mine, staring me down like I just took a baseball bat to his ego.

All I can do is smile through a suppressed moan, then Marc's lips break into a smile, too. "You ready?"

I nod instantly.

He asks, "You got my name ready?" and I nearly scoff out loud. *Like I could ever forget.*

Both his hands drop to my ass, pushing my cheeks together, and for a split second I worry he's going to do that thing. The thing I heard one of Shawn's friends, Chaz, complain about needing to do to an ex-girlfriend. He claimed he had to push her thighs together when he was fucking her just to feel anything and it made my stomach roil. Then the next time Shawn and I had sex, he did it to me and I cried myself to sleep every night for a week afterward. Giving birth changes a woman's body—all of it—and I thought that was why Shawn did that, because he had to, because I was the problem.

Spreading them apart just as quickly, Marc lifts me off my feet and my legs go around him on autopilot.

"Hey," he says, bringing me back to the moment. "Forget him."

Not even using the wall for help, he hits my clit with the base of his cock and helps me ride him while rolling my hips back and forth as he supports practically all of my weight.

I wasn't the problem. So many tears, so many years, just wasted thinking I was.

Marc and gravity play a nice little game of tug-of-war with me along his throbbing shaft and within seconds I'm chanting quietly in time with each rotation.

"Marc, Marc, Marc."

A light so bright bursts right before my eyes and I squeeze them shut, gulping a scream whole just as Marc slams his mouth to mine, trying to swallow it for me. A high-pitched noise makes its way out of my throat at the same time Marc rolls me onto him once more with a growl. A *loud* growl. Loud enough for Tysen on the other side of the door to knock again, asking if everything's okay.

"Shit. Fuck. Goddamn."

I let out a chuckle, kissing over Marc's lips still muttering curses from his own climax. After a moment, he places me back on my feet, testing the shaky strength of my legs before letting me go. As soon as he does, my skin goes cold. Cold and lonely. Like I'm missing warmth. Like I'm missing him.

Like a flame licking across the horizon…

Reality slams back into me with a cold snap of harsh truth, colder than the absence of Marc's skin against mine. I told him this was all I could offer, and now I need to put my mask back on, the one I let slip when I was too busy watching him without his.

Chapter 13

"**W**HAT ARE WE GOING TO DO ABOUT HIM?**" I whisper frantically while Marc slowly goes about cleaning up as if we have all the time in the world.

Um, hello?

Using my shirt, he bends down before me to wipe at my thighs but I wave him away, doing it myself. He waits patiently, then he fits his Henley from last night over my head, pulling my arms through as I stand frozen in place, openly gaping.

He's one of those—the guys that clean up after sex. I didn't even think those actually existed. I thought they were a myth, but nope, Marcos Vega is, of course, one. And a damn thorough one, too.

After I'm settled, he takes care of the condom and pulls his jeans back on and it's like waking up to him all over again. Marc in jeans and nothing else is like catnip to my libido.

This is why I tried. I fucking tried ignoring him. I knew, I just *knew* I'd make a mess out of anything to do with Marc. As amazing as this was, it was such a bad idea. The worst.

How can I do this? Really?

I already laid out the rules. I can't go back on them because of some sex. Mind-blowing sex, yes, but still, just some sex—exactly what I promised, and he agreed to.

Marc runs his hands through his wet hair, making tiny drops of sweat fly in all directions. At least he looks like he just got out of the shower. I look like I got fucked in the back of a barn. *Or against the wall of a cabin.*

He stops to look at me and I wonder what he sees, suddenly not giving a shit what anyone else thinks, but his phone's shrill ring causes me to flinch, ending the moment. The rest of the world does still exist and it'd like to remind us—now apparently. His eyebrows dip when he looks at the screen but then he just silences it, almost reluctantly.

Our eyes connect again, mine stripped and raw, his closed off and guarded. Or maybe it's the opposite, I don't know. I don't know anything right now.

He jerks his chin, asking, "I'll see ya?"

"I'm sure." I do work for him.

"I meant I'll see you out there." He nods his head at the door and I shrug. "Make sure you get dressed all the way before you let him in."

Simply bypassing him, I go around to the kitchenette to grab myself a glass of water.

"Are you serious?" he asks, and I take gulps from the glass, never once breaking eye contact with him. As much as I don't want Tysen to see me without underwear on, I really don't want Marc thinking he has a say in the matter. The second he walks out that door, I'm diving into the bathroom for a towel, but in the meantime, I'm clinging to that last shred of power I just discovered and am not ready to give up fully.

Ever. I'm not ready to give up ever.

I stand a little taller, letting the bottom of his shirt rise to show more thigh and preparing myself for the inevitable repercussion.

Only, it never comes.

Marc just says, "Fuck," then grabs the duffle bag with Tysen's stuff in it and rips open the door, inching his lean body—still without his shirt and still sexy as hell—through the thin opening.

Holding my breath, I hear Tysen's surprise before Marc closes the door completely.

"Here's your shit, so you don't need to go in there anymore."

"What? What's up with Bentlee?" Tysen asks.

There's a pause, then Marc says, "She's sick. Food poisoning from the prosciutto."

"No shit? I heard Paige talking about it smelling funky." I cover my mouth to hold in a laugh. That's not exactly how she put it. "Well, what are you doing then? Where's your shirt?"

"Who cares?" Marc counters, but I'm not sure which question he's referring to.

"Did she puke on it or something?"

Edging closer, I hear an unconvincing "sure" and I roll my eyes. Could he at least try?

"Damn, man. Thanks for taking a bullet for me. I don't do well with puke. Soon as someone even gags, I'm gagging, too."

Marc doesn't answer and I imagine him nodding in that quiet way he does but then the silence stretches so long I get secondhand embarrassment and I distract myself by going over to my suitcase, blindly reaching for some pants.

I get one leg in before Marc's phone rings again, making me jump and this time he takes it, first telling Tysen—again—not to go inside, then an easy "hey, little mama" to whoever it is on the other end.

Footsteps retreat down the front steps, each one crushing the progress I thought my heart was making.

But no. *Rest up, heart.* This was just…a practice run. There will be someone else. There will.

I hear Tysen mutter something unintelligible before he follows suit, leaving me to my thoughts and my dwindling adrenaline now that Marc's gone.

He's gone.

Without a backward glance.

Just like I wanted.

"Shit. Fuck. Goddamn," I murmur, having the sudden and completely inexplicable urge to scream.

What do I do now? And who did Marc call "little mama"?

"Oh my God. Ty told me everything." Paige rushes over to me as soon as I walk up the hill to the fire pit and a tingle starts at the back of my neck. "How are you feeling? Do you need some water? Do you want Beckett to go get you a sports drink? You need to replace your electrolytes."

Oh.

"Only if it's Arctic Blast," Beckett calls out, wearing a shirt that says *Grip It And Rip It.* "That shit's the best." Paige glares at him and he puts his hands up, telling her, "I see I didn't fuck all the angry out of you this morning."

"Baby, we both know it was me fucking you."

His face lights up and he shrugs, giving her the point, then to me, he says, "Whatever you need, Lee-Lee. Just let me know. I brought like fifteen different kinds of crackers and some ginger ale, too."

"Thanks," I mutter, not sure why he's calling me Lee-Lee.

Paige grimaces, rubbing circles on her chest. "Heartburn is kicking my ass right now. Between that and the morning sickness, I'm barely keeping anything down myself these days. That burger last night could've been a ball of fire between two buns for how bad it hurt."

Beckett steps up behind her, wrapping his long arms around her bump. Her eyes close as she melts into him, the sliver of animosity from a moment ago already forgotten.

When she reopens them, they narrow imperceptibly at something behind me and I follow their path, watching Marc as he walks up to join us, wearing a whole new outfit with his phone nowhere in sight.

"Marc, should I talk to Rosie about hiring you on as a nurse at Sunbrook?"

His voice soothes my rattled nerves. "I don't do uniforms."

Angela, standing at a table, yells over her shoulder, "You did one Halloween, Officer Vega."

The fact that they aren't sharing the photographic evidence of Marc in a police uniform right now should be a crime in itself.

"You'll never let me forget that, will you?" he complains before meeting my eyes with a half-smirk and I almost choke on my own tongue when I see the teeth imprints below his bottom lip. *My teeth imprints.*

"Yeah," Paige says, steering the conversation again, "I thought we'd have to pump fluids into Bentlee here after a night of food poisoning but she looks…"

My head whips around to pin her with a wide-eyed stare.

"Sated," she finishes with a proud grin just for me, then over my shoulder, she tells Marc, "You did good."

Some sort of acknowledgment comes from Marc that sounds smug as well but I keep my gaze trained on the ground. Everyone's a traitor this morning. Everyone.

"Is that a hickey?"

My hand flies to my neck a second before I realize it's not my neck she's talking about. It's Marc's.

For whatever reason, Beckett saves him from answering by saying, "Nah, that's ringworm. Probably from the wood. You know…cabins."

Paige side-eyes him and he laughs, waving a hand around at the cabins surrounding us. My face heats rapidly while I scramble to think of what other evidence I left on Marc.

"You're telling me, *a nurse*, that that gigantic hickey with a clear outline of a bite mark is ringworm?"

My blush intensifies until I feel like I might actually catch on fire. What is Marc doing right now?

Her fiancé nods solemnly, saying, "Some worms are more starved than others."

Closer to my back than I thought, Marc echoes, "Starved," sending an army of goose bumps to infiltrate every inch of my skin and I almost groan from frustration and from…something else that feels like yearning but stronger. *Starved?* Starved doesn't even scratch the surface.

"I don't know what you two are talking about but I can guarantee you, that's not what ringworm is," Paige says, shaking her head.

"Agree to disagree, dream."

They both look at me expectantly. At me? Behind me?

Why isn't Marc helping? This is exactly what I meant. He gets an assist while I get…I don't even know.

I don't even care.

Avoiding Marc and his friends' all-knowing stares, I go in search of food. He beats me to the food table though, and grabbing a plate first, he hands it over to me except when I take it, his fingers rub mine underneath, hidden from everyone's view and I freeze, unsure how to react. His penetrating gaze alternates between my eyes, causing my thighs to tighten.

He said it himself, I'm starved. But a girl cannot survive on Marc alone, even if that's exactly what my body's trying to convince me of.

I yank the plate from his hold, mumbling a quick "thanks," and with my plate full of griddle-seasoned pancakes, I find a seat next to Tysen, immediately apologizing for last night and this morning.

Such an inconvenience. *Always an inconvenience.*

I offer to treat him to lunch next week but he shrugs it off, saying, "Don't worry about it. Just pick me up a coffee one morning and we'll call it even."

Angela doesn't really like it when we show up with coffee from other places. I think she actually takes it as a challenge. There's only one coffee shop she says is competent enough to give our business to, a stand called Latte Da, but it's too far out of my way to ever give it a try, so I just give Tysen a tight smile.

Coty breaks up the silence to say, "So, Bentlee, Angela said you drive Hunter into town for school every day."

"It's crazy, right? Over an hour of driving every day to a school that's not a private school either. It's just public," Tysen tells him.

"You haven't had any luck finding something closer to his school?"

Coty asks me and I shake my head, stuffing a piece of pancake in my mouth.

"What about Creekwood?" Paige asks, coming over, and Tysen says, "That's what I told her. Marc could get her a discount."

Angela brings me a mocha in a big mug, made exactly the way she does it at work and I spy her espresso machine on the foldout table she's been standing at. It's got a long extension cord running from it to…somewhere. She distracts me by saying, "Or he could give you Beckett's old room."

I cough around the bite I'm chewing, washing it down with coffee and burning every surface inside my mouth in the process before saying, "I have Hunter," like that explains everything.

"And there's two open rooms," she says with a smile while darting a look in Paige's direction.

"That's right," she says, settling onto Beckett's lap with a pancake-filled plate of her own. "And Beckett's room is paid up through the year, so you'd only need to cover my old room. You're not gonna find a better deal than that anywhere."

Finding Marc's gaze fixed on me isn't surprising but him staying silent on the matter is. He can't want us living *with* him. That's just crazy. He'd be crazy.

"Whoa, whoa, whoa," Beckett cuts in before anyone else can. "Ty, don't you have a spare room at your place, too?" His eyebrows do a tap dance that make me squint in suspicion.

Tysen looks around, gulping down his own bite. "Yeah…one room. Diesel sleeps in the other." He looks at me hesitantly, saying, "Unless you'd be down to-"

"She can stay with me."

Oh, now Marc wants a say.

"*She* can speak for herself," I tell Marc, giving him an unamused look. "And *I'm* not moving in with anybody." I don't think.

"One room for the both of you?" Beckett muses out of nowhere, still addressing Tysen. "Just in time for those chilly winter months coming up."

Low and menacing, Marc's voice slices the head of the conversation clear off when he says, "You're not sharing a room with Tysen," and all I can do is watch as it rolls away awkwardly, the gore of it making my stomach knot along with the idea that Marc actually thinks he has a say over what I do. Or don't do.

Tysen stands suddenly despite his tone dropping several degrees in temperature to say, "You didn't let me finish, man. I was going to say the boys could share a room. I always shared a room with at least one of my brothers growing up and I bet Diesel would love it."

As sweet as that offer is, it's confusing as all hell. Diesel and Hunter are not brothers, nor will they ever be. And that won't help Tysen's situation with his ex. Not in the slightest.

I study the two men, then place my plate on the ground and get to my feet, wiping at my clothes.

Marc drops his arms from where they're crossed tightly over his chest to reach for me, asking, "What happened? What's the matter?"

"Just making sure I didn't get any piss on me from your little competition."

Marc's teeth line up perfectly with the imprint from mine on his bottom lip, biting to keep from laughing.

"Well, I think that sounds great," Beckett says off to the side and the same thunder from last night reappears, but with me looking right at its source, I see there's no storm at all, only Marc growling out his irritation.

Paige elbows Beckett and he makes an exaggerated howl of pain. "Actually, it's the perfect setup at Creekwood with Marc. Both you and Hunter each have your own rooms but you only pay for one. You get a separate bathroom, you're closer to school and work. If Marc's okay with it and you feel comfortable enough, then I think you should at least consider it. Seriously."

Angela chimes in, "I mean, he did help you recover from *food poisoning*."

"How did you know she was sick, by the way?" Tysen asks with a cold front still in place. "I was with her last and she looked fine."

Marc frees his lip to laugh, and not in a funny way either. "You weren't with her."

Tysen doesn't back down, goading, "How'd you know?"

Marc answers with a short, simple, and completely suspicious, "I didn't."

This time I do groan, dropping my face into my palms. What have I done? These people are impossible.

"I think I'm gonna take off in case Shawn lets me have Hunter early," I say, lifting my head. It's doubtful, very doubtful, but I'd rather be close to him anyway. I don't like being this far away in case something happens.

"What's Shawn's last name anyway?" Coty asks, looking genuinely curious.

"Mitchell. Shawnathon Mitchell."

Paige asks, "Shawnathon?" and I instantly tense, hoping she doesn't bring up anything I told her and Angela last night.

"What the fuck kind of name is that?" Marc questions instead.

"I don't know," I sigh. "His parents couldn't decide between Shawn and Johnathon so they combined the two." I've gotten this more times than I can count. When people bring it up to Shawn, things get…uncomfortable. He's sensitive about his name, to put it mildly.

"Didn't they ever hear of a middle name?"

"He's got one of those, too." Shawnathon Ryan Mitchell. It doesn't get any more vanilla than that. Truly.

Shawn insisted on naming Hunter himself after deeming all the names I'd chosen "not good enough" but I fought to choose his middle name—Mccoy. I found it on a baby name site, and seeing that it meant fire, it just kind of stuck with me. I compromised again by agreeing to give Hunter Shawn's last name even though we weren't married. Probably just another one of Shawn's little tricks he thought would make me want to marry him. With marriage there are no tricks though, at least there shouldn't be.

What feels like every eye in a ten-mile radius is locked on me and I realize someone asked me a question.

"What?" I ask but Marc's the one to answer, saying, "I can look at your truck before you leave if you want."

"Oh, thanks but no. It's fine." *I hope.*

"Think about it. Living with a mechanic's got its advantages." Beckett gives me a full smile but Angela butts in with, "Marc's a mechanic, too."

All of Marc's friends keep stealing glances at him, making it seem like everyone but me is in on some kind of joke regarding my living situation but joke's on them. I'm not even moving out right now.

Chapter 74

Bentlee

"YOU CAN'T STAY HERE ANYMORE."

I can't believe this is happening.

Actually, I can. Farm first, family second—that's the Graham way. Until I took a sharp turn and took off in a different direction. *Tried.* Tried to go in another direction.

I'm still trying and this proves why.

"You know the rules. Unless you-"

"I'm not giving up my child," I tell my mom and she rolls her eyes.

"No one said anything about giving up Hunter but you have to work here to live here. Besides, you'll only be going on a few trips."

"A few trips?" I almost scream. She wants me traveling all over Washington, Oregon, and Idaho for every state fair, festival, and holiday market possible. That's not a few trips. That's being an absent fucking mother and maybe, *maybe*, if I didn't have any other option and it was the only way to put food in my son's stomach, I would. I'd hate it but I'd do whatever I had to. But since I have another job—that actually pays me properly—I do have another option. In Graham terms though, that means I no longer get to live here, never mind the chores I've been waking up at four in the morning every day to keep up with.

Unfortunately, I haven't saved up quite enough to actually move out completely. That's why I was biding my time. I don't want to live at Graham forever but it's all I could afford when we moved in at the beginning of the year.

"It's only for the next four months. A small moment in an entire lifetime."

I shake my head. "Not a moment. *Moments*. With my child. My son." *My life.* "Moments with him I'll never be able to get back." I already lose time with him to Shawn and I'm not going to give up any more just because my parents are hell-bent on sticking to some archaic rule.

It'll start at four months just like my duties at Graham started as clerical. Each day turning into more and more and more until I'm drowning in milk while being told it's only temporary. It doesn't matter what you're told though because once it reaches your lungs, it's all over. There is no backing out when you've got nothing else to inhale. The promise of four months is just to test my lungs, see how long I'm willing to hold my breath.

She raises her hands then drops them. "Sacrifices must be made for this lifestyle."

"Maybe your lifestyle, but I didn't choose this life."

"As soon as you stepped foot back on this farm, you made the choice."

"You're forcing me to make another."

"And what about next time?"

Next time. Next time I fuck up.

Except I didn't fuck up, not the way she's alluding to anyway. Having Hunter wasn't a fuckup. Despite what everybody assumes, leaving Shawn wasn't a fuckup either. I waited as long as I could, trying to give Hunter as much of a normal childhood as possible, but when things became unbearable, I left.

But I did it without having a solid plan in place, one that didn't lead back here, and that was my fuckup. One I can promise I won't do again.

Even if Hunter and I have to share a room, I'll find something.

At my silence, she says, "Fine. Why don't you just quit at that shop…" My mind rebels against the very notion, refusing to consider the possibility of not working at Pop The Hood anymore. "…and we'll enroll Hunter in your old school? He can take the bus and we can keep an eye on him when you're gone. It's a better life than what you've been giving him. Constantly commuting back and forth. He could spend that time here instead, helping out."

Tricks. I can spot them now, practically smell them a mile away. Guilt trips are just that—a ride. Some take the beautiful route, others get right to the point.

I stop what I'm doing to peer over at her. "You don't even know what you're talking about. How could you? You don't know the first thing about bonding with your children unless it directly benefits this *lifestyle* you did *choose* by marrying Dad."

I don't fault her for who she fell in love with, only how she proceeded to treat her children after the fact, like our lives were a part of her dowry or something. If farming wasn't force-fed to me from birth, it's something I might've chosen for myself honestly. Hunter and I both love the animals. It's the blatant disregard of my own aspirations that ruins the experience from the ground up. That and the constant manipulations.

"Hunter and I talk," I tell her. "We dance. We make silly faces. We laugh. We bond on those daily commutes that I choose to make for him. To give him a sliver of what he used to have when I know I'll never be able to give him what we had before."

"I bonded with you girls plenty. You're just…different. Always have been. Always thinking you're better than the rest of us. Like you're too good to get dirty."

I scoff. "Yeah. That's it. I'm scared of getting dirty. Further proof that you know nothing about me because you've never taken the time. I'm more accustomed to the dirt than Sydnee. After all, I lived with a pig for years." Shit. I shouldn't have said that last part out loud.

She jumps on it though, using the opening to her advantage by twisting her own knife in the wound by saying, "That's your fault for getting mixed up with Shawnathon."

"Mistakes are not life sentences. Would you please stop treating mine like they are? I fell for a boy and it didn't work out. We had a beautiful baby together. Neither are a foreign concept nor do they warrant me being branded forever."

"A boy? Shawnathon was an opportunist preying on younger girls, plain and simple."

I open my mouth to argue but close it, considering her words carefully. Did Shawn prey on me?

It doesn't matter now, does it? Even if I could go back, would I?

The answer is simple. No, I wouldn't, because then I might not have Hunter.

But I would change how I let Shawn treat me. Since I can't go backward, all I can do is try going forward. Last weekend I felt a shift in myself and I feel it now, fighting against the handling, the constant handling of me, like I'm clay, molded however my handler sees fit.

"Mom," I say, meeting her eye. "Thank you for giving me and Hunter a place to stay while I got my feet under me again." I won't be sucked back into it. I can't. I barely made it out the first time. I'm older now. Wiser. I see the end result they're envisioning for me and I have to take my future into my own hands while I still can. "But I quit."

"Then you have until the end of the week to find somewhere else to live, however, my grandson's welcome to stay on."

Closing the distance, I stand almost toe to toe with my mother, telling her quietly, "The day I walk away from my son is the day you bury me in the ground. Do you understand? My son's never been a choice and he never will be." Not for me.

Her eyes flick between both of mine and she lowers her voice, too. "Who are you? I didn't raise you to be like this."

I turn away from her with a humorless laugh. "You didn't raise me at all." The heifers outside did a better job looking after me than she did. My aunt was more of a mother to me but she's sucked in, too. Her head's been fully submerged since she was a child and that's fine with her, just like it's fine with my mom, my dad, my sister.

But my mom's right about one thing, I am different.

It's only when she leaves the room that I take my first full breath. I take another one before the tears filling my eyes fall.

The first swipe of a mama bear's claws always takes the most effort. I just never thought I'd have to use them against my own mom.

Using my sleeve, I wipe my face, then pull out my phone to open the internet browser.

Time to find a new den.

After spending all morning scrolling through enough photo carousels to make my head spin, I decide to go outside for some fresh air.

Thankfully, Angela gave me today off after I called her last night to explain my predicament, leaving me the entire day to hunt for a place to live. I've already got a couple tours set up with places that are in my price range and by that I mean they're at the top of it—the tippy top.

Swiping some hair out of my face, I push through the screen door, coming to a stop when I see a familiar red motorcycle crawling up the driveway.

Parked in a cloud of fine dust, Marc dismounts, pulling off his helmet to stare at me.

"What are you doing here?" I ask when he finally approaches.

"Thought I'd help you move," he says simply.

How does he know already?

"I've got it taken care of." Technically I don't but I'm not admitting that to him. I'm not admitting that to anybody just yet. I will find something.

Those charcoal eyes of his sweep the front porch, his top lip curling at the overhead fly ribbons covered in carcasses. The bite marks beneath his lip are gone but the hickey on his neck is now yellowing against his beautiful dark skin.

"You're not staying with Tysen." It's not a question.

"Excuse me?"

He clears his throat, softening his voice to room temp butter. "I don't want you staying with Tysen."

"Neither do I," I mutter. Honestly, I never even considered that an option.

We both size each other up, wondering, assuming.

Marc keeps everything to himself but this is not the time for cryptic looks and secretive gestures. I need answers.

"Why are you really here?"

He traps his helmet between one of his thighs with his hand, pinning me with a hard expression that contradicts his next words. "To take you home."

I shut my eyes on reflex. *Home.* What even is that? *Where* is that? It's not at Graham Dairy. It's not at the old house I shared with Shawn. That never felt like home. He never felt like home.

"And by home, you mean…" I open my eyes to look at him.

"Creekwood."

Ah, yes. The elusive Creekwood. Creekwood did come up in my search but not with any immediate availability. He must've taken Tysen's suggestion to get me some kind of deal. I cringe thinking about what kind of strings he had to pull to secure one.

I clear my throat and lean against one of the columns framing the front door. "You shouldn't have done that."

"Do you need to pick Hunter up soon?" He changes the subject and I nod, watching him closely. "Then c'mon," his shoes scrape up the front steps until he stops beside me, cocking his head, "let's get you outta here."

Passing by me, he opens the screen door, walking inside my parents' house with more confidence than any one person should be allowed to possess and fulfilling another one of my fantasies—Marcos Vega barging into my childhood home to rescue me.

Only after I pick my jaw up off the decking do I hurry after him.

I take in the leather couch and coffee table and TV and stuff. There's stuff everywhere. Someone else's stuff.

"It's fully furnished?" I ask.

Not that I'm complaining since Shawn kept most of our furniture but this has to cost more than a regular unit would. Forget tippy top, this is way above my price range. There's even a long hallway with more doors than I could count in the quick glance I gave it when Marc first opened the front door. It's at least two bedrooms.

Just how many strings did he have to pull? *And whose?*

Marc glances over his shoulder, into the outdoor hall, saying, "Almost."

A voice that sounds like Coty's yells up the stairwell, "Are you gonna give me a hand or what?"

Facing me, Marc grins, telling me he'll be right back. Even after he disappears, his smell remains though, almost stronger, and I take a deep breath, letting it calm my nerves. I hate moving and this is the second time in the same year now.

Looking around the large space again, I venture further inside, noticing a glass on the counter—a used glass—then rush outside after him.

My rain boots hit the concrete sidewalk just as the words tumble from my mouth, "Does somebody live here?"

With his back to me, Marc doesn't respond right away as he lifts a mattress out of a moving truck before Coty jumps out, carrying the other half. I saw the truck when we pulled in but thought it was for someone else, possibly someone moving *out.*

"Hey, Bentlee."

I wave at Coty, having the sudden urge to hide. Even though I've grown close to Angela, I don't know him as well as the others and this isn't exactly the situation I wanted to get to know him in. He smiles though and I smile back as they pass my lead feet.

Uh. "Marc? Somebody's actively living up there."

"You know, for all the shit you talk, you don't say a lot," Coty tells Marc.

Stepping backward up onto the stairs, Marc says, "And for someone that talks a lot, you don't ever say anything worth a shit."

"You're thinking of Beck."

The friends break into easy laughter while hefting the mattress up the flight of stairs together.

Out of sight, Marc calls down the stairwell, "This is my place. Welcome home."

"His place?" I say to myself, turning to peek in the moving truck and finding a smaller mattress still in its wrapping.

Up the stairs and back in the—his—apartment, I follow them down the hall to a bedroom on the right. They drop the mattress onto a beautiful sleigh frame that's already built.

Since he clearly hasn't listened to anything I've said so far, I decide to use his preferred form of communication of keeping it short, simple, and directly to the point.

"No."

Standing, Marc uses the bottom of his shirt to wipe some sweat from his forehead, exposing his cut abs and my mouth goes dry before I can shut my eyes.

Tricks! He's using one…or eight, since it's technically an eight-pack.

That is what he's doing, right? No one just shows off their eight-pack naturally.

"Yes."

I open my eyes, narrowing on his.

"Marc."

He drops his shirt, saying, "Bentlee."

"This isn't a good idea."

"Yes, it is. You don't want to use the beds that were in here before."

Coty laughs, nodding his head. "That's for sure."

"No, not the beds. Wait, what do you mean beds?"

"Hunter sleeps by himself, right?" Marc asks suddenly, but without waiting for my answer, he continues, "Shit, I didn't even think about that. Fuck it, we'll finish setting the other one up, then you two can decide what you want to do with it. I just thought he'd want his own bed since we got the room."

"You let your son sleep with you?" Coty asks with an unreadable expression on his jaggedly handsome face. His hair's dark but not as dark as Marc's. He's also got crazy brown eyes that might have the same condition as mine except different. It's hard to explain but they're mesmerizing.

"Yes," I answer slowly, tearing my two-tone eyes from his two-tone eyes.

Hunter and I have been sharing not only a room but a bed as well since we moved in with my parents, but even before that, if he had a bad dream or felt sick, he was always welcome to sleep with me. It's not like there was anything else happening in my bed.

Surprisingly, Coty tells me, "You're a good mom," and I immediately start to respond with, "I don't," then stop myself.

The truth is I don't always feel like a good mom. I don't know if I ever feel like it actually. I try really fucking hard, all the time, yet I constantly feel like I'm coming up short, like there's an insurmountable standard I'm forever reaching for and failing to achieve.

"Thanks," I tell him quietly before turning to Marc. "I meant about us living here. With you. There's no way you want some mom and her kid imposing on your…lifestyle." Whatever that may be.

"I'll be outside," Coty excuses himself, disappearing out the bedroom door.

"Everything's already set up. I could use a couple roommates. You need somewhere safe and affordable to stay. What's the problem?"

"This just…looks bad. You know?"

He nods his head, rubbing his hands together, then says, "Coty's right. You're a good mom."

"Not if I move us in with some strange guy."

"You think I'm strange?"

"To Hunter, you are."

"And to you? What am I?" His piercing eyes track mine.

Hot. Bold. All-consuming.

Mysterious. Dangerous.

Like a flame.

Instead, I take a stab in the dark by saying, "A partier?"

He chuckles deeply, turning for the door and I follow after.

"That's the lifestyle you think I have, huh?" He laughs, not really confirming or denying it. "Even if that were true, things are changing. We're getting older now."

"I'm already older," I mutter, and he stops just before he crosses the threshold to look at me.

"Is age your hang-up?"

My hang-up? Not exactly. It's more of an observation. A fact—I am older than Marc. But with us both being well over eighteen now, I guess the age difference doesn't really matter like it used to.

We stare at each other for what feels like hours, then I say, "You know this can't." I motion between us. "We can't." It's as much for him as it is for me. Age may not be an issue but that doesn't mean I'm suddenly ready to get involved with Marc. Or anyone else.

My stance on that hasn't changed.

It hasn't.

He bobs his head. "Listen, I'm not here all that often. I," he rips his eyes away, glancing around, "travel, among other things that keep me tied up. For the most part, you and your boy will have the place to yourselves. I'll be out of town for the next few days, taking care of some business, so you two can get all settled in, then you can decide how you want to introduce me to Hunter when I get back. I know this kind of thing can be hard on kids," the space between his eyebrows creases, "but I don't want to upset Hunter. Or you. I want you both to be comfortable in your home. It's up to you if you wanna stay but here's the key," he hands me a key on a keyring, "and the beds will be here regardless, if you ever need them."

"You'd just have two spare beds? Just in case?"

His gaze collides with mine again and one of his shoulders lifts. "You get hit, I get hit, right?"

At my silence he cracks a smile like the sun breaching the clouds on a gloomy day and I have to force down a swallow. With amazing determination and a smile that could stop traffic, I don't think there's anything on this planet Marc couldn't get, if he wanted to.

My stance wavers. It wavers and it'll continue to waver the longer I'm around him. But if he's gone a lot, then maybe…

"Thank you," is all I say.

"That is, only if I don't hear you snoring again."

I shove his shoulder, squeezing by him, and he laughs, following me out to give a quick tour before going back downstairs to help Coty with the twin mattress he bought for Hunter. He managed to buy bedroom furniture for two rooms, procure a moving truck, assemble both frames and drive out to my parents' house to help me pack—all in less than a day.

But I already knew what he was capable of in that amount of time.

Lord help anything that Marc sets his mind to, including my wavering stance.

Especially my wavering stance.

Chapter 15

Marc

3.

2.

Keeping my eyes trained on the pin at the bottom corner of the starting gate, I watch the board in front of us out of my periphery, anticipating the moment it lowers as my YZ450F bucks beneath me, ready to go.

1.

I fucking rip it, flying over the gate the second it drops. The 450 circuit ain't for the weak, and if you don't get a good start…you need a good start.

Already in second gear, I tap into third, then fourth in quick succession with the inner edge of my boot, getting the jump on everyone and hitting the first double in the lead. Landing the jump cleanly, I notice someone behind me trying to cut into my line and accelerate that much more. *Fucking prick.*

Lowered to my seat, I sail around the bowl turn, my inside leg straight out and probably less than a centimeter off the ground, then I'm out of the corner and back on the balls of my feet, half-standing as I lay on the throttle.

I can't shake the asshole behind me and he's riding dirty with his constant zig-zags, so the only way to not get clipped—bad—or overtaken—worse—is to make sure I stay ahead of him the entire time which means staying off my brakes almost entirely.

The next turn approaches and I take it a bit too fast, my back tire trying to skirt out wide but I use my whole body to correct it, grateful I doubled up on core as well as thigh workouts this past week. Elbows out wide, I straighten just before entering another set of jumps, these ones bigger than the last. Airborne, time all but freezes allowing me to relax in the pause, feeling completely free and on top of the fucking world. Then I'm landing with the motherfucker stuck to my ass nearly coming down on top of me and I lose all that zen shit at once. Luckily, I catch myself before I can crank my head to the side to glare at him. The bike goes where my eyes go, and even though I'd love to park my Yamaha up his ass, I'm not willing to lose traction to do it.

Only a few more times around the course, then I'm crossing the finish line—first. As always, I keep my helmet on but the guy flanking me the whole race storms over as soon as he finishes second and tries to knock it clear off my head. With the chin strap still somewhat attached, it just jerks my entire head to the side, giving me a swift glimpse of vertigo along with an enticing taste of violence.

Oh, Imma eat alright. I've been fucking dying to catch this motherfucker.

Our fists fly at the same time, and while mine actually hit skin as I aim for his face, his connect with my midsection with rapid jabs that sting more than anything. Dropping down, his shoulder sinks into my stomach and he tackles me to the ground, knocking my helmet loose in the process. The second it's off, it's fucking on between us and we exchange blows like we're next in line for a title fight. He gets me with an uppercut to my jaw that rattles my fucking brain, my teeth clattering until I clench them and yank my head off the ground to head-butt his nose with my forehead. Blood gushes all over my face like a broken waterline and I throw an elbow across his cheek, finally getting him off me but his hand scrapes across my mouth on his way down, nicking one of my lips. Motherfuck.

"Next time stay the fuck outta my line," I growl, gripping his chest protector.

"Fuck you," he spits just as people intervene, working to break us up, then as if a mask falls from his ugly face, he laughs. Fucking laughs. What the fuck? "There won't be a next time. Your streak is fucking over, Vega."

What?

The commissioner of the motocross committee glares at me from across the track and I can feel his disapproval wash over me just as panic starts to swirl deep in my stomach. What did I do?

"Fifth fight in as many races? You're a fucking menace. A liability. Your number's getting pulled, brother."

"Don't call me that," I grit, not taking me eyes off the commissioner. Motherfucker ain't my brother, that's for goddamn sure. More like a fucking rat, setting me up.

I rise to my feet, tilting my head at him. Anthony Chease. He's like a mole in this sport, always slinking around the underground, popping up just for the hell of it. He's a good rider but cares more about clout on social media than actually winning. No doubt someone from his camp got some good shots of him fucking around behind me the whole race with every intention of posting them, if they haven't already.

They could be filming right now.

Reaching for my helmet, I tug it back over my head. My number may get pulled after this but I still won, and as the winner, I have certain obligations to fulfill, like pictures and shit. Not even the commissioner can argue that.

Only after a moment's hesitation, I take a step like I'm leaving—if I'm going out, I might as well make it worth it—then I twist and clip Anthony right in the nose again, not even bothering to stay and watch as he crumples back to the ground.

The whole time I'm signing autographs for a few of the local kids that are obvious diehards, I can't stop wondering what the fuck I'm going to do. This was the last motocross race of the season. After this I could either move on to supercross in arenas for the colder months or keep training for next year's outdoor circuit but I don't even know if either of those are realistic now.

What am I supposed to do? Just work at Pop The Hood before going home to an empty apartment every day? Wash, rinse, repeat?

Fuck that shit. I've been doing it since Beck and Paige moved into their own home and I'm already sick of it.

Maybe I could try to convince Kary to let Rebel stay over sometime. Maybe even have an actual weekend schedule or something, kinda like what Bentlee has with Hunter.

Unless Bentlee decided to actually stay.

I took off shortly after getting the beds ready and I've held off on contacting her so she wouldn't feel pressured. Whatever she decides, I have to accept. I made sure Coty hung around though in case she needed help with anything else. Not that she had much. It's fucking insane that her ex gave her next to nothing when she has a fucking kid to take care of. How can he not realize how much shit kids require? I know and Rebel doesn't even live with me.

With Rebel in mind, I take a stupid selfie and send it to Kary, asking her to show our little racer.

Shit.

Maybe Anthony caused some actual damage or maybe I'm just losing it but my father's words pop in my head again. *What's waiting for you?*

What if there is something waiting for me? And what if that something isn't a thing at all, but a someone? More than one, really.

What if this isn't an end at all and I'm just getting started?

A bead of hope blooms like an oil spill, and with my phone still in hand, I make a couple calls before leaving the complex to find my RV.

Hauling my feet up to my front door, I stop when I hear music coming from the other side. "Dance Monkey" by Tones And I pulses through the cheap metal and I frown for a split second before Bentlee's voice carries over the song, belting out the lyrics completely out of tune.

She stayed.

My lips spread into a small smile, then I wince, the cut on my top lip burning. It's nothing compared to my knuckles but much more no-ticeable and harder to explain away, unfortunately. Mechanics' hands are always a mess. Except for Beck's. Guy's always got baby-smooth hands.

The song ends only to start back up again.

Three more times and I'm still standing here, listening with my forehead pressed to the door and my heart pressed to my ribs, begging me to go in already.

Should I knock? Or is that weird?

The door behind me opens and my head pops up from my own. One of the tenants that took over Angela's old studio pokes his head out and with a stuck-up-as-shit eye roll, he asks, "Do you think you can keep it down?"

My face quickly settles back into my preferred scowl.

"No."

All the parties we've had and he chooses now to come out and complain? Shit.

A huff and a puff and a look that says he'd love to blow my house down, he chokes out, "I'll forward my complaint to Kary."

I check my smile, not letting it slip an inch to tell him, "You do that."

Another eye roll, then he closes the door, making sure to lock the deadbolt loudly. *It's fucking "Dance Monkey," Todd.*

I veer left, down the open-ended hallway, and rap my knuckles twice on the only other door on this level. Gary, our neighbor since we moved in, cracks the door and I give him a tight nod. Nobody sees much of him but that's the way he prefers it.

He sees though. Plenty.

"All good?" I ask.

He returns my nod with one of his own, looking past my shoulder and I follow his gaze, dropping my head for a second.

Fuck it. I'm already this far in.

"So, double then?"

He agrees and I hand over a wad of cash, this one twice as thick as usual.

"There are worse things than being surrounded by women."

"Name one," I challenge.

"Not," he says just before closing the door.

He's the only person I've met that speaks less than me, so when he does, it means something. I'm not sure what exactly happened to lead Gary here, living like a hermit crab that refuses to outgrow his shell, only that his particular set of skills helps me whenever I need to get away from Creekwood.

I consider his words on the way back to my own apartment. It wasn't my intention when I asked Bentlee to move in to surround myself with yet another woman but I'm not complaining either. Not yet anyway since this will be our first night living together. But if I don't open the door, I'll never find out.

Steeling my spine, I shake out my hands, then twist the knob, frowning at the way Bentlee insists on keeping all her doors unlocked. An image of opening her bedroom door late at night flashes through my mind but I tuck it away, focusing on the scene that's right in front of me.

Bentlee, hair up in a loose bun, wearing sweats that are a size too big but still fit all her curves just right, swaying around the kitchen while Hunter sits on the counter nearby. Both of them are brandishing serving spoons as microphones as they sing along as loud as they can to each other.

Now that I'm inside and I can make out the lyrics better, it's almost scary how accurate they are.

So fucking accurate.

The song picks up and Bentlee twirls, the biggest smile stretched across her bare face and all the air in my lungs leaves my body. One twirl. One fucking twirl and I can't breathe.

Why did I think this was a good idea?

Because I wasn't thinking about me. I was thinking about Bentlee being stuck. A feeling I've been avoiding as long as I can remember. When Angela told me about the position Bentlee's parents put her in, I knew. I knew they'd try that same bullshit my dad continues to try on me to this day and I couldn't just sit back and let it happen.

I've got resources. She doesn't. So I figured I'd give her some of mine. It wasn't even a conscious choice really. I just sprang into action, then next thing I knew, I was standing in her parents' foyer without any clue where I was going, only who I was taking with me.

A piece of Bentlee's hair gets stuck to her jaw as she stops and points to Hunter, swinging that ass of hers back and forth in time to the final chords.

I'd give her anything.

The song eventually ends and I take a hesitant step forward, not wanting to ruin the moment but feeling more and more out of place the longer I stand here, watching the private duet.

Bentlee's eyes round the second she sees me and she rushes to wipe the sweat off her forehead, saying, "Marc. We weren't expecting you." She grimaces. "I mean, we didn't know when you'd be back." To Hunter, she whispers, "Can you get it yourself or do you need help?"

With a stubborn shake of his head, he hops off the counter to open the fridge. Both hands full, he spins around, thrusting a homemade cake toward me.

My heart stutters and my eyes fly to Bentlee's to see them narrowed at me. She knows?

"We made it a couple days ago," *she doesn't know*, "but we kept it in the fridge, so it should be good." She gazes at her son. "We just wanted to say thank you for letting us crash your bachelor pad."

Hunter's face screws up in confusion. "What's a bachelor pad?"

Bentlee looks to me for help and I end up voicing the first honest thing that comes to mind, saying, "Lonely."

Her eyebrows rise but I busy myself by kneeling down in front of Hunter and the cake he's grappling to hang on to. Random chocolate streaks run across an otherwise vanilla cake and there's an entire fork-imprinted bite out of one corner.

Bentlee sees me notice and drops her head to hide a blush.

"Did you make this?" I ask him.

Hunter nods his head, his face brightening. "It's got a marble in it."

I glance back up at Bentlee and she laughs, explaining, "It's a marble cake. Vanilla and chocolate swirls. There're no marbles in it, I promise."

I bite the inside corner of my lips. "Looks good. Wanna split it with me?"

His eyes practically twinkle reminding me of how this was actually supposed to go.

Dropping my bag to the ground beside me, I unzip the top and grab out one of the two navy blue boxes inside.

I eye him for a second before asking, "Do you like stars?"

His head nods like it's on springs and Bentlee grabs the cake from his hold, placing it on the counter along with some plates and utensils. She keeps a watchful eye on us that I feel no matter where I'm looking. Something about it feels nice, too. I like her eyes.

I like her eyes on me.

Opening the box, I take out the projector and plug it into the wall, turning off the lamp as well.

"Watch this," I tell him, then hit the on button, grinning when he drops his head back to stare at the lit-up ceiling. Leaning back on one hand, I gesture above us. "Have you ever heard of Orion's belt?" Eyes still lifted, he shakes his head. "Orion's a grouping of stars called a constellation and it's one of the easiest to find. You just gotta look for the three stars in a straight line that make up the guy's belt."

Without pointing them out directly, I guide Hunter's attention in the general direction, giving him clues about what to look for, then when he finally finds them, I show him the rest of the constellation.

"He even has a sword," I say, pointing out Orion's Nebula under the belt. It's pretty blurry on the ceiling but I use my finger to draw in the air where it should be anyway.

"A sword? Cool."

I smile, peering over at him. "He's a hunter."

His eyes shoot to mine. "Like me?"

"It depends on where you go and who you ask."

Bentlee brings us each a plate, asking, "What do you mean?"

"Thanks," I say, accepting the cake. "In Greek mythology, Orion's believed to be a tall, good-looking dude with an unbreakable club."

"I thought you said it was a sword."

"He's got both." I show them the other part of Orion, said to be a club. "Lots of other cultures associate Orion with a hunter's image but the Egyptians thought Orion was some sort of gateway to heaven. You know the pyramids of Giza?" I ask Bentlee and she nods, her mouth full of cake. I shake away a smile. "Well, supposedly they were built to line up with his belt, with air shafts inside to make the transition for souls of the dead up to heaven easier."

She nods along, probably thinking I'm a fucking loser for knowing all this shit, but then after swallowing she asks, "What's another one?" and I get a high from it. An actual fucking high, I swear. She's looking at me like she's interested in what I'm saying, in what I know, and I have the urge to keep talking just to keep her eyes on me like that for as long as I can.

I never want her to stop looking at me.

I clear my throat, telling them, "The Aztecs called his belt and sword the Fire Drill, for their New Fire ceremony ritual."

"Whoa," Hunter breathes, gazing up, his fork caught halfway to his mouth. "Was there fire?"

I laugh lightly, catching sight of Bentlee's cheeks as they randomly turn pink.

"I think so." Some of the ritual isn't exactly kid friendly, so I leave it at that. I doubt people-eating spirits and sacrifices are the kind of fun facts that'll warm my new roommates up to me, especially right before bedtime.

Hunter launches into his own story about a shadow game his class played in gym today while I eat my cake, savoring each bite along with every moment of listening to him and stealing glances at his mom.

When he's finished, I set aside my plate and lie back, tucking an arm under my head while using the other to point out another constellation. Hunter follows suit but Bentlee stays on the couch, her head tilted back, too.

When she stands sometime later to announce it's time for bed, Hunter groans loudly, asking, "Do I have to?"

"Yes. It's already eight o'clock and you still need to brush your teeth and read to me."

Eight? I got home at six.

Hunter complains some more, so I get to my feet, unplugging the projector. "You can look at this anytime. It's for your room." My eyes touch on Bentlee's. "If you want. It's a nightlight." I got one for Rebel too because she burns through nightlights like I go through cigarettes. She's always got at least three on every night and somehow manages to choose ones that only run on batteries, so they die—often.

I hand him the machine and he smiles shyly, thanking me.

"You're welcome, little man," I say, ruffling his already messy hair.

Bentlee and I watch him drag his feet down the hall, dropping his new light off before disappearing into the bathroom. The second the door closes, Bentlee rounds on me, her face turning murderous.

"What happened to your face?"

"A door?" I have no idea why that comes out as a question.

"A door kicked your ass?"

I scoff, grabbing my bag off the floor. "*I* wasn't the one that got my ass kicked."

"You got into a fight? Why?" She eyes me like there's something wrong with me. Like she should be scared of me.

I hate it, but I can't actually tell her the truth. Can I?

"Thanks for the cake," I tell her instead, avoiding her questioning gaze on the way to my room.

The click of the lock on my door is only followed by another click, then the door is open with Bentlee striding through it like she has every right to.

"That shit was locked." What the fuck?

"If I'm going to be living with you, if my son is going to be living with you, then I need to know what kind of person you are. Why did you get into a fight?"

"Are we not gonna acknowledge the fact that you just picked my bedroom lock?"

"Do we need to? You're already aware I did it. What else is there to discuss?"

I frown, dropping my bag to cross my arms over my chest. "How? How'd you pick it?"

She brings her hand up, touching her thumb to her lip. "Tell me why you fought and I'll tell you."

"You go first," I demand quietly, aware the water running in the bathroom will be shutting off soon.

That same hand reaches over her head to reveal a bobby pin pulled from her hair.

"Party trick?"

She shakes her head, a few more pieces of hair falling from the bun and lying on the part of her neck that I wish I would've sucked the absolute fuck out of last weekend just like she did to mine. My cock twitches from the reminder.

God, what I wouldn't give to have her skin on mine again. What I wouldn't give to have her.

My fingers itch but I flex my arms to hide it.

Boundaries, motherfucker.

"Not exactly," she admits, bringing me back.

How did she learn to pick locks? And why? She did it with next to no effort and in almost less time than it took to even turn the lock to begin with.

Nothing in my room is safe anymore.

Why doesn't that thought scare me like it should? Like it used to?

Bentlee's eyes take me in, possibly checking for other injuries, maybe just checking me out. Either way it's strange—the sensation— like her attention hurts, but in the best way possible.

Cigarettes. I probably just need a cigarette. Or fifty.

"Your turn," she whispers, not hiding her inspection at all.

"Another rider got a little too cocky."

Her eyebrows crease. "Motorcycle?"

I jerk a nod. *Close.*

She approaches me and I freeze, every muscle in my body seizing the fuck up. Touching—what are the rules for touching here? Because my hands are literally fucking shaking with the need to touch her and I never shake.

Except when it comes to Bentlee.

The thumb that was just pressed to her own lip brushes mine, smoothing over the cut and I close my eyes, relishing the way it hurts so good. Best pain I've ever felt.

Then in an instant, the pressure increases and my eyes pop open as I rip my head away, glaring at her.

"One. That's one lie to me, Marc." Her face fills with a different kind of pain. One I wish I knew the cause of so I could put an end to it—an apocalyptic end with no chance of ever hurting her again.

Still, I didn't lie. Not technically.

I didn't *try* to lie. Staying silent about shit is easy, so easy that after a while I don't even have to try at all. Being tight-lipped is my norm, and easier to convince it isn't outright lying…to everyone else. To me, I know. I know but I can't help it. I can't help it all the time.

Maybe this time's different.

"I always have one on me," Bentlee whispers, holding the bobby pin between us, studying it as she all but vanishes in thought. "If there's not one in my hair, I've got two in my purse and a spare in every pair of jeans I own. I didn't use to but I started to…because of lies."

My scowl deepens as her eyes refocus on my face.

"Lies, and deceit, and…tricks."

"I'm not trying to trick you, Bentlee." That, at least, isn't a lie. Or even an attempt at one.

She stays quiet for so long I think she's done. Done with me?

"Fine." Fuck. *Am I really doing this?* "Another rider ran his mouth, put me," and my money, "at risk, then tried to catch me with a cheap shot. Any one of those things alone would've pissed me off enough to retaliate, but all three? Yeah, I beat his ass. It's what I do. I fight when I need to." And sometimes when I don't. I don't take anything lying down and rarely standing up.

Gargling echoes from the bathroom and a shadow passes over her face.

"Can you promise you'll never put Hunter in danger?"

Hunter? What about her? But then I look into her eyes, really in her eyes, and I see legitimate fear there. Not fear of me or my fighting.

But fear that she made a mistake moving here. That she's the one putting her boy in danger when all she wants is to protect him, even if it costs her own safety.

But I'd give my life to save either of them—gladly.

Closing the distance, the tips of my shoes touch her toes and I lower my voice, promising her, "I won't let anything happen to either of you as long as you're under this roof. At my hands or anyone else's." It's a promise similar to the one I made before and have yet to break. If I change now, I risk that security and I can't. I won't. Some things are that important. Bentlee understands that as much as I do or she wouldn't be bringing this up.

"I don't care about me—"

"I do," I say, cutting her off. "I care." I don't know how exactly or why, but I somehow started caring about Bentlee in a way I can't even begin to describe to myself, let alone anyone else. She wouldn't be here otherwise. Doesn't she see that?

"You know we can't…" Her slender fingers gesture between us as she struggles to voice the same concerns as before.

"We won't." I didn't move her in here with the intention of fucking her. Of course I want to, but just because I want to touch and hold and please her, doesn't mean I think I get to. I do have some boundaries. I'm not entirely sure what they are yet but I can follow someone else's lead for once. *Probably.*

"You're still holding back," she says, her eyes flicking between mine as she backs up, the door down the hall opening.

"So are you." I know for a fucking fact she hasn't been as upfront as she's asking me to be. The hypocrisy isn't lost on me. Neither is the way her gaze sweeps my room, taking in my wall covered in maps, before she spins on her heel, leaving me with a fresh burst of peppermint and…trees. Does she really smell like trees? Fucking trees? Whatever it is, it's got my cock hardening by the second.

A light laugh trails after her while one of her hands lifts above her head like a victory flag waving in the air. "Welcome home, Marc."

As soon as her mouthwatering ass disappears from my sight, I max out my lungs, wondering how the hell I'm actually supposed to keep up with all this. I'm rock hard for a woman I can't have, that I invited—no, *insisted*—to move in with me and she just left my room to read bedtime stories to the only man she seems to give a shit about. Aside from Tysen—maybe.

A smile ghosts my lips. *At least she's not sleeping with Tysen tonight.*

Bentlee's staying here but this living arrangement doesn't technically rule out the possibility of her sleeping with anyone else. Even though she was ready, willing, and motherfucking eager with me, she's made it clear that she sure as fuck isn't planning on doing it again.

The smile disappears without a trace.

Welcome home.

Chapter 16

SHUFFLING SOME PAPERS IN MY HOLD, I WALK OVER TO the car wash portion of Pop Two, keeping my eyes downcast. Marc's been here every day this week. And last week. Working. Where he used to just stop over in the mornings, he now works here all the time, putting in as many hours as the rest of the crew, and the only times he's not at Pop Two is when he says he's leaving for Pop One.

He said he'd barely be home. *Lie.*

All day, every day, whether we're at work or at home, he's around.

And as much as I've been telling myself I don't mind, I do.

Angela sees me when she's just finishing up with wiping down a car and says, "Hey."

"Hey. Can I get tomorrow off?"

Luckily, Angela promoted me to full time as soon as I moved out of my parents' and I've been able to add to my savings.

She grows serious, tossing the towels in a bin. "Is everything okay?"

"It's fine. I just need to do something."

Regarding me for a moment, she sticks her hands in her back pockets. "Is it anything I can help with?"

I shake my head, risking a look behind me before telling her, "I wanted to look at some more apartments."

She rushes forward, asking, "What'd he do?"

"It's nothing like that. Marc's…fine." Or at least he was for our first couple nights as roommates.

Sometime after that though, it seemed to have changed. Marc seems to have changed. He's been seen alright, but not heard.

It reminds me of Shawn and how he used to come on really strong to lower my guard, then return to his usual self, treating me like shit when I no longer had my barriers in place.

While Marc hasn't treated me like shit—not even once—the indifference is eating away at me, more than I'd like to admit.

I can't figure out why either. He hasn't laid any guilt trips for me to walk into blindly. He hasn't asked for any favors that benefit only him. He hasn't done or said *anything* to me. Which somehow hurts just as much. Maybe worse?

Also, this is the first weekend in a while since Shawn's actually taking Hunter, so he won't be with us to break up some of the otherwise strained silence. I never thought silence could be so loud until I moved in with Marc. He's as beautiful as a statue but as silent as one, too. He's downright impenetrable, and the more time I spend around him, the more I find myself wanting to chip away at his obstinate veneer. Which is exactly the opposite of what I should be feeling right now, and if he was out of sight, he'd be out of mind entirely.

Another lie.

I just want my life to go back to normal, whatever that may be. The normal before Shawn but not the normal of living at Graham Dairy.

I need to find my new normal—make it if I have to—but that can't happen while living with Marc and obsessing about him.

Absently, I rub my upper arm, tugging on the long-sleeve waffle-knit shirt when I realize what I'm doing.

"Then what's wrong?" Angela asks, her hazel eyes full of genuine concern.

"Damn, bro," Beckett booms across the garage, talking to Marc who's just coming out from under the hood of a Chevelle.

"I just think it'd be better if I lived on my own."

"Where's little miss Lee-Lee?"

Tuning out Beckett's obnoxious voice and nickname—*are they talking about me?*—she takes a deep breath and says, "Of course. Anything you need. But I'm sure whatever it is, he'd fix it if he could. These boys don't back down easily."

"We don't back down at all," Marc says over my shoulder, making me jump. To me he asks, "What needs fixed? Is it your Cummins?"

"Is it just me or did that sound dirty?"

Angela, Marc, and I all say at once, "It's you," to Beckett and his head jerks back like whiplash with his arms going all different directions.

Marc ignores his friend's theatrics to study me, asking seriously, "Is something wrong?"

Angela pipes in though, announcing, "Bentlee and I are pulling a sick day tomorrow."

Beckett stops to sputter, "What now? You haven't taken a day off since we opened the doors at Pop One. What's the emergency and who are we burying?" He punctuates his point by cracking his knuckles loudly, reminding me of Tysen's habit.

Casting a quick glance in my direction, Angela says a little too nonchalantly, "We're going shopping," and Beckett mumbles, "There's the emergency."

"Bullshit." Marc's low tone has me fighting a shiver. "You don't shop."

"That's why Bentlee's going with me. Duh." She waves a hand at my outfit. "I need better style."

Marc and Beckett exchange identical looks, then Beckett pulls out his phone, unlocking it and pressing a button. "What you need is a better alibi, girl. I thought we taught you better than that, but damn, this got ugly real quick."

"What are you doing?"

"I'm calling Coty to tell him his girl's cheating."

"Don't do that!" she screeches, smacking his phone out of his hand and watching wordlessly as it sails through the air before plopping into a bucket of water. "I'm not cheating on Coty."

"You're suspect as fuck right now, Angie," he accuses, pointing at her face, not even bothered that his phone is currently sinking in a foot of water. "We should take her temperature," he says to Marc.

I finally speak up, saying, "I'm taking tomorrow off." This is ridiculous. Beckett is ridiculous. Her *temperature*? Really?

Marc's response is immediate. "Why?"

"To find an apartment."

"For what?" Beckett asks while Angela and Marc both fall into their own versions of silence.

"To live in," I sigh, sneaking a peek at my roommate. His charcoal eyes harden and his nostrils flare as he meets my gaze head-on.

"Oh, fuck. Lee-Lee, you did it now."

"Sorry, girl. I tried." Angela tugs on Beckett's arm after retrieving his phone from the bucket, telling him she's got a bag of rice in her office to put it in.

They leave us alone and I watch the spot where they disappeared, wishing I was anywhere but here.

"Did I do something to upset you?"

I shake my head, unable to speak.

"Did somebody else do something to upset you?"

Another headshake, this one more adamant.

"Then what happened? What changed?"

"Nothing changed. I appreciate everything you've done for us but…"

"But what? The truth, Bentlee."

The truth. I cannot admit the truth to him. I cannot even admit it to myself. It doesn't make any fucking sense. I'm the one that said I couldn't give him anything else. I'm the one that set the same confines that are restricting my own throat.

The papers in my hand crinkle by my hip. "You told me you'd be gone a lot."

Marc's lips twitch. "You're mad I'm not?"

"I'm not mad."

"But you don't want me around?"

"I-" I do. I so do. But I want *him* around and he's not giving that to me. The very fact that I wish he would is why I need to move out. "I just think it's better this way," I say, pasting a fake smile on my face and heading for my office without further explanation.

With hands that feel swollen and achy, I lock my door as soon as I reach it and slump against it. He asked for the truth but whatever I just told him couldn't beat a polygraph while wearing a thick layer of antiperspirant. *The truth?* I don't even know what that is anymore.

The next morning, I wake up to the smell of food being cooked. There's a distinct sweet smell with a hint of smokiness.

What is that?

With my robe around my back, I'm pulling my arms through when I enter the kitchen, halting altogether when I find the source.

"Am I interrupting?" I ask Marc, tearing my eyes away from his plain white tee and sleep pants that outline his ass nicely. This is the first time I've even considered what it might look like if Marc… entertains.

Oh, God. What do I do?

His back shakes with an easy chuckle but he doesn't bother stopping whatever he's doing as he asks, "You don't remember?"

Oh, God. What *did* I do?

Did my sleep talking start back up?

After meeting Shawn last night to hand off Hunter, I spent way too many hours scrolling through my phone while lying in bed, then fell asleep. I wasn't necessarily hiding from Marc but having a break from seeing him for a few hours was nice.

More lies.

Holding up a waffle, he finally faces me, saying, "Buttermilk. With chocolate chips."

The meal we talked about in the cabin.

"And omelets?" I ask a little too hopeful.

He points to a platter full of fluffy eggs in perfect semicircles, then shrugs, returning to the waffle machine in front of him. *We have a waffle machine?*

I cast another glance around. "Are you expecting someone?"

Halting all movement, he stares over at me, saying, "No. Are you?"

"I have bedhead, morning breath, and a hole in my crotch." His eyes drop to my sleep shorts instantly and I smirk, moving behind the breakfast bar. "So, no. No company for me."

"Perfect," he says, lifting his gaze to mine, then he gestures to the back balcony. "If we eat outside, maybe I won't be able to smell your morning breath."

He grins when I chuckle.

"And the other issues?" I ask, resting my elbows on the counter to stare at him. Let's be honest, a little fresh air definitely won't help the situation on my head and it'll probably only make the hole in my sleep shorts that much more noticeable.

Mirroring me from the other side of the counter, Marc leans in and I do the same without meaning to.

"I don't scare easily, mama."

My heart does a somersault in my chest and I straighten, causing it to land on its butt instead of its feet. *So out of shape.* Not that I was ever great at flirting but this might be my all-time low.

Is this flirting?

"I'll bring everything outside," he tells me with his own chuckle, turning his back to me.

The apartment has two balconies. One facing the parking lot in the front and one overlooking the pool area that sits in the middle of the apartment complex. Beyond that is a random high school. A little fun fact I wasn't aware of until moving in is the anxiety-inducing bells continue to ring even during the weekends and I'm guessing the holidays, too.

When Marc finds me sitting at the round patio table a few minutes later, I jump from my seat to get the slider but he turns down any other help from me, putting the plates down by himself before going back in for the rest.

With a knee bent, I keep one foot on my chair while tucking the other underneath me to watch him. It's colder than I anticipated. It is the beginning of October but it's been pretty mild so far.

"Is it too late to get breakfast in bed?" I joke when he reappears.

"Which bed?" Marc asks and I drop my forehead to my knee, hiding my smile. "I'm just kidding. I'll be right back."

He's only gone a moment, then he returns with my faux-fur boots and a thick throw blanket I've seen next to the couch. Dropping the boots beside me, he places the blanket around my robe-covered shoulders.

I rotate my head so my cheek is on my knee again and thank him. He nods it off, taking his own seat across from me.

"Aren't you gonna eat?"

Still leaning on my knee, I tell him I will, then gaze out at the courtyard, afraid if I move, or blink, or breathe, this moment will end.

But that's what I should want, right?

And yet, I don't. Not in the slightest. In fact, I wish this was my life. Always. A man—a sexy, confident man—making me breakfast, keeping me warm, all without me having to even ask. All without any strings attached—the kind a puppeteer uses on its ignorant puppet.

Too bad that's not real life though. Definitely not one I've ever seen.

I remain in the same position a little longer, taking in the view of the other apartments and pool area.

Wind sweeps past the alcove, its fingers sending tiny chilly tendrils along my neck and onto my scalp, causing me to shiver in a pleasant way.

"Are you still cold?"

I cover another smile.

"No." Then when I see a woman walking over to fix a sign on the pool's gate, I lift my head to ask, "Who's that?"

Marc's staring at her, too, his hold around his fork twisting tighter.

Just when I assume he's not going to answer, he says, "Kary," and it's like he's working to keep his voice level.

I try to get a better look at her but end up only catching the side of her face before she walks quickly away. The little bit I could see I thought looked familiar but now I'm not sure. She definitely isn't much older than us. Maybe even around my age.

And she manages this place?

"Her name's Kary?"

The air around us seems to freeze and I do shiver, this time in an entirely different way.

"Yeah. Why?" His voice turns harsh, his restraint from a moment ago gone.

Maybe she has a sister or cousin. Sydnee and I used to get confused for each other all the time when we were younger.

I shrug, picking up my own fork to pierce a grape. "Isn't the guy down the hall named Gary?"

Pausing, he finally jerks a stiff nod, and I joke, "Don't tell me there's a Larry and Mary around here, too."

Luckily, it does the trick and Marc visibly relaxes.

What can only be described as a bitter pile of mush fills my mouth and I contemplate plugging my nose just to get the grape down.

"What?" he asks suddenly and I gulp down some water instead, clearing my mouth of the taste.

"What?"

"You made a face." *I did?* "I thought you liked grapes."

"I do, it's just I prefer them cold. Like frozen, if possible." And how'd he even know that?

"For real?" He eyes me suspiciously and I laugh.

"They're better like that, I swear." I don't like mushy grapes. They're the worst. Cold and crisp is the only way to go.

"In jam is the best."

I practically gag making him grin before taking a drink of the coffee I bet Angela made for him somehow. She keeps the guys at the shop stocked, especially her main trio.

A bell at the school goes off at the same time he asks, "What's your plan today?" like he doesn't even notice it.

"Don't you have to get to work?" He should've already left by now. Homeroom just started but first period's quickly approaching.

I should probably look into buying myself an actual clock when I move from Creekwood. It's clear I've become dependent.

"Didn't plan on it."

Our eyes collide like magnets. I have the day off...and he has the day off.

His grip on the mug tightens, then he swings his gaze over to the school building, saying, "I thought I'd do some shopping," he squints one of his eyes at the flagpole, "for apartments."

"Oh." With me? "Um. No, thank you?" That's fifty shades of awkward and one shade of absolutely not.

He swings his gaze to mine and I'm sure many, many people have tripped over themselves at this kind of thing—Marc giving them his best *I'm serious* look—but I'm sitting down, so it has no effect on me. He sure is cute when he's all smoldery though.

"I don't need any help. I can do it myself."

"Never said you couldn't. But if you won't let me come with, can you at least tell me which places you're planning on looking at today?"

I'm listing off the third one when I realize my mistake. I gasp dramatically, saying, "You wouldn't."

Marc's sexy mouth curls into a wicked smile and he says, "I would."

"When Angela said you didn't give up easily, I didn't know she meant stalking."

He holds his hands up, dropping his fork to the plate with a clang.

"Hey, I'm just a concerned roommate who wants to make sure his employee and her son aren't moving into some shithole, especially because she has a really bad habit of not locking her doors."

"I think you just described the plot to a romance novel."

His chest shakes with laughter and I can't help but laugh, too.

"Are you sure? There's a lot to check out." I give it one last half-hearted try. I could use someone else's opinion.

And aside from yesterday when I actually did lock my office, the door thing is true. I think because Shawn kept everything locked up all the time, I rebel against the very notion of locks now. Plus, I've had to pick so many, I know how false the sense of security locks provide actually is. They give you momentary peace of mind but not long-term safety. If someone wants in bad enough, they'll get in.

Marc's right though. I should start locking my doors anyway.

"I got nowhere else to be today," he tells me, sitting back in his seat. "Consider me yours."

Are locks on emotional doors just as faulty because today seems like a good day to find out.

"But, Bentlee?"

"Yeah," I say, tugging my boots on my feet and looking into Marc's suddenly serious face.

"Think you can put some underwear on before we go?"

My thighs squeeze together tightly, remembering the hole in my shorts, and I press my lips into a flat line.

Talk about a false sense of security. Marc can probably shed panties like I pick locks—without effort.

"I can." *Doesn't mean I will.*

Chapter 17

Bentlee

"**N**o."

"What do you mean? It's nice."

Marc gives me a flat look, starting the engine of his BMW. "Put your seat belt on." He waits until I do, then backing out, he says, "The tenants are on a first-name basis with the roach control dude. His van has its own reserved parking spot." He slows down next to it on our way out, emphasizing his point.

"Maybe they're just being proactive," I say in vain even though I can't lie. It was gross. We had to dust off our clothing before getting back in Marc's car.

"It's a no."

"You said that about the last five we looked at."

"For good reasons."

Good reasons. According to Marc, one wasn't up to "code." I'm not sure which code or how exactly he knew that because all he said was "shit's not up to code" and went right back to his car. Another had a sleazy maintenance man that even I found alarming. There was an unidentifiable smell coming from the vents in another that Marc just *knew* meant something bad. Oh, and my personal favorite—the water pressure sucked.

I lean my head back on the headrest. I know he doesn't want me and Hunter living in a "shithole," but water pressure? Really?

"I've got three more to go still."

Not missing a beat, he says, "Tell me where I'm going," and for the rest of the afternoon we continue with similar results. Marc finds something—anything—wrong with each and every one, and by the time we pull away from the last apartment complex, I don't know if I'm more exhausted or entertained from the entire experience. Eight places to tour, eight places to watch Marc rip to shreds using some list of impossible standards he refuses to share out loud. Just critiques. Lots and lots of critiques about how they're not good enough for me and Hunter.

"I gotta make a stop. Is that okay?"

He glances at me and I pretend to think about it. "Will you feed me?"

We had a quick lunch between tours but that was hours ago. I was prepared to pay since Marc made breakfast and drove all day, but he beat me to the register and paid for both meals before I could even get my wallet out. Honestly, it was hot. Marc is hot.

His lips spread. "Of course."

So hot.

I'd never admit it to him but even the way he dismissed all the apartments was hot, too. Like he thinks I deserve better, maybe even the best. It doesn't help my living situation but it was hot nonetheless.

"What's the meaning behind your tattoos?" I ask, tracing his flame half-sleeves with my eyes.

"A truth for a truth?"

Shit. I didn't think about that. But maybe he'll want a different truth.

"What do you want to know?"

"What does your tattoo mean?"

No.

I try to wipe the sweat from my palms onto my thighs before giving up to grab my purse off the floor. What's that acronym again? KISS. Keep It Simple, Stupid-ass-who-asks-too-many-questions-for-her-own-good. I'm pretty sure that's how it goes.

Gaze fixed on my purse while I hunt for…gum, I mumble, "It's a reminder."

Easy peasy.

"A reminder for what?"

Or not.

I abandon my *search*, exhaling loudly. "That there's more. That there can be more."

He frowns but keeps his eyes on the road and I ask about his, hoping he takes the bait.

His thumb and pinky tap the top of the steering wheel as he re-adjusts in his seat. "You know how this state gets a ton of wildfires?" I nod. Wildfires have always been a problem in Washington but each year it only seems to get worse. "Even when a wildfire's contained, it can still burn from the inside, waiting patiently for its moment to grow bigger than anyone could've ever expected."

Something deep within me tugs, drawing me to him, to his confident words. I have no doubt he'll live up to his inked prophecy. Marc will surpass us all. He's just quiet about his upsurge.

Noticing a little too late that we're on the same road that leads to his friends' houses, I open my mouth to say something but then we pass them and Marc doesn't acknowledge it, so I remain quiet, waiting to see where he's taking me.

With the houses gone from sight, Marc eventually turns onto a dirt path, silently putting the car in Park before studying me.

Avoiding his penetrating stare, I inspect a large temporary carport next to a foundation for what looks like a house.

"Is this yours?" I ask, nodding out the windshield and noting his head do the same. "Will that be your house?" I don't know why but the inside of my mouth sours and I swallow multiple times, trying to rid the taste. It's like warm grape, but worse.

Not bothering with an answer, he pops his door open and climbs out.

After a moment's hesitation, I follow after, glad I wore my boots today. The toes on his bright white shoes kick up dirt but he doesn't seem to mind as he strolls over to the opening of the carport. Next to an RV is a cargo trailer that's attached to a lifted Ram, all three the same color as his car and motorcycle and the last dirt bike I saw him on—a deep red. *His color.*

"This just stays out here?" There's nothing else around. One broken window, a couple of wires rubbed together, and this could all be gone.

Marc laughs darkly. "Nobody's touching my shit."

"How do they know it's yours?" There's no identifying marks or signs on anything. If I didn't recognize the color, I wouldn't have known it was his. Is all of this even his? And why? What does he do with it?

Something he said about practicing out at his dad's comes to mind.

"They don't need to," he says, pointing up at the metal ceiling. Small, unassuming security cameras dot each corner. "Streaming to my phone twenty-four seven. Like I said, nobody's touching my shit."

"Ruby red," I murmur but he shakes his head, telling me, "Not ruby. Garnet."

Garnet red.

Taking in everything again, my eyes snag on the back door of the trailer.

Rider. He told me he got into a fight with another rider before.

"I'm gone a lot." Marc's words catch me off guard and I pry my eyes away to look at him. "And I don't always share where. Or why."

"Do you race?" I blurt, my heart dusting off an old pair of running shoes to suit up. "Is that where you went?"

Slowly pivoting, he produces a key to unlock both padlocks securing the hasps.

My heart hustles into a crooked little wog—a walk-jog—trying to keep pace with the rest of me as I automatically step closer, helping Marc lower the ramp.

Is it inside? I've never seen his dirt bike this close before.

We lay the heavy metal onto the ground, sending the familiar scent of stale dirt along with the tang of gas into the air, then I see it—Marc's dirt bike—except it's not the one from long ago and there's two.

I shoot to the tips of my toes.

Three.

Maybe four? It looks like there's another one in front of the three main ones but maybe a different size. I can't tell with all the handlebars and number plates blocking the way.

"You race motocross, don't you?" I say, breathless, my heart gaining speed. After all this time, it is still possible. All of it. He's still burning just as bright as he did before. Maybe more. "That's where you disappear to?"

With an arm propped on the side wall as he leans inside the trailer, he says, "Sometimes," and my heart stutters to a stop.

He drops his arm, standing up straight. "I'm not doing anything that'd put you or Hunter in danger, I swear. You just have to trust me."

"I don't."

"You don't trust me?"

"I don't have to trust you. We're not," I wave a hand spastically between us, "anything that requires trust."

He scoffs. "We're roommates. That sure as fuck requires a certain amount of trust."

"Not for long," I say, making him frown even deeper. There are levels to Marc's frowns, about seven that I've counted so far, like a seven-layer cake but without frosting. Just dry, frustrating crumbs. Seven layers of irritation and every single one is more attractive than the next.

Why are Marc's frowns better than any other man's smiles?

We're both quiet for a while, his jaw flexing every so often, then he says quietly, "Don't go. Don't move out."

"Why? I thought you didn't even like us there."

"What made you think that?"

"You stopped talking to me!" I throw my hands up. Did I just imagine the last two weeks? Sometimes silence is the loudest sound there is and Marc's is fucking deafening. I *hate* it. I didn't even realize how much until today, talking with him, laughing with him. Finally getting to witness him let down his guard today, I don't know if I'll be able to handle him putting it back up tomorrow.

"I know. But, it's easier like that."

I shake my head, growing more irritated with myself by the second. I want him like this all the time. I like it. I like him.

"Right? You said we can't push this any further," he accuses, his voice rising higher than I've ever heard it.

Instead of flinching though, I take a step in his direction, my chest heaving with the power I feel more of when I'm in his presence.

He matches my step with one of his own, the hands at his sides shaking, reminding me of the last time I got him to lose his mind.

"And for good reasons," I throw his words right back at him, hoping they stick better than they did when he used them. Bullshit is bullshit no matter who flings it.

His eyes flash as he snarls, "Oh yeah?"

"Yeah."

One of those hands grasps the belt loop at my hip, dragging me the rest of the way to him.

"Tell me one."

I wet my lips, buying time.

"I can't."

"You can't tell me or you can't think of one?"

"Both," I whisper.

His hold on me tightens—everywhere—and he drops his voice to match mine. "I like you living with me. I like you being there every day. Every night. I like your smell." Eyes glued to my wet lips, he inhales softly. "Peppermint and…"

"Tea tree oil."

"What the fuck is that?" He cracks a smile, raising his eyes to mine.

"It's in my shampoo."

His other hand comes up to finger a curl. "Don't leave." The plea comes out as jagged as I feel—hard edges with no hope of being smoothed over anytime soon.

"I have to." I need to.

He releases the curl, dropping his hand to my throat, his thumb rubbing back and forth along my racing pulse.

"What can I do to fix this?"

At first, I don't say anything, and without removing either hand, Marc tries to push me away, thinking he's overstepped. It's only inches but feels like heartbeats. Broken heartbeats, the kind that don't heal with something as simple as time and definitely not with distance.

My body physically reacts before my mouth even can—before my brain even has a chance to—by pushing back into his space and he welcomes me back, bringing me in with both hands, his fingers curling possessively around my neck and hip as his breath feathers my face.

"*Tell* me." He needs to tell me what's wrong. Why he's stopped talking to me after showing me what I thought was the real Marc.

"I want to touch you. Kiss you. I see you playing with your son, and I see you at home in the kitchen and on the couch and all I want to do is wrap my body around yours. You said we can't and I've been trying to respect that but the only way I could was to avoid you completely."

I bark out a laugh. "I've been working that angle since we met."

"Why?"

"Because I want to touch you, too. Kiss you, too. I see you any-where, everywhere, and all I want to do is wrap my body around yours, too."

His hand slides to the back of my neck, then yanks me forward to close the gap, our mouths hovering against each other's with equal amounts of compressed need. We've been holding back for days. For weeks. Longer.

So much longer.

"Now *show* me."

Marc smirks cockily and leans in to capture my lips but I twist my head over my shoulder, regarding the dirt bikes filling his trailer.

His gaze follows mine, asking, "You want to see me race? That might be a problem."

"You brought me out here for a reason."

"My own family doesn't even know I race." He slides his eyes back to me. "I'm practically ripping myself open right now."

"I don't need to see you race. I just want to see you ride." Again. I want to see if it's still the same now as it was back then—the feeling. The one I had tattooed on my body to serve as a constant reminder. The one I need reminded of now more than ever. "Just...be you. For me."

"You'll stay?"

I disentangle myself from his hold, telling him, "I didn't say that."

Running his hands over his short hair, he grips the back of his neck roughly. With our toes still lined up and our pounding hearts calling to each other's, I reach up to press a quick kiss to his lips.

An impatient growl rips from his throat as he leans in for more but I pull back, saying, "Show me what's inside your chest and we can talk after."

I hear him say "fucking shit" on my way past but I don't stop to look back. I can't. Here I thought I was making Marc lose his mind but I forgot to keep ahold of mine all along.

What am I doing?

What I want to do. What I've always wanted to do.

Chapter 78

Bentlee

S TOPPING IN THE MIDDLE OF A LARGE FLAT PORTION OF the field for a better vantage point, I take a deep breath, spinning in a circle. There's nothing else around, just me and Marc and countless bare acres—exactly like it used to be. Not even his friends' houses are visible from here. Why *is* his house being built this far out from theirs? I thought they had plans to raise their families close to each other's.

My mouth sours all over again, this time refusing to go down with a few mere swallows, and I have to spit a bunch out.

The sound of the dirt bike starting up sends shockwaves of déjà vu through my entire body down to my toes, and just like that, I'm a teenager again, anticipating my next glimpse of the cute boy next door, except this boy's now a sexy man with a door that's much closer and doesn't require a key—for me anyway.

Marc's fiery red dirt bike flies past, sending my hair sideways and I audibly gasp, my arms hugging my ribs to keep myself from going to him.

I'm in so much trouble.

But I like trouble—Marc's kind of trouble in particular—and I end up taking a step in his direction without consciously making the decision. I'm *drawn* to him. Now more than ever before. And in ways I can't even explain because I've never had to. If we keep on this path, I will though. It will all come out, everything, and I'll need to answer what I never thought to question because I didn't care. Marc gave me something to look forward to—a possibility.

Up until that point in my short, inexperienced life, I'd never seen anyone look so happy, so free, so unapologetically themselves. And now I see the exact same thing, but so much more. I see Marc for Marc, not just a possibility. Marc's heart is full, fuller than I could've ever predicted from across a deserted meadow, and now that I've seen it up close, I can't pretend otherwise.

I tried avoiding him.

He tried avoiding me.

It didn't work.

Maybe I'm not the only one being drawn in. Maybe he was drawn to that same meadow without even knowing why.

Back then, I needed him, what he represented. Today, I want him, *all* of him. Or at least the parts I can have in private, without the outside world demanding those same questions.

Charging up a steep incline behind me, I twirl to watch him, my mouth falling open as my feet continue to pull me toward him automatically. He's still fearless and I'm still in awe. He's still magnificent and I'm still just me, watching on like an invisible spectator.

All my life people have tried to make me feel like that's all I was good for. Except Marc. Whether knowingly or not, he's always made me feel like something. Like someone. And not just when we had sex. It's in the way he puts his hand on my back when we're crossing a parking lot, ready to pull me out of harm's way. It's in the way he makes sure I'm buckled before moving his car. It's in the way he bought and assembled beds for me and Hunter without even knowing if we had any to begin with. It's in the way he refuses to let us live in a place with something as inconsequential as weak water pressure.

But I'm done feeling invisible. And I'm done being a spectator. I'm ready to be an active participant. In my own life. In it all.

He coasts back down the hill, a trail of dense dust left in his wake like a cape for the unintentional superhero.

Doing donuts, he spins steadily around me, giving a wide berth, and I can just feel his stare behind that helmet of his. When he finally comes to a stop and beckons me over, I'm already walking for him, my heart going fifty in a school zone.

I try to get on behind him but he scoots back, telling me, "Your turn."

With a nervous laugh, I get on in front of him, and once I'm seated, he places his helmet over my head.

"Don't you need it?"

"Don't worry about me."

"Someone has to," I mumble, feeling him tense momentarily behind me before going over all the basics of how to operate the dirt bike. From far away, it looks really simple, but up close, it's scary. Marc races this machine against other riders and…wins?

"How many races have you won?" I ask in the middle of his instructions.

"Enough," he says, pointing out something important but my mind gets stuck and I interrupt again to ask, "Enough to what?"

Marc's forehead drops to my back and turns from side to side before he lifts it to say, "To learn a few things."

Recognizing the same words I told him in the river, I gaze out at the landscape before us, shaking my own head. "We're quite the pair." Not only are we both watchers, we're also omitters. We omit. It's like lying but less punishable because it's not *technically* lying. Some things are better off buried and omissions make for great temporary top soil but why's he trying to conceal his winning streak? Or racing at all? He should be proud. I would be. I am. I'm proud of Marc.

His hands cover mine on the handlebars, his front pressed to my back and I can feel his heart. It's just like mine, but faster, of course.

"You know I could just look it up, right?" Now that I know what I'm looking for, I could easily search Marc's racing career on the internet.

He tenses again.

"You said you wanted to see what's inside my chest. You won't find wins there, not those kinds anyway. I don't hold on to competition wins, not like that. I hold on to…other things. More important things."

"Like what?" That's what he's supposed to be doing, *showing* me.

One of his hands drops to my stomach, pulling me into him more. "Like this." My heart pulls up short. *I'm in his chest?* "Now I'll kick the starter for you with my right leg but remember all the gears will be with *your* left leg."

The bike starts right up for Marc, warm and eager to move for him, and for the first time in my life, I can say I wholly identify with a dirt bike.

After I shift into first gear just like he explained, he says, "Alright, she's in first. Slowly release the clutch and *slowly* give it gas. I'll tell you when to shift again."

I do as instructed, sucking in a breath when the front tire rises off the ground several inches. Instead of chastising me, Marc just laughs and tightens his hold on my waist, not in a reprimanding way either. Far from it actually.

We level out and soon I grow more comfortable, making the ride less jerky but just as nerve-wracking. Continuously gulping, I strain to focus on the precious balance between clutch and gas while hovering a finger over the brake as well, but Marc's grip, both protective *and* possessive, is distracting as is his crotch against my ass. He's distracting, in the best and worst of ways.

We ride around, exploring a small fraction of his four hundred acres, and surprisingly, it's even better than watching Marc do the same. It's *the* feeling but amped up several notches. I love it. I love the way it makes me feel, the way Marc—so patient, so caring—is content in letting me take over. No, not just letting me, encouraging me.

Marc's supportive, not so much vocally, but emotionally, physically. He lets me lead when I try but isn't afraid to take charge when needed either. I wish we could've been like this from the beginning—not the beginning that I know of, but the one he does.

With Marc, I get to be bold. Daring. Just like him. I get to be… me. More me than I've ever felt.

Coming to an abrupt stop, the engine cuts off with neither of us rushing to say anything as we sit atop the garnet red bike in charged silence. I don't know who moves first but all at once the helmet is off my head and tossed to the ground next to Marc's shirt with mine following soon after.

Without getting off the bike, he pushes to standing and I do the same, twisting so I can see him.

Marcos Vega, in nothing more than riding pants and boots—*when did he change into those?*—staring at me like he's about to eat me whole, rasps, "Lose the pants," and if I had any underwear on, they'd be toast.

With his flexed pecs and eight-pack on full display, it's hard to concentrate but then that delicious V disappearing beneath the waist of his pants catches my eye and my attention falls to where it leads.

I swallow thickly before trying to dismount but Marc catches me, shaking his head.

On a dirt bike? Is he serious?

"But I can't-"

"Just pull them down over your ass, I'll do the rest."

A couple hip wiggles later and Marc hisses through his teeth when he sees my pants strangling my thighs—with not one hint of underwear to be found.

I suck my bottom lip into my mouth to keep from smiling, then release it on a moan when Marc's palm glides down my spine, over my cheek, and settles between my thighs, cupping my pussy from behind.

"Is this the part where we talk?"

Marc's chest rumbles against my back, one of his dark arms wrapped tightly around my light middle, keeping me in place as he gathers my wetness with his other hand, rubbing circles over my lips.

"I'm listening," he tells me, slipping his middle finger in while his palm rubs rough circles on the entrance to my ass.

"You, uh," I rock against his hand shamelessly, "didn't like any of the places we saw today?"

"I don't like *anywhere* that isn't Creekwood."

"So another unit there would be okay?" I choke out, feeling the ache in my core intensify greedily.

All movement halts for a moment, then he stiffly shakes his head—thankfully. I don't want to be anywhere but next to him. I don't know for how long but the thought of stopping this hurts. Deep. An overdose of Marc sounds a thousand times better than never getting another taste at all.

My veins aren't even fully prepped yet and I'm already addicted.

I tense at the idea and Marc releases my middle, shoving another finger inside my opening as he bends me forward, over the handlebars, putting me on full display.

"I want you at my house. In my bed. Under my sheets. Nowhere fucking else." He groans on a thrust before asking, "Got it?"

"I'm…" Legs shaking, I squeeze my eyes shut, breathing out, "About to come." Already. I'd be embarrassed if I could focus on anything other than the feeling between my legs.

I back up into him, capturing his wrist between us and making his thrusts that much harder.

His free hand covers my mouth, and I suck his thumb between my lips, moaning around the digit as I come apart on his other hand, everything blurring to a rosy shade of reality.

Marc's forehead rests between my shoulder blades as his breaths come out as shaky as mine feel and I bite the tip of his thumb.

"Goddamn it, Bentlee. You almost made me lose my shit and I'm not even done with you yet."

He slowly removes both hands to undo his own pants while I suppress a grin.

"You watched me." My backbone stiffens and I push onto my elbows, giving him a look over my shoulder as he pulls his riding pants over his solid erection. "Now I want to watch you…" *What?* "…come…"

"You just did."

"…all over my cock."

Oh.

"But I don't have a condom on me."

Oh.

He eyes me with something unreadable and I half laugh, saying, "That's fine."

"Fine? If it's not a fuck yes, it's a fuck no. You need to tell me."

The ache in my core I could've sworn he just satisfied pulses hard and demanding. I need him inside me again.

"Fuck," I say quietly and he starts to tug at his pants, misunderstanding. "Yes," falls from my lips on a whisper, stopping his hands with one of mine.

With eyes flaring as bright as an actual wildfire, he yanks me to him, saying, "After I get you there, I can just pull out."

I shake my head, facing forward again and placing my hands on the inner part of the handlebars. "I'm on birth control." The pull-out method robs me of one of the best parts and I don't want to miss the feeling of Marc losing control inside me without any barriers hindering the sensation. "It's still a fuck yes," I tell him, chasing away any last doubt.

Feeling his mouth on my back, kissing and blowing, he tangles one hand in the back of my hair, then tilts my head to the side, snatching my lips up with his in a kiss I can feel in the rest of my body.

His hard length pokes between my thighs, teasing my sensitive seam as he breaks the kiss to lean back and spit. Actually spit?

Um, what?

I cast a look behind me, watching as he strokes himself with his spit and my pussy walls clench in anticipation. Catching my eye, he smirks, then yanks my hips to him, lining himself up with my aching entrance. With one quick thrust he's inside and my arms give out just enough for me to fall onto my elbows.

"Oh my God."

My legs quake beneath me, threatening to give out and we haven't even started moving.

"Christ," he grinds out, pulling back just enough to slam back into my pussy, filling me completely. "You're so goddamn tight."

His hand glides along my back up to where my shoulder and neck meet, grasping on for leverage as he repeats the move. It's slow, calculated, and I know he's holding back. *Always holding back.*

My back arches down with my ass sticking out and I back up into him, meeting his thrusts with my own.

"Fuck," he groans. "I can't promise to be a perfect roommate, but I still wanna try."

I hesitate for a split second, looking out in front of me before slamming backward into him again and closing my eyes on a lung-robbing gasp.

"So do I."

Marc holds me firmly to him one-handed, circling his hips with his cock buried deep inside me. "You're staying?"

Unable to form any real words, I bite on to one of his knuckles at my shoulder to keep from screaming and jerk a quick nod.

"Say it," he growls, circling even harder and this time I do let out a scream.

"Yes. I'm staying."

Without me holding his hand hostage, he drops it to rub my clit and I warn, "Marc," in a high-pitched tone, knowing I won't survive if he keeps this pace. I'll fucking explode. All over him. While he watches.

Just like he wanted.

"Marc!" I scream out, my head thrown back as he leans his torso away just enough to do exactly what he said he would.

"Fuuuck, you're fucking drippin.'"

He pounds into me unchecked, and screams like I've never heard before rip from my throat. With only a couple more jerky thrusts, Marc curses and collapses against my back, his cheek resting on my shoulder blade as I begin my return to earth a little bit more reluctantly.

After a few minutes, he straightens, taking me with him.

"Let's get you fed."

Food? That's what he's concerned with? I'm floating—zero gravity, zero appetite, zero thoughts about what's next—but that's how Marc is. He worries about everyone else, all the time, and not for the first time I wonder who does the same for him.

We disentangle ourselves and I wince, thinking about the mess running down my thighs but Marc hops off the bike and quickly scoops up his discarded shirt before his pants are even fastened all the way. Turning it inside out, he presses it between my thighs, checking the rest of me over for any marks with gentle fingers and kind eyes.

Little does he know, the marks he leaves behind aren't visible. They're internal and they're permanent, more permanent than the ones I've ever left him.

Chapter 79

Marc

I SNEAK IN AN ASS SQUEEZE ON MY WAY PAST, CHUCKLING when Bentlee shoots me a nasty look. *He didn't see.* Hunter's in his room watching the week's most viral videos featuring farm animals. It's an entire montage, and after the first seventeen minutes of trying to watch it with him, I gave up. I already sat through four episodes of some baking competition for kids earlier today with Rebel.

I got something I need to do anyway.

"I'll be out front," I say, still grinning.

We've been sneaking around for a couple weeks now and her worried expressions when she thinks we might get caught never get old. I can behave, I just choose not to…the second we're alone. Anytime someone else is around though, I keep my hands, mouth, and dick to myself. But when it's just us, all bets are off. I've even started sexting Bentlee, telling her all the shit I want to do to her, in explicit detail, just to get through the day. That, by far, is the most amusing because by the time I do get my hands on her, she's already halfway there herself with need.

Working regularly at Pop Two has its advantages, like being able to take my lunch break when Bentlee takes hers. Or putting that lock on her office door to use—a lot—and I can honestly say I don't miss working out at my dad's.

Since I skipped out on work today to be with Rebel while she's got an ear infection, I didn't get to do any of that with Bentlee, so I'm getting my fun in now.

Sometimes I find myself wishing we didn't have to keep this thing between us a secret though, especially times like today, when I'm meeting her ex.

She doesn't want to confuse Hunter by springing a boyfriend or whatever on him but I'm the one left feeling confused lately. We live under the same roof and we work together and we eat all of our meals together and we fuck whenever we can manage but we're not exactly dating, I guess. I don't know. It feels like we are to me. It feels like we're a lot more than dating to me.

Because I respect the hell out of the reasoning behind Bentlee's decision along with her determination to stand by it, I go along with it. I'd lose my shit if Kary was introducing guys left and right to Rebel. I'd lose my shit if she introduced *any* guy to Rebel.

I stride down the stairs to Bentlee's piece of shit that leaks like it came straight from a fucking aquarium. I prefer to work on it here since every time I try putting it on the lift at Pop Two, Tysen takes it as some sort of personal invitation to piss me the fuck off. Him continuing to butt in where Bentlee's concerned will be the death of him one day—soon, if he doesn't rein that shit in.

The slider to our front balcony opens just as I hit the bottom step and Bentlee pokes her head out, surveying the lot before looking down at me with wide eyes to ask, "What are you doing?"

I frown, gesturing to her Cummins. "Checking the oil. What are *you* doing?"

"Can you go to the store?"

"Right now?"

"Yeah."

"Why? What do you need?"

"Apple cider."

Coty and Angela invited Bentlee to join us for Friday family dinner and they want to try out some drink with cider and caramel vodka.

"We can pick some up on our way," I tell her, turning for the truck but then she rushes to say, "I need tampons," and I freeze in my tracks. Bentlee doesn't have periods because of the kind of birth control she's on. I know because we've talked about it many times, and since I haven't worn a condom with her since the first time we had sex, that'd mean she went off it and could possibly get pregnant.

Warmth starting in my chest spreads so fucking fast, heating the rest of my body faster than a first-place win.

Does she want to get pregnant? By me?

I turn slowly, glancing up at her.

"I can…but if it's an emergency, you can check under the sink in my bathroom for now. I got anything you might need in there."

Her already flushed face darkens.

"Why do you have feminine products in your bathroom?"

"Same reason why the kitchen's stocked with food and water," I tell her, a little confused by the turn in conversation. Is she off her birth control or not? Am I going to the store or not?

To add to the confusion, she slams the door without another word.

Okay…

How did this get turned around on me? And so damn fast?

Bentlee has it in her head that all men are terrified of anything even remotely feminine. Why the fuck would I care picking up some tampons? Or keeping them on hand? If a woman needs them, she needs them. I wouldn't deny her or anyone else a basic necessity, so why would I draw the line on an item just because I don't particularly need it myself? I blame her ex. I could see him thinking something like a woman's natural fucking cycle is an obligation for *us*. Like we're the ones being inconvenienced.

I blame him for everything actually. When I stub my toe, when I lose the remote, even when there's traffic, I mutter his stupid fucking name. *Shawnathon.* It already sounds like a curse all its own, so it fits most shitty situations. Plus, I hate the guy, basically on principle alone considering Bentlee refuses to tell me much about him…aside from the fact that he never went down on her, which honestly, is enough in my book.

I shake my head, going over to pop the hood on her truck. If she really needs something, she knows where to find me.

Gary said it best—I'm practically surrounded by women. It'd be fucked if I didn't keep that kind of shit on hand, so why did it seem like she got mad about it?

Then it hits me. All the *other* women she's probably assuming I keep it on hand for. But I always make sure my partners are good. Once, I was with a girl for a while who bled after every time we had sex, something about a surgical procedure that left the tissue in there sensitive. Of course, I'm gonna take care of that. I'm not about to leave anyone bleeding and embarrassed.

What the fuck do I look like? Shawnathon?

Maybe she's jealous.

Now that's an interesting twist I can get behind. That…among other things.

We're gonna need to talk after Shawn picks up Hunter, hopefully before we head out to Coty and Angela's.

Eyeing the entrance to Creekwood, I spit next to my foot. Bentlee's ex is supposed to be here any minute and this will be his first time even coming to the apartment. He always makes Bentlee meet him somewhere else, somewhere that benefits him, but today he agreed to come here and now I get to officially meet him. Get a good read on him.

A much smaller wad of spit lands next to mine and I turn to find Hunter standing directly behind me.

"Oh fu," I catch myself just in time and end with, "dge."

"Fudge?" The blue eyes behind his glasses squint even though I know his sight's significantly better since he started wearing them.

It was the best I could come up with on the spot. What the fuck?

"My dad says bad words in front of me, you know?"

"Your dad's a," I catch myself again, "not here." I'm not gonna talk shit on the kid's dad in front of him. That's pretty damn low. Now

Beck, Beck would talk shit on Shawnathon up one side and down the other without hesitation. To the guy's face though, like a fucking seal on a rock—showy, loud, and not giving a single fuck who hears. Me? I'm the shark. I don't make a single sound because I don't need to. I just attack when I've had enough. And by then, you'll know exactly how the fuck I feel without me ever needing to say a word.

"What are you doing right now? Wanna help me out 'til he comes?"

He shrugs, climbing onto the front rusty bumper. I wedge my knee under it and lean in, telling him what I'm doing as I do it. I never liked when people taught *at* me. Teach me what you're doing while you're doing it so I can see the problem, then consider all possible solutions in order to comprehend the end result for myself.

Every so often I notice him glance over my shoulder and I stop to ask, "Am I boring you or something?" I thought he liked getting dirty.

He shakes his head, doing it again.

"Then what's up, little man? You got a date I don't know about?"

His face blushes as red as my Ducati beside us. Damn, guy's got a crush.

"Is it a kid from school?" I don't know if he's into boys or girls and I don't want him feeling pressured to correct me if I get it wrong. I'm all ears either way but that's gotta be on his terms.

"I don't have friends at school."

I noticed. Not just from that day at the farmer's market either but from the general lack of playdates. When he's home with us, he's home with us. I try my best to keep him busy when I'm here but nothing beats a friend your own age.

Turning around, I lean against the grill and cross my arms over my chest. "My best friends didn't go to the same school I did."

"They didn't?"

"No. We met riding dirt bikes though. What do you like to do?"

"I like taking care of the animals at Grandma and Grandpa's."

He's selling himself short here. Hunter's that person. The one that believes any life, no matter how small, is priceless. Bentlee told me he asks her to stop anytime there's a dead animal on the side of the road, just in case they're still breathing, and if they're not—*they never are*—he cries.

I glance around the complex. No way could we get away with an animal here. We barely got by with Beck.

"Hey, if you could have an animal of your own, which one would you pick?"

His eyes drop. "Mom won't let me get one."

"Just tell me anyway."

"Goat," he mumbles.

"A goat? As a pet?" I thought maybe a dog. Guinea pig at absolute worst. A motherfucking goat?

He looks up at me, immediately telling me about a kind of goat that faints. They legit just stiffen up and fall over and he promises to show me videos of them doing exactly that when he gets back from his dad's.

"Fainting goats, huh?"

He nods.

"And you think that'd give you a way to make friends?" Pretty sure Bentlee said she was in a club for agriculture shit when she was younger. If not, it's a hell of a conversation starter.

I never joined anything like that—I don't do clubs.

"Well, there is one person I could play with." His eyes trail across the lot and this time I realize it's not out of the complex he's looking, it's just at another building.

"What's the name of your school again?" I ask, trying to keep my voice steady.

"Old Mill."

Old Mill? Never heard of it.

Because we're in the district, Rebel takes the bus to her school which is some dude's name, Howard something, but she calls it Howdy for short. Bentlee still takes Hunter to his school every day but her commute is nothing compared to what it was when she was out at Graham Dairy. I know Bentlee prefers to drive Hunter back and forth herself otherwise I'd offer to look into the district boundaries. It doesn't help that I don't even know where Old Mill is either.

"You've seen the little girl that lives here?" I ask on bated breath and he nods eagerly. "Alright, tell you what. When you get back from your dad's, maybe I can see about introducing you two." Rebel should be better by then. Going to school after being around next to no people, she's sick every other week, I swear.

"You *will?*" There's pure hope in his voice that makes me smile as I jut out my jaw, thinking this over.

It's time Rebel made a friend anyway. Her mom and I can't be it for her forever, even if that's exactly how Kary would prefer it. And what better place to make one than Creekwood? I can't see her objecting to that. Hunter literally wouldn't hurt a fly and could benefit from having someone close by too since his school's obviously a bust in the friend department. *Bunch of little shits.*

Speaking of shits, Shawn's Audi pulls in, parking across from us—diagonally, like a poser trying too hard—and I help Hunter down off the bumper, telling him to run up to get his mom. She packs a bag for him and likes to go over all the shit Shawn will end up ignoring anyway. He lives to get under her skin and I live to make her forget he even exists.

We are definitely not the same.

I wait until Shawn gets out, then walk up to him, saying, "What's up? I'm Marc." *The real man of the house. The guy that shows you up in every single category. Nice to meet you, fucker.*

After giving me a once-over that borders on patronizing, he sticks his hand out. "Shawnathon."

I don't take it. And that shit ain't bordering anything, it's patronizing as all fuck.

"Johnathon?"

Bentlee told me how uptight the guy is about his name.

"No, *Shawn*athon."

"So, just Shawn then."

"No, man, it's Shawnathon."

I let a moment stretch a little too tight between us before saying, "Got it."

"Do you?" he sneers and I narrow my eyes.

Trust me, motherfucker, I do. Earlier today I stepped in an oil spill and I annunciated each letter of his name clearly as I wiped the sludge off my brand new shoe. *Fucking Shawnathon.*

I don't bother with a response and he doesn't bother waiting for one as he looks around, blowing out a loud breath like he can't believe he has to wait thirty fucking seconds. No need to act high and mighty on my account though. That shit don't work here.

When Bentlee and Hunter first moved in, three weeks went by where Shawn didn't see his kid and not once in that time did he even try to call Hunter on the phone. Not once.

He's got shit brown eyes and shit brown hair that looks like it hasn't been washed in a while, and against my better judgement, I inhale through my nose. *Smells like shit, too.*

Sick of looking at him, sick of smelling him, sick of him in general, I take a step back, glancing into his backseat and notice the booster seat sitting crooked.

"Do you need help with that?" I ask, pointing through the window.

He barely spares a look back. "What are you the fire department?"

"Nah, but I could get 'em here to show you how to properly install a child seat." It's not that fucking hard. There's instructions *on* the fucking seat. How do you miss that?

Oh yeah, by being a piece of shit. Or a Shawnathon. Same face, same eyes, same hair, different name.

Seriously, I've known honeydews I liked better than this guy and I fucking hate honeydews. *Such a pathetic imposter of cantaloupe.*

Bentlee and I have *a lot* to talk about tonight, starting with her raging jealousy and ending with mine.

"Hey," Bentlee says then, sounding out of breath as she descends the stairs, and before Shawn can even respond, I open the back door to his sedan and get to work fixing Hunter's seat.

"What are you doing?" I hear him screech behind me. "What is he doing?"

"It looks like he's buckling Hunter's seat the correct way. Remember how I showed you?"

As I make the necessary adjustments, they continue talking in low tones that I keep one ear trained on in case he steps out of line. I don't give a fuck what he says to me or even how he says it, but if I hear him disrespect Bentlee or Hunter, that's a different story entirely. Then it's time to hunt.

Swim, motherfucker, swim.

When that's all taken care of, I have Hunter sit in it to adjust the back to fit his height. It's the kind that grows with the kid but Shawn sucks at paying attention to his kid at all, so it's no surprise the seat's a couple inches off.

"All good?" I ask Hunter, still leaning over the backseat to tug on the seat belt. A pamphlet on the floorboard catches my eye but I can't make out the exact wording as Hunter nods, thanking me. There's an infant on the front though, so I can guess what it's about. Has he really had it in here for fucking years? Shoved half under a seat, collecting dust? No wonder guy doesn't know anything about kids if he can't be bothered to read a general informational guide from the start.

"Who does he think he is? Bent?"

Bentlee just shakes her head, wrapping her arms around herself, almost like for…protection. But why? Doesn't she know I got her?

I keep my eyes focused on her but jerk a thumb at Shawn's car, telling him, "I know a place you could get this washed for a good price. Inside and out. Looks like it's been a while." A long while. Angela'd have her work cut out for her if he hasn't even vacuumed it in seven years—or longer—but she'd gladly do it if it meant Hunter wouldn't have to sit in filth.

"It's brand new."

I tear my gaze away from Bentlee to see Shawn rolling his eyes so hard I want to bitch-slap him but then I regard the car again. It's not fresh-out-the-showroom new but he's somewhat right, it is a newer model. A lot newer than what I was thinking originally.

Then what's with the pamphlet? Is he having a baby? Or planning to?

Bentlee hands him the backpack, murmuring, "Play nice," and I study her.

Shawn asks, "Can you show me how?" in a voice that belongs in a bedroom. Under sheets. Doing things. Things he might've done with Bentlee once upon a time but sure as fuck isn't doing with her anymore.

Right?

The hairs on the back of my neck rise and I have the urge to post up on him or tuck Bentlee away from the eyes currently trying to undress her. What. The. Fuck.

If Hunter wasn't watching, I'd have done both already.

He leans toward her and for a second I think he's going in for a kiss, then he straightens fast enough that I let him live.

I wait to see Bentlee respond with some of that fire she uses on me, but all she does is fold in on herself even more and cast an overstretched smile at Hunter, saying, "I love you. Have fun."

"We have more fun with you," Shawn says.

Motherfuck. Is he really hitting on my girl right in front of me? *Is she my girl?*

To me, she is. To Bentlee though? I don't know.

Closing Hunter's door after telling him my own goodbye, I look between Shawn and Bentlee who squirms in her spot, then say, "Didn't Bentlee tell you? She's taken." I wait a beat before adding, "Tonight." And every other night. I don't give a fuck.

Bentlee's arms drop by her sides and I have to bite the inside of my cheek to keep from smiling. *There's that fire.* It's weak but it's building and I can't wait to feel its full strength. She saves it for me, knowing I can take it.

Fucking bring it, mama.

Shawnathon could never handle Bentlee's heat—luckily. I may not know exactly what happened between them to cause their breakup but I don't have to. This motherfucker's to blame one way or another. I can feel it in my bones. And for whatever reason, Bentlee's covering for him by not telling the truth about his dumb ass.

That thought alone should piss me off more than anything, except I'm holding out, too. My hands are tied because once I put the pressure on her to confess the rest of her secrets, she'll press right back and that ain't happening. Even if I wanted all this to play out another way, ultimately, it's not up to me. So, we keep our secret while I keep my secrets and Bentlee keeps hers; and the entire time, I still want to knock every last one of Shawn's teeth out if only for the simple fact that he knows more about Bentlee than I do and is trying to hold it up to my face like a participation award earned in a one-person race right now.

Also, and I'm not just saying this, but he just sucks overall, in every area as far as I can tell. Except on clits. Guy don't suck on those, now does he?

I let loose a small smirk.

But is she hiding anything else about Shawn? Something that could affect *us*? Like the fact that he's got a baby pamphlet in his car the same day Bentlee's talking about having a period. She did get her period, right?

Or was she just trying to keep me from meeting him?

"She didn't say anything about being taken, tonight or otherwise, and we've talked *a lot* this week."

My eyes fly to Bentlee's but she's not here anymore. At least not the real her. Not the Bentlee I know and…like. This Bentlee's cold. This Bentlee's unrecognizable.

"It wasn't that much," is all she says. Not *you're lying through your teeth*. Not *I am taken*. Nothing.

Shawn opens his door, winking at her and nodding dramatically. "Sure. Say bye to Mom," he says to Hunter and Hunter listens, telling us both goodbye while Shawn rolls his eyes again like an arrogant asshole.

Something squeezes my heart. Like something's wrong. Like I shouldn't be here at all. Like I'm a thorn in this family's side.

But that's not true. Is it?

I mean, they're not *my* family. Not according to Bentlee. Not according to anyone when you think about it.

The band around my heart tightens.

The second the car's out of the lot, Bentlee turns on her heel and takes off up the stairs, but before she can disappear into the apartment, I yell up, "How about you have Shawnathon go to the store for you?"

Her spine finally solidifies but the only noise that follows is the front door slamming shut.

I'm not sure why I said it or even what I meant by it but whatever was just wrapped around my heart coils into a ball and sinks to the bottom of my stomach, making me feel like I'm gonna puke.

If I could rewind the last half hour, I would. I would and I'd erase it from all of our memories because as much as I thought I hated Shawn, in this moment I might hate myself more.

Chapter 20

Marc

"I need tires. Lots of 'em."

"Any kind in particular?"

"Big."

Coty nods. "By?"

"End of week. Sooner." Depending on how fast I can get everything to come together. I can't shake the feeling that I'm on some kind of timeline. I gotta get this right. I gotta *make* this right.

"Shouldn't be a problem. Okay, I got pink, green, or black. Don't ask why those colors. I don't even remember buying them," Coty says holding up cans of spray paint I asked him for.

"I'll take pink."

He tosses it to me and Beck walks into the spacious oversized garage slurring, "Whose house we taggin'?"

"When have we ever spray-painted someone's house?" Coty deadpans and I grin.

Beck shrugs. "It's never too late to start. Suburbia could use a little…flair."

"That's not flair. That's crime."

"And this isn't suburbia. This is the sticks," I tack on.

"Fuck yeah it is. Bro, there's no one out here." Beck takes a sip of his drink and says to me, "When can we expect you to join us out here anyway? You'd love it, especially with your *four hundred acres.*"

"Why the rush? You need somewhere to crash when Paige kicks you out?"

He scoffs. "Paige doesn't kick me out." Coty and I glance at each other, holding in laughs, then he says, "She kicks my ass, sure, but not out. The makeup sex is too good to pass up." He winks, making Coty laugh but I stay quiet, thinking about Bentlee and what happened earlier.

Tonight was supposed to go a completely different way, not whatever the fuck that was with her ex. Now, to make matters even worse, she's ignoring me. She knows I hate that just like I know she does, too. So why bother? Just tell me why the fuck you're calling your ex behind my back and I'll start digging his grave somewhere on my *four hundred acres.* Simple shit.

And if there's room for some of this makeup sex Beck's talking about, even better—after we discuss the birth control thing.

"What? You and Lee-Lee haven't had makeup sex yet?" he asks, bringing me back.

"Stop calling her that." I don't usually care when he uses his nickname for Bentlee, but tonight, everything's pissing me off.

I shake my head, getting to my feet and weighing the can in my hand to make sure there's enough.

"'Cause you guys haven't had a fight yet, or..."

I stare at him blankly but he just gives it right back with a lopsided grin.

Coty gets between us, looking at Beck. "Marc would tell us if something was going on between them." Then he faces me, asking, "How's the ringworm treating you these days?"

My hand finds my neck and they both crack up.

"Maybe tell Bentlee to ease up on the teeth."

"I'd rather die," I mumble, pushing him into Beck and making them laugh even harder.

"It's for the best." I frown at Beck, missing his meaning. "Word on the street is she and Ty are getting closer by the day. But you already knew that since you spend all your time at Pop Two now, right? When you're not at home anyway."

Coty shuts up but because I can't help myself, I ask, "What street is that exactly?" Tonight's just full of revelations. Maybe I should borrow a shovel from Coty, too. Sounds like I might have two graves to dig.

With a straight face I know he's working hard to keep, Beck says, "Sesam-"

"Don't even say it, you cheesy fuck," Coty cuts him off, chuckling but watching me closely. "You know that's not the only place Marc goes."

"Oh, yeah." Beck snaps his fingers. "You mean when he tells Angie he's going to Pop One but then never shows at either location."

Coty grimaces in my direction. "You do know we talk, right? Like morning, noon, and night."

Now that I don't have my dad's farm as an alibi, I got people keeping tabs on me. Like I give a fuck. Less than a fuck. A micro fuck. They still don't know who I'm with or why though and that's all I do care about.

"Then there's today. You called in sick but you don't look it."

"I am sick. Sick of your ass."

Coty chuckling, asks, "Strip club or craft time?" then points at my forehead, wiping a piece of glitter from it.

Dammit. I spent two and a half hours on the floor this afternoon playing with Rebel and her stupid fucking sparkle ponies while she was supposed to be resting on the couch. My head next to her made for an ideal landing pad one too many times and now I'm sparkling. Fucking sparkling.

I scrub my hands down my sparkling face, telling Beck, "You got something to say, spit it out."

"Fine. You're fucking around with Lee-Lee and you don't have the balls to admit it. Not even to us."

Beck's posture straightens and suddenly the spiked cider isn't hitting him as hard.

Out of the corner of my eye I see Coty's do the same like he expects us to fight. Over an accusation that's half true? I don't think so. I'd love to hit someone tonight but neither man in front of me fits the bill.

"Bentlee's a mother," I say, looking them each in the eye. "She has responsibilities. A reputation. A fucking child to think of." They have no idea what that's like, putting someone so small, so innocent, so fucking helpless before themselves and what they want. What they need.

"Funny thing is, so does Ty."

I move so fast I don't even know where I am until I'm nose to nose with Beck.

"Take it easy." Coty tries to get between us again but I don't budge and neither does Beck.

His blue eyes flick between mine. "Are you sleeping with her or not?"

"You don't have to answer that. As long as the thing with you and Kary is…whatever. Just don't tell us you're cheating on one or both, dude."

Coty lets that hang in the air and I give a quick headshake to ease his concern. I'm not like his dad or Beck's mom. I don't cheat. Not that me and Bentlee are in a *real* relationship. If we were, that phone call shit would've never happened. Fuck Shawnathon.

"Yes, he does. He gets away with too much and I'm not letting him get away with this."

"Why do you care? Who the *fuck* made you Bentlee's keeper?" I press into him so hard our noses mash together. I gotta give it to him, not once does he so much as blink.

Coty shuffles on his feet next to us, his hands at the ready to slip between our bodies the second one of us makes a move for the other.

"You said it yourself, Lee-Lee's a mother. A young mother. She deserves better than someone who sneaks around, answering to no one but himself."

My head snaps back several inches but my gaze remains fixed on his. "I know that. You don't think I know that?"

"Then let Ty-"

"You finish that and I swear-"

"What?" He pushes back into my face and I growl, my free hand clenching into a tight fist. "What are you gonna do? Beat my ass? Beat Ty's ass? Beat everybody that glances in her direction's ass? Yeah, I've been there, bro. Just like our boy when Angie moved into Creekwood." Coty nods off to the side, still cocked and ready to act. "You're with her, aren't you?"

"It's. Not. Your. Business," I grind out.

He holds my gaze a beat longer, then closes the distance to press a tight-lipped peck against my mouth before pulling back just as quick and chuckling. "You're fucked, just like the rest of us."

I throw wild eyes at Coty who's holding his stomach in laughter. "What the fuck was that? Was a kiss necessary?"

"No, that was a bonus. You're welcome."

"You're not thanked, asshole."

"I'll put it on your tab." Beck shrugs, then states simply, "You love her," and picks his glass back up. I didn't even notice him put it down.

Too shocked that he kissed me, I can't even respond appropriately. I shouldn't be. He does everything for shock value. *Wait.* "Is that what you've been up to this whole time? Putting Bentlee at Pop Two? Trying to get her to move in with Ty? Constantly talking your shit?"

"I told you Lee-Lee was going to be my sister-in-law, didn't I?" Tipping his glass my way, he proceeds to knock the rest of his drink back.

"She ain't marrying Ty." That I do know. For a fucking fact.

Both my best friends give me sympathetic looks that drag against my nerves like a scouring pad. What am I missing?

"He's not the brother I was talking about."

Me?

"You're crazy, man," Coty laughs. "If you tried that shit with Angela, you would've been put down long before now."

Unconcerned, Beck tells him, "That's 'cause you didn't have anything to lose. Marc does."

I feel my heartbeat in my throat and I shake the can in my hold, trying to buy some time but knowing I'm out of it. They're done waiting, but I can't give them everything. Instead, I give them something…else.

"Are you talking about me racing motocross?"

Neither one reacts save for a matching pair of shit-eating grins. I knew Beck was on to me, and I may have shared a little too much with Paige one night when she first moved in, but I didn't know Coty was in on it, too.

"When did you find out?" I ask him.

"Just before we opened Pop Two." Coty drops his eyes. "Angela searched everyone up. She wanted to make sure what she was attaching her name to."

I nod numbly but then he walks over and pulls something off the wall above his work bench, saying, "I bought it off some kid online."

Hidden underneath the sign he had up is an autographed photo of me racing. My head's cranked over my shoulder, looking directly into the camera while I'm airborne in the middle of a jump.

"Someone was *selling* it?" My autograph?

Beck bursts out laughing from right behind me, saying, "I got one almost identical to that up in my garage, too. Probably from the same kid." Impressed, he studies the picture while I try to wrap my head around the fact that not only did both of my best friends know, but they're not even mad. They're proud.

Also, someone's out there making money off my signature and that's surreal, too. Suddenly, I don't feel so inconsequential anymore. Why didn't I tell them sooner?

"Then, you know, that whole fight with Chease kinda went viral, too."

"Yeah," Beck says. "I watched that shit on repeat. Motherfucker went *down*."

He taps my knuckles with his and I shake my head. Leave it to Anthony "the Clout-chaser" Chease to blow my cover.

"Where were you keeping all your gear before you moved it out here?"

I tell them about the different hiding spots around Vega Farms. I figured they'd catch on once I started storing my racing gear on my own property, I just didn't care as much. Not once I shared it with Bentlee. She makes me want to be more open. Whether in hopes of getting her to open up, too, or for something else entirely, I don't feel like holding back as much anymore.

"Damn, dude. You're a sneaky bastard."

"Well, it's done now. Pretty sure my career's over, so make sure to hold on to these." As painful as that is to admit, at least I know I'll still be involved in Rebel's racing. There's no way that girl won't have a long, successful career in motocross—if that's what she chooses. If that's what we can make happen some-fucking-how, considering the state of the only moto-track we have access to in the area.

"Then that isn't the only thing you have to lose."

Beck's back on his bullshit about my secrets. Thirsty motherfucker.

"What else is there?" He knows everything now, right? But he better tread carefully here on out. One wrong word about Rebel and there won't be any kisses other than the ones glued to my ass as I walk the fuck away from every-fucking-thing, brothers or not.

"I don't know yet. I'm sure you'll tell us one day. After you tell Bentlee I'm guessing."

I finally let out my breath, giving my lungs a break. So much for a fun night.

"I'm not marrying her either." As soon as it's out of my mouth, I want to rip my own tongue out just so there's no chance of ever hearing myself say it again.

"Not today."

Coty hangs his head, agreeing with Beck softly, "Not today," but I don't know if he's talking about me and Bentlee or him and Angela.

"Why *haven't* you asked Angela to marry you yet?"

"I have. Every week I ask her." He laughs but it's not funny, it's sad.

"On your knee with a ring and everything?"

"No."

"That's your second mistake," Beck mutters.

"And what's the first, fuckhead?"

"Asking at all."

I scoff. "He's not making Angela do anything. Look how well that works out for us."

"It's not about making her marry him, it's about showing her why she should."

"Are you stupid? What part of my life doesn't revolve around her?"

"The part where you continue doing what you fell out of love with."

Coty and I exchange equally confused looks.

"Listen, we all know my place is under the hood, but that's not where either of you belong. Not anymore." He waits a beat, then says, "Marc just told us where his heart is."

I did?

"I'm okay at Pop The Hood," Coty states and even I have a hard time believing him.

"Okay?" Beck pretends to dry heave. "Dude, what's up with all those damn blueprints you're always drawing up only to hide them away?"

"I don't hide them."

"You don't do *anything* with them!" Beck's hands rise, then drop. "This house, my house, they show your true passion." He points at Coty's chest, knowing under his shirt are tattoos that stand for that very virtue. "You're wasting time doing something you outgrew, and Angela's scared you're doing the same with her."

"Stop talking like you know her," Coty growls.

"Stop acting like you don't."

"So, what are you saying? You want us out of Pop The Hood?" I guess.

"I want my brothers to be happy with their lives and not feel held back because they think that's what's expected of them. Isn't that what we've been fighting against our entire fucking lives?"

Fuck if he doesn't have a point there.

"Is that the real reason why you hired Bentlee? To see if you could swing it yourself?"

"Fuck, bro, and you all say I'm the stupid one. I hired Lee-Lee because I knew you'd never act unless you had to. Enter the perfect setting, along with Ty, the sacrificial lamb-"

"Some brother-in-law you're gonna make."

He shrugs. "My loyalty's not to him. Only to my real brothers."

"Dude, would you stop? You're getting your growth and knowledge all over the place." Coty gestures to the entire garage and we all laugh, each of us getting lost under the weight of that truth. Where's my growth? Keeping the status quo isn't growing. It's stagnant and it's starting to get old.

"Sorry about keeping my racing from you. I just-"

"We know. You're an onion, full of layers." I frown as Beck rubs his hands together, the smirk on his face growing. "And now that we have the right knife, we're finally getting somewhere."

"What knife?" What the hell is he talking about?

"Lee-Lee."

I'm just finishing up spraying the lines on the ground when "Go Crazy" by Leslie Odom Jr. starts playing from the cab, floating out the open doors of Bentlee's Cummins as the headlights shine on me and my handiwork.

Sitting on the hood, with her legs bent and spread wide, Bentlee leans forward between them, her wrists together and asks, "Are you marking where your track will go?"

She's looped from drinking the last few hours away and I thought was still pissed at me. This is the first time she's even spoken directly to me all night.

After leaving Coty and Angela's, I parked us out here at my property to make a few placement marks. It's dark and cold, and even though I told her to stay inside her truck, she's out here, watching my every move as I try my hand at spraying semi-straight pink paint lines. At least she's got a leather jacket on.

"Track?"

"You've got enough property for it. And if you can't race at anyone else's, you could just," she shrugs, glancing around the pitch black, "make your own."

Make my own…

"No, that's not what I'm doing," I tell her, hoping she doesn't ask what I actually am doing. This was never part of the plan—not that I necessarily had one—but now that it is, I don't want her to know about it until it's ready. Until it's done. If she even *wants* to see it.

I stand, checking out the parts of the haphazard perimeter I can make out in the dim light. I'll have to come out here during the day to make sure it's as big as I'm picturing but I wanted to get the general idea out while it was still fresh in my mind. Maybe I'll even have Coty come take a look. And get his opinion on a track, too. It'd definitely fit out here, and while I could give input on the construction, it's the execution I'd need help with. If he's serious about design, it might be the kick in the ass he needs.

A couple thumps have me looking over at Bentlee and, finding her dancing on the hood, I grin, walking over to watch her. My mouth goes dry as she turns around, her hips swaying her ass in a mesmerizing dance to the song.

Over her shoulder, she smarts off, saying, "Let me guess. You want me to get down."

Using the sketchy-ass front bumper to place my foot, I climb onto the hood behind her, pulling that fat ass against me. Her breath hitches from my sudden contact and she turns in her spot to face me.

"I don't want to keep you from doing anything. I just want to keep you safe."

We look between each other's eyes, our bodies moving together just slightly, then the headlights flicker before cutting off completely, along with the music.

Cloaked in darkness, I say, "Bentlee," but she pulls away, complaining about the shitty battery. She's back on the ground the next second, diving into the cab to try the key.

It makes the telling sound of a dead battery and I jump down, too, asking her to pop the hood while pulling my phone out of my pocket for light.

Here I am claiming I just want Bentlee safe yet she's still driving this fucking truck every day. It's so old and run-down and unreliable. Just thinking of her and Hunter in it gives me anxiety.

Heading to the driver's door, I start to tell her "We're taking my…" but when I find her curled up on the bench seat, fast asleep, a different kind of anxiety creeps in, except this time she's not in an ounce of danger—I am.

Through the dark, I carry her all the way to my truck, get her in and get her home, and it's only when we're halfway up the stairs back at Creekwood that she wakes up, huffing, "I can walk now," despite her grip on me not loosening whatsoever.

I wait until we're on the other side of the front door before putting her back on her feet, telling her, "I know." I didn't feel like letting her go just yet. I don't feel like letting her go at all.

She turns away but I grab her again, drawing her close and gazing into her eyes. "I'm sorry for what I said earlier."

"Which part?"

"Any part that might've hurt you."

"You basically told Shawn we were fucking."

I scowl, caught off guard. He started it by openly flirting with her. Of course I'm gonna let the fucker know where I stand.

"You agreed we'd keep this a secret."

"And I have."

"Then why couldn't you just stay quiet like you do with everybody else," she throws in my face. "Why bait him?"

"Why do you care so much? Are you worried I hurt *his* feelings?" It sure seems like it to me. Poor piece-of-shit Shawnathon needing Bentlee to baby him and his micro-penis feelings. And she does. Just covers for him and caters to him and *calls* him. "Is that why you called him? To make sure *his* feelings were okay?"

Tearing her arm out of my hold, she glares at me as she spits, "Screw you."

She makes a beeline to the fridge, yanking it open and saying, "He did what he always does. He twisted the situation to fit his narrative, to make me into something I'm not. I didn't 'blow up his phone.'"

She stops to meet my eyes while I lean against the counter, listening intently. This is the most she's ever spoken about him. "I called him *once* to ask about Halloween. This year," she faces the fridge again, "will be different. Just like everything else."

Her breathing intensifies as her back looks like it's about to give out from the weight put there by…I don't fucking know. Her? Him? I just want to know what happened and what I can do to fix it already. *Can* I fix it?

Before I get the chance to even try, she spins around again, sticking her finger at me. "But if I call my son's *father*," I flinch before I can school my features but some-fucking-how she doesn't notice as she continues, "that has nothing to do with you. You don't get to act like a dick because of it."

"Yes, I do," I say before I can think better of it. Did I just admit to being a dick? And justify it? This girl's making me crazy. "It does have to do with me."

She barks out a harsh laugh, turning away. "No. It doesn't. You're not some fill-in dad, Marc. You're a fuck and a secret one at that. Know your role."

If words could kill, I'd be six feet under, looking up at my killer and she'd have no fucking idea why. Nobody would.

My entire foundation shakes, threatening to collapse into the grave of my own doing, and I push off the counter, heading out to the front balcony before I do something I'll regret. Before I say something I'll regret.

A week-old sponge would be a better dad to Hunter than Shawnathon but I didn't think I was even in the running to fill his goddamn spot. I never even said as much.

I never say anything.

And look where that's gotten me so far. Misunderstood, misjudged, mis-fucking-taken for someone not worth replacing if they can't even fill the role correctly themselves.

I put a cigarette between my lips, lighting it in the next breath. Inhaling until it hurts, I hold it all inside.

I keep everything inside—everything—but with each passing

day, the load I'm bearing only continues to get heavier, not lighter. Even when it feels like my lungs are gonna explode if I don't let it out, still, I keep it all in.

But that's my choice. I *chose* that and will continue to do so. Bury my body, burn my soul, but watch me still find a way to protect those I love most, scorching the fucking earth in my efforts to keep them safe. I'll never go down easily when it comes to my family.

If I could just make Bentlee understand, she'd know—she'd fucking know—that any overstepping I've ever done wasn't for my benefit.

She appears at the sliding glass door, coming right out to snatch the cigarette from my mouth.

I release my breath, the smoke rushing out between us in a thick, intrusive cloud. I don't say anything though, I just watch her, seeing what she's going to do next.

Tearing her gaze from mine, she swipes it across the lot below us, and I know the second she sees my truck in the spot where hers should be.

She puts the cigarette up to her gloss-covered lips, then the end flares even brighter and I'm out of my chair before she has the chance to swallow the smoke down. With her cheeks full, I can tell she didn't inhale properly but I don't care, I pinch the cherry red tip anyway, extinguishing the cigarette with my fingertips before plucking it from her and tossing it over the banister. I'll pick it up to throw away in the morning but right now, it needs to be out of my goddamn sight.

Bentlee rotates her head to the side and deliberately blows the smoke into my face and I debate kissing the fuck out of her. I don't but only because it'd hurt her right now and I'd never, ever intentionally do anything that hurt her. Would never. Could never.

I'm not like them.

Except for today.

My chest rises and falls rapidly as I watch the back of Bentlee's head hanging limply between her arms as she leans against the banister. She's staring at the wood like it has the answers to this shit. *I fucking wish.* I'd do anything to have someone tell me what to do right now. How to navigate this swell of emotions I'm not equipped for.

"I'm sorry," I whisper, feeling a part of myself break off like an iceberg thawing.

"*I'm* sorry," she whispers back, sounding just as affected.

Closing the gap between us, I press my nose against her ear, rasping, "I don't want you to call him because I don't want you to need him." My arms come up to frame hers. "Anything you want, anything you need, I want to be the one to give it to you. Just me."

She spins in my arms. "You want to control me."

"No. It's not like that. I told you, I just want to protect you."

"And by protecting me, you want me to drive your truck?"

I hesitate then nod.

"Then quit smoking."

"What?"

"Who protects you, Marcos?"

I don't give her an answer because I don't *have* an answer to give her.

"That feeling you just had when you saw me smoking, I feel that knowing you smoke. *I* worry about *you.*"

My eyebrows sink. "I don't need you to protect me."

"And I don't need your truck." She ducks under my arm, skirting past me to go back inside.

I find her at the kitchen counter, her jacket now gone with a bowl of frozen grapes in front of her. I make sure to always have grapes in the freezer now. The piercing in her nose flashes in the overhead light just as bright as the anger on her face.

"You know who else refused to compromise?"

If she says Shawnathon…

"Shawn."

Motherfuck.

It's not that I can't compromise, it's that I don't see the need to in this one particular instance. Who cares if I smoke? I barely even do it anymore anyway.

But that's exactly what she's trying to tell me. She cares. She cares because I mean something to her like she means something to me.

Coming up behind her, I flatten my hand against her stomach, rubbing the soft material of her sweater as I hold her to me.

"The title will be switched over to your name on Monday."

"What about the smoking?"

I lower my hand, skimming just inside the waistband of her jeans and loving the way she quivers with the need for more. I know her body better than I know my own at this point which should prove I'm not just some throwaway fuck. If she needs more proof though, I'll give it to her.

I need to prove it to her just as much as myself anymore. I am good for something else. I am good for something.

"Done. I quit." She starts to argue but I slide my hand further down, over her pants though, just above her sweet spot.

"Just like that?"

"Just. Like. That. I want you safe." Doesn't she see that? I'd do fucking anything for her.

Almost anything.

"Marc," she whimpers, covering my hand with hers and pushing to get me closer to where she wants me.

I groan against the side of her face while giving in slightly by thrusting against that ass I've been watching all night. I'm not a fucking saint and I'd never claim to be one.

"Why?"

I freeze up, removing my hand to place on her hip.

Why?

Does she really not know?

I don't know how coming home to an empty apartment ever held any appeal. The sounds, the smells, the feeling of walking into *home.* Bentlee and her boy took this apartment and flipped it on its head, showing me what it was missing the entire time. What I was missing. I walked in on them that first night and now I don't want to walk in any other way. I can't go back to what it was like before. I want them here. I want her.

I need her.

She doesn't try to escape and I take the opportunity to lift her onto the counter so she's facing me. Then we stay just like that, neither of us so much as moving as we regard the other quietly.

Without taking her eyes off mine, she grabs a grape, popping it into her mouth.

"Because you're mine," I all but whisper, testing the words out on my tongue and liking them more than I ever thought I would.

My face hardens when she simply chews without any other reaction, pretending like she didn't even hear me. The act is too much to take yet isn't anywhere close to enough. Yell at me, scream at me, show me you feel this, too.

"Bentlee."

"What's wrong with saying we're just fucking? Why do I have to belong to you?" She studies me closely, letting the façade slip just a bit.

"I don't know. You just do."

Her eyes flutter closed as she breathes, "That's one of the worst things you could've said to me."

I need her to understand what I'm trying to say just as much as *I* need to understand what I'm trying to say. It's just that...I don't know how to actually say it. I've never done this.

"What's the best thing I could've said?"

Those clear blue-green eyes open again and stare into me like only she can. Like only I let her.

"You want me to write you a script?"

She rolls her eyes trying to appear unaffected again and goes for another grape but I intercept, tossing it into my mouth first.

"*That* was mine," she gripes and I steal another one, earning a death glare as I attempt to swallow the cold-ass fruit whole, wanting it washed down already. Grapes are not better frozen. They taste like nothing. No flavor at all. Not like...

"You don't have to be mine openly," I tell her as I rip off another grape from its stem, keeping it in my hold as I watch her. "We can be 'just fucking' to everyone or no one, I don't care. But to me, you being with me, here, there's no one else."

"For just me though, right?"

I frown, standing to my full height. No. I never said that.

"And what about all your overnight guests you keep your bathroom at the ready for?"

Making sure I don't blink, I say, "I'm not going to apologize for being prepared for the women in my life."

"Angela and Paige don't live here anymore. Your obligation is over to them."

"Now that sounds like a Shawnathon move. Stop comparing me to your ex, Bentlee. Not all of us are as useless as him."

After a moment's hesitation, she shakes her head, her hair falling in front of her face. "I know. Ugh, what am I saying?" She pushes the hair back, her eyes finding mine. "It's sweet that you do that. I like that you're not like him. Don't ever change. Don't be a Shawnathon."

I fight a smirk.

"It's just that I'm expected to stay true," her eyes fill with water but she blinks and it's gone, "but you get to continue doing 'what you want.'"

What I want? She's still not getting it. I like sex but I love sex with Bentlee, and this is so much more than that. She is so much more than that.

I tell her honestly, "This is exactly what I want. You are exactly what I want."

I drag the frozen grape along her collarbone and Bentlee hisses, then so quiet I almost miss it, she says, "That's the best thing you could've said," and my eyes jump back to hers.

Dropping my hands onto her hips, I go in for a kiss but she leans out of reach, saying, "That still doesn't mean you're mine though."

Not breaking eye contact, I pull my shirt over my head with one hand at the back of the neckline. With my arms out wide, I tell her, "Bentlee, I'm fucking yours. You have my word."

"Your word's as good as mine," she whispers painfully.

I drop my head into her lap before popping it back up, asking, "Do you know what I wanted from you since I first met you?"

Her eyes land on my straining cock in my pants.

"No." She tilts her head and I chuckle. "Yes, but no. I wanted you to see me."

Those same eyes rise to mine and widen.

"Remember when you asked me what I like about your eyes?"

"You said 'everything.'"

"I like the way you look at me. I like how you *see* me."

"Me too," she whispers, this time not blinking away the tears that appear. "That's all I've ever wanted."

Ever? Is she talking about Shawn again?

Her hand comes up to brush above my eyebrows and I remember the glitter too late but then she continues on, her fingers tracing my lips while saying, "Lie to me with your mouth but never with your eyes. Never with your eyes."

"Never." Eyes hold more truth than our words ever could. "You have my eyes as long as I have yours. I don't want you seeing anyone else while we're together and I promise the same." She can take that however she wants. Whatever "together" or "seeing" or "just fucking" means, bottom line is I'm not sharing Bentlee and I'm definitely not sleeping with anyone else.

"Okay."

"Okay?"

She nods and I lean into her space, pushing until her back is flat against the counter. We work together to remove her pants, then I do the same, shedding mine in record time. Grabbing another grape, I bite it in half, partially chewing the pieces quickly before letting the freezing juice drip off my lips onto her clit.

"God, Marc," she moans, her sweater riding up as her back arches clear off the counter.

With one hand on her stomach to keep the material out of the way, I kiss a cold trail from her navel to her clit, then swallow the grape halves. The juice runs down over her already glistening slit and I'm quick to lick it all up, sucking until there's an actual flavor, my favorite flavor—her. I only stop once that's all I taste and Bentlee's ripping at my hair.

Standing again, with a grape between my pointer finger and middle finger, I drag it along her pussy lips, using my mouth to chase away the cold. I kiss and suck both the grape and her, sometimes even getting my own fingers until it's an all-out feeding frenzy and Bentlee's mindless begging forces me to climb onto the counter as well.

The second we're lined up, I ask on a rasp, "Did you really go off birth control?" then hold my breath.

Embarrassed, she shakes her head and I push away my disappointment to slip inside her pussy, feeling remnants of the cold around my cock like an icy tease and we both moan loudly, our foreheads connecting in their own kiss.

"You see me now, Marc?"

"I see you, Bentlee."

"Good. Never stop looking."

Her arm hooks around the back of my neck, then she rolls her hips up as she grinds into me, drawing my cock that much deeper into her sweet pussy.

I spend the rest of the weekend learning just how good makeup sex can be.

Chapter 27

Bentlee

"**M**E NEXT! ME NEXT!" HUNTER CRIES AFTER MARC finishes spinning the same little girl around in the courtyard that I've seen a few times now. I'm assuming she lives somewhere in the complex but I'm not sure where exactly. She's got blonde hair that looks like it hasn't been cut in…maybe ever. It's so long I doubt she's had a single haircut in her life. She sounds like she's around Hunter's age but is so much smaller than him that it's hard to tell. I do know her clothes are more expensive than mine though considering her entire outfit is comprised of brands I can't even afford. She's wearing the latest sneakers that nobody in the area could get a pair of because they sold out *before* they even hit the shelves.

The apartments making up Creekwood are nicer than others, especially the ones Marc and I toured, but still not fancy by any means and I have to wonder which residents are keeping their daughter in such expensive clothing, particularly to play in.

But, looking around now, there's no parents. At all. I've been outside on our back balcony, watching the three of them for going on twenty minutes and still have yet to see anyone check on her. I don't even see a nanny or older sibling watching nearby. Same with the other times she and Hunter have played, too.

When I first saw her, I thought it was just a happy coincidence but now I'm not so sure. Marc must know her somehow, especially with how friendly she's being, has been every time she's around. Marc's great with kids. Or, he's been great with Hunter anyway.

Although, he handled Diesel with ease, too. He's just one of those people who's naturally good with kids even though most people wouldn't think it by looking at him. Tatted arms that are usually gripping one motorcycle or another, his own clothes dripping in swag—even at work—a resting bitch face that could sharpen metal, and his old smoking habit that's thankfully a thing of the past.

More squeals fill the courtyard and I drop my chin in my palm, leaning in my seat to get a better look at them. If I didn't know them, I'd assume the little girl was Marc's daughter, the way he is with her—familiar, natural—like he genuinely enjoys playing with her. And Hunter, too—but I already knew that. Not once has Marc ever acted inconvenienced by Hunter wanting his attention. Not even after a full day's work when Hunter's bugging him to tell him more about the stars. Or his travels. Or his races. Marc knows a lot about a lot but doesn't hold it over anyone. Only shares when prompted. And my son, he prompts…a lot.

You'd think the sound of Marc's deep, intimidating voice would scare kids off the way it seems to adults, but no. Of course kids are drawn to the scariest-sounding man who isn't actually scary at all. Not when you get to know him. Not when you fall for his unassuming charm. Not when you start to fall for him, period.

For a moment I let the dream take over, the one where these are our kids, together, as they laugh and play while I watch on, loving our life. Loving him.

A text alert from my phone ends the fantasy before it can even begin though and I shake my head at myself.

Telling Marc he was just a fuck was one of the hardest lies I've ever had to tell because the only person it protected was me. Lies to protect Hunter roll off my tongue like water on a duck's tail but that lie was self-serving. And hurt. Not only myself but Marc as well. I could tell even if he didn't outright say it. The lies that followed about us "seeing" each other were just as bad but easier to swallow as we both spewed them with practiced proficiency.

How can you see someone that isn't really there?

We're both hiding important parts of ourselves, or at least I am. But Marc's not forthcoming either, and for a reason. Maybe even multiple. I don't know, just like he doesn't know what I'm keeping secret which goes to show we do not actually "see" each other. We see what we're shown, what the other is willing to show. We see a manipulated version of the truth shaped by our own hands which does not make for a viable relationship foundation, let alone marriage.

Marriage. I wouldn't even marry Shawn and I had a good reason to…according to society. According to our families. According to everyone looking in from the outside. Spending life with the man whose last name my son carries would be easy on paper. It's what's "right." But it didn't feel right. Not to me.

Marc and I are having fun for the time being. We're enjoying each other's company while the rest of the world continues on as if forgetting us entirely. His friends are moving on. My ex is…did…he did move on. Even if he's working double time to hide it, I can tell he did, just like I could tell when we were still living together.

And maybe Marc's friends did the same. Maybe Marc wasn't ready to grow up and grow out at quite the same time. Maybe he's playing house with me just to feel it out. Try it on for size and see if the settled-down life is the right fit.

Watching him now, I'd say it is. It fits him very well.

Is that just another delusion in a string of deceptions my mind is trying to feed me though?

It's hard to tell because the deceit's anticipated anymore. Expected. I stared a liar in the face and didn't turn to stone, only hardened myself from further disappointment. Hurt. Pain.

But…what if I'm hungry for this one trick, absolutely ravenous for it?

A few more minutes pass as I sit silently, taking in the trio. Hunter's glasses fall onto the ground and the words sit on the tip of my tongue just as the little girl rushes over to grab them, giving them back to him. It's such a sweet gesture that I choke up, sliding my hand over my face to cover the sudden onset of tears trying to fall.

After wiping the few that escape, I look down again only to find the courtyard calm with Marc's back to me as he walks the girl… home, I guess. Before I can see which apartment he goes to, our own front door slams shut with Hunter already talking a mile a minute about Marc sending him and his friend up to the moon and back all before dinnertime.

Meeting him inside, I have him wash his hands, trying to keep up as he describes his new friend. I ask her name, and after answering with "Rebel," he bounces away to his room, apparently done with sharing. I feel myself growing just as excited, if not more excited, about what might just be his first non-meowing, real-food-eating human friend and more tears fill my eyes, these ones spilling over before I can catch them.

Another text chimes from my sister at the same time Marc strolls through the front door, and with my heart filling my entire chest, I ask if he wants to join us tonight, never once considering the consequences. Or why his smile matches my own.

Chapter 22

"WHAT KIND IS THIS ONE?" MARC ASKS, BENDING down to slip a hand through the wire fencing that specifically states not to reach past.

He pets the goat's head while Hunter launches into a full description of the Alpine goat, tripping over his words in his rush to get them out before Marc loses interest. Only, Marc never does. He just waits patiently at each pen for Hunter to educate him on whichever animal's inside, then and only then do we move on to the next. And the times when Hunter remembers something Marc just *has* to know, Marc's quick to give him his full attention again. He does make faces occasionally and I've seen him wipe at his nose about a dozen or so times to know he'd rather be out in the open air than stuck in here with pigs, goats, and rabbits, but he never lets it show otherwise, especially not in front of Hunter.

We haven't made it into the big building yet which is where my sister will be with the Graham cows, and not even the earlier high of Hunter's newfound friendship can keep my anxiety at bay about the possibility of running into my parents. Sydnee said they weren't here yet but I know they often stop in. It'll be the first time I've seen them since I moved out.

But, ever since Hunter could walk, I've been bringing him to the

Fall Fest and I wasn't going to miss it this year. It's the same festival I used to work at when I was a teenager, the same one I met Shawn at actually. It's easy work as far as manual labor over an extended period of time goes but that's just it, it's a very long extended period of time. Pulling twenty-hour days for four days straight with only fair food for nourishment might be something a teen can pull off but it's not the life I'd want now, which is what my parents expected me to travel around doing in order to stay at Graham.

"You can milk them," Hunter says, panting as he struggles to catch his breath, and Marc yanks his hand back.

Hunter giggles uncontrollably at Marc's horrified expression and I tell him, "Yeah, some breeds of goats are used for milking, too. This is one."

"What about these ones?" he asks, pointing at two stocky-looking goats in the next stall.

Reading the laminated placard, I smile over at Hunter. Without even needing to say anything, he claps his hands together just once but loud enough to startle the little guys and they both stiffen before tipping over into the high mounds of hay surrounding them.

"What the-" Marc starts forward only to stop when the attendant on duty appears, shaking his head with a grin.

He comes over to stand beside me and Hunter, saying, "I've been waiting all day for someone to do that," then laughs. "How'd you know they faint?"

All evening, Marc's hand has been brushing mine every so often and I've had to work to hide my reaction to the feel of his hot skin against mine. It's like dipping into a bath full of too hot water—shocking at first, then comfortable, then soothing. Before long you seek out the warm spots, wanting that heat more than any other feeling you've ever experienced, burns be damned. In such a short amount of time, my skin's already acclimated to his heat, desensitized to anything less than Marc's fire, so when his hand finds my lower back in that moment, I sink into it without even realizing my mistake.

The farmhand frowns, glancing between us and I pull away, dropping my hands onto Hunter's shoulders to answer, "They're his favorite." I think he'd even own a few as pets if I'd let him. He'd own anything as a pet if he could.

"These are the goats you told me about, huh?" Marc asks, gazing at Hunter who nods absently as he watches the goats come to and stand back up as if nothing even happened. "They stink." His nose scrunches up in disgust and Hunter and I laugh along with the attendant. They all stink. You either get used to it, or you don't.

I didn't know Hunter told Marc about them though. Maybe he showed him some of those videos he's always cracking up at. Marc often goes out of his way to ask Hunter what he's watching like he's genuinely interested, and after watching him with Hunter all day, it's easy to believe he might actually be.

We wave to the attendant, then Marc opens the main door, holding it to let us through first.

"I'm hungry."

"Okay." I grab Hunter's hand, telling him, "Let's find something to eat then."

Marc stops us, handing me a fifty and says, "You two go ahead and I'll catch up."

Studying his blank canvas of a face, I frown when he refuses to meet my eyes directly. *He's not going to go smoke, is he?*

But he's gone before I can ask, so Hunter and I weave through tents full of handmade crafts and other local goods, stopping every now and then to make a purchase. Then, before I can redirect us, Hunter's already tugging me toward the one labeled with Marc's last name at the top.

A man almost identical to Marc but older steps around from the back, coming right over to help Hunter. The only times I've ever seen Joaquin Vega was from a distance greater than when I used to watch Marc ride, but it didn't matter. You know who you're looking at when Joaquin's around. His presence is large, heavy, like he knows everything. Marc probably knows just as much, if not more, but holds himself differently. He's still just as arrogant, but not about his intelligence. That he keeps to himself.

"I don't think we've had the pleasure of meeting in person." I put my hand out. "I'm Bentlee. Bentlee Graham."

"Graham? Our neighbors? The pleasure's all mine. Joaquin Vega." The smile that lights his face is the same as Marc's though—pure magic.

"Not anymore," Hunter tells him, eyeing a peach that's been cut up. His voice warbles when he says it and I gaze down at him. I thought he liked living at Creekwood. There aren't any animals but there's Marc. And now Rebel.

Joaquin frowns, the lines on his face etched a whole lot deeper than Marc's from more years of use. These Vega men and their frowns. They should trademark them. Nobody frowns like a Vega man. Nobody. It's what makes their smiles that much more special.

"You're not the Grahams down the road from us?"

"We are." I don't *think* they disowned me after this last go around.

"So, you're both farmers, carrying on the family tradition?"

I'm pretty sure stars fill his dark eyes, darker than Marc's.

"We," I gesture to myself and Hunter, "just moved out is all."

Without breaking eye contact, he hands Hunter a piece of the cut-up fruit then another the second Hunter swallows it. It's automatic, taking care of Hunter—also just like Marc.

His frown deepens as he asks, "For what?" and hands Hunter another piece of peach.

Marc steps up from behind me, dropping down beside Hunter and saying "me" as an answer.

Joaquin pins me with those midnight eyes, and mine go as wide as the Granny Smith apple Marc's now got in his hand.

"Welllll…" I motion my hands around in a wide circle in front of me that nobody can decipher. "It's not exactly. There's just. We have." On my fourth attempt to form a complete sentence, Marc glances up at me, his own signature frown in place and I barely refrain from mouthing the word "help" to him.

"Tu novia?" Joaquin asks Marc, gaining his son's full attention.

Novia? What does that mean again? My Spanish teacher from sophomore year would be so disappointed right now.

Girlfriend…I think. Is that what he just asked? Am I Marc's girlfriend?

I stare at the side of Marc's face, the muscle in his jaw twitching while his silence roars around us.

"We live together," he states plainly before jumping into his own description about the Granny Smith and its fluke origin. While his enthusiasm doesn't reach anywhere near Hunter's about animals, he's just as knowledgeable.

And now I really am in need of help. Why is Marc making it sound like we're together-together when we're not? Not really. Certainly not enough to tell family members about, especially Joaquin. He looks like he paints everything in his sight with disapproval—liberally.

I clasp my hands behind my back though, smiling as wide as my lips will stretch.

Marc always measures his words very, very carefully, so this shouldn't come as a surprise. Still, he could've just as easily shook his head at the girlfriend question. Right?

"Las cuidas?" Joaquin asks after watching Marc and Hunter with their heads together but this question isn't familiar at all.

Marc's back stiffens, then so small I almost miss it, he nods his head.

When Joaquin speaks again, it takes me a second to realize he's not talking to me, but to Marc as he asks, "And what do you do?"

Even though this one's in English, I still don't know what he means. Doesn't he know what his son does for work? He did work out at Vega Farms before he made Pop Two his main priority…I thought.

Marc stands, telling him, "Live," like it's the obvious answer and I guess it kind of is. We do that. We do that happily actually. I hadn't even realized until this moment how happily we live.

While my life is nowhere near perfect, I can honestly say I am happy, this past week more so than all others.

Does Marc feel the same?

Joaquin scoffs like it's ludicrous but Marc doesn't bite, he only gazes over at me, his charcoal eyes threatening to ignite everything in their path. My breath gets stuck in my throat as my smile dims in brightness but not in depth.

"Wow, Marc, look! He's got as many medals as you do." Hunter slices the tension in half by pointing out the many medals decorating the back wall of the tent.

"Medals? What medals?" Joaquin asks, and Hunter's quick to answer, saying, "Marc's the best motor-cross rider ever."

Marc pulls his eyes from mine to his dad's, then to Hunter and just when I think he's going to shut down and go quiet again, he… jokes. Openly. About something he confessed to me like a sinner in church. "It's motocross, little man, and I'm not the best. I just win more than I lose."

He ruffles Hunter's hair and Joaquin's frown relaxes, actually relaxes, watching the exchange.

"The vehicles que escondiste." Marc's entire demeanor stiffens all over again at his father's words. "You think I don't know what's in my own orchards?"

Marc is the most noticeable person I've ever laid eyes on. He's got this *presence* that can't be ignored or hidden or forgotten. His signature garnet red racing gear is just as unmistakable, so of course his dad would recognize the vehicles stored on his property.

Marc's not meant to blend in, not when he stands out everywhere he goes. Doesn't he realize that?

Choosing to tease Hunter about the motor-cross comment again, Marc fools absolutely no one with his avoidance of his father. If he'd just look at him, he'd see Joaquin isn't trying to insult him. Joaquin looks impressed actually.

He tells me and Hunter to pick out some fruit, saying, "This is the best you'll find around."

His dad crosses his arms, a grin tipping his lips. "Best you'll find in the state."

They're both wrong—Vega fruit is the best in the entire Northwest—but as two great walls of power facing off, neither willing to budge by admitting fault or wrongdoing of any kind to the other, I doubt we'll be hearing any such thing from either of their mouths.

"And it's on the house, so take whatever you want. Anything for Marcos's," he nods at me, "friends."

Acid burns my throat from the bottom up. *Friends.* We are friends. But not. Much like being together—together.

It's complicated.

"I'll pay. We're not gonna-"

"*We're* grateful for your kind offer. Thank you," I interrupt, giving Marc an unimpressed look that he ignores too as he breathes through his nostrils.

I pull him aside, letting Hunter and Joaquin fill a bag.

"Listen. Your *me* statement was adorable in a prehistoric sort of way but the *we* statements end here. Your issues with your dad are just that—yours. If you want to wage war over some Red Delicious apples, you'll have to do it on your own behalf." Marc barely blinks and I wonder if he even heard me. "Now, if we were talking Golden Delicious, I might allow it," I add and he finally breaks, relaxing his rigid frame on an exhale. "And I'll take your dad out myself for some Honeycrisp."

"I think I saw some in the back." His dark eyebrows egg me on by lifting once in a taunt. "Why don't you show me what you're made of?"

"Stand back, Vega."

I start forward only to pull up short when he catches me easily, saying, "Not so fast, Graham."

With an arm around my stomach, holding my back to his front, we both laugh, losing ourselves for a minute. These sixty seconds though, they're like nothing else I've ever felt. It's like the planet beneath our feet comes to a complete stop to freeze everyone in place while Marc and I share a private moment, succumbing to the pull of each other's arms instead of the gravity keeping us on the ground. Like it's inevitable. Like *we're* inevitable—the *we* I just told him we're not and won't be.

"If you want Honeycrisps, I'll take you to Minnesota where they were invented. Best you'll ever taste."

The fantasy from earlier appears before I can stop it, coating my vision with notions of not just living happily, but living happily ever after—together.

I don't bother responding. I can't.

"Looks like that ringworm is contagious," Marc says quietly, his fingers brushing the back of my neck and making me shiver. Without having to ask, I know he's talking about the hickey he gave me a couple days ago on a lunch break where the only thing on the menu was me.

It's a good thing the weather is finally cooling down and I can wear a hoodie around the clock. *If only they could hide the inner mayhem he causes, too.*

Even after righting myself in his hold, Marc doesn't let go right away, but when he does, I'm left spiraling, out of control, wishing for that tether I had a second ago as much as I wish I never did to begin with. You can't miss what you've never known. You can't ache for what you've never had.

I ache for Marc—*ache*—and while I always have, it used to be manageable. It was malleable back then, like young hearts that haven't been crushed to bits yet. Now it's hardened just like my tired heart and I can't manage shit. Not how I react to him. Not how I feel about him. Not how this entire thing was supposed to go. He was not supposed to be better than I ever imagined. Yet he is. Marc is so much better, so much more, and that's what scares me because I don't even fully know him, not really, not yet. What if Marc is the trick? What if he's the delusion I'm grasping for in my desperation for something, anything, real?

"What did your dad ask you? About me?"

Keeping my eyes held hostage with his, he swallows and says, "If I take care of you."

I nod just as he had, not exactly sure what to do with that.

"What about the girlfriend question? Why didn't you answer that?"

His eyes round just slightly, proving I was right. Maybe my teacher would be proud after all.

Before he can respond though, a commotion pulls our attention back over to the table where Joaquin and Hunter were just weighing a bag of produce except Joaquin's no longer on the other side, he's on the same side as Hunter, standing in front of him. Shielding him.

Marc's there quicker than I thought possible and throwing a guy back several feet, causing him to land on his back.

Rushing to Hunter, I check him over, seeing he's perfectly fine. His glasses slipped down his nose about an inch but, otherwise, nothing's out of place at all.

Joaquin and Marc form a united wall between the guy and us, glaring down at him simultaneously.

"What's your problem?" Marc rages down at him but the guy looks a second away from pissing his pants while his friends nearby scatter, giggling like immature teens. After a closer look, I'm pretty sure they are immature teens.

"Was it an accident?" I ask Hunter and he nods, telling me about how the teens were pushing each other when one lost his footing and almost toppled into Hunter. Judging by Joaquin jumping over the table, I'm guessing he caught the guy before that could happen.

"I don't care," Marc says after hearing Hunter's explanation, then spits, "You need to watch where you're going around here," to the kid.

"Or you won't be coming back," Joaquin threatens, his words hanging by a strand of discomfort.

The teens scurry off and both Vega men turn around as one, their faces identical electrical storms full of moody thunderclouds as well as blinding flashes of danger.

"You meant to the festival, right?" I ask Joaquin and he shrugs noncommittally. I shoot my eyes to Marc only to find the exact same unapologetic attitude.

Not one hair on Hunter's head was so much as touched but that doesn't matter to them. To either of them. I already knew Marc was fiercely protective but his dad only just met us.

I study them a beat longer, only seeing the vast similarities between the two now.

The very thing Marc resents his father for, he inherited directly from him. I understand the urge to buck the system and go your own way—just like Marc, I've had it in me as long as I can remember—but there's a big difference between Joaquin and my dad. If there wasn't, Shawn wouldn't be breathing. That I have no doubt. Joaquin loves his son, maybe too strongly because Marc loves just as hard, if not harder. You can see it when he's on his dirt bike, how intense it is for him. But how he does it and shows it are his choosing, no one else's, and that's where they butt heads.

Also, their delivery could use some work. Most people don't respond well to terrifying threats.

It isn't disapproval Joaquin leads with, it's fear. He just doesn't know how to show it without trampling all over his son. And his son…doesn't get trampled over. Not without a fight.

They eye each other, gathering the charges in the air around us, and just when I start to worry they'll create an actual storm, the atmosphere settles into a low buzz of compatible energy.

Brushing off my thighs, I stand, asking, "Got any Honeycrisps?"

"My g-" Marc starts and my eyes fly to his. "My roommate's got a thing for Honeycrisp."

Joaquin looks around conspiratorially, dropping his voice. "We don't have a lot left, but what we do have, I keep in the back."

"Great. Maybe you both can tell us all about your medals."

Marc side-eyes his dad, gauging him, and Joaquin nods stiffly, dragging his fingernails across his thickly stubbled jaw.

"We can do that."

Meeting my eyes, Marc says, "Yeah, I guess *we* can," then teases my hand behind his back as he passes, making sure it's out of view of Hunter and Joaquin.

I know what he's thinking. If he and his dad can come together as a *we*, then maybe he and I have a chance, too. But he and Joaquin are family. *We* are not. They at least had some kind of bond started long ago. *We* did not.

Unless we're counting the feeble one shrouded by lies. A lie. My lie.

On instinct, I lift a hand to my shoulder, then forget it's even there as I watch the Vega men bond about something they probably never knew they had in common—succeeding.

When we finally make our way over to the big building, I breathe a sigh of relief finding Sydnee by herself.

Hunter races straight for his aunt and catches her from behind with a giant hug.

"Hey, munchkin. I was wondering if I'd get to see you." She snags my eye over his head, giving me an unreadable look.

"How're you doing?" I ask, glancing around at the calves she's in charge of. "Need anything?"

"I could use something that isn't deep-fried and glazed." Her face turns a light shade of green and the repulsion washes over me like it was yesterday. Fair food sounds good until that's all there is to choose from.

Marc holds up one of the bags from his dad's tent. "We've got fruit."

"Vega fruit? You're a god." She even bows dramatically in front of him, making me cringe.

Thankfully, Marc just chuckles, handing her the bag without any Honeycrisps in it and gives me a wink when he sees my apprehension.

"Marc, look! It's Marcus."

Marcus, the bull, is here, too, and I smile at the reminder of Hunter naming him. Every calf born at Graham gets named, and despite Marc hating the name Marcus, I didn't feel right changing it.

Marc leans down beside Hunter, grabbing the little bull's face in his hands. "Think he'll earn some medals, too?"

Around a bite of apple, Sydnee breaks the news to him, saying, "He's not here for competing. He's here for eating." She scrunches her face, then corrects herself. "He's here to be eaten."

"What?" Marc looks at me, equal parts horror and confusion.

"Sydnee's right, although she didn't have to say it so bluntly." She shrugs, forgetting that normal people don't talk about slaughtering animals quite so easily. "Graham's a dairy farm. They don't have use

for bulls." Everything serves a purpose there. Marcus's is a nice price…
hopefully. "He'll most likely be sold to a butcher."

Hunter drops his head. He hates the fact that Graham doesn't
keep every calf. He'd raise each and every one if he had it his way.

"Or, somewhere that impregnates heifers like the place we use,"
Sydnee says, pointing with the half-eaten apple. "Then they won't kill
Marcus. They'll just milk him for all he's worth."

I slice my hand across my throat, telling her to shut the hell up.
Again, she needs to think about who she's talking to before she speaks,
especially at a public event. It's probably one of the reasons my parents didn't want her to run all the markets and festivals. She knows
her stuff with the calves but it's the humans she struggles to connect
with. Having more bovines than humans around can do that.

Hunter frowns up at me. "I thought you said bulls can't be
milked."

Marc stands so suddenly, holding his palms up in front of him
and saying, "I'm gonna find the bathroom."

After scowling at my sister, then giving Hunter a tight smile, I
turn to watch Marc's shaking back, wondering where all those *we*
statements are now.

It's not long before he returns though, not even bothering to wipe
the grin from his face.

Sydnee's just finishing mixing up electrolytes with three baby as-
pirin in a bottle of warm water for one of the calves whose manure
color is off. Just like human babies, calves can get sick at the drop of
a hat, so you have to be prepared to treat them as best you can, even
if that means getting creative for things like heating water.

"So, how'd it go with Shawnathon when you saw him?" she asks
like she can't hold it in any longer.

"What do you mean? When?"

"He was literally just here before you showed up. I thought you
would've passed him. Well, them."

"Dad!" Hunter pushes between me and Marc, then I hear the
"oof" of him jumping into Shawn's arms.

I don't look though. I don't turn around at all. I don't even re-fill my lungs.

She said "them."

Meeting Sydnee's sympathetic eyes is a mistake.

Coming here was a mistake.

Bringing Marc was a mistake.

Thinking this wouldn't explode was a mistake.

Assuming I ever had a say, any say, was the biggest mistake of all.

"I thought we might find you here."

I don't even know who my ex is talking to but I squeeze my eyes shut, wishing a hole would appear and swallow me and my stupidity whole so I never have to find out. He planned this? Of course he did.

Opening my eyes to find Marc already turned around and facing Shawn, I slowly do the same, telling him, "We'd never miss it." Which he knows.

"Ready to meet your sister?" Shawn's words are for Hunter but his eyes are locked on mine, refusing to let go as the world speeds up, making me dizzy from hearing him say "sister."

Just let me go already.

I return his weighted gaze despite seeing Marc staring at me as well out of the corner of my eye.

Hunter let it slip a while back about the pink room his dad was painting but I didn't...I didn't want to believe it. I still don't.

I definitely didn't think the baby was here already. I thought—I hoped—the birth was months off still.

It makes sense, why Shawn even bothered with that overly nice guy act before. I thought it was for Marc, but now, I know. Just like always, he was pulling the bag over my head while preparing to pull the rug out from under me, wanting to make my fall that much more pointed. That much more painful. But, even if Shawn used his bare hands to break my rib cage apart and expose my insides to everyone in this circle, I'd be in less pain than I am right now and I wouldn't even need the bag at all.

Despite every molecule in my being telling me not to, I drag my eyes from Shawn's over to the woman beside him, then run my gaze the length of the baby currently snuggled in the carrier strapped to her chest.

Hunter takes one soft-eyed glance at the sleeping baby and I fix my focus on him instead. What is he thinking? How does he feel about having a…sibling now? Does he understand what this means yet?

No, he doesn't, and I hope he won't for a very long time.

With a grin so bright it hurts to look directly at, Shawn finally speaks to me, saying, "Bent, you know Windy, right?" He releases one of his arms from Hunter to slide it around his girlfriend's back.

Know her? How could I? Shawn never let me near the house to ever meet her. And now I know why.

"Not officially." He knows I'm aware of who she is but I'm not sure she does. "Hi, I'm Bentlee."

She smiles softly, dropping her face to kiss the top of the baby's head sticking out and says, "Oh, I know. Hunter talks about you all the time."

"Congratulations," I say through the agony coursing through my body.

"Thanks. We're still getting adjusted."

She gives me a flustered look I feel down to my toes. Those first few months after birth are both exhausting and exhilarating.

Marc shifts beside me but I don't dare look in his direction. If only he was still in the bathroom. If only he wasn't here at all. If only I'd never gone to that gender reveal party and gotten mixed up with his entire friend group. *If only.*

"Hunter, help me with this bottle," Sydnee says unhelpfully. She's trying to give us a moment. I don't need it. I don't want it. I've wasted enough time with this. So many moments gone forever on thinking and overthinking, guessing and second-guessing. At the end of the day, look where it got me. Look where it fucking got me.

"Marcus, was it?" Shawn snipes and I automatically correct him, saying, "It's Marcos," not because Marc will get mad like Shawn, but because Marcos is a beautiful name and Marcus…is a cow.

"I go by Marc," Marc tells Windy after an awkward pause. Then it's as if I'm underwater listening when he asks, "How, uh, how old?" gesturing to the baby and I wish I was.

Eyeing the trough in the corner that's foaming with cow saliva, I contemplate sticking my head in it just so I don't have to hear her answer.

"Seven days."

Shawn dropped Hunter off to me early on Sunday but didn't give a reason and I wasn't about to question his decision to give me more time with my son. Turns out it wasn't for me or for Hunter, it was because he was busy having another baby.

"Newborn smell is the best," I murmur, watching her smell the baby's head. Both my words and the ground around me shake with yearning. I love that smell. I *miss* that smell.

"Tell them the name," Shawn says, the smile on his face revealing his true intention—spite. That's why he's here right now, to torture me. My penance for leaving him will never end.

"Bryanne."

"Brian?" I look between them, confused. I can't see the baby's face but with the mention of a pink room, I kind of assumed…

"No, her name's Bry-anne. Like Cheyenne."

A muffled chuckle next to me has me dropping my chin to my chest, trying to hide mine as well. This is *not* funny.

Shawn might've unknowingly given Hunter an oxymoronic name but our son's the only one of us with a normal name that's easy to say and spell correctly.

"Yeah, so anyway, can I get Hunter tonight? Next weekend doesn't work anymore."

I pop my head up, narrowing my eyes; but Hunter, trying to balance the bottle on his forearm like a fancy waiter offering up expensive wine to the calf, speaks up, saying, "I thought we were camping tonight?"

I finally, finally look at Marc. Camping? Since when?

Luckily he's focusing on Hunter to tell him, "We can do that anytime."

I rip my gaze away from Marc to stare at my ex.

"Shawnathon. It's Halloween."

Shawn huffs, "Fine, we'll watch him next weekend. Whatever."

Watch him? Like he's babysitting someone he's saddled with, not enjoying quality time with his own flesh and blood. He's acting like he's doing me a favor somehow when really I'd give anything not to have to share Hunter on Halloween. But we already talked it all out. Hunter's looking forward to both of us coming together again to go trick-or-treating.

"At least this way you'll have more time to find a routine. You know, without a seven-year-old underfoot, too."

Both Shawn and Windy give me blank stares. They didn't even consider what it'd be like taking care of Bryanne and Hunter at the same time. I'm long past thinking Shawn gives a single shit about me, but the fact that almost eight years in, he still acts selfishly without considering Hunter, not even for a second, has never been more apparent than right now.

After a few more minutes of forced small talk, they say their goodbyes, but even after they're gone from the building, I keep my gaze fixed on the ground, pretending this was all in my imagination.

"When did you guys break up again?"

How could I imagine something so awful though? And why?

"January first," I say without looking at Marc. I don't need to. I can practically feel the questions coming from him.

How long did they wait after Hunter and I moved out? Hours? Days? Did they even wait?

But I actually know the answer to that last one. It's one of the reasons why I moved in the first place. It's *the* reason why I learned how to pick a lock.

I close my eyes, willing the tears beneath the lids to go somewhere else, anywhere other than my cheeks, and when I open them again, my parents are heading right for me, my mom's eyebrows scraping the ceiling.

Is that trough still available?

Chapter 23

Bentlee

"And here's your bed." Hunter points to a flattened spot in the mass of blankets covering the living room floor. This is what they meant about going camping. Sleeping under the stars…on the ceiling. "You get to be between me *and* Marc."

My eyes dart over to the side of Marc's face as he sets up the star projector. He still hasn't said a single word to me. He introduced himself to my parents but didn't speak to me otherwise. It's been…heartbreaking. If that organ wasn't already beating erratically from Shawn and Windy's surprise appearance, Marc's repulsion to me would've done the trick all its own.

"The couch looks nice," I say, pointing to it. "I think I'll just sleep here, if that's okay."

I've been a trembling mess since Sydnee mentioned Shawn's name. It feels like my bones are rattling inside my body like that Halloween glow-in-the-dark skeleton hanging on our neighbor's front door. Except instead of glowing, I'm just sweating.

After going to get changed into my pajamas, I'm walking back out to the main room when I hear Marc talking, so I slow my steps, losing myself in his deep voice.

"Farmers were the first people to use the stars."

"Really? Like your dad?"

Marc laughs. "You gotta say that to him next time you see him, okay?" There's a pause, then, "He's not *quite* that old, but yeah, farmers like my dad. They'd watch the stars to know when it was time to harvest."

"Wow. What else?"

My back to the hallway wall, I slide down until I hit the floor with my legs out in front of me.

"Animals. The sky's full of them. We probably can't see all of them with this thing but let's see. Okay, there's a crab, a scorpion, a lion, and a unicorn somewhere but I've never been able to find it. Here's one you'll like. Remember Orion?" Hunter must point it out because then Marc says, "Good. So now you look for the V-shaped cluster. They're part of the Taurus constellation."

"A Taurus? What kind of animal is that?"

"A bull."

"It's Marcus!"

Together they laugh and I close my eyes, committing the sound to memory. It sounds like Christmas morning—magical—and I never want it to end.

"Sure." There's still laughter in Marc's voice. "The bull, or Marcus, is said to be protected by the goddess of love."

"By *love?*"

Hearing Hunter's skepticism I can't help but smile.

"Trust me, I used to think the same thing. Then I learned that love is one of the strongest feelings there is. It's faster than light. It even outlasts death. It makes people do crazy things they wouldn't normally do."

I lean my head back, looking at the wall opposite me.

"Like what?"

Marc's quiet for a long time, then so low I have to strain to hear, he says, "Pretend."

There's some rustling, then Hunter whispers, "One time I pretended to like Mom's potato soup, does that count?"

Marc chuckles softly while I frown. He really had me fooled.

"Yeah. That was you protecting her because you love her and didn't want to hurt her feelings."

"I love my mom *so* much."

"I know. You hit the jackpot."

"Would you pretend for her?"

I push off the floor, clapping my hands together to drown out any answer he might give. Or not give. Either way I don't want to hear it. Not tonight.

"Alright, I'm ready to get my gaze on," I say as I enter the living room, flopping onto the couch with a loud bounce.

Marc mock-whispers, "Mom joke," making Hunter laugh and I throw a couch cushion at them, knocking over a stack of DVDs instead which only makes them laugh harder.

Marc obliges by continuing his star tour all the way up until light snores replace Hunter's questions.

The silence when he does finally stop digs under my skin and I have to close my eyes against the feeling.

Careful to keep my voice low, I say, face to the stars, "Two doors down there's this sweet old lady that invites us in every year to show off her Christmas nativity set. It doesn't matter that it's only October, she spends the whole month decorating her entire foyer. Knowing she doesn't get many visitors, she does it in time for Halloween so she actually has people to show it to. We've been going there since Hunter's first Halloween and every year she points out all the new decorations she's added. Even if we don't technically live there anymore, I can't imagine not taking Hunter to keep up the tradition."

"That's the real reason…"

"The *one* time I called Shawn, it was to see if he was planning on bringing Windy trick-or-treating, too. I just wanted to prepare myself so something like today didn't happen." Today, I was blindsided and it gutted me.

"Because of the baby?"

I press my palms into my eyes like it'll keep the tears from forming.

"I didn't even know there'd *be* a baby." Aside from our old neighbor's tiny baby Jesus, all nestled in the handmade manger. "When I brought up Halloween, Shawn didn't even mention Windy, and since he's never been forthcoming about her being pregnant at all, I thought we were safe. I thought I was safe from the *look*, the same one I saw tonight."

"Who cares what your old neighbor lady thinks? It's none of her business."

That's true, but it doesn't stop the fact that she'll still be doing the math in her head, just like Marc did. Just like my parents did. It doesn't stop the scrutiny she'll be broadcasting when she looks at me over her Christmas decorations. When they *all* look at me.

Judgement. How do we measure up against each other? Did Shawn trade up or down?

Pity. Being replaced is one thing, staring your replacement in the face while having to keep a smile plastered to yours is just brutal. Today proved that.

Suspicion. What really happened? Was it something I did?

It doesn't matter what's true and what's not, the questions will still be there, and I won't be able to answer any of them because I'll be too busy pretending like everything's okay because one of us has to think about Hunter.

"It's not like-"

"Yes, it is. It's exactly like what everyone's wondering." Including him. I know he wants to ask. "She might've become pregnant after I left, but…but she could've just as easily before."

I let that sink in, feeling like I'm naked. Naked and afraid. Why do people find that so entertaining? It's fucking humiliating.

"It's embarrassing," I voice, barely above a whisper.

"What do you have to be embarrassed about? That was *his* choice."

It was Shawn's choice to cheat but what made him feel like he even had the option? Nobody can tell me I didn't play a part in that.

"I wish it was that simple." I wish I had Marc's confidence. He doesn't seem to care what anybody thinks.

"When did you know?"

"Last fall." The night I went out to my parents' looking for answers and ended up finding Beckett instead.

Automatically, my fingers go to the tattoo on my shoulder, rubbing the meaningful ink.

Movement from his spot on the floor echoes throughout the apartment, then Marc's voice reaches out to me even though he does not. "Why didn't you leave then?"

"I didn't know how. Physically. Emotionally. Financially. I didn't know how to get both of us out with as little damage as possible but I tried. I tried." I shake my head against the pillow.

I knew where things were going, had for a while, I just didn't know how exactly to make the necessary moves to get there as safely as possible. A breakup between two people is manageable. It's treatable. A breakup within a family can be irreparable. I didn't know how to ensure that this time wasn't. I still don't really.

After that night, when I stumbled across Marc's best friend, when I proved to myself that I was capable, that what seemed impossible wasn't always, I became motivated.

So, I waited. I adapted. I looked outside of myself and my heartache and I saw what really mattered—my child. Once the holidays were over and I finally had my bookkeeping certification, I channeled all of that and I left Shawn for good, giving Hunter a mother that was split wide open but not broken. Never broken.

"How'd you find out?"

Something about not seeing his face makes this easier and I keep my eyes shut tight to take a bobby pin from my hair, tossing it on the table between us, unsure where it lands exactly, just that it tings atop the wood surface a couple times before going silent.

I picture him nodding his head, trying to piece it all together.

"Do you still love him? Is that why you cover for him?"

I finally open my eyes, letting them focus on the star-covered ceiling again. Do I *still* love Shawn? The more time I spend away from Shawn, the more time I spend with Marc, the more I wonder if that was even love at all.

"I don't out Shawn about the affair because I don't want Hunter to question his worth like I did." *Like I still do.*

If I admit what Shawn did as a way to make myself look better, it won't actually *feel* any better. It'll only hurt worse because it'd hurt Hunter. Shawn didn't just cheat on me, he cheated on his family, on *our* family.

"I don't want Hunter to think what his dad did was acceptable or, even worse, that it's his fault, but I'm not stupid. I know he'll figure it out one day. I'm just hoping by then he'll be able to tell right from wrong and that the unconditional love I provided him was enough not to ruin his entire childhood."

"And what if Hunter blames you for keeping the truth from him instead?"

"That's a risk I'm willing to take." One of many. Parenthood isn't based on certainties. It's not a one-size-fits-all guarantee. It's trial and error followed by more trials and more errors. It's hope based on gut feelings and lessons taken from personal experiences. No one child is the same nor are the parents raising them. We're all learning at the same time. Some people are just better at faking it.

Some chances are riskier than others. Will showering your child with the love you were denied make them see how much they mean to you, or make them resent you, too, for projecting your own insecurities onto them? Will giving their father more credit than he deserves make them distrust everything you tell them? I don't know. But I never truly know what will happen.

The one thing I do know is if I should ever fall along the way, I won't quit because there is no length I won't go for my son. If I lost my eyes, I'd stumble blindly to him. If I lost my voice, I'd listen closely for him. If I lost my feet, I'd crawl endlessly, searching for him.

As long as I have my heart—the heart that never tires for Hunter—then that'll never steer me wrong. Of that I have no doubt.

While Marc was right about love being the strongest emotion, whoever said love was easy couldn't have been more wrong. Love is the ocean, continuously ebbing and flowing with stubborn resilience. Love is the sky, beautiful and reliable but moody and dangerous. Love is physically demanding battles, internal and external. Love is simultaneously the easiest and most exhausting tornado to get caught inside of. Sometimes you choose to be swept away by the contrasting chaos of it all. Sometimes you never get the choice at all.

Isn't that what Paige and Angela were trying to tell me at the bonfire?

But how can I expect Marc to understand? Until he has a child of his own and has to make sacrifices that don't make sense to anyone else, he won't. Yes, Marc's mature and kind and generous but he doesn't get what it means to love someone so wholly that you forget you even exist.

I swallow thickly, telling him, "There's…something else."

Footsteps fall against the carpeted floor like a train eating up railway sleepers on its nighttime journey, then he's standing above me, a perfect statue of enigmatic beauty—not a god like Sydnee claimed, but a fallen angel, too tempting to refuse.

Chapter 24

Marc

A HUNDRED THOUGHTS, EMOTIONS, *SECRETS*, WHIR IN that pretty head of hers, each one stronger than the last as she deliberates below me, weighing whether she should tell me the truth or not.

I slide my arms behind her back and under her knees, lifting her off the couch in one easy motion.

"What are you doing?"

I don't know. I don't have a fucking clue what I'm doing at all anymore.

But I do know one thing.

"I want you with me."

"But Hunter-"

"Is asleep. Don't worry. I'm not gonna try anything."

Settling her on the part Hunter specifically saved just for her, I take up her other side, turning so we're facing each other.

I'm fucking terrified to hear what she's about to say. Terrified because if she says what I'm thinking, then this might be our last night together. If Shawn so much as laid a hand on her or Hunter, I'll be in jail before first light hits tomorrow morning.

My eyes study hers. "You don't have to tell me." I want her to and I don't. I need to know but it could change everything. It would change everything.

She closes those eyes, denying my need for them, and whispers, "I don't talk about the other reason I left because it'd show just how weak I really am when all I'm trying to be is strong."

After a moment, she opens her eyes again, meeting mine and there are even more emotions, even more pain in them. *Christ.*

"Shawn always wanted things the way he wanted them, and if they weren't, he'd twist reality so that they were. He'd do and say *anything* to get his way. He was so…persuasive, at least that's what I thought for a long time. That he was passionate, compelling. It wasn't until I started noticing just how manipulative he was that I saw the damage he was doing with all of his so-called persuasion."

"Did he ever use physical force? On either of you?"

I'm already imagining my keys in my hand, my helmet on my head, flying down the stairs to my Duc. I won't even take a weapon with me—I won't need one.

"That's the thing, he didn't seem to do it with everyone, just me. Like it was me specifically that he wanted under his thumb."

Her gaze narrows, lost in thought.

"Bentlee." I keep my voice low but say each word clearly. "Did he ever hit you?"

Thankfully, she shakes her head, breaking the spell to say, "No, it never got that far."

We both fall quiet for a while, then I break the silence by telling her honestly, "You're one of the strongest people I know."

To smile in the face of the one responsible for piercing your heart takes courage. To walk away with your head held high while you're still bleeding out, that takes strength—a lot of it. And Bentlee was able to do both. Twice. I watched her do it tonight.

"It doesn't feel like that to me."

"It never does."

Her eyebrows crease. "What do you mean? You're so confident and fearless all the time."

"People aren't brave. People choose to be brave. And that choice?

It isn't always made intentionally, sometimes it's made in the moment, out of necessity."

"You make it look easy," she grumbles, and I grin, telling her softly, "I've just got more practice."

Shawn tried so hard to fuck Bentlee up. That's what they do. They play mind games. They victim blame. They blur the facts and manipulate the events until the women believe they're the cause, the problem, the ones that brought the mistreatment on themselves. He probably even has her thinking she's the reason he cheated. That's classic abuser mentality. Yet, Shawn's still got a hold on Bentlee without her even realizing it. I never would've believed it either if I hadn't seen it with my own eyes last weekend when Bentlee completely shut down the second Shawn tried his bullshit on her out front. Because how she is with me, she's different. She's brave, strong, a fucking force that doesn't back down from what she wants. She makes *me* bend. She makes *me* compromise. The difference is I do so willingly—for her.

Shawn's the one that's weak. Even the way he tried to finagle their visitation agreement today just so he could feel the slightest bit of control. It's not about being with his kid. It's about seeing how high he can make Bentlee jump, even still. She didn't so much as budge—luckily—but that was one time in what sounds like a long history of him pushing, nudging, goading her to. He's a piece of shit I wish Bentlee and Hunter didn't have to deal with, but unfortunately, they do.

Which means I do, too.

"I could go with you." I'd just need to work it out with Kary first. It's one of the few times she doesn't fight me on taking Rebel out of the complex. I won't miss Halloween with them but I want to be there for Bentlee, too.

"Trick-or-treating?" She's already shaking her head. "I don't think that's a good idea. It's already confusing as it is. We're just-"

"I got it, Bentlee," I bite out, well aware of the fucking score. Keep this—keep us—to secret meetups, stolen glances, and hidden touches. That's all I'm good for—a fuck, as she likes to remind me. "It doesn't mean we can't be friends outside of my bedroom. If you need me, I'm here." Always.

She lied to protect the person she loves most. I know what that feels like. I know what that does to a person, how it tears them up but fills them at the same time. To know your loved one is safe, happy, healthy, there's nothing like it. To know you have a hand in it, the sacrifice it takes, it's an honor not everyone's privileged to.

She blows out a breath but I start talking before her tongue can lash out and strike me fucking dead. "Do you know why I like the stars?"

"Because you are one?"

I laugh, feeling some tension leave my body for the first time since the Fall Fest. "Nah, not even close." I don't have to tell her about life growing up on a farm because she gets it, more than most, so I just share some of the more memorable trips I've taken.

"It doesn't seem like you even like people very much."

I shrug. *That's fair.*

"I don't have to be social to still notice and appreciate both the differences and similarities between people. I think you find out more about people by not interacting. By just sitting back and watching, you can learn a lot about someone. That's when people are unguarded and show their true selves."

She gives me a long look that I couldn't decipher if I tried.

"Anyway, there are certain things that every person on earth sees the same way."

"Like stars?" she asks, covering a yawn.

"Like stars."

I tuck my hand between her thighs, keeping my distance from being downright inappropriate but still staying close to what Bentlee thinks I like most about her. It's what I always do before we fall asleep together.

"You can look up at the sky and know that somewhere out there, someone else is seeing the same stars you are and it doesn't matter where they are, or what language they speak, or how they were raised, or how much money they make, or even what their last name is. You're never really alone when you look at the stars because we're all being held captive by the same show. We've just got different seats."

After a secretive smile, her eyes flutter closed, and just like every other time, I wait a few minutes until I see the movement behind her lids stop, then I remove my hand, sliding it up to her chest to hold against her sternum, over the part I love most about Bentlee—her heart. There's nothing else I'd rather fall asleep to than her heartbeats, and on the nights we don't share the same bed, sleep doesn't come as easily for me. Not anymore.

I didn't get the chance to answer Hunter's question earlier.

Would I pretend for Bentlee?

I already do.

"Go ahead. Give it your best shot."

"Really?"

"If you don't, I will," Bentlee threatens and I smirk, about to do it myself if Hunter doesn't hurry up.

With a smile the size of Texas, he tosses the rubber ball over his head, folding in half with laughter the second one of the goats seizes up and falls over.

Damn. What if they really do die one time? Is there a way to tell the difference?

Its head is still trying to move, so there's that, I guess. Whatever. I'll figure it out eventually.

Slipping between the newly built fence, Hunter chases after the ball, zig-zagging between the goats—fainting goats. A few chill in some tires I half buried in the ground while the others just try to avoid the ball—and Hunter—at all costs. I don't know why I thought they'd go after the ball like dogs. They're fucking scared of everything.

"Can we get some slides?"

"Slides?" Do they even sit?

"For them to climb."

"They'll climb anything," Bentlee says, her hair dirty blonde reflecting the afternoon sun.

She looks over at me and nothing else matters but this moment.

"Sure," I tell Hunter without taking my eyes off Bentlee's. Fuck it. I'm not about to start half-assing this shit now.

"I don't think you know what you got yourself into." She turns away to watch Hunter run around, talking to the goats with zero hesitancy or his typical shyness, but the whole time I just keep watching her, thinking, *yes, I do.*

With only my nighttime rough-sketch to go off of, I had a team out here for the last week and a half, getting this entire area mapped out properly before they actually began construction, building the fenced enclosure along with some pens. My goal was to have it all done before Halloween and here we are already getting the goats settled into their new home three days ahead of schedule.

It actually worked out perfectly. Angela's birthday party over at her and Coty's earlier gave me a great excuse to "check on my property" without tipping Bentlee off about the surprise awaiting her and Hunter once we got here.

I know Bentlee's still nervous about Halloween and I wanted her and Hunter to be able to hang on to this, knowing I'm here for them. Shawn's a douche who pretends to give a shit. I gave them goats.

Technically I didn't *give* them the goats. I bought them and own them but they're for Hunter, so he can have friends. Whether in the goats themselves or if he wants to use them as his excuse for joining some kind of club, I don't care. They're his to have. His to love. His to be loved by…if they stop fainting long enough to get to know him.

Holy fuck, they faint a lot.

Maybe Bentlee was right. What did I get myself into?

"I guess this explains where all those tires missing from Pop Two went." Bentlee gestures to the tires currently housing goats and I nod. "Where'd you get the goats though?"

I check out the tops of my shoes, telling her, "The Fall Fest."

"That's where you disappeared to? Back inside to make a purchase?" She lets out a laugh. "You and your secrets, Marc. You're just full of surprises." The way she says it though, there's a slight bite to it that brings my eyes up, raking over every inch of her.

"You don't like it?"

"I think you're nuts. Hunter's always wanted goats but you didn't have to build this on your property. Or buy goats at all." Glancing over her shoulder, she says, "It's so far from your house."

I follow her gaze, seeing the foundation in the distance.

"That's not my house."

She eyes me skeptically, asking, "What is it?"

"Not my house." What the fuck am I supposed to say? It's not. I have no plans on living there. I knew it was only a matter of time before I built it out here, and I needed somewhere to run electricity to my security cameras for my gear, so I started there first. It is what it is, but what it is isn't something I'm ready to share. Yet.

The fact that I want to tell Bentlee doesn't matter. I can't.

"Is it a garage?"

My sudden laugh causes a nearby goat to tip over. "Any garage of mine will be twice the size of that."

"So…" She looks around. "That's not your house." I shake my head. "But you have a goat…I guess we can call it a farm."

I see where she's going.

"I'm not a farmer," I tell her, keeping my voice stern.

"Right. Not a farmer but has a farm. Got it."

I lick my lips, wishing I could kiss her smart mouth.

"And you're going to have a gigantic garage…somewhere. What *are* your plans anyway? Will you ever live out here?"

"Eventually."

"So, there's no rush to leave Creekwood?"

"No." I shrug my shoulders. I couldn't leave if I wanted to. Not until everything else is lined up and I don't know when that will be. *If* it will ever be. I can only do so much. I can only want, and plan, and try so much but it's not my decision when it comes down to it. Kary holds all the cards, even if I wish I did, too.

"Because…you like the neighbors?" Her sarcastic little smile nearly does me in and I almost kiss her anyway. Hunter's so busy he wouldn't see. Maybe.

"Roommates actually."

Bentlee's smile slips.

"Marc. If we're holding you back-"

"You're not."

"But-"

"I do what I want, right? And I *want* to be at Creekwood."

I want to be near Rebel. It's like what Bentlee said about their trick-or-treating tradition. I wouldn't miss something like Halloween, or Christmas, or even her first school play which is coming up. I could still make it to all those without living nearby but it's not just the big things. I don't want to miss *anything*. I'd happily take a day with Rebel when she's sick and achy and needs to be spoon-fed soup that she blanches at because, like Hunter, she doesn't like it either.

"I'll move out here one day," I say. "When I'm ready."

A heavy silence creeps between us, twisting my insides and I can tell we're both thinking the same thing. What will that mean for her and Hunter when I move? Will Bentlee sign a new contract with Creekwood or...?

What if I want that or? What if I don't have a fucking clue what that is, but whatever it is, I want it to be with me? I want her to be with me. I want them both to be with me.

I want them *all* to be with me.

Maybe that's the real reason why I bought the goats. To give me a reason to keep Bentlee and Hunter for myself that much longer because I'm a greedy fuck.

That invisible timeline ticks even louder, making me frown. Who's out of time though?

Time is such a fucking thief but I like everything I have right now.

Hunter clutches his stomach giggling at one of the goats trying to bite the ball and Bentlee laughs, too, shaking her head and ducking between the fence slats to join him.

I *love* everything I have right now.

But how much longer will I have it? And why can't I keep it?

Beck said we were keeping Bentlee but he didn't say for how long.

"At least you still have enough land to build your track," she says, trying to lighten the mood.

"That's next," I tell her seriously but she doesn't hear me as she tries to coax the ball out of the goat's mouth. I get caught up watching her, the way she leans over the goat, handling it with such practiced care. She's a natural, just like Hunter. She may not want a career that's forced onto her because of her last name but there's no question that she and her boy love animals. They belong out here.

I could always just change that last name of hers, then they really would belong out here…with me. Forever.

A trailer carrying the final delivery pulls in and Bentlee's gaze shoots to mine, a million questions building beneath those blue-green pools.

Sydnee drops down from the driver's side, waving a hand at Hunter as he stops what he's doing to tilt his head to the side, a couple questions of his own simmering. Once the back door of the trailer is opened and the bull comes into view, they all disappear.

"Marcus!" he yells, sprinting so quickly the wind couldn't outrun him.

"You didn't think I'd leave my man hanging, did you?" I call out to Bentlee, the ball in her hold dropping from her fingertips as quickly as the bottom half of her jaw.

Now I'm a motherfucking farmer.

Chapter 25

Backing into a spot at Creekwood, Shawn parks his Audi, then lowers the volume on the radio, asking Hunter for a black licorice while I try not to gag. I can't believe someone had the audacity to pass that crap out, to children of all people. Giving out black licorice on Halloween is like gifting coal on Christmas.

Windy opted out of trick-or-treating to stay in with Bryanne and hand out candy at Shawn's place—their place—instead. I thought it'd feel better. I thought I'd feel better. It's what I wanted, Windy out of the picture for a few short hours where I could pretend everything was a shade of normal.

Or so I thought.

Things felt worse than ever and I caught myself wishing I'd taken Marc up on his offer to join us more times than I care to admit. Without Marc, everything just feels…wrong.

I gaze out the front windshield, wondering what he's doing right now. His car and bike are both parked in the lot which I hadn't even considered. I thought he'd be with his friends at the very least. Or one of those biker parties he's told me about. Apparently there's always a big Halloween one with costumes and dumpster fires and crazy burnouts, all at whatever abandoned warehouse they can find.

Catching movement from the courtyard, my eyes focus on what looks like a mini princess with a long braid draped over her shoulder and she's got a leather jacket over the top of her purple gown. For some reason Hunter's friend Rebel springs to mind, and when I peek at the backseat, I find his gaze aimed in the same direction.

Pieces of wispy blonde hair blow away from her face to reveal it is Rebel, smiling over at someone like they've given her the moon, the stars, and something else, something just as intangible but even more impressive.

With a sword in each hand, she's anything but the typical princess. Or maybe we're all fitted for swords, we just wield them differently.

She disappears from sight, and not a moment later, Marc strolls around the side of the building, coming from the same spot Princess Rebel just was.

"Can I go up and get my bag now?"

Before I can say I'll get it for him, Shawn asks me to stay behind a minute. His seemingly altruistic offer to drive us tonight is starting to make sense now.

I nod tightly, telling Hunter to look both ways before crossing the lot and reminding him not to eat any of his candy until one of us can check it all. I wish I could trade places with him. I don't want to sit here another minute with Shawn. Not when Marc's right there. Not ever.

Silently, we watch Marc wait for Hunter, his inflatable-cowboy-on-a-horse costume dragging behind him now that the fan is off. After making eye contact with me through the thick glass, Marc leads him upstairs, casting a few more looks over his shoulder before going inside.

As usual, Shawn sprung this whole carpool idea on me at the last minute or I would've told Marc beforehand.

"What's that guy's deal? He looks like he wants to stomp the life out of me just so he can revive me himself to do it all over again."

I bite my lips between my teeth. *He probably does.*

"Is that what you wanted to talk to me about? How my roommate feels about you? You could've just asked him yourself." Okay, that part's a stretch. Marc doesn't waste words, especially not on someone like Shawn. The last time he even bothered at all, Shawn wasted enough words for all of us.

A deep cringe contracts my entire body remembering that day and how Shawn was being, like there was still something between us.

I guess it wasn't all bad though, considering how it got Marc to reveal some of those deep-seated desires of his. Marc doesn't display his emotions on his sleeve. He tucks them so far out of reach, you'd pull a muscle trying to find them yourself, but that night he opened up enough to put up some boundaries around our…relationship. I have to admit, it was sexy hearing Marc say he wanted me all to himself. It was even sexier when he said I had him all to myself.

I fan my face, gravitating toward the chill emanating from the closed window. It's finally one of those perfect fall days with stray leaves swirling outside around the car in a cold gust I wish I was feeling instead of just watching.

"Your roommate? You're telling me there's nothing going on between you two?"

"I'm not telling you anything because that's none of your business."

His laugh is bitter and harsh, colder than any breeze. "You think he actually wants you?"

And just like that, his hands are on the rug beneath me, ready to yank.

But…I didn't let him slip the bag over my head this time. I can see what Shawn's doing. I can see Shawn for who he really is now.

Marc has said several times that he does want me. He's also followed through by showing me he does which is more than I can say for Shawn. Of course, there will always be that little doubt made bigger by comments like this though.

I remain quiet, hoping to weather the storm that much quicker if I don't engage.

"Bent, guys like that don't have the first clue what it takes to run a household. In case you've forgotten, you're not some hot single catch. You have a kid. *My* kid. You think any guy in his right mind would actually want to take you *and* your fucking baggage on?"

Baggage? Is he serious right now? How can he even say that? Hunter's not my baggage. Shawn is.

That's not even mentioning the fact that Marc "taking us on" has never been discussed. I've never expected anything like that from Marc.

There may have been moments of intense weakness here and there where I've imagined it, but to actually put that kind of responsibility on Marc…I wouldn't. Couldn't.

"Let me be the one to break it to you. The answer is no. Especially that guy." He points up at the front balcony just as Marc steps out onto it, leaning his forearms against the banister as he stares down at us openly. "No way."

"Why do you keep saying it like that? *That* guy. You don't even know Marc."

My own bitter laugh leaves me and I shake my head. There is so much more to Marc, even from what I used to think and I used to think pretty fucking highly of him.

"Neither do you if you think he's gonna swoop in and be your hero."

Hero. Marc already saved me—twice. And both times he did it unknowingly. I don't need him to save me a third time. I…have my own swords. Don't I? I just need to start wielding them better.

"You want to talk about what it takes to run a household, Shawnathon?" I feel myself stepping off the rug, ready to stand on my own. "It doesn't include pretending to work late while going to fuck somebody else. It doesn't mean ignoring your own child to sneak around only to knock another woman up with one more child you plan on ignoring."

"So, you think you're the hero here? Saint Bentlee, saving one bastard child at a time."

Tears fill my eyes and threaten to clog my throat. My fingers arch into claws on instinct, wanting flesh. Wanting blood. My child, our child, is off-limits.

"Fuck. You." I've never been so happy not to be married to Shawn than I am right now. I'd rather have a bastard child than a son of a bitch for a husband.

"At least you've upgraded from begging to actually offering now."

"It wasn't an offer." I'd never sleep with Shawn again. I used to think sex with Shawn was just that, sex. After being with Marc though, I know how wrong I was. That wasn't even sex, it was just pathetic. Shawn is pathetic.

He gestures to Marc, drawing Marc's eyebrows together ever more. It's obvious we're talking about him but thankfully he can't hear us. This is bad enough. Me knowing I was with this person is bad enough. "Is that how you get him, too? With your constant guilt trips and pity parties about how you're not getting enough attention?"

I lean my head as far back against the headrest as it'll go, past the point of pain—in my neck, my head, my fucking heart. It takes my eyes from Marc's but I don't want him to see this.

"I'm going to find someone that I don't have to beg, to plead," my voice cracks despite my efforts to keep it even, "to *guilt* into wanting me." Marc proved that already. And if he can, then maybe somebody else might, too. My chest aches to cave in at that thought above all the others but I press on, telling Shawn, "And you'll just be *that* ex. The one he asks what I ever saw in. And I'll laugh and it'll hurt, not because I can't bear the memory of us, but because it'll be forced because I won't have an answer." Water spraying off my lips from the tears, I twist my neck to look him in the eye, saying, "I don't have an answer."

"You forget, Bent. *I* was your original hero. *I* was your way out. Without me, you'd still be washing cow pies from your hair."

"What do you want from me then? You want me to thank you, is that it? Really? Why am I even here?"

"I don't know!" he yells suddenly, making me flinch. "I don't know. I just… You made me be with Windy. You made me this. She was *nothing* to me but now because of you, I'm stuck with a fuck trophy that won't stop crying and Windy, who also never stops fucking crying. I can't take it anymore."

"Don't put this on me. I didn't make you be with her. I *never* made you be with her!" My head flies off the headrest and through blurry eyes I see a figure drop from the second story.

What the hell was that?

"Yes, you did. We'd still be together if it wasn't for you making me go to her. Making me crawl to Windy like a stray fucking dog. I rescued you from your parents and you repay me by handing me off to a side piece?"

"I was planning on leaving you even before I found out about Windy."

His knuckles turn white against the dark of the steering wheel and the menace in his voice has me feeling the first real spike of fear as he says quietly, "You wouldn't have though."

"Yes, I would've." I so badly want to believe that. "We weren't working long before Windy entered the picture."

"What if Windy wasn't in the picture anymore?"

Huh? But she is and she always will be because she has his child. How does he manage to make us all seem so indispensable? Because he believes we are.

"Even if she wasn't, I still don't want to be with you."

The passenger side door jerks open but Shawn reaches across me, his arm pressing the wet fabric of my shirt against my quivering stomach as he scrambles to hold on to the handle.

"God. What the fuck? Can we get some privacy?"

"No." Marc yanks so hard, the movement takes Shawn with the door as he stretches across my abdomen, struggling to wrestle it from Marc. My stomach roils from it all.

"I'm trying to talk to my girl."

"I'm not-" I start only to be cut off by Marc saying, "She's not yours anymore. She's *mine*."

My chest expands beneath Shawn's weight. Marc's not supposed to talk like that out in the open, not to other people, and yet, I can't bring myself to care. Not right now. In this moment it doesn't matter if Shawn knows or not. It doesn't matter who knows. I let Marc's words settle over me, as warm and reassuring as the scent of spices in the autumn air filtering in.

Bending down, Marc face-palms Shawn and shoves—hard—causing Shawn to jolt back on his ass before he tells him, "So, keep your fucking hands off her."

With a flurry of elbows, Shawn bounces around in his seat, yelling profanities and, with the door still open, I worry Hunter will come down and see this, never once considering my own safety from Shawn's manic flailing.

Ducking inside, Marc shields my body with his as he guides me up and out of the car, telling me to go upstairs.

"No. Marc, he's-"

"It's okay. Just go upstairs, Bentlee."

He slips back into the car, taking up the passenger seat he just pulled me from and closes the door, never once taking his eyes from mine.

Hearing Shawn's voice rise even more, I shake my head, wishing he'd just stop already. What was the point in this? Any of this? He doesn't really think there's hope for us, does he? After everything?

With a final nod from Marc, I make my feet turn away, my body following shortly after with my mind still planted firmly inside the car. What's he going to do?

Across the lot, I suddenly hear all noise cut off at once and I whip around to see Marc's hand wrapped around Shawn's throat, his lips moving as his head gestures in my direction. My hand flies to my mouth, then a second later Marc's releasing Shawn and stepping out of the Audi, slamming the door shut behind him.

He waits until Shawn starts up the engine.

He waits until Shawn pulls out of the spot.

He waits until the car disappears from sight.

Then and only then does he turn to face me and what I see has me wavering all over again.

Somehow I become rooted to my spot, absolutely riveted as he approaches, his eyes an inferno as they scan me. Is he mad? At me? At Shawn?

At himself?

I tried to tell him. So many times. Seriously, what did he expect?

Shawn was right, I'm a fucking mess. A basket case with baby daddy drama. Who the fuck could ever want that?

"What about Hunter? He's supposed to go with Shawn this weekend."

One hand cupping my jaw, he tilts my head up as his chest brushes mine, the heartbeats there pounding just as hard as my own.

"Shawn wanted me to tell you he's not feeling so good and he'll take Hunter next weekend, if he's up for it and it fits your schedule."

If I wasn't still wiping tears from my face, I'd laugh. Shawn would never.

His voice drops to say more seriously, "He's not driving anywhere with Hunter right now. At least not until he cools off."

"About what you said…"

My eyes find his but he lowers his to my mouth.

"I don't want to hide this anymore, mama. I'm done hiding."

"You don't know what you're saying."

Our eyes collide with the subtlety of a crack of thunder and he says, "I do."

My heart skips a beat at those two little words before I can stop it.

"You don't know what you're getting into."

"I do."

Something inside me strains, reaches out, wanting to return the sentiment so bad. *I do.* I never wanted to say those words to Shawn. I wasn't even sure I'd want to with anyone. Now they sit on my tongue, ready to launch us both into uncharted territory.

Something else holds me back though. Something I'm still hiding from him.

His thumb rubs a tear along my cheekbone, studying it.

"It fucking crushed me seeing you and Shawn and Hunter together like a perfect little family. Then I saw you with Shawn and it felt even worse, like someone had stolen my lungs out of my fucking chest. I couldn't *breathe*, Bentlee. When I saw you crying, because of him, I wanted to kill him, take the breath away that he was robbing me of. Him touching you almost put me over the edge but I knew it'd hurt Hunter. Which would hurt you. And I never, ever want to cause you pain. I," his eyes lift to mine slowly and I hold my own breath, "love you, both of you. A lot."

I watch helplessly as that seed of doubt Shawn just planted sprouts, growing rapidly into an entire seedling made up of delicate leaves of insecurity.

With all of us living together, basically playing house for the last couple months, I guess those kinds of feelings are inevitable. Of course we'd develop feelings toward one another. We blurred lines that wouldn't have been touched otherwise. So, is that it? Or is this real?

If it was, I wouldn't be questioning it, would I?

If it was, I wouldn't be questioning him at all.

"What were you doing when we pulled in?" I whisper, watching his eyes, the ones he promised me.

Unsurprisingly, some of that fire diminishes.

When it's clear he's not going to answer, I tell him, "You're not done hiding," and pull his hand off my face. How can you love someone if you won't share yourself fully with them?

A voice in the back of my head echoes back, how can *you* love someone if you won't share yourself fully with them?

I step away but he follows just as quickly, saying, "I deny you nothing."

"You deny me answers, and if you loved me, you wouldn't."

"Don't do that. Don't put conditions on my love. That's something Shawn taught you but I'm not him. I'm nothing like them."

What Shawn really taught me is love without trust isn't love at all. It's a ruse and I'm done deluding myself.

"I'm not doing this sneaking-around shit anymore." With his arms spread wide, he says, "I'm with you, Bentlee. I'm all fucking in with you. Are you with me?"

A part of me wishes we could be together like he says he wants.

Sadly, a bigger part of me knows he absolutely is still doing the sneaking-around shit. If he wasn't, he'd be able to tell me where he was tonight. Because even though I do trust him, trust that he's not doing the same thing Shawn did, I wonder if I should. Marc's great at grand gestures, phenomenal even, but what if they're not grand gestures at all? What if they're just distractions?

"I'm not sure."

"You have-"

"Your eyes, I know. But what about your chest? Why don't you want me to see? What else are you keeping there, Marc? *Show* me." He did last time.

Those very eyes harden though, refusing to compromise, and I sigh sadly.

"You're not done hiding," I repeat, knowing what I'm saying is true.

He's worked to weave himself into every aspect of my life, a complicated thread that can't be unraveled easily, and he thought I wouldn't want the same access. Why?

He shakes his head, a deep frown setting in. "Shawn fucked you up more than I thought."

I know that, I do, but it still hurts hearing it for myself. Maybe because even though he's saying Shawn, in this moment it feels like he could just as easily be saying Marc.

"This isn't about Shawn." *Is it?*

"They're all the same," he says almost to himself, and I ask, "Who?" That's the second time he's said "them" or "they." Who else are we talking about here?

Gripping the back of his neck, he retreats further into himself, a mask slipping over his face while his voice loses any previous emotion.

"He made you doubt real feelings because what he gave you was a cheap replacement for what I could."

Could. Sounds like a cheap replacement to me. Because he's not all in like he claims. Not yet. Not until he's ready to let me in all the way.

How fucking dare he try to convince me otherwise, especially after what Shawn just pulled.

I can't build a life on wishful thinking and inflated possibilities. I need a foundation as sure and strong as the one out at Marc's property, the one he won't tell me about because he's still very much hiding.

He pulls his keys out of his pocket, the metal jingling aggressively loud in the calm evening air as he says, "I've got some stuff to take care of."

"Out of town?" I suspend an exhale, hoping he'll stay and fight. The disappearing act when confronted with hard truths is all too familiar. The similarities are there; I just need to figure out why. If he's not cheating, then what else could he be hiding?

Pinning me with serious eyes, he says, "I'm not going anywhere," and I relieve my aching lungs.

As reassuring as that should be, I don't even know where Marc is when he is here. Not really.

Chapter 26

IT'S SO DARK I CAN BARELY MAKE OUT MY PURSE BESIDE my feet but my shoe sticking to the floor tells me I just put it on some kind of spill. The school's cafeteria doubles as the auditorium, so it's anybody's guess what I'll be cleaning off the bottom of my purse later.

I fight a shiver as I peer down the tight walkway, looking both directions for any hint of Shawn. The last thing I want is to sit next to him for the next forty-five minutes but Hunter wanted us both here to watch his school performance, so both of us he'll get.

Maybe.

I go to text Shawn, but before I can hit send, he's squeezing between me and the seat in front of me to get to the one I saved beside me.

"Parking," he says in answer before I can actually question him. Except for the text Shawn sent me demanding he get Hunter this weekend to make up for last weekend, we haven't spoken since the parking lot incident.

"How did you find me?" The dim light streaming from under the closed curtains on the stage isn't enough for those of us toward the back.

He taps my phone. "It lit up your face. I followed the scowl."

"I'm not scowling," I mutter, immediately thinking about Marc and his perfectly perfected scowls. We haven't spoken since Halloween either. We've spoken but not about anything important. We also haven't touched at all which somehow feels even worse because one touch from Marc doesn't feel like one touch from anyone else. It feels like the sun itself left its outpost in the sky just to graze my skin, making it practically sizzle in need for more. The immense longing the second it's gone is agonizing though and I've been writhing in withdrawals all week, so much so that even now the faintest hint of his scent has the rest of me aching for him.

The smell grows stronger and I cast a look around just to make sure. Since he's working at Pop One today, I only told Angela where I was going. Hunter's school puts this play on every fall. We watched the exact same play last year but he had a different part in it, so here we are, getting ready to watch him be Pumpkin #3. Last year he was a leaf. Kindergartners are leaves, first graders are pumpkins, and I'm not sure what the other grades are. I'm sure we'll find out as they don't seem to switch things up around here all that often.

A man breezes by and, even in the dark, I recognize the walk. Marc doesn't walk, he more so strolls confidently. He's holding a bouquet of flowers that make me stretch my lips wider than they've been all week.

Did Hunter tell him about the play? It wouldn't surprise me. Hunter was very excited about his role as a gourd. Or fruit. I'm not sure what pumpkins are actually but I do know Marc showed up to watch my son imitate one and he even brought flowers.

And just like that, the last week is forgotten. This is what Marc excels at. He does care. And that care sounds, looks, and feels a lot like love, even if it is hard to believe. *Hard to believe? Or accept?*

I search around, trying in vain to find an empty seat nearby, but when I peer back down the walkway, Marc's already making his way down a row closer to the stage. Bringing my phone back up, I decide to text him instead, both to thank him and maybe see if he can snag a few closeups of my little pumpkin.

Light pours out of the curtains as they open halfway and everyone in the audience collectively groans at the sudden brightness. My eyes finally adjust to the light in time to see Marc smirking at the person next to him. They're several rows up, maybe eight or nine, but the blonde hair is somewhat familiar.

The woman turns her head to smile back at him and my entire body goes numb, the noise around me fading to white noise.

Kary?

What's-

"Hello. My name's Johnathon Baker." Shawn scoffs beside me but I ignore him, trying to divide my focus between the man speaking on stage and whatever the hell is happening between Kary and Marc. "I'm the principal here at Howard D. Miller Elementary School, commonly referred to as Old Mill. Welcome."

Marc's neck stiffens and his head swivels from side to side… searching?

Someone in the back yells, "Howdy!" and the principal chuckles, saying, "Good to know the kindergarten parents are with us today." The audience laughs knowingly. It's tradition that the whole school uses "Howdy" as the morning greeting in honor of the founder's childhood nickname. Coincidentally a lot of the kindergarteners end up thinking the school is actually named that. Hunter did for a little while.

Like I said, they don't change things up here, hence *Old* Mill being the real preferred nickname.

Mr. Baker drones on about the history of the school and how it was founded one early November day which is the inspiration for today's play, but I tune him out, watching the back of Marc's head as he continues to glance around while Kary's head beside him remains still, her attention locked on the speaker. The light from the stage might as well be a spotlight on Marc and our apartment manager because they're all I see.

Why are they sitting together? Was it purely coincidental? Why is she even here? Did he invite her?

My right leg bobs furiously, the stickiness infecting my sole noticeable each time I lift my heel off the ground.

Shawn's hand clamps down on my thigh, squeezing with his fingers. "Everyone's looking."

Not everyone.

I smack him off, gritting between my teeth, "Don't touch me." He lost that privilege the same day he lost me.

"Fine," he hisses. "Just don't send your whack-ass boyfriend after me again. He's lucky he caught me on a bad day."

Despite his overly bold tone, Shawn's hand rubs the front of his throat. The fact Marc left his windpipe in working order shows just how lucky Shawn is, not the other way around.

"Without further ado, please enjoy this afternoon's presentation."

The cafeteria/auditorium erupts in applause and the lights cut out again as the curtain closes. When it reopens again, the stage is full of wiggling kids camouflaged as fluttering leaves and the audience claps even louder. Not Kary though. Her hands are too busy holding her phone toward the stage, capturing one long stream of continuous photos. And Marc? His phone's recording a video.

Eyebrows pinched, I sit forward, leaning my elbows on my knees as I scan the stage. After only a few unfamiliar faces, I spy the wispy blonde hair—Rebel's wispy blonde hair. She's shorter than the rest of the kids on stage but she fits right in among the other leaves, pretending to sway in the nonexistent breeze.

I sit back so fast my shoulder blades hit the chair with a thump.

He can't be. He would've told me.

Wouldn't he?

There's no reason why he wouldn't. Why he couldn't. I'm a single parent with a complicated situation with my ex. Why would I mind if he was, too? Out of everyone, I'd be the most understanding, maybe even the only one to get it fully.

Unless.

Unless Kary isn't an ex.

Unless Kary was the part he was hiding.

But he told me there was nothing between them.

The curtain closes and I barely notice, my eyes not even reliable anymore.

"Which pumpkin is he again?" Shawn asks when the curtain re-opens, reminding me the rest of the world didn't just short-circuit like I did.

"Number three," I say on autopilot, lifting my phone with dead hands. I can't feel any part of my body actually, only my lips as they pull into a smile, seeing Hunter sitting like a perfectly regal pumpkin. Just when the curtain starts to draw to a close, he breaks character at the last minute to wave at me. The people around me laugh but I don't react at all. There are already enough bad actors in attendance.

When the curtain opens again, I can feel him. Just like before, I can sense Marc without even needing to see him.

My eyes find his through the crowd as easily as he can spot constellations in the sea of stars. The pain I see staring back at me is just as deceiving as those balls of gas. Some are so much further away than they appear. Some have already blinked out entirely—our eyes just see the figment of what was really there.

I force my eyes closed, making them see what my brain already knows. He's not mine. He never was.

The rest of the play passes in a series of light-induced torture. That's what it feels like anyway. This whole thing is torture and I can't wait to get out of here. I have to stop by Creekwood to get Hunter's overnight bag for Shawn, but after that, I'm gone. I'm so gone.

I'll go, hell, I'll *run* back to Graham. I can never go back to Creekwood again knowing what I know now. I once thought Kary looked familiar, like I might've known her from my past, little did I know she'd be plaguing my present and possibly even the rest of my future.

The curtain opens for the final time and the crowd gets to their feet, applauding…I'd assume loudly but the pounding in my ears makes it impossible to tell.

I just want out. Now.

The harsh overhead lights flick on as a voice over the speakers gives instructions for finding your child which the students ignore by rushing off the stage at once, forcing me to put all my focus on locating Hunter in the G-rated mosh pit. The sooner I find him, the sooner we can get the fuck out of here. I can't face Marc's…face. Or any other part of him. Ever again.

Hunter appears just before his small arms wrap around my middle. "Did you see me?"

I laugh. "I did. In fact," I gaze down at him, "you were so believable, if you were a real pumpkin, I'd pick you."

"Mom joke," I hear beside me and stiffen, my nose stinging with tears.

Hunter, oblivious to Marc's treachery, pulls away, saying, "Marc! You saw me, too?"

My eyes try ever so slightly to lift in the area I've just deemed completely off-limits but I catch them when his pants come into view and avert my gaze immediately.

"You did great, little man. I took some pictures to show my dad what his pumpkins should look like."

Hunter giggles but my eyebrows rise on their own, apparently not aware of Marc's betrayal either. Despite everything, I'm glad Marc and his dad are on better terms.

Someone brushes my backside and I straighten, trying to step to the side with no luck since bodies are packed in here tighter than sardines.

"Dad!"

Hunter hugs Shawn beside me and I settle my gaze there instead.

If I don't look at him, he's not there.

"Did you see me?"

What does Hunter think we came here for? To stare at the backs of liars' heads?

Well…

"I tried but Mom was practically jumping out of her seat trying to see you better."

"Mom, I thought you said you saw."

"I did. Just someone with a big head was in front of me." A big, lying head. "It was hard to see past."

"Don't worry, I helped her out." Shawn laughs and I pull a face.

Marc growls but covers it with a cough and I almost break into hysterical laughter. The fucking irony. The audacity.

"Bentlee, can I talk to you for a minute?" he asks suddenly, and focusing on his Adam's apple, I shake my head stiffly, telling him, "I don't think so. I already know everything I need to, um, know."

"What does that even mean?" Shawn asks, studying me with a bowed upper lip.

I don't know.

"Can I get punch? And cookies?" Hunter tries to dart away but I grab his shoulder, clutching for dear life.

"No, hold on. We need to leave," as soon as humanly possible, "and I-"

Shawn shuttles Hunter out of my hold, saying, "I could go for some free cookies."

When his shoulder bumps into Marc's, it takes everything in me not to get between them, then I hear Shawn mutter something about not planning a honeymoon just yet.

What?

I almost ask Marc about it before remembering I don't care. I can't.

"Well," I say, turning to leave because contrary to what I used to believe, I'm not okay with being alone with him. *Alone in a crowded cafeteria/auditorium.* Somewhere in here are Kary and Rebel, and I can't stop my eyes from roaming, seeking out that blonde hair of theirs.

In an instant, Marc's front is plastered to my back as something is put in my hair. If it's a flower from that bouquet he had earlier, I will lose it. I'm already on the verge of losing it, losing everything.

A bobby pin—my bobby pin, that I put in my hair this morning—appears in front of my face as Marc says against my ear, "Never stop looking."

I take it from him, then he's gone, moving through the crowd without a backward glance and I allow my lungs to fill fully for the first time since he walked past me. Strolled. Strolled past me.

Marcos Vega, why'd you have to stroll back into my life at all?

Shawn bumps into me, his attention on something behind him.

Steadying himself, he points through the mass, saying, "I could've sworn I just saw Karina."

Without looking, I know who he's talking about. "I thought the same thing." Now I wish I never knew her at all. "It's not her though. It's Kary." The sneer saying her name should embarrass me but then I remember I don't care about that either.

I've been slapped with humiliation so many times, I should be numb to its sting by now.

"She looks a lot like-"

"I know. But it's not." Granted, I never knew her that well, but what I did know is nothing like Kary. The girl I knew was full of life and energy. The one time I saw Kary, she reminded me of a ghost. She was alive, but not.

"Kary… You're sure?"

I shrug, not really sure about anything anymore.

"Let's get out of here," I say, putting an arm around Hunter and hoping Shawn will just drop it. I don't want to know about Kary. I don't want to face the fact that I might very well be the other woman this time. Here I was so worried about Marc not being a Shawnathon, meanwhile I was a Windy all along.

What's taking him so long?

Shawn was supposed to be right behind me but he's still not here. We've been packed and waiting for him for the last twenty minutes and I don't think I have another twenty in me. Marc could be here by then.

Why isn't he here already?

Because he's probably with her.

He's probably with *them*.

"Let's go wait outside," I suggest after checking my phone again, then stop to throw a glance toward Marc's room.

Why did he give me the bobby pin? I haven't used one on his room besides that first night when I did it in front of him to prove a point. I've spent enough time in that room, and still, I never had the urge to search it like I did my old house. Never. Not once. Even knowing Marc was keeping secrets, I never broke that thin thread of trust between us.

Trust.

Never stop looking. I said that to him because…because he didn't use to see me. Then once he finally did, it felt too good to ever go back.

Those days of staying hidden while watching him ride seem the most euphoric because this *hurts*, like a flame licking across the horizon, except this time it's not the meadow catching fire, it's my skin and it's spreading—fast. Faster than any blaze ever could. Now I feel like I'm engulfed in flames so high I can't escape and I've never wanted to disappear more.

How could he do this? Why? What was there to gain from making us move in with him? Giving me his truck? Getting the goats? Marcus?

Why would he do those things, pretending they were for us? He has his own family to take care of. Why bother with mine at all?

Outside, descending the front stairwell, I hear a loud voice, yelling, "Karina!" and my steps quicken, grabbing Hunter's hand as we hit the pavement.

"What did you do?" I demand the second Shawn eases from his car.

"I thought he should know," he says, glancing at his friend, Chaz.

"Know what? I already told you, it isn't her."

Shrugging, Shawn sidesteps me and I turn to follow, pulling Hunter along behind me.

"Get your friend out of here," I tell my ex.

I hate Chaz, always have. The way he talks about women is sickening and I never liked him coming around when we lived with Shawn. The only time I could somewhat stomach him was when he was with his ex, Karina, but even then, there was always something off about him. The way he watched her like she was a bug he couldn't wait to squash one day. I don't know what happened with them, only that they split not too long after I gave birth to Hunter. Or maybe it was before.

"Karina! I know you're here!"

What the hell is this? Is he threatening her?

It's not even Karina.

We all follow him into the courtyard between buildings.

"Chaz, you have to leave before you get me kicked out." I was planning on leaving anyway but I don't need to get a bad mark on my renter's history on my way out, especially over Chaz Price.

"Karina!" Chaz's voice booms off the exterior walls.

"It's not her!" I yell, glancing back at Hunter and hating the fear I see there.

Why did Shawn say anything to him anyway? It doesn't make any sense.

This entire day doesn't make sense and I just want it to end already.

"Shawnathon, get him. This is insane."

My ex acts like he doesn't even hear me as his gaze flicks around the complex.

A motorcycle pulling in followed by car doors slamming shut draw my attention over to the parking lot.

Great. Just great. Just what this today needs—a bigger audience.

Beckett and Paige exit the Tahoe, then Coty and Angela dismount Coty's black motorcycle. Angela takes a little longer, carefully balancing her cat-ear helmet on the bike's seat while Coty just hooks his on a handlebar, then they're all moving together, both men with a hand on their female counterpart as narrowing gazes take in the scene.

"Hey," I say with a tight smile, simultaneously stepping away from Chaz's general vicinity. "What are you guys doing here?"

Coty answers me while keeping his eyes locked on Chaz. "Thought we'd surprise the birthday boy."

My eyebrows bottom out.

"Marc," Paige supplies, also watching the Creekwood intruders.

"Oh." He didn't tell me it was his birthday today. He didn't tell me a lot of things. His car is still missing from the lot though. "He's not here," I tell them, the bite in my tone able to cut raw meat.

Angela tilts her head. "I knew you were at Hunter's recital today and with Marc 'working' at Pop One, we just assumed. Well, we thought we'd find him with…" She trails off at my confusion.

What does that mean? Has he not actually been working at Pop One when he says he is?

She tugs on Coty's hand then, nodding over my shoulder but he remains silent, shooting a look at Beckett.

"What's Gary doing out here?" Beckett asks with a scowl on his face, and following their gazes, I find an older man, not as old as I would've expected, leaning casually against the back corner of our building.

From the way the others would talk about him, I always thought he was in his seventies or eighties but this man's maybe in his fifties, early sixties at most, but fit and active from the looks of it.

It's starting to feel like someone let the crazies out and I'm too confused, too irritated, and too tired to be the warden.

I cast a glance down to Hunter, wondering what I should do. This technically has nothing to do with us.

If Shawn would just…

"Shawnathon, it's time to go."

"Is this your ex, Lee-Lee?"

At first, I tried to object to the nickname Beckett gave me, until I realized he gives them to everyone. It's like a rite of passage with him, I've learned. While he gives ones that directly relate to the person's name for the people he actually likes, he gives out straight insults to the ones he doesn't. I predict he'll have a particularly creative one for Shawn.

Shawn finally pulls his attention over to us and I give him a wide-eyed look, trying to convey the severity of this situation…whatever the situation actually is. Above everything, we have a child we have to consider here.

"Yeah, I'm Shawnathon. Who are you?"

For answer, Beckett bursts into laughter, wiping at imaginary tears and saying, "I thought Bentlee made that name up. It's so much funnier that she didn't though."

With his head down, Shawn leaves his wingman post, approaching us and I warn him to let it go, gently nudging Hunter behind me and noticing the guys do the same with Paige and Angela.

"Karina!" Chaz persists, making everybody, except maybe Shawn, that much more uncomfortable as he spins in slow circles.

"Oh, good. Daddy's home. He can take out the trash," Beckett says suddenly, flicking a pretend tear at Shawn who reluctantly stops his advance.

Daddy. He knew. They all knew. Everyone but me.

Beckett repositions his hat so the bill's facing backward, whispering something to Coty that I can't make out. Coty nods and they both look over to one of the other buildings, the front building actually. There, Marc bypasses the stairs methodically and I'm guessing coming from the other side of the building where another parking lot is located. Is that where he parked? Of all the times I've pulled into Creekwood, I've never even bothered looking over there. I didn't think I needed to.

Jerking a subtle nod over at Gary when he enters the courtyard, I end up losing all the nerve I thought I was building back up at the prospect of seeing him again, feeling like nothing more than a wilting flower in his presence.

Those charcoal eyes touch on everyone in sight, lingering a hitch longer when they reach me.

"Boys," he greets calmly and both Beckett and Coty surge forward, and despite my best efforts, I do, too. Even though his face, his tone, his entire demeanor hint at nothing being wrong, something inside him calls to something inside me, telling me there is. Something is absolutely wrong here but I don't know what.

My head protests adamantly the idea of helping Marc while my heart yearns to go straight to him, ready to battle whatever evil may come.

I choose somewhere in the middle of the two, and keeping Hunter completely behind me, we join the courtyard of chaos, sticking to the outskirts in case any violence erupts. I don't know why it would but the atmosphere surrounding us promises carnage.

"You know where Karina is?" Chaz demands, aiming a finger in Marc's direction and I groan internally.

"She's not-" I try again, getting cut off by a feminine voice asking, "What do you want, Chaz?"

Chapter 27

Bentlee

THAT VOICE, THE ONE I'D ALMOST FORGOTTEN ABOUT, HAS everyone sucking in their breath at once except for Marc who hasn't reacted whatsoever, save for the narrowing of his eyes on Chaz.

Karina, who I was told was Kary, leaves the covered stairwell area to join Marc in the grass. Standing in front of us is a fortified version of the Kary I've only caught a glimpse of before but, at the same time, a mere flicker of the girl I knew long ago. A glitch. *A ghost.*

What happened to her?

"Karina." Chaz appears to sway on his feet as he blinks at her dazedly, asking, "Where've you been?"

"Mommy?"

Instantly Karina's eyes grow frantic while Marc surreptitiously places himself between Chaz and Rebel as she skips into the crowded courtyard.

"Rebel!" Hunter calls excitedly, slipping out of my grasp to run over to his friend.

Trying to go after him, I end up stopping short when Shawn swipes at my arm, holding me back.

Coty's there in a flash though, shoving Shawn away and telling him, "Yeah, we don't do that here. Hands off the women."

"Who are you?"

"I'm the nice one." Coty smirks. "But I'd be happy to let Marc explain the rules to you instead."

Marc, showing the first real emotion all day, is absolutely fuming as he regards Shawn from his spot.

Behind him, Rebel's holding the bouquet of flowers Marc had at the play, smiling at Hunter as he runs his fingers over her costume, oblivious to the adults and our drama. The fake leaves sticking out from Rebel's sleeves are orange, gold, and red, and shimmer in the sunlight just like her pale hair and skin. They only see the pretty, the fun, the shiny, and in this moment, I envy them.

Beckett passes by with a swagger only a man his size could pull off, muttering, "Nice one, my ass." Then loud enough for everyone to hear, he says, "There's obviously some stuff that needs sorted out but I got two buns in my wife's oven that trump the rest of," he gestures around wildly, "this. So, Auntie Paige is gonna take all the kids upstairs. Even this one." He looks down at Rebel with a raised eyebrow. "Mini Kary." His eyes rise to Marc but Marc doesn't so much as blink, refusing to give anything away.

So, they didn't know?

"Anyone that has an issue with that can stay right where you're at and I'll be happy to assist you in a moment." He winks at Angela who positioned herself between Shawn and me without me noticing and tells her, "Customer relations," smugly.

She scoffs. "Even at a time like this he has to show his ass."

Paige walks past, murmuring, "Only 'cause it's such a good ass."

Beckett hears and grins at her before dropping down to a knee to talk to Hunter and Rebel quietly. Whatever he says has them perking up, then he tosses both of them over each of his shoulders. Giggling, the pair bounce upside down as Beckett tramps across the yard easily, meeting up with Paige next to our building. A private look passes between the couple with Beckett dropping his usual humor-laced armor to show something other than playfulness—fear.

Once on the ground again, Hunter turns to me and I give him a gentle smile and a thumbs-up. *Go ahead.*

I swallow thickly, watching him reach out to Rebel with an open hand. Seeing Hunter's glasses falling down his nose from being upside down, she pushes them back up, then takes his hand, swinging their arms back and forth.

I know Paige will keep them safe but I can't help but wonder who will keep her safe. She's pregnant with twins.

Why does it feel like she *needs* to be kept safe at all? What am I missing?

Marc catches Gary's eye in a silent conversation as well before Gary tries to turn the same way.

"Whoa. Where you going?" Beckett asks the man, but Gary doesn't answer Beckett. Marc does.

"Let it go, B. He's with me."

Beckett's head shakes side to side as he grumbles, "Motherfucking onion," under his breath, letting Gary follow the waddling woman and the ducklings in her wake upstairs.

Chaz gets exactly one step in Karina's direction before Marc intervenes, shielding her with his body and shaking his head. "You're good right there."

Chaz scoffs, his neck jolting. "And who the fuck do you think you are?"

Shawn shifts on his feet with Angela mirroring his moves so she's still between us. I want to tell her I'm fine and that I don't need her protection, or whatever she's offering, but Karina silences everyone when she speaks, asking again, "What do you want, Chaz?"

"I want to know where you've been." His arms swing out wide. "Why you've been hiding? But mostly I'd like to know who the fuck that was?" He rams a finger in the direction Rebel disappeared and things start to fall into place—sort of. It's still like trying to fit cube blocks into circular holes though. The timeline of when I last knew they were together and Rebel's age are close…maybe. It doesn't match up perfectly, but it *could* be possible.

Honestly, Chaz was always tight-lipped about it, and Karina, almost like she died.

Or disappeared.

"The last time I saw you-"

"The last time you saw me was the night before I woke up in a hospital bed," Karina cuts him off, making my eyebrows practically jolt off my face. From the safety of Marc's cover, she says, "The hospital bed you put me in," and one of the holes morphs into a square suddenly, eliminating exactly one block from the pile.

Chaz didn't clam up about Karina because he was heartbroken. He was guilty.

"Oh, fuck. I knew you were a shitbag," Beckett says, cracking his knuckles and licking his bottom lip.

Angela stiffens beside me, reaching out her hand and I take it. I don't know why. It feels like someone is grating my heart with a potato peeler and I can't imagine what Karina feels like. Minutes ago I hated her, envied her, now I wish I could hold her tight while sending Chaz back to the hell he escaped from.

"That was," Chaz stutters, at least having the decency to look ashamed. "That was an accident."

Tears fill Karina's eyes as she shakes her head. "What about the time before that?"

"It was..."

"Or the time before that? Or the time before that?" Her voice breaks on the last part and a small gasp escapes me. I had no idea he was hurting her. I had no idea. She was so lively and beautiful and she always smiled so big when you spoke to her, like she was hanging off every word that left your mouth. And maybe, it's because she was. Because once everyone was gone again, she'd be back at Chaz's mercy.

"It wasn't supposed to go that far. I didn't want it to." Chaz's backbone hardens, anger oozing back in to replace the momentary shame he seemed to have just felt. "You were constantly going on and on about getting out of where we grew up, like you were too good to stay put with the rest of us."

Chaz registers my presence for what feels like the first time since arriving as he meets my stare head-on and says, "Like you were going to leave."

I don't dare break eye contact with Chaz. There's fire in his gaze, like hot tar slinking through the streets, but it's nothing compared to the firestorm sure to be swirling in Marc's at this very moment. I can feel Marc's intensity and it's not even directed at me.

He's right though, I did leave my family and everything I knew once I got pregnant with Hunter. I didn't do it for Shawn, I didn't really even do it for me. I did it for Hunter and the prospect of being able to give him a better life. But if Karina was planning to do the same thing, whatever her reasoning, then the only thing I regret is not being there for her sooner.

The question eating at me now is, did Shawn know? Because while Chaz is lining up a sniper shot aimed at my forehead, preparing to unleash a direct accusation between my eyes, Shawn hasn't so much as blinked.

Chaz finally rips his gaze from mine to Karina's, her head shaking while tears stream down her face.

"Is that her then? Is that the baby you kept from me?"

Kept from him? How close do the dates line up?

Marc says so calmly, so confidently it raises every hair on my body, "She's mine," and everyone aside from Shawn and Chaz squeeze together, tighter, the crowd practically swelling with unspent energy.

As much as it physically pains me to hear him say it, I still breathe a sigh of relief that Rebel isn't actually Chaz's.

A new timeline forms in my head that adds even more blocks to the pile. Karina's older than me by at least a year or two. Marc's… not. He's younger than me. That'd put Marc at sixteen or seventeen when Karina conceived Rebel.

Again, it *could* be possible. I was that age when I got pregnant with Hunter and Marc did mention being "friends" with people in my grade and higher.

Even knowing that though, the blocks aren't fitting into the holes completely. Why?

Chaz sneers, "Doesn't look like it," with his beady eyes dragging over Marc.

"Aye, did you guys feel that?" Beckett asks, dead serious. "Little dick energy just joined the chat."

"Uh-huh." Angela beside me says, "It felt kinda like a prick. But smaller."

Coty chuckles menacingly, putting his hands in his front pockets and rocking on his feet in a move that shows exactly how much of a threat he thinks Chaz and Shawn really are. "Yeah, man, 1940 called, wants its scumbag back."

"Who are these fucking idiots anyway?"

Shawn chimes in, saying, "For real. Just fuck off already. This doesn't even concern you guys."

Pot, meet Kettle.

I bite my tongue, disgusted to even be associated with either of them.

"This is my family," Marc speaks low but everyone hears him just fine as Beckett nods and Coty jerks his chin, switching between glaring at Shawn and Chaz equally. I don't know if he meant to include me in that sentiment, but despite everything that's happened, I still warm at the possibility.

"I'll get a paternity test," Chaz spits suddenly. "Once I have that proof, there won't be anything you can do to stop me from claiming what's mine. They're both mine."

Karina whimpers from a lost memory digging its way back from the grave she tried burying it in and Marc flexes visibly but Angela races to get between the two men, holding up a shaky hand to each.

"Wait. Think about this. Do you really want to do that?" I assume she's asking Marc but then she turns her head over to look Chaz in the eye. "If you're right and that little girl up there is yours, you'll be expected to pay all that back child support. Every penny from the day she was born. They'll take your wages without you even getting a say and they'll keep taking them until you're paid up in full. That's thousands and thousands of dollars, not to mention the thousands you'll be paying until the day she turns eighteen." Chaz starts to say something and she rushes to add, "Or until she finishes college. Some orders are by age, some are by schooling. What if she decides to be a doctor? A lawyer? One cotton swab could change your entire life. You could be on the hook for all that whether you like it or not."

I can't see Angela's face but I hear her sniff abruptly all the same.

Coty alternates between looking pissed at her for putting herself in a precarious position and like he's breaking from not being with her in this moment.

Something about what my boss just said nags at me though. Shawn's been adamant about not going through the courts to figure out a visitation schedule but now I'm thinking that was just an excuse so they wouldn't make him pay child support. He's never paid me a dime but I never pushed it because I thought he was letting me have Hunter full-time. He made me *think* he was letting me have Hunter full-time.

"Is it really worth it to you?" Angela questions.

Marc's gaze searches out mine and this time I don't shy away from the connection, feeling like he's trying to tell me something. Like he's been trying to tell me.

Is he really the one keeping the blocks from fitting correctly? Or am I?

"I can afford it," Chaz says smugly, then asks Marc, "Can you?"

"You got the money?" Marc lurches forward, wrapping his forearm around Angela's middle like he's getting ready to move her out of harm's way. "What about the blood, the sweat, the fucking tears it takes to raise a kid? I'd go bankrupt in all of it ten times over for her. Every fucking bit of it." Past Chaz's shoulder, Marc makes eye contact with Shawn that sends a shiver up *my* spine before a deep sadness seeps into my bones, making them exceedingly heavy.

This isn't going to end well for any of us, but the worst part is, the kids will suffer the most.

Each of Marc's friends standing here—even myself—have scars our parents caused. Those wounds take the longest to heal and the journey to recovery isn't always traveled alone. Sometimes it takes a village.

Rebel and Karina are lucky, not only because they have Marc but with Marc comes his hand-built family—his forged family.

I don't know if Marc and Karina are together, were together, or just made a beautiful daughter together, but I don't care. I don't need to know. The blocks don't have to match up today. Not right now. Right now he needs us. She needs us. All of us.

We are her village and we'll shelter her, care for her, help her. Whether I'm technically considered a part of this family or not doesn't really matter because I'm choosing to be, right here, right now. Another choice I'm taking, and making, by myself.

Tomorrow I can crumble. Tomorrow my own walls will fall. Tomorrow I will mourn the death of the life I pictured for the briefest of moments where Marc and I actually had a chance at being something spectacular.

Then, the next day, I'll start the rebuild, just like the one I did earlier this year but much more painstaking as this time I'll be doing it knowing I lost an amazing man.

In my first breakup, I never felt like I lost Shawn, only myself.

Out of the corner of my eye I notice Coty inching closer, his eyes never leaving Angela or the two men sandwiching her, and with Marc still focused on Shawn, Chaz decides to use the opportunity to launch himself at him.

In one smooth motion though, Marc spins, lifting Angela and taking her with him so the brunt of Chaz's assault hits him from behind. Angela lets out a curse so loud it rings throughout the complex like a bell at a boxing match, then Marc's spinning back around without her to pull Chaz to the ground.

Coty closes the distance, yanking Angela out of the way completely at the same time Beckett bounds over to grab Karina, too.

Beside me, Shawn makes for the two men on the lawn now exchanging brutal hits like they really are in a ring, the intention in his movements clear and calculated, and I automatically kick my leg out, snagging both his feet at once. He hits the ground with a thud and I lean over him, careful to keep out of his reach.

"Did you know?"

Groaning and rolling onto his back, he glares up at me. "What?"

"Did you know he was hitting her?"

"Bent, what other couples do–"

"Did. You. Know?"

"Fuck!" He sits up abruptly and I fight a flinch. "The guy had a temper, okay?"

"You asshole," I grit, shaking my head and feeling my stomach churn. A temper? A temper is getting frustrated when your pocket gets caught on the drawer handle for the fifth time in a row and you yank the material free a little harder than necessary, then swear to never wear the stupid pants again because…obviously it's the pants' fault. A temper isn't putting your girlfriend, someone you supposedly love, in the hospital. A temper isn't causing a woman to go by a different name for years as she lives in absolute terror that you'll find her again.

"You barely even knew Karina."

Grunting noises and curses almost cover the sound of body blows in front of us—*almost*—and my stomach churns even faster, knowing Marc is on the receiving end of at least some of them.

"Even in high school, she acted like she was better than the rest of us. Then she got pregnant and she acted like she couldn't wait to leave, make something of herself. She thought she could just forget where she came from."

Wait. So, she was pregnant. *Before* Chaz put her in the hospital? He could've killed both of them.

That also means…

Never stop looking.

Marc wanted me to look deeper. He wanted me to see what he wasn't able to tell me, whether because he couldn't or wouldn't. Rebel's not his daughter—not biologically.

"That's not how that works. There is no excuse for what he did, Shawnathon. You don't get to crush someone's spirit just because their light is too bright for you," I tell him but absolutely no remorse registers on his face. None. Not for Chaz, not even for his own transgressions.

Marc was right. *They are all the same.*

"You used to be the same way," Shawn sneers, and the way he says it, it's like he's proud of something. Like he's bragging.

Although I wasn't trying to get pregnant with Hunter, I never questioned how it actually happened. My dream was to get out of Graham Dairy but becoming a teen mom in order to do it wasn't part of the plan. Honestly, it never even crossed my mind. I'd always wanted to be a mother one day but not like that, not so soon, and under such—I didn't know it at the time but—duress. Being so young and naïve, I kind of took it as an honest accident. A twist of fate that I was meant to be a mom early.

Looking down at Shawn, I'm questioning that, too. Shawn's used a lot of different techniques over the years as a way to control me, to keep me right where he wanted me, but how far back does that actually go? The night we conceived Hunter? Did he sabotage the condom he swore he used that night? Because he could've—easily. It was my first time and it was pitch black in the backseat of my truck. Being underage and under curfew, we were rushing and I just remember the smell. I'd had to do temp checks, rectally, for all the heifers in the dry barn and I couldn't get the smell off me even after I'd showered and changed. It was overwhelming everything else and I held my breath for most, if not all, of the forty-five seconds it took for Shawn to finish his jabbing hip thrusts while I stared at the ceiling of my cab, wishing we were outside so I'd at least have the stars to look at. *The stars.* Marc's stars.

Whereas Chaz resented his and Karina's unborn child, Shawn might've found a way to use ours to his advantage.

You forget, Bent. I was your original hero. I was your way out. Without me, you'd still be washing cow pies from your hair.

"Lawyer up," I tell Shawn. "We're going to court. And Hunter's staying with me until then."

"The fuck we are." He springs into sitting and this time I do recoil, watching as he stumbles over his words, trying to find a new angle as he turns it around on me, saying, "You already kept him last weekend. If you keep him from me again, you'll be the one in trouble and missing Hunter, not me."

"Then call the cops!" I scream, spit flying from my mouth. "And make sure to report a murder because the only way you're getting Hunter this weekend is over my dead fucking body."

His hands tremble as his face flushes a deep red and I stand back up to my full height, asking, "What about you? You got a temper, too?" I swallow down hot bile, hoping he doesn't actually try to hit me. I've let so much, so fucking much, slide for Hunter's sake but I won't let that go. I'd never let that go and the fact that Shawn knew what Karina was going through and didn't do anything to stop it, sickens me. He sickens me.

"Knife!"

I turn away, seeing Chaz on top of Marc, both men bloody and gasping as Chaz pulls a knife from his pants, the metal glinting in the late afternoon sunlight.

The drawstring bag in my hold crinkles from my tight grip, reminding me I still have it. If only there was something in it that could help.

In it…

I start ripping the stitching apart as fast as I can, praying I'm not too late.

Chapter 28

Marc

THIS MOTHERFUCKER. HE BROUGHT A KNIFE WITH HIM. For what? To use on Kary? Or even worse, Rebel?

Five of the people I love most—basically my entire fucking life with the exception of the three upstairs—are in the same airspace as this crazy motherfucker holding a knife.

That's too fucking close.

I can't take any one of them getting hurt, let alone stabbed. I won't. If anyone's taking a blade, it's me.

One swipe. One swipe and I can stop him. I just need it to be deep enough that he can't pull the knife back out easily but not catch something vital.

And if it does…hopefully Beck and Coty can get to him in time. They have to. There is no other option.

Making myself relax under Chaz, I prepare my body for impact, my hold on him loosening just a fraction before he's yanked backward, out of my grasp entirely. Still horizontal, his knife swings down in a tight arc and I manage to roll out of the way in time for the blade to meet grass as he's dragged across the ground.

What the fuck?

His body comes to a stop with his head just below my feet and I jerk my legs out of the way in time as he immediately rolls violently from side to side, trying to reach for something. Bentlee rushes over, her lips moving like she's counting as she watches him, and as soon as he's on his left side with his back to her, she drops onto both knees, putting all of her weight on top of Chaz's right shoulder, effectively trapping both his arms against his body.

Bentlee pitches forward so suddenly, I scramble up from the ground, my body buzzing with the need to protect her. He's got a fucking knife and she just threw herself on top of him.

Back on my feet though, I see her hands holding his wrists… tying them together with a thin cord. She's working so fast, a blur of fingers and cord, but the knife is still moving in Chaz's grasp, so I kick it away, noticing an almost identical cord tied around his ankles when the blade skitters past his feet.

Stuck there in the fetal position, he grunts loudly, telling Bentlee he's going to kill her.

And that's strike three.

Almost killing Karina seven years ago was strike one. Showing up today—armed—was strike two. Threatening to kill my girl? He's fucking done. If his night doesn't end with him in a jail cell, he'll wish it had.

Bentlee secures the cord, then pops back into standing directly behind him. With beads of sweat dotting her hairline, her wild eyes meet mine and she looks like she just got kicked out of heaven and spent the entire journey to earth kicking ass. She's the most beautiful thing I've ever seen and my body pulls me toward her with a not-so-invisible line. Not now. Not ever again. I'm never hiding how I feel about her again.

I can't believe I was able to as long as I did. I love her so goddamn much.

I just hope I didn't ruin everything.

Her eyes drop and I'm almost positive I did. Today was not the way I wanted her to find out about Rebel. Today was not the way I wanted anyone to find out about Rebel.

Quickly pivoting, she bends at the waist and pukes in the grass.

Beck stands beside me, staring down at Chaz as he flinches away, trying to avoid the splash from Bentlee's puke and I have to fight the urge to kick his ass all over again. What a useless excuse of a human being.

Bentlee straightens, carefully wiping her mouth on her shoulder and I frown, watching her, wanting her. I just want to hold her already but can't without explaining some stuff first. I don't even know where her head's at right now. She's barely met my eyes all day.

I can't even blame her either. The school play followed by this shit, it's a lot to take in.

How the fuck was I supposed to know different kids call the same school different things? Yeah, Howdy's a dumb fucking name for a school but that's what Rebel called it—a shortened version of the founder's name, Howard D. I didn't know people shortened his last name to Old Mill, too. Shit's so stupid. Almost as stupid as naming your kid Shawnathon.

"Damn, Lee-Lee. Is that how you got me on your UTV? By hogtying my ass?"

Her head shakes. "No. I've never done that before. I've only seen it done on livestock in competitions but I always hated it." She looks between us, saying, "We'd never handle any animals like that at Graham."

Beck nudges Chaz with the toe of his shoe. "What does that say about you, asswipe?"

No wonder Hunter's so gentle. His mom's physically ill from hogtying someone that was posing an immediate threat to her…

What does she even consider us? What does she consider me?

I told Chaz this is my family and I meant it. Every person that showed up today is my family, including Bentlee—*especially* Bentlee.

Except Shawnathon. Guy doesn't even know the meaning of family.

One of Bentlee's hands flies to her mouth, her back arching and shoulders bunching as she dry heaves violently. Once she finishes, her hand falls away, leaving a bloody handprint on her face behind and I dart forward, stepping over a thrashing Chaz like I'd step over a pile of dog shit.

"You're bleeding," I tell her, but she just says, "So are you," like it's even remotely comparable.

I blink a couple drops of blood away, finally noticing—and ignoring—a cut above my eye, to look down at her hands. Both palms have matching angry gashes across them and her thumbs and pointer fingers are sliced up pretty bad. She fucked herself up trying to tie him down. Trying to save me. Even after everything. All the shit I refused to say last week and all the shit being revealed today. She still put herself on the line, put herself in direct danger, to save me.

Fuck.

"My pain…it's nothing," I tell her, shrugging. "It means nothing to me." I'd suffer voluntarily for the ones I love. Already have been for years now. "But yours," I bend, meeting her eyes to tell her, "your pain hurts worse than anything I've ever experienced." Especially knowing it was because of me. For me.

That was the one line I hadn't planned ever crossing—hurting Bentlee—and it's so much worse than I could've imagined. It's fucking agonizing. The cuts on my face, the bruises marking my body, none of it matters. It doesn't even register. All I want is for her to be okay.

But she's not. Because of me. Physically, emotionally, I know Bentlee's suffering right now, even if she refuses to show it openly.

She takes a step in my direction and I can't help it, I get my hopes up that maybe I didn't fuck this up completely and that I still have a chance to make everything right but then the sound of police sirens in the distance have her tensing up.

I hear some movement behind me before Beck warns, "Don't even think about it, bro," and I don't have to look to know who it is. I can smell him from here. Fucking Shawnathon.

Coty joins us, telling Shawn, "You brought Chaz here. You're gonna explain to the cops why."

Him being friends with someone like Chaz makes a little too much sense. I just wish I would've thought so before.

Before what?

Would I have changed anything that's happened with Bentlee if I knew there'd be a connection back to Chaz?

I love her. That I couldn't change if I wanted to.

But I love Rebel, too.

It's not either/or. It shouldn't be. Yet, that's what it constantly feels like lately.

"I need to go," Bentlee says.

"What? Your hands are fucking wrecked."

She tries to sidestep me, not listening.

"Bentlee? Bentlee?" It's like talking to one of Rebel's dolls as she stares blankly in front of her, not acknowledging me at all as she scurries away, wet eyelashes and all. "Bentlee!" I shout, scowling when she only speeds up.

She won't look at me, maybe ever again.

I don't have her eyes anymore.

What's worse is they're currently fucking veiled by tears. Tears I had a hand in putting there.

"Give me time to explain. I just need time." My voice cracks like my rule against begging for anything in life. I'm ready to beg, negotiate, surrender. She wants to see what's in my chest? Hell, I'll carve out my heart and hand it to her myself. It hasn't been mine since I fell into those pools of hers anyway. I'm fucking *drowning* in Bentlee and I never want to come up for air.

She doesn't even seem to hear me though as she disappears around the corner of our building.

Fuck, fuck, fuck. I'm out of time. I'm out of fucking time.

My lungs struggle to fill completely as my chest rises and falls in short, aching spurts. They fucking burn with need. They don't want air. They need blue-violet and nuclear green depths.

Without them, without *her*, I'm just lost. So fucking lost.

I avoid meeting anybody's eye as I turn back around. There's no way Karina doesn't blame me for this, too. At least part of it. Pushing for Rebel to go to public school after living so carefully for so long. She didn't even like Rebel racing and that was with a helmet covering the girl's face the whole time. Then inviting Bentlee to Creekwood, which ultimately led to Shawn's sorry ass being here as well.

I admit I made some mistakes, but damn it, I can't find it in me to regret a single one. Not after I saw the smile on Rebel's face today when she was up on that stage. That wasn't a mistake. She wasn't born to live in the dark. She won't thrive there. Her roots may have been steeped in the shadows for her first six years but the spotlight is just waiting to welcome Rebel with open arms. I knew it the first time she got on a dirt bike.

This was bound to happen sooner or later, and as much as I hate the way it did, I'm glad it was with my family around. Everything feels more manageable with them by my side.

Not a minute later, Bentlee's pulling away in my old Ram.

Christ.

Gary comes downstairs, telling me, "The other two are still up there but did you want me to stop your girlfriend? She took her boy."

I shake my head.

The police will probably want to talk to her but even I couldn't keep Bentlee here. I don't know why she was so determined to leave in the first place but I'll cover for her as long as I can. As long as I need to.

Gary's gaze takes in the scene, landing on Shawn sitting with his head in his hands, then on Chaz still tied up and fuming. Bending down, he inspects the knots but I don't care. Chaz isn't moving 'til the cops get here because if he does, it'll be the last move he ever makes. He brought a fucking knife to my home.

A. Knife.

Hopefully Bentlee's knots keep. I got shit to fix and Chaz has already ruined enough.

"Bentlee shouldn't get to leave," Shawnathon whines like a bratty kid, and I tell him, "Shut the fuck up," not wanting to hear one more sound out of his stupid fucking mouth.

"Can you watch them?" I ask Gary and he gives a nod.

Beck pipes up, saying, "Girlfriend? You hear that?" He elbows Coty as we make our way over to Karina and Angela. "Our boy's got himself a girlfriend and a daughter and didn't think to tell us about either."

I hate the hurt in his voice, too. I hurt everybody when all I wanted was to protect them all.

"Marc," Karina says and I don't know what she's feeling or

thinking. I don't know anything right now. It feels like a bomb just went off in my face and I'm searching through the smoke, trying to piece everything back together. Piece myself back together.

"Are you okay?" That's all I really care about. As long as my family's okay, we can figure everything else out.

She shakes her head, saying, "He knows now. He *knows*."

"We all know things that we didn't before," Beck says.

Angela shifts, wringing her hands together and telling him, "This isn't about you, Beckett."

"Yeah, that's been made clear. This isn't about any of us because this motherfucker," he jabs a finger at me and I flex on instinct, "didn't think we needed to know about his super-secret daughter or his super-secret girlfriend or his super-secret life. We could've helped. We could've known what the fuck was happening instead of standing around with our thumbs up our asses!"

I've never seen Beck so angry and I know he could probably use a minute but...

"I need you," I tell him, tasting the words on my tongue for the very first time in my life.

"It's a little late for that." He gives me a hard stare, turning to leave but I step in his way.

It's not. It can't be.

I need more fucking time.

"I need you to call your dad." He works to keep the surprise off his face which only makes this next part harder. "She's... She's not..." I look at Karina, feeling my throat clog like a dam. "Rebel's not my daughter," I manage to croak out, hating that truth more than any other I've ever told. "Not technically. She is in all the ways that count... to me. But not to the court, if Chaz takes this there."

I'd seen Karina through passing at a couple parties in high school. She was older and was always with her boyfriend but hung out with some of the same people I did when Beck and Coty weren't around.

Karina and I weren't even friends back then. We'd barely met each other. So when I walked into Creekwood years later, looking for a place for me and my boys to live, it took me a minute to place her.

Once I did though, she started spinning some web of a story with a fuckload of loose ends and mismatched threading that I wasn't buying for one second. Before she could finish it though, her little girl woke from a nap, royally pissed someone had interrupted her beauty sleep.

That was the first day I ever fell in love. Hook, line, sinker—I was a goner. So wholly, so completely, I never stood a chance against Rebel, the girl who refused to die.

Karina was pregnant with Rebel the last time Chaz beat on her, landing her in the hospital, fighting for both her own life and the life of her unborn baby. Karina eventually confided in me that Rebel wasn't supposed to make it. The injuries Karina sustained were too great, the odds stacked against both of them too heavy, but Karina wanted her daughter more than anything, wanted a better life for her, wanted *a life* for her, so she fought. She fought for her life and for Rebel's. Rebel was delivered prematurely and spent the next several months in the NICU. It was enough time for Karina to find the help she needed to finally escape Chaz. She wanted to disappear but didn't know how. How do you start over as a whole new person? Any job is gonna need identification. Housing, everything.

Luckily, during Rebel's hospital stay, Karina got close to one of the pediatric nurses…who just so happened to have an uncle that was looking for a building manager for one of his properties. He lived in Florida and was mostly hands off with Creekwood, so he was hard up for help. The nurse put in a good word for Karina and with the new job came an employer that didn't ask a million questions along with a place to live rent-free while she could heal not only herself but also her preemie daughter. For a long time, she was able to manage Creekwood largely by herself as well as fly under the radar.

But it was lonely. She was lonely. And exhausted. When I stumbled across her and Rebel, she'd never even used a babysitter because she didn't trust anyone.

It was only after she reluctantly agreed to let me and my boys move in that Karina and I became friends but only under certain *strict* conditions. Well, one. One condition. I couldn't tell *anybody* about her real identity or her daughter's. I started helping her out every now and then, watching Rebel for her while she chipped away at her never-ending laundry list of managerial duties. Then, one day it all just kind of shifted, like two tectonic plates, setting off a life-changing earthquake and I no longer saw it as babysitting anymore. Honestly, I'm not sure I ever did.

Even back then, Coty, Beck, and I could've afforded a place twice the size and double the cost as Creekwood, but it was Rebel that sold me.

Suddenly, I wanted to spend time with Rebel even when Karina didn't need me to. I wanted to be there as she grew up, witnessing all the milestones as if I was always supposed to. As if she was *my* daughter and I was meant to be there for her. I cherished every one of Rebel's firsts just like Karina did. Then later I got to teach her how to blow bubbles in her chocolate milk when her mom wasn't looking. How to say the word remote correctly. She's always said it as merote and I finally got her to say it right this summer. We're still working on cinnamon but I think once her front teeth come in, she'll get it. I also taught her how to skip. How to ride dirt bikes. How to race motocross and beat the boys.

But she taught me, too. She taught me what it is to love someone else more than yourself. Not because you have to but because you don't.

A piece of paper can tell you you're a biological father but it can't make you a dad. I've been Rebel's surrogate dad, stepping not only into the position but up to it. It's a steep fucking climb being a parent, one that never ends and I'm not about to let Chaz breeze his way to the top without a fucking fight. Not everyone that makes a child deserves them. He sure the fuck doesn't.

"I need your dad's help keeping Rebel out of his hands," I tell Beck, motioning toward Chaz, unwilling to even say his name anymore. "Please. If not for me, then for my little girl. And Karina."

You'd think it's an easy concept to grasp—abusive, homicidal parents shouldn't get custody of their kids but that's not always the case unfortunately. Biological parents have rights, a lot of them, and some judges are lenient, too lenient. I don't know how this is going to play out but I'll throw everything I have into keeping Rebel safe from Chaz, starting with hiring Beck's dad to represent Karina. Beck's dad is one of the best family law attorneys money can buy. I probably should've had him on retainer already but I was cocky. And I fucking failed.

Angela throws herself at me, hugging me tightly, and I hold her, keeping Coty's eyes the entire time.

She whispers, "Thank you," before releasing me and I ask her what for.

"For being what I always needed but for somebody else."

"Yeah, we're in. Let us know what we can do to help," Coty says, then thumps Beck's chest. "Call your dad, man."

He pretends to rub at the spot Coty hit, saying, "I already did. He's on his way."

"How did you-"

"I didn't do it for you." He frowns at me. "I did it for Lee-Lee. Shit got tense between her and Dumbathon before she manhandled Chaz the fuckin' Spazz."

"Womanhandled," Angela corrects, stepping under one of Coty's arms.

"What do you mean? What'd he do?" I scowl, looking over my shoulder at Shawn.

"You mean besides fall like a ton of bricks when Bentlee tripped him?" Coty laughs.

What? She tripped Shawn?

"What'd he do to her?" I repeat so low I'm surprised anyone can hear me but Angela's quick to fill me in on Shawn acting jumpy, like he thought he'd get one in on me while I was busy fighting his boy.

Not once, but twice Bentlee physically protected me today. She had reason enough to let the wolves fucking have at me but she didn't.

Where is she? I need to talk to her.

"We couldn't make out what they were saying until she yelled something about Hunter staying with her from now on. He's been pissy ever since over there," Angela explains. "What, uh," she glances at Karina, "what are you going to do about Bentlee?"

Karina speaks up, her voice raw and hoarse, saying, "You're going to have to tell her everything and then you're going to have to grovel. I'm sorry, Marc. I'm so sorry."

Goddamn it.

"You have nothing to be sorry for. None of this is on you. I knew what I was doing the entire time. I'm sorry, okay? I'm…" So fucking sorry. I thought I could take on the world alone and win, but I was wrong.

But the truth is, I'd do it again. Without question. Meeting and getting to watch Rebel grow over the last five years, I wouldn't trade that time for anything.

I'll grovel. I'll grovel and grovel and grovel. I'll grovel until Bentlee agrees to at least hear me out but I won't apologize for sticking by my little girl. If I know Bentlee, I know she'll understand that. She may still decide I'm not worth the trouble I've caused her but she'll know that my heart was in the right place. The heart that now belongs to her. I just hope she doesn't throw it back in my face before I can actually get to the groveling.

"So, you two," Beck motions between us, "aren't a thing?"

Karina's eyes drop but I shake my head, answering him. "No. We're not. It's never been like that." Not for me anyway. For all the time we've spent together, my feelings for Karina never developed past our friendship.

After a silent pause, Karina excuses herself, wanting to check on Rebel.

"I'll text you when the cops are ready for your statement," I tell her before she can leave.

"Thank you. For everything. I just," a hiccup interrupts her, "don't know what we're going to do after this."

"I'll take care of it," I promise her. The house out on my property that I was planning to be for Karina and Rebel isn't even close to being ready but I'll figure something out. They're not staying here anymore.

"*We'll* take care of it. We got you now," Beck says out of nowhere, and Angela and Coty both nod.

I wait until Karina's gone to tell him "thanks," then we turn to face the two piles of shit on the lawn. Thankfully, with Gary's eagle eye studying them, they're still in the positions we left them in.

"I love you but I don't have to like you right now," Beck deadpans and Coty laughs under his breath. I just shake my head. He's always gotta be so fucking dramatic. Always. "Seriously, I could've been a funcle."

"A funcle?"

"A fun uncle!"

"She's not my blood."

"When the fuck has that ever stopped us?" he asks, incredulous.

"I'm with Beck. We could've helped, dude. Before today. Before all this went down. It's pure luck we were even here today."

"Why were you?" I ask.

"Happy birthday, fucker," he says and I breathe out a laugh. Oh. Yeah. With Bentlee barely speaking to me and then Rebel's first performance, I sort of forgot about it being my twenty-fourth birthday today.

"Rebel," Beck says. "What a perfect name for our first kid. Why would you keep her from us? Do you really think so little about us? About me?"

"I trust you guys with my life but you weren't ready for hers."

"It's never been about being ready with us," Coty says. "Only willing."

We all nod our heads silently. I get it. I fucked up. If the roles were reversed, I'd be pissed. More than that, I'd be insulted. I didn't mean to make them feel less than. They're my brothers, my chosen brothers, and they're anything but less. They're more than I could've asked for. More than I deserve. But still…

"It wasn't just my choice." If Rebel was my biological daughter, there's nothing on this planet that could've stopped me from sharing her with the rest of my family.

Nobody speaks for a while, then three cop cars pull in at once, their lights illuminating the surrounding buildings.

"Mind telling us what the deal with Gary is? I thought he was a recluse."

I laugh quietly, heading in the direction of the police officers stepping from their vehicles. Another secret that isn't mine.

I tell them what I can though, saying, "He is," *mostly*, "but Gary and I have an arrangement. He keeps an eye on Creekwood when I can't."

"You mean for Kary and Rebel?"

I shrug.

And Bentlee and Hunter when they moved in. If only I would've had him watching out for Angela, too, then that whole thing with her boss showing up at her door probably would've never happened.

I look over at Coty, remembering how freaked out he was that night. He'd fallen in love with our neighbor girl and thought he'd lost her. I'd never seen someone look so hopeless.

Now the tables have turned and I'm the desperate one. I need to talk to Bentlee—soon.

Coty stops and we both look back at him.

"Did he used to be a cop?"

"Something like that."

I'm not exactly sure what position Gary held, only that he was on the police force before retiring sometime before we moved in down the hall from him. Although he doesn't openly interact with the other residents here, he's never let me down watching over Creekwood whenever I've traveled.

"Think these guys are his friends?" Beck asks, sounding hopeful but there was a domestic disturbance. I could go to jail just as easily as Chaz.

"We're still talking about Gary, right?" I ask and we all look over to see Gary holding a clipboard I hadn't noticed before as he jots down notes on a sheet of paper.

Angela breaks from us, heading toward Coty's R6, and when he asks her what she's doing, she says, "Grabbing the footage."

Footage?

Chapter 29

Bentlee

SEVERAL PIECES OF MY HAIR FALL UNPROMPTED FROM MY bun and flop against my forehead before lazily drooping over my eyes.

Figures. It's only fitting I look as awful as I feel.

I got Hunter to sleep at my parents' house a couple hours ago, and after driving the RANGER to *the* hill, I've been sitting out here ever since. I finally decided to power my phone off thanks to Shawn and his obsessive calls. And messages, and threats, and…

The things he's said tonight further prove why Hunter shouldn't be anywhere near him right now.

Headlights heave across the skyline and I turn to see a low-to-the-ground car making its way over the uneven landscape. They're obviously coming from Graham but no one would actually brave this terrain in a car that size. So, who is it?

Then it hits me and my stomach bottoms out. Shawnathon must've followed through on his threats to tell the cops I kidnapped my own son.

Never mind the fact that it's been an outright fight just to get Shawn to even take Hunter on a regular basis, but now he gets to report me for not handing him over one time? Really?

I push my hair out of my eyes, then put my hands out in front of me, spreading my fingers as wide as the dressings will allow, and walk down the hill, slowly approaching the patrol car. The closer I get I still don't see any lights on top though and start to wonder why they'd send an undercover officer.

Am I not getting arrested?

I raise one bandaged hand to my eyes, trying to see the make and model, and as soon as I identify the emblem, I lower both hands, feeling nauseous for an entirely different reason.

Cutting the lights, his door opens and closes, then he's out and walking toward me. Not walking. *Strolling.*

"How'd you find me?"

Marc looks around, his own wounds bandaged from being treated. "I just had a feeling." I swallow an ironic laugh and he asks, "What are you doing out here?"

"Thinking."

"About?"

I let the laugh out to say, "Everything."

He comes closer, his hands out in front of him similar to what I just did when I thought I was a wanted fugitive. Did I look as guilty as he does?

"The cops want to get a statement from you but I told them I'd bring you down to the station to give one tomorrow. Using the footage caught on Angela's helmet cam, they were able to see everything that went down."

So that's what she was doing.

"What about Shawn? Did they see..." Because I struck him first. Although I was only trying to save Marc from further injuries, Shawn didn't technically hit anyone. Not while I was there anyway.

Marc shakes his head. "The camera mostly caught my fight with Chaz and since Shawn was just out of shot, they didn't really have anything to go off of because it was his word against...everyone else's."

I breathe the biggest sigh of relief.

"But," he says, coming closer, "I know what you did. Thank you."

"It was..."

"It was badass. You took both Shawn and Chaz down by your-self. *You're* a badass."

If that were true, wouldn't I feel like a badass? Do badasses puke? Do they cry? Because I did both. I puked—in front of everybody—then cried all the way out to Graham Dairy.

I eye my gauze-wrapped hands. It was a natural reaction what I did. A basic instinct to defend Marc. It was a split-second decision in the moment that I made out of necessity—just like he described.

I unsheathed my own two swords and went to battle protecting the man I love but I was too hopped up on adrenaline to feel any-thing. The boomerang effect afterward caused by that same surge of adrenaline depleted me not only physically but emotionally, too, and now I'm left feeling too much.

"I'm sorry," I blurt, and he chuckles, reminding me how much I miss his chuckles. I haven't heard one for a week and it sounds like home. My home.

"I say I love you and you question me. I say thank you and you apologize."

"I know. I am sorry though." This apology sticks out to me above all the others because it's true. I've been apologizing for so many things—even existing at one point—for so long that I think I for-got what it felt like to apologize for something I actually did wrong.

Tears I hadn't noticed building fall, wetting my windblown cheeks.

"I'm sorry for making all this so much harder on you. For bringing Shawn and Chaz back into Karina's life. I had no idea. If I'd known-"

"Bentlee, stop. It's not your fault. None of this is your fault. I'm the one that's sorry. I fucked it all up."

There's so much pain in his voice it hurts my own throat.

"How's Karina doing?" I wanted to be there for her but as soon as I heard the police sirens I panicked. The only thing going through my mind was getting Hunter to safety, and in that moment, noth-ing else mattered.

"She's okay. She and Rebel are staying with Coty and Angela until their house is ready."

"Their house?"

He grins. "Remember that foundation you asked about?"

"The one on your property?" The one he was adamant about not living in himself but vague about it in every other way.

"That'll be theirs, yeah, when it's finished. I was hoping to get them situated out there before-"

"Before you thought of yourself."

Our eyes meet and he nods slowly. Marc's the prime example of what airlines don't want you to do in an emergency landing. You're supposed to put your own oxygen mask on first before assisting anyone else, but for Marc, the thought to save himself would never even cross his mind as he worked to help everybody around him.

"I just wanted to make sure they were still close. Still safe. You know, in case Chaz…"

"Yeah, I know." *Now.* I wish he would've told me but I understand why he didn't.

Again, now I do.

"Karina and I are not dating. We never dated. We've never even slept together. Not. Once," he says, looking me directly in the eye, and I wait a minute before saying, "I know that, too."

After Shawn's slip, I knew Rebel wasn't really Marc's but knowing he tried to claim her anyway, despite the fact that he wasn't even with Karina, only warms my heart that much more.

"But I thought you-"

Now I'm the one shaking my head, telling him everything Shawn said and why I actually ran out earlier.

"I met Rebel when she was only a year old and I've been in her life ever since," he confirms with a tremble in his voice, like it's his first time admitting it out loud. And maybe it is.

I understand what Karina did—becoming Kary, becoming someone foreign, all for her child's sake—she did what she felt she had to do, and I respect that. I admire that. I admire her. And I admire Marc for taking Karina and Rebel under his wing when not many nineteen-year-old single guys could've. Would've.

Not many would've. He's one of a kind.

But I already knew that. I'm just finally getting to see him in his entirety now.

Who would ever want to take on a single mother with crazy baby daddy drama? Who would be tough enough, amazing enough to do it twice?

Marcos fucking Vega.

By the time he's done explaining his connection to Karina and his genuine love for Rebel, my face is drenched and all the blocks have finally matched up with their holes. All but one.

I still have one confession I've been putting off but I'm not sure how he'll take it. Will he be mad? Will he understand?

How *do* I tell him without butchering the real reasoning for keeping it from him to begin with?

Interrupting my thoughts, he asks, "So, now that you know everything, do you want to be with me? For real this time, not just in secret. I know this wasn't supposed to be anything serious but it's serious. I'm fucking serious about you."

I questioned his love when he wasn't sharing all of himself with me. How can I confess my own feelings and expect him to believe them if I'm not either?

"Or maybe I got it all wrong," he says, sounding more hurt than before. "Maybe I really was just a rebound. You said it yourself, but I didn't want to listen. Five years ago I fell for one girl that wasn't mine and now I'm starting to think I did it all over again."

He really has no idea.

"Can I show you something?" I ask softly, wiping under my eyes with the sleeve of my shirt.

He looks like he's going to refuse, then he jerks a stern nod. Following me up the hill, the moon above us lights our path and then the meadow below us once we're at the top, and I stop to take a deep breath, preparing myself.

With Marc scowling one of his signature scowls, I ask him if it looks familiar even though his face says as much. Now that I can decipher his seven layers of frowns, I know just how expressive his face really is.

"I used to ride out here," he tells me, and I bring my thumb up to my mouth before realizing it's bandaged.

I drop my hand by my side, saying, "I know."

Turning to me, he waits me out.

"This is where I'd come to get away from everything, everyone."

His quiet laugh bounces around inside my chest. "Same."

"I'd been coming out here for a while and never saw anyone else but then, one day, this red dirt bike came tearing out of nowhere. The rider was wearing red, too, and he looked like a flame licking across the horizon, setting off this fire all around him. It caught instantly, spreading to me—inside me." I let us both sit with that for a minute. "After that, I started coming out here more often, hoping to see the boy that made it feel like things could be different. I saw him and I saw a way out, someone that was going to make it. Make a name for themselves that had nothing to do with their family. Someone that could live a life bigger than what one farm holds. That things could be better. He made impossible obstacles seem possible and I was addicted to watching him ride. I was addicted to watching *him*." A nervous laugh tickles my lips. "I spent so much time out here, this became my hill." I look at Marc, my heart thundering. "It became our hill, yours and mine. You just didn't know it."

His jaw flexes but I continue, knowing there's no turning back. If this ends us, at least it'll be the real us—finally. "Last fall, when I found out Shawn was seeing Windy, I'd never felt so helpless, powerless. I knew I needed to leave but I didn't know *how*. So, I came out here again. After years of being gone, and knowing it was a stretch to see you riding, I still hoped for that same reminder. That same inspiration that I could do hard things. That I could make it. That's when your friend turned up, flying across the same landscape I'd watched you on so many times. At first I thought it was some cruel joke."

Marc chuckles and I close my eyes, savoring it all over again. "Sounds about right. Beck would be the butt of some cosmic joke."

Opening my eyes, I laugh, too, then we both fall quiet. Marc stuck in his head. Me swimming in mine, trying to make sure I get this right.

"That night changed the course of my life. I helped someone else out of what felt like an impossible situation and it gave me the hope I'd been looking for. It gave me the strength to go home, make a game plan to get myself out of what also felt like an impossible situation, and actually follow through with it."

Badasses don't feel like badasses in the moment because they're too busy being an actual badass to notice. It's only in hindsight that you realize you were a badass at all, and by then it's already rooted in you because the decision was already made. Being a badass is a choice and you can make it whenever you want to, or need to.

I glance over at Marc with blurry eyes, telling him, "That night also led me back to you. You were never a rebound, Marc. You were worth the wait."

His own eyes shimmer in the moonlight as he swallows, asking, "This is your tattoo, isn't it?"

Pulling my shirt over my head, I keep it in my hold, the material getting stuck to my bandages. Down to a thin tank top, I shiver, turning to show him the hand-sketched picture set against the real-life inspiration.

"I got it as a permanent reminder. The same one you unknowingly inspired years ago. That it's possible."

"What about the butterfly?"

I feel his fingers graze the inked skin, soothing the goose bumps produced by the cold November air.

"It's a moth," I admit, dropping my eyes and holding my breath. He bared his soul to me but I just handed him mine. What will he do with it?

"Like a moth to a flame," he says almost to himself and, exhaling, I lift my head, meeting his charcoal gaze as he steps in front of me, blocking the meadow from view.

He's all I've ever seen anyway.

"I'm sorry I never told you before."

"What exactly are you telling me?" he whispers, his hot hands gliding up my exposed arms and warming the skin with his touch alone. "That you were drawn to me, to what I represented."

"That I loved you before you ever knew I existed. That I never stopped loving you. That the love I felt back then is nothing compared to what it is since I've gotten to know the man beneath the helmet."

"Like *his* moth to *her* flame." He hums enigmatically. "Is that still true? How do you feel about me now?"

"Consumed." Utterly fucking consumed. Like the wildfire the firefighters mistakenly assumed was contained, Marc came back into my life with a vengeance, burning everything else—every touch, every promise, every preconceived notion—to the ground. He claimed me so completely, I'll never fully recover.

Today all our secrets clashed together like they were on an ancient battleground, just devastation among the chaos, but through it all, my love for Marc is the one thing that's come out unscathed.

His lips crash against mine, a cut somewhere on his mouth adding a coppery taste to the otherwise perfect kiss. When he draws back, that fire from earlier reappears, but brighter. Stronger.

"I fucking love you," he says, and I smile, telling him truthfully, "I love you, too."

I kiss him then, taking as much as I give, and feeling like a true partner for the first time in my life. It was never like this with Shawn. I think a part of me knew it was never supposed to be like this with Shawn because we weren't meant to be together. Not like this. Not with twists and turns and jumps and dips put there to test us, not break us. Marc and I managed to get through it all and now that the blindfolds are off, we're able to ride into a future together knowing we fought for everything we have.

"There's just one last thing I was wondering about," I break the kiss to say.

"Name it."

"Why was Shawn talking about a honeymoon when we saw you at the school?"

"That day in his car…"

"When you?" I gesture to my throat, and he nods, saying, "Yeah. I was just letting him know what would happen if I caught him putting his hands on you again."

"But what does that have to do with-"

"He didn't believe I'd be around to see it, if he did touch you again."

When I'm still not getting it, Marc's lips spread so wide the white of his teeth rival the moon's brilliance in the sky and he says, "I told him I'd always be around because I'd be marrying you one day. I'm not going anywhere, Bentlee."

Leave it to Marc to fulfill another one of my fantasies, this one putting an end to all others. He really is mine.

Finally.

Epilogue

Marc

Two years later

TALL GRASS SWAYS ACROSS THE MASSIVE HILL LIKE FANS in a stadium doing the wave as they prep for the big moment, the action they came for.

It's almost time.

Rebel breaks into amused laughter, bringing my attention back to her as she watches Hunter chase the goats. His mom would flip if she knew he was in the pen with them, getting dirt and mud and who knows what else on his suit. At least Rebel's still on the fence, otherwise her mom would be pissed, too. This isn't the first time Rebel's wearing a dress but it's definitely the most expensive one she's rocked.

Hunter almost trips over one of the goats when its legs freeze up, falling over right in front of him, and I flinch, but luckily he catches himself, playing it off. Rebel covers her face, cracking up, and almost tumbles backward off the fence she's hanging on to.

For fuck's sake.

"Dude, I'll never get used to seeing these zombie fuckers come back to life after playing dead."

"They're not playing dead. Their muscles just lock up when they get scared." Or excited. Or when they go down one of the slides

Hunter insisted we buy. Or if the wind changes direction. It doesn't really matter, these goats faint over fucking everything. "It's hereditary."

"They get it from you then, Daddy?"

I shoulder-check Beck, mumbling out a "fuck off" just for his ears.

Just like its owner, Beck's house looms over ours, but in the distance; and when he's not inside it chasing Paige and their twins around, he's either at one of the two Pop The Hood locations he and Angela now run together or he's here. Not here with the goats. He's here at the motorsports complex—my motorsports complex—Ride It Motorsports, or Ride It More for short, thanks to Beck's obsession with nicknames. It's been in construction for the last year after I hired Coty to design the best race tracks in the area using three hundred of the four hundred acres I originally purchased.

Karina and Rebel have a few dozen acres of their own with the house I had built for them, too. Rebel's itching to compete in the first pee-wee race as soon as we're officially open to the public, but for now, she's enjoying being able to practice on the course any chance she gets.

Since everything came out, Karina's been a little braver. She's been getting out more, even if it's just over to the track to watch Rebel ride or to visit one of the three other houses out here. Literally, the only other neighbors we have besides each other are the aggressive-as-fuck tumbleweeds constantly blowing around. Angela, Paige, and Bentlee welcomed her into the fold seamlessly though—thankfully. We're currently trying to figure out if she should stay at Pop The Hood full-time since Bentlee's been training her there or keep her close to home and have her work at Ride It Motorsports once it opens. I think I know which one she'll choose. She's branching out but she's not back to her old self. I doubt she ever will be.

Chaz has been behind bars ever since that day at Creekwood and will be for a long time. We haven't heard anything more about him pushing for a paternity test but we'll be here and ready to fight if he does.

Karina and Rebel's stint living with Coty and Angela may have inspired something none of us saw coming and now Angela wants to be a foster parent. With over ten thousand kids in Washington State alone in need of temporary or adoptive families, she wants to give to others what she never got as a child in need herself. And since Coty would wrestle the sun bare-handed from the sky for her, they started the process months ago and are preparing for their first kid. We're all excited to meet them whenever they show up. We've got the open land, the open minds, and the open hearts. Bring 'em on.

Bentlee and I finally made the move out here, too, with the goats along with Marcus, the bull, and Hunter, my boy. We have him almost full-time after Bentlee took Shawn's ass to court. Thanks to court-ordered anger management and therapy sessions, it came out that Shawn had been using what's called narcissistic domestic abuse on Bentlee since they met basically. Even though we can't really prove it, Bentlee thinks he purposely got her pregnant to trap her, then once he had her all to himself, he used any form of coercion he could on her—emotional, financial, sexual—as a way to keep and control her. He still gets to see Hunter, it's just supervised visits now, and until he gets the help he needs and can prove he's not a watered-down version of Chaz anymore, it'll stay that way.

We invited him today but I don't know if he'll show. A part of me hopes he doesn't so I don't have to see his ugly face on one of the happiest days of my life, but a bigger, pettier part of me wants him sitting front row.

Beck's dad came through in a big way for us. For my family. It tore a piece of my soul to ask for his help but I'm glad I did. I don't think I'd even have my family, the way it is now, if I hadn't and that's fucking priceless.

"Boys?"

Coty, Beck, and I turn our heads to see Angela wearing her white bridesmaid dress. Coty sucks in a breath next to me and I smirk, knowing I won't be any better. Hopefully I'll actually remember how to breathe when I see Bentlee.

"It's time," she tells us.

Time. Something I was quickly running out of but now have more than any man has any right to. I've got all the time in the world with the people that matter most to me, and after today, I'll get to spend it with my wife by my side.

Beck's daughter, Terra, waddles over to her aunt with Paige hot on her heels. While Paige still keeps her hair dyed red at the ends, Terra's got a full head of chocolate curls already. Their son, Harley, who has a shade lighter hair with a lot less curl to it, is over with the Christensen men, probably being passed around from brother to brother. Paige is dressed in a similarly colored dress as Angela's with only a slight variation at the top and Beck curses, moving for her, but Coty and I both grab an arm, jerking him back. We got kid duty, we *all* got kid duty, and he's helping wrangle these fucking kids. I swear they multiplied somehow and now there's faces I've never even seen running around out here.

Diesel's one of them, but the rest, I don't fucking know.

"You're so screwed," Paige says, pointing behind us and I turn to see Rebel bent over, helping Hunter up. They're both inside the pen now and they're both covered in wet, brown…something.

Jesus fucking Christ, this farmer shit isn't a lifestyle, it's a fucking curse filled with dirt, mud, and shit. So much shit.

"Their moms are gonna kill me," I mutter and Coty and Beck chuckle.

"What are you waiting for? Go get your kids." Beck grabs at my elbow and I rip it away from him.

"Only two are mine," I argue, earning a pair of laughs from my supposed friends.

Motherfucker. It's my wedding day.

It seemed like a good idea to host both the ceremony and reception here at home…until this moment. Now I'm thinking some clean building with squeaky floors and zero animals would've been nice.

Yeah, right. Then it wouldn't have been us.

"What are you gonna do when you make this a petting zoo?" Coty asks, and I frown, telling him, "Not let people inside the fence." Fucking duh.

Looking down at my all-black tux and red high-tops, I cringe.

What the fuck? Why did we even bring them over to see the goats anyway?

Because they wanted to. Because we give them everything they want. Because I'm a fucking sucker when it comes to my family, specifically the kids.

Coty just shrugs innocently like he's not planning on ditching me the second I hop the fence and I eye Beck next.

He laughs, saying, "Divide and conquer, bro. That's the only shot we got here. Which ones you going for?"

Angela yells at Coty, telling him, "You better help. Remember what Beckett did last time."

"Angie! I wanted to go down that slide face-first, okay?"

"Uh-huh," Coty says to Beck, stepping onto one of the lower slats after I do.

"I did. It lowered their guards."

"By making them believe you're just a kid yourself," Angela says, walking away with Terra's tiny hand in hers. She's going to be such a good mom when she allows herself to be.

"You smelled like shit for a week," Paige complains over our shoulders before turning away, too.

"That's…" Beck shakes his head, finishing with, "Beside the point," as he steps up between us.

"What *is* the point?" I ask, swinging a leg over.

They both follow suit and we drop down on the other side at the same time.

"The point is…" Beck trails off.

"Ride it?" Coty asks, using our usual motto about riding life instead of letting it ride you.

"Ride it," I agree, knocking his knuckles with mine.

Beck rubs his hands together, his eyes practically sparkling from the challenge before us. "Ride it more."

I shove him, saying, "Try not to get too dirty. I still gotta get married after this."

As a unit, we start forward.

There's this theory I learned about when I went up to B.C. once about trees in forests and how they're actually an interconnected community. Not visibly though. Their links are underground, hidden out of view—at their roots. There's a Mother Tree, or several, in each community that feed vital nutrients to the other trees they've formed connections to. Essentially, they look out for them, help them grow, protect them from outside factors, and sacrifice their own resources when needed most. They don't have to be the same age or even the same species, they just make this deep connection below the surface, all without needing a specific reason. They just fucking do.

This family, my family, we're all connected in ways others don't understand. Don't even see. Coty, Beckett, and I, we became each other's family, providing each other with what we were in need of most—unconditional love, unwavering protection, and indestructible loyalty. As our circle grows bigger, because of our solid foundation made up of intertwined roots, we're able to offer up that same exchange, but on a larger scale now. We step in when one is struggling, we lift when one is weak, we fight when one is threatened, and we never, ever let anyone collapse.

As I look out over our guests here today, it's hard to tell exactly where our tightly woven web ends, or if it even does. With each new addition, the bond widens to include more people into the fold, making them all a part of our story, a part of our family.

Next to my sister, my parents give me matching smiles that I return before throwing one over to the other side of the aisle where Bentlee's parents are sitting with Sydnee.

Scientists even believe that trees that are no longer active parts of the community, like stumps, can still be involved in the connection so long as it hasn't been severed completely. Many of those weaker links were invited today but not all made the effort to stay united. The ones that did though, I can feel their support like I can feel the sun on my face as I wait for my bride so we can reinforce our own connection—officially anyway. That shit's already in the bag. This is all just for pictures and memories and so I can finally show everybody what all I keep in my chest.

"Twenty-Somethings" by Judah & the Lion starts up, causing the guests to turn in their seats to face the back.

Angela makes her way down the aisle first, holding Coty's gaze the entire way. We wanted the women in our lives to have their own spotlight while we stand up here, eagerly anticipating them to join us. Even from here, I can see the panic in Angela's hazel eyes at having this many people focused on her and I try not to laugh. The small bouquet of wildflowers in her hands doesn't so much as move and I know she's got them in a death grip. She blushes, probably from Coty winking at her but my attention shifts to the pair behind her.

Harley and Terra begin their own journey to us with Paige right behind them, patiently redirecting them every time they get distracted. They're supposed to be the flower children, but at only eighteen months old, the petals are just getting stuck in their tiny clenched fists. They make it about halfway down the aisle before Beck abandons his spot beside Coty to help out, saying, "Come to Poppa." He bends down to scoop them both up and gives Paige a kiss on the lips that has some of the guests fanning themselves. With a twin on each arm, he returns to his post while Paige goes to stand off to the side of Angela.

Beck waited exactly six weeks after Paige gave birth to marry her. He planned it perfectly so that the day the doctor gave them the thumbs-up to have sex again, they'd be celebrating their honeymoon. He would've loved to have a big wedding like today, but with Paige's mom's health still not improving, they had an intimate wedding up at their house with only our immediate family members in attendance. No bells, no whistles, just a ton of tears at the most emotional ceremony I've ever been to. Seriously, *I* cried.

Coty ends up taking Harley when the kid snatches the purple cloth in his breast pocket and throws it on the ground. Beck's is blue and Terra immediately starts chewing on the stiff fabric.

I have no idea why they chose those colors. We're all wearing black-on-black tuxes with our own spin on shoes. My pocket square's garnet red—*obviously*—and I kind of assumed they'd be doing the same color scheme, but no, they did their own thing, as fucking usual.

Rebel's next down the line as she steps up with the entire bottom of her white dress now stained brown.

From her seat, Karina shoots me a look over her shoulder and I hold my hands up, fighting a grin. What does she expect?

In typical Rebel fashion, riding boots peek out from underneath the dirtied dress with each stride she takes as she wastes no time whatsoever getting where she wants to go. It doesn't matter that I just bought her the newest shoes by her favorite basketball player or that her mom found some fancy white strappy sandals to specifically co-ordinate with her dress, she still prefers her riding boots. The pillow that's supposed to be carrying the rings is nothing but a white blur of tulle as she spins it around on one hand like she's making pizza dough. She only stops to look up at me when I snatch it clean off her and I let my smile free, grateful I'd already pocketed the rings this morning.

"You look beautiful, little mama," I tell her. I don't care that her dress is filthy or that her shoes don't match the occasion, she's staying true to herself and she's happy doing it, which is all I want. All I've ever wanted for her.

She beams, telling me, "Thanks, Dad," and with her lisp finally gone it comes out perfect…just like her.

I bend over to cup her head, kissing her forehead and handing the pillow back to her.

Karina and I explained to Rebel that although I wasn't technically her dad, she could call me that if she wanted. She'd been drawing me into all her family portraits for a while and I didn't want her to feel weird calling me something that felt right to both of us. I'll be her dad as long as she'll have me.

And even after that because even though meeting back up with Karina might seem like it was just a chance encounter, it felt like fate to me. Rebel was supposed to be my daughter and now she always will be.

The beginning notes of American Avenue's cover of "Ocean Eyes" floats across the yard and my heart changes its tune altogether. It beats so fucking hard like it's trying to lead me to where it really belongs.

It's time.

Bentlee waits at the end of the aisle, holding Hunter's hand securely in hers. She wanted Hunter to be the one to walk her down the aisle and I can't think of anyone better for the job.

This is my first time seeing her white lace dress so I run my gaze over it, lingering on her meadow tattoo before moving on to the garnet red sash tied around her middle. It's a stark contrast to her simple sleeveless gown but matches the color of my pocket square perfectly. Out of all the outfits I've seen Bentlee in, this is undoubtedly my favorite.

Later, when I'm stripping it off her, I'll have to remember to tell her so.

Hunter says something to her, and she turns to wipe some mud off one of his lenses, revealing more red fabric behind her. Her blonde hair's half up in a complicated braid she told me in a text this morning gave her a headache with the rest half down in loose waves that frame her glowing face. Starting at the top of that braid though and draped all the way to the ground is a red veil longer than the dress itself. Murmurs kick up as soon as it comes into view and I find myself just as obsessed with wanting to know the reasoning behind her fashion choice as I was all those mornings I used to spend at Pop Two, hoping to catch a glimpse of her.

Facing forward again, her eyes meet mine just as the song's beat rapidly picks up and I swear my knees almost buckle as I stumble forward, wanting to go to her.

Of all the locations I've traveled, Bentlee's eyes are the one place I've never wanted to leave. The most amazing place I've ever discovered and it wasn't even a place at all. It was a person. My person.

Together, mother and son start walking, the veil fluttering from the movement and fanning out behind Bentlee like a growing flame, igniting everything from the ground up. Igniting her.

Holy fucking shit.

Flashes of bright red surround her as she stays perfectly calm, fearlessly accepting her fate of being consumed.

How do you feel about me now?

Consumed.

Almost two years later and nothing's changed. She's the moth to my flame and I'm the shark to her depths. She's consumed and I'm fucking immersed.

I clutch my heart, willing it to stay a little longer so I don't miss a second. Once I have Bentlee back in my hands, it's free to leave, go back to its true owner, but for now, I can't risk it. I need to see this, commit it to memory so I'll never forget.

"Dayum," I hear behind me, followed by a whispered, "That's a quarter, Funcle Beckett," from Rebel.

"Worth it," Paige says softly, and with my hands shaking at my sides, I nod, too mesmerized to do anything other than stare at the rest of my life making her way to me. Bentlee's worth everything. She is everything.

A long time ago some asshole made her question her worth. Now I get to spend every day making sure she knows how much she means to me. How much she means to all of us.

As soon as she's within reach, I grab for her, sealing my lips against hers. Laughter fills the air around us but I don't give a fuck. I deepen the kiss just to prove it.

Laughing against my mouth, Bentlee pulls back to look up at me, whispering, "You couldn't wait?"

With a smirk, I tell her, "We're done with waiting, mama," before wiping her lip gloss off my lips and bending to press a gentle kiss to her stomach.

Only three months along, we haven't told anybody yet but now we don't have to. We just had our first appointment last week and I made damn sure to keep my phone in the car. No fucking way was I getting pulled away from hearing my baby's heartbeat for the first time.

After some gasps, a chorus of "congrats" follow several "I knew its" but I block it all out, dropping onto a knee to look Hunter in the eye.

"Thanks for bringing me to your mom," I tell him seriously.

"I thought I was bringing her to you." He chuckles, making everyone else laugh, too.

"Not today. I mean when we first met. Thanks for bringing me to meet her. You were right, I did need her." He gives a proud little nod, remembering our first meeting. "I know you're supposed to be giving her away to me today but I don't want to take her from you." I sit back to look at both him and Bentlee. "Do you think, maybe, you could share her with me instead?"

He considers it as Bentlee sniffles above us. A couple others nearby do, too, but I focus solely on Hunter, waiting for his decision. Bentlee was in my blind spot, had been for years, and if it wasn't for her boy catching my eye that day at the market and bringing his mom to the forefront, I don't know if I ever would've seen her.

"Okay, I guess I can," he finally says, setting off a round of applause.

Crushing him to me in a hug, I say, "Yeah?" and he nods his forehead against my shoulder, his little ribs shaking in my hold as he cries.

I give him—and myself—a minute, then push to standing, dusting some of the dirt from Hunter's tux off my just as dirty, if not dirtier, tux. Those kids gave us a run for our money and I have a feeling they're just getting started.

After hugging his mom, Hunter rushes over to Rebel, his face relaxing into pure happiness once he's next to her again. The tears cause his glasses to slip down his nose but Rebel pushes them back up for him, grinning at him then over at us.

Bentlee's blue-green pools continue to spill over, but unlike the Blue Lake's sacred waters, I can touch these, so I wipe the tears with my thumbs, asking her, "You still see me?"

Smiling, she says, "I do."

Books by
A. MARIE

You can find the latest information regarding A. Marie titles,
including how to order signed copies, here: amarieauthor.com.